I Found You

Erica Marselas

Copyright 2018 Erica Marselas

All rights reserved. No part of this publication may be reproduced, distributed, or transmitted in any form or by any means, including photocopying, recording, or other electronic or mechanical methods, without the prior written permission of the publisher, except in the case of brief quotations embodied in critical reviews and certain other noncommercial uses permitted by copyright law.

This is a work of fiction. Names, characters, businesses, places, events, and incidents are either the products of the author's imagination and used in a fictitious manner Any resemblance to actual persons, living or dead, or actual events is purely coincidental.

    Editing: Kristen Your Editing Lounge
    "I Found You" Lyrics written with Leslie Middleton

To the ladies who gave me the strength to keep going and write the story I wanted to be told, no matter how different it seemed. Who some days held my hand, offered me help, and gave me their guidance. Thank you-I couldn't have done this without you. This is for all of you... you know who you are.

To my husband: You always have my back, encourage me and let me vent. I know this story drove you insane as much as it did me, but now that it's done, you can have your wife back----well, 'till the next book ;p.

The past is an outline for our future. Sometimes we can learn and grow from it or you can let it consume you.

But I can tell you one thing....

True love does win in the end... uh-huh

ONE

January 3rd, 2002

Violet

My boyfriend, Cooper, dropped me off a block away from my house wanting to avoid my mother giving him a hard time. She wasn't happy when Cooper and I left two days after Christmas for Los Angeles to spend the rest of our winter break and New Year's together. She tried to forbid me from going, but I was going no matter what she said or did. So, I know I'm about to get an ear full and be grounded until summer.

Whatever.

Nothing could bring me down after the week I had with Coop. We spent most of our time locked in a hotel room, naked in bed. When we weren't, we toured the city, which will hopefully soon be our home.

Yep, nothing could bring me down from soaring.

Well, that's until I flew straight into a large yellow moving truck sitting in my driveway.

Two bulky guys in blue overalls carry our couch to the back of the truck. I move behind them and see most of our furniture sitting inside.

What the fuck is going on? And what's the possibility we're getting robbed in broad daylight?

I march into the house, but suddenly my feet are frozen to the ground. Every hair on my body stands on edge in fright seeing all the boxes lined up in the living area. There in the middle of all the cardboard squares stands my mother, talking to her boyfriend, Jeremy West.

I'm not a fan of this jerk-off.

For one, he's not my father, and second, he's a douchebag. The man owns a bunch of sleazy car dealerships in California and Arizona. I have no idea what my mom sees in him, and now looking at my packed house, I realize he has something to do with this sudden move.

Wherever the hell they're going, I'm not.

"What the hell is going on?" I shout, grabbing their attention.

"Oh, good you're home, just in time to help us finish packing up the rest," my mother says with a forced smile.

"Pack up what? I'm not going anywhere."

"Oh, yes you are. Jeremy and I got married over New Year's."

I pale and my eyes dart to the new shining diamond on her left hand. She got married and didn't think to fucking tell me? We don't always get along, but I could've sworn my mother loved me enough to want to me to be present for her wedding.

"He's opening a new lot in Tucson and we're going with him."

I shake my head and try to keep the tears from falling down my face. I have five months 'till I graduate and she thinks it would be okay to just uproot my life now? I'm not eighteen 'till October, but Goddammit I shouldn't have to obey this.

"You don't think you should have talked this over with me? Or gave me an option to stay? I'm almost done with high school and you want me to uproot everything I know because you decided on a whim to marry this

I FOUND you **JANUARY 3rd, 2002**

asshole?"

Jeremy has the nerve to chuckle before he kisses my mother's cheek, telling her he'll let her handle this. Once he's left the room, throwing a glare my way, my mom takes a few steps closer to me.

"I was going to tell you, but you ran off with that boy. You won't listen to reason when it comes to him, so what better chance for you to fix your life, then by starting over, as I start mine."

"I don't want or need to start over, mother. And Cooper isn't ruining my life. It's you and his mother doing that to us. I'm not going. And screw you. You should've told me all this before you got MARRIED!" I scream the last part out, the venom in my voice doing nothing to convince her of what she's done wrong.

She crosses her arms over her chest and squints her eyes at me. I stand my ground, pushing my shoulders back, mocking her stance.

"This isn't up for debate, Violet. We're moving, and it's happening bright and early tomorrow morning. You're my daughter and you have to do what I say. Your father isn't here, so it leaves you with no other options to stay."

"I'll live on the street then, I don't care," I argue and look away for her.

I'm sure Cooper will let me hide somewhere in his room.

"I know what you're thinking, and you need to get over it. You think his parents will allow you to live under their roof? They won't. Who's going to pay for your college if you stay here, because it won't be me. Hell, Violet, you haven't even picked one yet. You have no clue what you're going to do come June. As your mother, I have to do right by you and also for me. You can't keep following in his so-called footsteps. You really think his fleeting music career will take care of you with no degree

to fall back on?" She tilts her head and thinks she won.

Cooper and I made plans to run off to L.A. along with his brother Brody, and work on getting Cooper's music career started. I know he has what it takes and the drive to be successful. I still planned to go to college; we even did a tour of UCLA while we were visiting this week. There's also community college to start if I had too. Whether or not I had it all figured out, my life is my own and I'm going to do what I want *to do.*

Sometimes in life, you have to take a leap of faith.

But now my leap is crashing down on me before I've even jumped.

"Why can't you let me live my own life, make my own mistakes? Why does it bother you so much that I'm with Cooper? It's been over two years and you still won't give the guy a chance. He loves me, why is it so hard to understand? Here you are marrying some dickwad car salesman, who I'm sure is going to use you for every penny you have."

"He won't do that, but I'm an adult, and you are a child, Violet. End of discussion. I've already had your *belongings packed."*

"You packed my stuff?" I scream, my fists clenched at my side. "You better not have thrown anything away, or I swear mother."

"Don't worry, I didn't throw any of your precious mementos." She sighs and scrubs her hands down her face. "You'll be eighteen in October. 'Till then, you'll be living in Arizona with me. If you're really meant to be with Cooper Reid, well, I guess he'll be able to wait the next ten months for you, but I wouldn't count on it. Hopefully, you'll see how much better of a life you'll have without him bringing you down."

A piercing, fiery, roar bubbles in my chest and leaves my throat. If only I was a dragon I would've burned her to a crisp with my anger.

I FOUND *you* **JANUARY 3rd, 2002**

"You're ruining my life, and I'll never forgive you for this." I run towards the door, needing to escape, needing Cooper.

"You'll thank me one day." My mother calls when I make it past the threshold, where a moving man blocks my path.

I stop and face her, glaring at her with tears in my eyes. "That's never going to happen," I sneer and bolt around the confused man in overalls to race down the street.

Finding a pay phone, I dial Cooper's number. It rings a few times before he picks up.

"Hello?"

"Coop," I try to keep my voice from shaking because I don't want him to worry. He doesn't need to add worry on top of the heart I'm about to shatter.

"Ace, what's wrong?" There's a slight panic in his voice.

Guess it didn't work.

"Meet me at White Park, please," I beg. "I'll explain everything when you get there, but I need to see you."

"I'm on my way," he says quickly. "I love you."

"I love you, too. Please never forget that." I whisper the last part before I hang up.

Hues of orange, yellow, and red filter from behind the trees of White Park in Riverside. Cooper has me wrapped tightly in his arms while we admire the array of colors as the sun continues to dip below the horizon.

Neither of us says anything as the cool night breeze dances across our faces and the whippoorwills call into the dusk.

I pull Cooper's arms tighter around me, snuggling deeper into him, wanting to inhale his scent; a mix of Irish Spring and cinnamon. He presses a kiss into my temple, mindlessly, as if he knows I need his comfort. I smile and my heart warms because he always knows what I need without saying it. Glancing up at him, I try to memorize every inch of his face. From his wild untamed blond waves, which are still wet from his shower, to all the fine hairs of his five-o clock shadow. My smile falters and I'm not sure how I can make it without him.

He's the center of my universe and I'm seconds away from telling him news that will destroy our perfect bubble.

I've been with Cooper since we met our sophomore year, when he saved me from being attacked by Thomas Ryan.

That was the beginning of our love story. Yet, it has been difficult at times due to our parents not wanting us to be together. They believe we aren't good enough for each other, for reasons I'll never understand.

Even though Cooper rescued me from being physically attacked, my mother despises him. She thinks he's a violent "thug" with severe anger problems.

Cooper has a reputation for being a bad boy, but I don't know how anyone can't see how he has changed since he met me.

If it isn't bad enough that my mother hates him, his parents dislike me as well. They think I'm helping him throw away his potential, but it's actually Cooper who wants nothing to do with their visions for him. He has even bigger dreams that they don't recognize as more than pipe dreams, and they're making me out to be the bad guy because I encourage him to reach for the stars.

With his dad being a successful lawyer, his mom a doctor, and behind them a long line of powerful and influential family, they've been trying to mold him into

I FOUND YOU **JANUARY 3rd, 2002**

some kind of suave businessman or a politician. To them, it's the only way for him to succeed in life.

How can they not see it's them *standing in his way, making him unhappy, and not me?*

Sure, we both like to party, and we've gotten tattoos, and we drink, but we're young and adventurous. Our moral compass isn't broken; other than our first meeting, we've never been in trouble with the law. We both keep our grades up. No, we're not pounding out the A's anymore like our parents expect; now we just get more B's tangled in with those A's. No big deal. Overall, I say we're pretty damn good kids.

Even though our parents push back, we've made it. But now, sitting here in Cooper's arms, watching the final rays set behind the trees, my heart breaks...because maybe our love won't be enough to survive me moving hundreds of miles away.

It seems my mother is finally getting what she has always wanted by ripping us apart.

My father, the only person who is willing to listen, accepts and supports our relationship, and could help us, is gone. He got stationed overseas in Afghanistan and will be for another six months.

With no money and no place to stay, I know I have no other option than to go.

"My mom is making me move with her to Arizona. We're leaving in the morning. I don't have a choice," I blurt out, ripping it off like a band-aid.

His whole body freezes as tension ripples through him. "In the morning? How? I mean, don't you need to pack?" Hurt, shock, and anguish cloud his blue eyes. It's as if the glass house that surrounded our relationship has been hit with the final stone and it's shattering around us.

"It seems she had someone do it for us while we were away this week. I came home to a packed house and moving truck." I frown remembering the argument with

my mother that had ended with me running off and calling Cooper to meet me here.

"You can't leave." He holds me tighter and his voice cracks. "Maybe we could get married..." He ponders the same thing I've been thinking since I saw the large yellow truck outside my house.

Though there's nothing more I want in this world, we can't. No way in hell our parents would allow it. Well, my dad would, but sadly my country needed him more than me, so we're in screwed-ville.

"We can't get married before we're eighteen without our parents' permission, and I don't think that's going to happen."

"I'll kidnap you," he says seriously, and I can't help but laugh. I have no doubt that he would, but living on the streets in the cold isn't ideal for either of us.

"I really wish we could," I muse.

We sit in silence a little while longer. The sun has disappeared, and the sky has gone black. The stars twinkle above us, and I close my eyes, wishing upon all of them I won't have to leave; my home is here in this man's arms.

My hand glides across my flat stomach, remembering the loss of our baby last year. It still makes my heart ache and my stomach twist when I think about our little angel. Cooper is the only one I can talk to when I'm feeling down about it. The only hug that puts me at ease, and the only one that understands the pain it brings. He's my heart and soul, and now I have to move a hundred miles away from him. I don't know how I'm going to make it, how we're going to make it, without each other. We've only ever had each other in our worst of times.

I'm doing everything not to cry, but the ache is too much and I fail miserably, letting the tears fall from my eyes like rain. Cooper grabs my face and brushes them away with his thumbs. His lips gently kiss my nose and cheeks, but the flood keeps coming.

All I want to do in bury myself in him and never leave. Why do our mothers have to hate our relationship? Why can't they see what we see.? That the two of us are nothing without each other?

"Ace, baby, stop."

I shake my head and nuzzle myself into his chest. What seems like a lifetime later, my shuddering sobs cease, but stray tears still fall. When I lift my face to gaze at the man I love, his face is also wet and stained from tears. I wipe them away, and kiss him the way he did me. I've only seen him cry once before, after losing the baby, and now he's losing me. Seeing him so affected, gives me hope we can make it through.

"I need you to promise something," he whispers, looking me dead in the eye, his hand tangled in my hair around my neck.

"Anything."

"Promise me you'll write me every day, call me every day, and when you turn eighteen come back to me."

"I promise. I love you, Cooper."

"I love you too, Violet. I always will. You're my girl. My only girl, and one day I swear I'm going to marry you." His wet lips kiss the side of my neck, as he pulls my body closer to his.

My heart leaps and the tears fall again at his words. All I want is to always be his.

"And I promise to say yes."

May 15th, 2006

Violet

*"I've never stopped loving you.
You're the only love I've ever known
You're my soul, my air, my everything...
And I need you back to live again."*

A guitar riff for the chorus plays through my headphones before it's met again with a rich baritone voice that melts my panties. I'm listening to my favorite song "My Everything", on repeat. It always makes me feel better, and worse, at the same time. I don't know why I torture myself with listening to this man's sweet voice. His lyrics send something straight to my soul and it's like he's singing to me—only to me.

*"You went away, but in my heart,
you're always here.
I close my eyes hoping you'll come back to me
Because I can never stop loving you
with everything I have"*

I miss *him*.

My feet tap on the bed as the sexy, soothing voice continues to pipe into my ears. I'm starting to realize my life is not what I expected it to be at this point. I snort, knowing this is nothing like I had planned when I was seventeen. I graduated from Tucson University four days

I FOUND YOU **May 15th, 2006**

ago, earning my degree in business management. I've been searching for months for a job leading up to graduation, without much success. It's disappointing because I thought it would be easy.

On top of being jobless, I'm now boyfriend-less. Last night I broke up with my boyfriend of six months, Darren. I don't know why I ever put up with his arrogant ass. I caught him sleeping with someone else. I mean *fine*, I know I wasn't putting out very much—because frankly, he sucked at it—but he could've broken up with me before he slept with someone else. It wouldn't have been such a total loss.

"Say you still love me. That you'll always be mine.
Because I miss the way you taste
and the way your eyes used to shine.
My everlasting love, my number one,
my everything."

I was once his Ace.

Damn this song. Damn the emotions it gives me. Damn it all.

I throw the headphones out of my ears and they fall to the mattress. Softly, I hear the lyrics start again, and turn off my mp3 player. I need to stop torturing my poor soul.

I need to move on—past him.

My door crashes open and my roommates, Julie and Alexa, stumble into my room, giggling like loons. They have been my best friends and roommates for the last three years. The two crazies are already drunk. Julie flops onto my bed, beside me, making the both of us bounce.

"About time you dumped his ass," she exclaims.

"Yeah, I caught him in bed with Teagan." I shrug, not caring. Life is full of heartbreaks, this isn't one of them.

"Are you okay?" Alexa sits next to me and squeezes my hand. Her green doe eyes look at me sympathetically.

"Yeah. I have no idea why I put up with him as long as I did. It's done and dusted and I can now move on to the next dope," I chuckle softly.

"That's the spirit!"

"Whatcha listenin too?" Julie grabs my MP3 player from my lap and starts scrolling through it.

"Your future *husband*," I tease.

"You bet he is." Julie swoons and falls back flat on the bed. Her brown hair fans out everywhere, placing the player over her heart, lost in a daydream. I swear I see stars in her eyes.

The girl is nuts.

A pillow goes flying in front of me and hits Julie square in the face, waking her from her fantasy.

"Hey, me and my husband were about to jet ski off into the sunset." Julie sits up, crossing her arms over her chest in a playful huff.

"Anyways…we have an idea." Alexa rolls her eyes, ignoring the nut beside me. "The three of us. Vegas! My dad has some free room vouchers, and asked if I would like to use them."

"Wait, your dad *wants* you to go to Vegas? Sin City?" I ask raising my eyebrows.

My dad would never *want* me to go to Vegas. He would think I'd end up gambling all my money away. Or think the bright lights of Vegas would turn me into a stripper.

Or I'd get married to some stranger on a whim.

"Okay, not really, but when I told him I wanted to go for an after-graduation celebration with my two best girls, he offered to pay." Alexa shrugs. "He knows if I'm with you Vi, I won't get into any trouble." She smirks, and I smack her leg.

I have no clue how I got the goodie-two-shoes badge. There was a time some parents thought I was the cause of trouble.

"Well, gee thanks…I think."

"Come on, we worked so hard these last four years. We studied our asses off, missed some great parties, and you graduated magna cum laude. I think we deserve it, don't you?"

"Yeah, it could be fun…" I say, getting excited about the idea. Sun, swimming, liquor, gambling, and sleazy nightclubs. What else could be better than dancing in sin?

"WOO VEGAS!" Julie screams, doing a seated jig.

"Maybe we can find you Mister Right, Vi…" Alexa interjects, shoving my shoulder.

"ME?" I screech. "What about you two? You're having the same luck in the love department as I am."

Hell no, I'm not hooking up with anyone in Vegas. The only thing I want my lips on is the glass holding my *Jose Cuervo*.

"Maybe we'll all get lucky. Now come on, I already broke open the wine and Tess and Uma will be here soon." Alexa yanks my hand, pulling me off the bed.

Who knows, maybe Vegas is what I need to get out of this small slump I'm in. Have some fun, then face the real world head-on.

Erica Marselas

Vegas Baby
May 19th, 2006

I haven't found the sin yet, but I have found the fun. The lights, the excitement, and all the noise and chatter of the city have really been good for my soul. The three of us arrived in Vegas early this morning and hit The Strip first thing. We did the zip line, were drunk by noon, and now we are at The Bellagio's bar, drinking and dancing.

I'm wearing a royal blue, mini-dress with spaghetti straps, and a low V-neck showing off the perfect amount of cleavage. Alexa insisted I needed this dress when we spotted it this afternoon. Her words had been, "you're not going to attract *anything* looking like a nun." I personally saw nothing wrong with my long-sleeve, high neckline, black dress, but I do feel incredibly sexy now.

I've been feeling eyes on me all night, and men have been all over us as we dance. So far, no one has made an impression on me.

"Guys," I yell over the pumping music, fanning myself, "I need another drink."

"Me too," Alexa yells back, and we grab Julie to head back to our table.

We all order waters and a round of tequila shots. I dance in my seat as "Don't Cha" by the Pussycat Dolls plays, ready to get back on the floor.

There's a sudden burst of commotion; surprised hollers and 'oh my gods' fill the bar. The three of us look around wondering what's going on. There's a mob of people flowing to the VIP area, but all I see are black suits, protecting whoever is between them.

"Wonder who the VIP is?" Julie muses, as our waitress returns with our drinks.

My skin prickles with familiarity. The air shifts as

well, making it hard to breathe. There's a magnetic pull, drawing me to the person who just broke away from his guards to stand at the bar. My heart hammers in my chest, not believing what I'm seeing. I rub my eyes twice to make sure he's not an illusion.

It's him. It's really him.

"Oh, my god," I whisper, my mind still in a state of disbelief. My whole body is trembling, I'm lightheaded by all the possibilities that could take place. This might be my only chance to talk to him again.

No matter what, I have to do this.

"Violet, you going to take your shot?" Julie asks, grabbing my shoulder.

"I'll be right back," I say, not turning my attention to her. I hear her asking me what's up, but I ignore her, letting my heart lead the way to the opposite end of the bar.

With each step, my heart thumps erratically. I swear it's about to burst out of my chest. My hands are clammy and I'm worried he might disappear like a wisp of smoke.

Four years.

Four years since I've seen his chiseled face, and the single dimple in his right cheek. Four years since I've heard his husky laugh, or seen his blue eyes that shined into my soul and lit up my life. I've missed the way he made me feel complete.

He's even more handsome since the last time I saw him, and even if I didn't recognize his face, I would have recognized his firm ass in those dress slacks.

I get to the velvet ropes of the VIP lounge when one of the guys in a black suit stops me.

"Ma'am I can't let you over here," he tells me firmly and stands a tad taller.

"I just wanted to say hi—"

"I'm sure you did. That's what they all say. Now please." He points me to the other side of the bar, gesturing for me to get lost.

I shake my head at how quickly I've forgotten he's a big, famous singer now; untouchable, surrounded by bodyguards and groupies. I sigh. It's all he's ever wanted to be. His dream came true while I faded away.

I need answers though. I need to know why he let me fade when he continued to shine brightly in my life.

"I know you get all kinds of people trying to talk to him, but we went to high school together." I start to explain my heartbreaking tale to the uptight guy who I'm sure could use a drink—or eight. The man crosses his arms and looks away from me.

"I can't blame you for not believing me, but could you just tell him Violet Spencer wants to say hi. I beg you. And if he tells me to get lost, I promise I won't bother you anymore."

He was my one true love.

"Violet Spencer," he murmurs in awe. I don't quite understand his reaction as he moves in to look at me more closely. Like really close, where I can taste the mint on his breath. He nods his head, and without saying another word he walks over to the bar, grabbing Cooper's attention before whispering in his ear.

His head snaps in my direction, and our eyes lock as realization dawns all over his handsome features. He knocks over the barstool when he jumps to his feet, and strides over to me like a man on a mission. Before I can even process that after all this time he's standing in front of me, his lips smash into mine.

Holy crap.

My mouth parts to let his tongue in and explore. My heart soars and my body heats up, tingles shooting through my skin. He moans, pressing himself into me, encouraging me to kiss him harder, and I tangle my hand in his hair.

He tastes and feels just like I remember. All the love

we had before lingers in this heated, passionate kiss—it's as if no time has passed at all.

Maybe the last four years had been a bad dream and when we break apart we'll still be on that picnic bench where we last saw each other.

He pulls away, resting his forehead on mine, and his dark blue eyes bore into my own, recapturing my soul again. "My Violet," he whispers against my lips.

"Cooper," I pant. He still takes my breath away after all these years.

"God, you're more beautiful than the day you left." He rubs my cheek with his thumb. "I lie, you're fucking sexy. This dress…fuck." His eyes roam over my body. My skin heats at his traveling eyes and now I'm really glad Alexa made me buy this dress.

"You're not so bad yourself. And I've been hearing good things about you." I grab the lapels on his jacket wanting to keep my hands on him.

"I've missed you…" he breathes, his eyes still exploring mine, I'm sure verifying that I'm real. "Why don't me and you go to my room so we can talk without all these people listening?"

All these people.

The words bring me back to reality. My eyes dart around the crowded bar, suddenly feeling a million eyes on us.

"I think we have a lot to catch up on, Ace."

My heart skips a beat and I'm trying not to surrender to the tears caused by the elation I'm feeling when he calls me by my old nickname. There's nothing I want more in this world than to be his number one girl again.

"I would like that," I croak out causing him to smirk.

I look back to the table where I left my friends. Friends who are now gawking at me and I'm sure have a million questions after witnessing the show of a lifetime. I'm never going to hear the end of it from them.

Vi, you got a lot of explaining to do.

I turn back to him, my heart expanding again at the sight of his sly grin. "I just need to tell my friends."

"Hurry…" he urges, brushing his hand across my cheek. "I don't want to waste any more time."

Words escape me and I nod. He places a kiss on my cheek before I walk back to my table in a daze.

I glance back at him, needing to make sure it hasn't been a dream. He's talking to his security guy and pointing to me. We smile at each other and he blows me a kiss with a wink. I giggle thinking the Rockstar moves have gotten to his head.

When I arrive back at my table, Alexa and Julie stare at me wide-eyed, with their jaws on the floor.

"Oh my God! What the hell just happened there? Why was Cooper Reid's tongue down your throat?" Alexa shrieks. People around us spin their heads to look at us.

I wonder if this will be in every tabloid tomorrow.

I blush. "We used to date in high school, for a couple of years before I had to leave for Arizona."

"And you didn't think to share this information with us? The hottest singer in the whole world was your boyfriend?" she narrows her eyes at me, but her voice is still screeching. I'm having a hard time telling if she's mad or still in shock.

I'm still in shock. The guy I loved was ripped away from me and I *never* thought I would get the chance to see him again.

"I know, I'm a terrible friend for not telling you about me and Cooper, but it was always so hard to think about how I lost the guy I thought I would be with forever," I tell them sadly. "Seeing him in magazines and hearing him on the radio didn't help because I still loved him. We never broke up, just kind of lost touch."

Not a complete lie. Once the letters and phone calls

stopped, I moved on.

That's a lie too, I never really moved on.

"When you walked over there, the last thing I expected was that. I thought you were being nosey. Damn."

"I'm sorry. Don't be mad, please."

Alexa gasps at me and shakes her head, pulling me into a hug. "Of course, I'm not mad. You just have to explain it all to me later."

"I will, I promise." I look back towards the VIP area, and Cooper is talking to one of the other bodyguards. "I just need to know what happened first, myself," I mumble.

Turning my attention back to Julie, she hasn't picked her jaw off the floor since I returned. I decide to close it for her. "You okay?"

"You…you…and him…you lucky bitch!" Julie always had the biggest crush on Cooper Reid. It sometimes got to the point I would wonder if Julie loved him more than I did.

Nah. Nobody could…

And the kiss we just shared proves he might share the same feelings for me.

A love that can never be forgotten.

"I didn't say anything because I didn't want to break your heart." I stick my tongue out at her, playfully.

"Holy fuck," Julie whispers her jaw popping open again.

The hairs stick up on the back of my neck and there stands the only person who can cause that type of electricity in my body: Cooper Reid. His brother always used to say we were magnets; always stuck together at the hip and attached at the lips. I only wish the magnetic energy crossed state lines.

His muscular arm drapes around my waist, pulling me tightly to his side. The scent of cinnamon and rum tickle my nose and warms my belly. He smells fantastic, and I wish I could bottle it up to keep it with me always.

"You ready?" His voice is low and husky, and his stormy, lustful eyes dampen my panties.

"Um yeah…Cooper these are my friends Alexa and Julie."

"It's nice to meet you both." He shakes both of their hands.

Julie giggles like a schoolgirl and stares at her hand then back at him. I'm sure her everlasting fantasy of meeting her crush isn't going the way she planned, but she's handling it pretty well. I was almost convinced I'd have to fight her for him.

"Would you guys mind if I went with Cooper? We kind of need to catch up…"

"I promise to have her back down in a little while. If you want, you guys are more than welcome to go over to the VIP section. Drinks are on me…" Cooper offers.

"Really?" Julie and Alexa chirp. Their eyes light up at the offer of free drinks.

"Yep. I already told them you might be coming over. Help yourself." He gives them both his winning, dimpled smile then looks down at me. "Come Ace," he tells me in *that* voice, the one that tells me I'm seconds away from being naked.

Yes, please.

Alexa and Julie hug me, double checking I'm going to be okay before running off to the bar. Free drinks make everything better, including to help them forget their best friend hid a famous boyfriend from them.

Cooper guides me to the elevator banks with his bodyguards in toe. They join us in the metal box and one of the big guys pushes the button for the 23rd floor. Cooper pulls me towards the back corner, his fingers caressing my ass from under my dress. Shivers skate down my back as he moves dangerously close to my heated core.

I peek over at the backs of the bodyguards, and my cheeks heat, knowing we have company, even though the guards appear stoic and uncaring.

"Is this what it's like for you now? Always have people following you around? No privacy?" My arm crosses over his to grab a handful of his firm ass in return.

"Yeah, but it's for my safety. Some of the fans get crazy." His fingers travel under the small sliver of my thong.

I bite down on my lip, suppressing my moan, as his fingers run across my wet slit. It's been so long since I've been touched like this. The last months with my ex were sexless, but even so, the only person who stood a chance against Cooper Reid's magic touch was Cooper Reid.

"You always did have a problem with girls throwing themselves all over you. I'm glad you have protection now."

In high school, the girls were always all over him, especially after a show. It used to drive me crazy, but he always made sure I was his number one girl. He always made me feel like a queen.

"You were and still are the only girl I would want all over me." He winks at me, removing his hand from my panties as the elevator doors open to the twenty-third floor. I don't want it to end, but then again, we are going to his room.

"Let me guess, you got the penthouse-presidential-high-roller suite." I giggle as he takes my hand to two large, white, double doors.

"It's all part of the life, baby." Cooper turns to one of his guards as he swipes the room key. "Collin, we should be good."

The bodyguard nods and we enter the oversized hotel room.

The door closes behind us and in a blink, Cooper has

me engulfed in his arms, latching his lips to mine, in a desperate, fiery kiss. My hand grips the back of his neck as he pulls me closer as if making us one. I've missed his deep hungry kisses, the way his touch gives me goosebumps, and the feeling of his dick pushed into my belly. It feels so freakin' good to be in his arms and I don't know how I survived this long without him. But I know there's no going back now.

A loud moan escapes from my throat as he grabs my ass from underneath my dress. I wiggle against his stabbing erection, trying to convey how much I want him without words, refusing to separate my mouth from this never-ending kiss. I'm dizzy from this high and I stumble back hitting a wall causing our lips to separate, and we are left panting.

"I can't believe you're here." His hand runs down my cheek and his thumb traces over my swollen lips.

"I can't believe it either," I say breathlessly, my head still spinning. "I keep wanting to pinch myself."

"Four years…It has to be some miracle that you're standing in front of me. I can't tell you how much I've missed you." His words are like a bucket of cold water being poured on me, reminding me why we're up here in the first place. I push him away before he can kiss me again. He looks at me confused and tries to take me in his arms again, but I step back shaking my head. It's as if his initial kiss and his touch wiped my memory clean of the past heartache that he caused me when he stopped responding to my letters and calls. I need answers to why he ghosted me.

"If you missed me so much, why did you stop writing me?"

He sighs heavily and rakes his hands through his dirty-blond waves. When he looks back at me I can see the shattered look in his eyes, but I don't understand since he's the one who left me hanging.

I FOUND you **May 19th, 2006**

"At the end of Senior year, I got a letter from your mom with a bunch of pictures of you with some guy. Your mom said you moved on and wanted me to stop writing."

"What? I didn't date anyone my senior year. The only people I hung out with were Alexa and…Mark." It all clicks now. Mark became a good friend, and I ended up going to prom with him, so we didn't have to go alone.

"So, the fucker has a name." Jealousy swarms in his eyes and I smack him lightly in the chest. Nothing has changed about him in the past years, that's for sure. He always was jealous before he even knew what was going on. Though, I know if it was the other way around, I would have been upset too.

"Mark is gay, just so you know. I can't believe this. So, you just gave up and ignored me? After everything? I wrote you for almost a year after, hoping you would answer."

"I did write you and I tried calling you a bunch of times, but your mom would answer or I'd get a voicemail. As for your letters, I didn't get them." My face falls at the memory of my mom taking my phone away from me because she couldn't afford the bill anymore. And now I guess it's easy to say my mother also hid his letters from me. "It killed me that I didn't hear it from you, but yeah, I thought you gave up on me."

"I would've never given up on you. I thought you knew that."

"A part of me did. That's why I went to see you in Arizona before graduation. I came to your house with flowers in hopes of seeing you. Your mom answered and told me you were out on a date. In love. I waited for you to come back, and when you did, you were laughing with the guy in the pictures." He shakes his head with a frown and my heart rips in half. We had a chance and I missed it because my mom wanted—*what*? I'll never understand what she got out of us being apart.

23

"I knew I had to let you go; thinking, if you were happy that was all that mattered. It hurt like crazy and I hate myself for not kidnapping you, but it would've killed me more if you told me you didn't want me anymore. Even though it was a dagger to my heart, I had always held on to hope maybe it wasn't true, and you would come back to me, wanting me again. I even tried to hate you, but after the first week, I gave up. I couldn't. I didn't want to."

"I always wanted you." My voice cracks and his hand moves to my face wiping away the stray tear. "And I never loved anyone else but you." My eyes close, thinking back to how many times I thought of and dreamed about him. Though it ate me up inside every time he crossed my mind, I held out hope we could be together and in love again.

When I see my mother again, she's going to have a lot to explain, but only if I don't end up strangling her first. I can't get over the fact she caused my heart to break more with each passing day, knowing why it broke, and hadn't done anything to help repair it.

"I can't believe my mother knows no bounds."

He pulls me into a hug and kisses my forehead. We can't fix the past, but damn it, we missed out on all those years, and now we carry around so many what-ifs.

We stay silent, holding each other, before I finally break away. "I get it now. It all seems so clear." I reach up to touch his face, running my fingers against his stubble. "So, what did you do after graduation?"

He moves to the bar to grab the bottle of Jack, and pours us both a drink. "Once I graduated, I got a gig in Los Angeles, and then next thing I knew, I had a record deal."

My lips lift into a proud smile. We might have missed out on time, but his dream had come true. No matter what, it's what I wanted for him. He worked hard and he earned it.

"How did your parents take that? You were supposed to go to Princeton," I say mockingly in his dad's voice.

"Yeah, we both knew that wasn't ever happening." He snorts, handing me a drink and I chug it back quickly. The burn from the Jack instantly heats me up and relaxes me.

"What do they think of your big success?" I ask as he pours me another drink.

"Oh, they say they couldn't be prouder now." His eyebrows rise and he looks to the ceiling, not amused.

We both take another shot before he takes my hand and leads me over to the couch, where we sit down with our knees touching. Suddenly I feel shy around him, as if we're on a first date.

I don't know why I'm getting shy now; our first date in high school ended with us fucking under the school bleachers.

"What have you been up to?"

"I finished school. Graduated with highest honors in business management, but I still can't find a job. We can't all be superstars." I nudge him playfully.

"That's amazing, Ace. Though, I have to say, I'm surprised you picked business management for your major. What happened to studying advertisement?"

"I got a minor in advertising, but I always had an interest in management. So, I took a couple classes and fell in love with it. Also, if I remember correctly, I was supposed to be your tour manager or PA, or whatever. Maybe I had a lingering idea that a job could lead me to you." I shrug. It's not a complete lie.

Cooper's pearly white smile nearly blinds me. I'm sure he pays someone to make them so perfect.

"And what brought you to Vegas?" he pushes.

"Alexa thought we needed to live it up before we start having grown up responsibilities. But really it's because we're all recently single and she wanted us to meet Mr. Right..." I trail off, biting my lip, knowing I've said too much. I'm hoping he didn't catch my slip, but when I see the grey clouds rolling into his blue eyes, I know he didn't miss a word.

We might not have been together, but I know it's going to bother him that I was with someone else. Just Mark's name set him off.

"So, you've been dating..." he mutters, taking a swig of his drink.

"Cooper...you can't be upset. I know you've probably had your fair share of women. Plus, I haven't heard from you in, what, three years and haven't seen you in four?"

"I know..." He sighs regretfully. "I've never gotten over you. I tried to move on...but I couldn't. I was still in love with you. *I'm still* in love with you." His body shifts closer to mine and he moves the fallen hair out of my face.

"I feel the same," I admit. "I tried relationships, but nobody even came close to holding a candle to you."

Cooper's hands lace through my hair, pulling my face to his, and he kisses me lightly. "I want to show you just how much I missed you," he whispers against my lips, his eyes dancing lustfully with mine.

"Yes, please."

He lifts me off the couch, and our lips connect hungrily, as he pushes me backward to the bedroom. There's a loud thud when Cooper's hand connects with the bedroom door, opening it, and it slams against the wall.

"I'm going to ravish the fuck out of you, Vi," he murmurs only millimeters from my lips. I can't reply because he's quickly sucking me back into his lascivious vortex.

The back of my legs hit the soft mattress, and his mouth descends to the side of my neck. A deep, primal

I FOUND you **May 19th, 2006**

moan leaves both of our throats; a sound all too familiar, that only we could make together. A sound I didn't realize I'd missed 'till I heard it again.

His hands run down my chest grabbing a handful of my breasts, massaging them in his palms. My nipples strain against the fabric of my dress and his thumbs rub over the hardened peaks. "Cooper," I gasp, wishing his mouth would wrap around them to ease their ache. Darkened blue eyes stare at me, showing his desire for me, and a knowing smirk plays on his lips. It's a look I remember well, telling me he has me right where he wants me, which only dampens my panties more. My legs press together, needing the friction against my throbbing core.

"I've missed you so much," he breathes before his lips crash back into mine.

Calloused fingers run down my shoulders, pushing the straps of my dress down, and his honey lips make their descent down to my now fully exposed breasts. Cooper wastes no time latching his mouth around my nipples relieving my yearning—something I had been silently begging for. He nips and sucks as his hands push the rest of the dress down my body and it pools around my feet. I step out of it, now standing before him in a tiny blue thong.

Cooper detaches himself from my breast and steps back. His eyes trace over every inch of me, each of his blinks is like he's trying to take permanent pictures to frame in his mind.

"Fuck. You always did have the perfect body. That hasn't changed one bit. If anything, you look even hotter," he hisses through his teeth and falls to his knees in front of me. His nose face plants into my core, rubbing against my lace thong, as he inhales deeply. "Heaven." Looking up at me, he's grinning wickedly, while his thumb traces my left hip bone. His soft lips place a kiss over my tattoo, which reads *Cooper*, in perfect calligraphy,

"I'm glad to see you still have it," he growls and grabs the strings of my thong, pushing them down my legs, and helping me step out of them.

"Of course I do."

"I bet all the other boys hated this." He smiles smugly, his eyes gleaming, looking as if he just won the lottery.

Oh, they did.

"What about you? I've seen pictures of you…topless and in your underwear and I didn't see it." If he got rid of his, I think my heart will break a little bit more. It was one of our forever connections to each other.

Standing, he undoes his belt and takes off his pants. The white cotton briefs make his package look amazing and I can't wait to wrap my lips around his dick. I almost forget about the tattoo, until he lowers the hem of his boxers exposing his left hip bone; and there it is, written in the same calligraphy: *Violet*.

"They airbrush it off. No matter how many times I tell them not too."

My fingers trace over the black ink, and it seems like only yesterday when we got them. It was Cooper's seventeenth birthday and he had talked about getting a tattoo of my name for months. He tried to convince me to get one as well. We each had fake ID's which we'd made to get into clubs and all kinds of other trouble.

I thought it was a crazy idea to ink each other's names into our skin, thinking it would be a curse to a break-up. Though once the guy finished the 't' in my name I was sold on getting one myself. Funny how we did end up separating, but at the same time knowing we could never forget each other even if we ended up thousands of miles apart.

"I think it's only fair if you undress for me. I want to admire you too."

"Whatever you want, baby," He slips off his shirt and

tosses it to the ground and then pulls down his boxers. His dick springs free, already at attention, waiting, wanting me.

Yep, he's still as big as I remember.

My mouth waters, wondering how good he would taste in my mouth again. I reach out, fisting his cock in my hands, pumping it, noting how velvety it feels against my palm. He groans and his hand moves to the back of my neck, urging me down.

Who am I to say no?

I fall to my knees and lick the trace of precum dripping from his tip. I hum my appreciation of his salty seed before taking him in my mouth and letting him slide down my throat.

"Fuck, Ace. I've missed your mouth..." My head bobs, taking him down as far as I can, tears escaping my eyes from the gag. I suck and slurp like crazy enjoying and savoring the hard, veiny, length of his cock. My hand falls between my legs, rubbing my achy nub.

"Oh, no, baby," he moans. Grabbing my hair, he tugs me off his cock. I whimper, missing my delicious lollipop. Hauling me up to my feet, I can feel his grin against my neck, while his fingers brush against my sensitive clit. "This is mine and I'm going to make you come so fucking hard tonight."

One of his digits slips inside of me, then another, working me over. I cling to him, my nails digging into his back, relishing in the feeling of our bare skin meshed together. "I want you," I plead.

His fingers fall from my drenched core and he sticks them in his mouth. His eyes close as he slurps my arousal from his fingers. "Mmm...strawberries. Just as I remember."

I feel my entire body flush at his words. He used to claim it was my hair color which made me into some kind of strawberry flavored goddess. I've tasted myself on his mouth and skin hundreds of times, though I think I taste good, I wouldn't call it strawberries. Then again, who am I to complain about the compliment?

Cooper lifts me and gently lays me on the bed. He crawls to hover over me, and his fingers run down my face. "I'm going to enjoy every inch of you. I have years of making up to do."

Wet, hot lips attach to the side of my neck, working their way down my neck over collar bones to my chest, taking his time sucking and nipping at every inch of my skin. My body withers underneath him, a fire igniting in my core I thought had burned out long ago. I've missed this man's mouth so much.

Slowly and teasingly, he works his way down to his goal between my legs. His tongue flicks my clit and his fingers go back to working their magic power over my core like moments ago. Threading his hair through my fingers, I push his face further into me, wanting to smother him between my thighs. "You taste so fucking sweet." His voice is muffled and his fingers pump inside me faster, "and you're still fucking tight."

With a hard suck on my nub, I explode, "Coop, yesss!" I scream, my body convulsing.

"That's my girl," he murmurs, removing his fingers from me. My arms reach out for him, needing, wanting him fully inside of me, expanding and stretching me out.

"Cooper...I want…"

"What do you want, baby?" Warm kisses move their way back up my body, 'till he's finally hovering over me, his dick poking me right where it needs to be, teasing me. I thrust my hips urging him in without any questions.

"I want to hear the words, Ace. Tell me," He takes his dick in his hand to stop it from touching my needy, wet core, giving me a wicked dimpled grin.

How I've missed this smartass bastard.

"You inside of me. I want to feel you again," I beg

and wrap my arms around his neck, pulling him down. I don't care about foreplay right now. I want him. All of him.

Now. Now. Now.

"Shit!" he mutters, trying to pull back out of my hold, but I don't let him.

"What??" I whimper, wondering why he's stalling.

Get in me, Coop. Freakin' fill me.

"I don't have any condoms."

Oh.

"I'm still on the pill Cooper...I'm clean, I swear...I've never gone bare with anyone else."

Cooper's forehead wrinkles as he cringes at the thought. *Okay*, maybe not the best thing to mention when we're in the middle of having sex, but he needs to get a clue—at this point, he could knock me up, and I wouldn't care, as long as he starts pumping that cock of his inside me—now.

He shakes off the uncomfortable thought and kisses my cheek. "I haven't either, but I've been checked. You sure?"

"Yes, please. I *need* you. I can't wait any longer." I thrust my hips into him again, showing him how desperately I want this.

Blowing out a sigh of relief, he smiles widely at me. "I know the feeling, baby. This is going to be fucking amazing."

With his elbows on each side of my shoulders, I wrap my legs around him, urging him with my heels, as he slowly slides himself into me. A loud vibrating moan escapes my throat when he completely fills me. When his balls hit my ass, he stills. My eyes flash open, and he's staring down at me earnestly.

"This is where I belong," he groans. "This is my home."

"This is my home too, but I beg you, move...please."

"As you wish..." His thrusts are painstakingly slow and I can feel every ripple of his cock as it moves in and out of me. I know right now he's trying to drive me wild, wanting me to beg for more. There's no way this man has forgotten I like to be pounded and made sore for tomorrow.

"Faster...enjoy me later. Fuck me now!" I demand frustrated. He shakes his head, his blonde waves dancing around, messing with me. My fingers grip in his hair, yanking it hard, feeling a couple strands breaking off in my hand. "Give me what I want, Reid. Take me."

A pleased smile spreads across his face. "That's my girl. Always knowing what she wants." Planting a kiss on my nose, he pulls out, and I feel his tip at my entrance. "Hold on baby, I've got you."

He slams into me violently, filling me to the hilt. My head hits the soft backboard and my hand releases its hold from his hair from the aggressive hit. "Yes, yes..." I scream, begging for more and harder. I need more.

He repeats the rhythm, but each time his thrusts become stronger and more frantic. My heels dig into his back trying to hold on to him. The bed creaks below us, the scent and the sound of our rough love making fills the room.

My nails run down his back; I'm sure leaving a permanent trail of red marks as I fall over the brink and call out his name in the most powerful orgasm I've had in years. My whole body shakes, making me weak and tired, but I want more.

"Now that's the best sight ever," he tells me through his panting. "I love that I can still do that for you."

"The only one!"

And it's the truth.

"Fuck, baby." His lips latch onto mine in a scorching kiss. The aftershocks of my orgasm, meeting his long punishing strokes are about to send off another earthquake.

"That's it, baby, let it go. Come with me."

"I—I can't—" My pussy grips his cock, sucking him in and holding him in place. He's barely moving inside me. It's enough though, all I need…

"Yes, you can Ace, you're right there again. Scream for me, baby." Cooper breaks through the tightened walls and sends me off again.

"Fuck, yes!" he hisses and spills himself into me, chanting my name like a sweet prayer.

He falls and rolls to his side, taking me with him in his strong arms.

We don't say anything as we listen to the sounds of our breathing; both of our chests rise and fall as our heartbeats calm from the amazing high. Our souls have connected again. He's here, I'm here, in this bed together, where I finally feel whole again. His hand brushes down my cheek, pushing my hair back.

"I love you. I could never stop loving you. I'm not letting you go again, Violet."

"I don't want you to let me go either. I love you." I roll my body on top of his and kiss him with everything I have. He grabs a handful of my ass and pushes me into his already growing erection. I guess someone else missed me too and is eager for more.

"Again?" I bat my eyes adoringly.

"Do you really have to ask?"

"We should get back down to the bar. I'm sure your friends are wondering where you are." He rubs his hand up and down my naked shoulder, both of us content—well for now. The musky smell of our lovemaking lingers in the air.

"I bet they don't even know that I'm gone with all the free drinks I'm sure they're drowning in."

Alexa and Julie are probably having the time of their lives right now, and I'm grateful; the last thing I planned on was leaving them to hook up with my high school boyfriend.

Cooper chuckles and places a kiss on the top of my head. "You might be right, but we're in Vegas. We should be partying it up."

"I thought that's what we were doing?" I bite my lip and wiggle against him. I'm perfectly fine partying in this bed, naked, 'till I can't walk again.

"Oh, it is. But if Brody finds out that you're here and he doesn't get to see you, he might kill me."

"Brody's here?" I shoot up and clap my hands. I missed that bum.

Brody is Cooper's older brother who was also like a brother to me. We always had Brody's support when we were dating. He never understood why his parents disliked me, and covered for us all the time when we went out or would run away for the weekend.

"Yeah, he's my manager."

"Good. Then I don't have to worry about you not being in good hands and some crook trying screw you over," I tease and leave small kisses on his neck.

"I don't know...sometimes I wonder," he jokes back, and I smack him playfully. Brody would be the last person to fuck him over. "Come on, get dressed. I promise to bring you back here tonight and the next and so on and so on. You know I'm not letting you go now that I have you back." His hand tangles in my hair, his eyes telling me how serious he is.

"Cooper..." I start and trail off, glancing down at the mussed up sheets on the bed.

I FOUND you   **May 19th, 2006**

I don't want to let him go either but I don't know how that's going to work. I live in Arizona and he's in L.A. On top of everything else, he's always traveling.

"Come on," he lifts my chin to look at him, "we can talk later and figure it out. I know you don't want this to end. This is forever now."

I run my finger along his tattoo of my name. "Forever," I whisper, making my lasting commitment to him.

"Forever," he whispers back, kissing me softly on the lips, sealing our devotion.

Once we re-dress, we make our way back to the bar, with Collin, the bodyguard in tow.

Cooper takes my hand as we walk through the club to the VIP area. The music blares louder and there's double the number of sweaty bodies on the dance floor now. Cooper leads me over to the VIP bar and taps the shoulder of a guy with wild, long, curly, blond hair. Brody: the boy was always in need of a haircut.

He turns around and looks at us with a drink to his lips. "Look who I found," Cooper grins, pulling me to his chest. Brody's eyes grow wide, with quick recognition. He places his glass down at the bar, shaking his head in disbelief.

"No!" he exclaims and Cooper laughs.

"Yes."

"Violet! Holy Shit!"

"It's me." I hold out my arms for him. "Miss me?"

Brody quickly gathers me in his arms and spins me around. Once he's done making me sick, he places me back onto the ground. "It's so good to see you." He grabs my face and squishes my cheeks. "Look at you. You're really here, jellybean."

Cooper groans beside me. He always hated the nickname Brody picked out for me, saying I needed something more *fitting.* Brody kept doing it to drive him insane and honestly, I didn't mind it.

"God, how are you?" Brody drops his hands from my face, allowing me to answer.

"I've been good. How about you?"

"Great. Cooper keeps me busy. Thankfully he pays me well." Brody looks between us and grins. "I'm so glad to see you. Because this man," he claps Cooper's shoulders, "has never been the same since you left."

"Shut up, dick." Cooper shoves Brody away

Brody puts his arm around my shoulder and leans down to whisper in my ear. "He's never gotten over you. Not that I can blame him."

"The feeling is mutual." I glance over at Cooper who winks, showing off his dimple, reminding me again why so many girls go wild over him.

"You, my friend, need a drink." Brody waves down the bartender and orders us a couple shots of scotch. My liver and stomach protest, even if it's the expensive shit.

The bartender pours the amber liquid into the shot glasses and slides them over to the three of us.

"Cheers," Brody says. We click our glasses, and toss them back. Thankfully, I'm already drunk, so it didn't taste as bad as I was expecting, but I have no control over my *yuck* face when I slam the glass back down.

"Still not a fan I see." Cooper kisses my cheek and I shake my head, the burn settling in my chest.

"Never will be."

A loud feminine squeal comes from behind us: Julie's. I turn and see Alexa and Julie in the middle of the dance floor, grinding on each other.

I FOUND YOU   **May 19th, 2006**

"Brody, you need to come and meet my friends." I grab both their hands and pull them towards the dance floor.

"Alexa, Jules!" I shout over the thumping music.

"Violet, you're back!" Alexa cheers excitedly. "You've been missing everything." She glances at Cooper beside me and bites her lip to contain her laughter. "Never mind, I forgot already."

I redden, remembering the naked fun I was having moments ago. "I want you guys to meet Brody. He's Cooper's brother."

Brody fixes his collar and gives them his full white smile. "Hello, ladies. Room for one more?"

"You bet!" Alexa pulls Brody between her and Julie, sandwiching him in.

"Cooper, will you dance with me?" I bat my eyes and run my hands up his chest and around his neck.

"It would be my pleasure, baby."

Cooper grabs my ass and pulls me flush against him. The rhythm and the pulsation of the music take control of my body, and I grind myself into him. Soon, our hands and mouths are all over each other's exposed skin, and then I don't think we're dancing anymore, but fully making out; Cooper's erection poking me in the stomach.

It's not 'till we hear the hoots and hollers of my friends that we break apart.

Yeah, we were seconds away from taking each other in the middle of the dance floor.

Being in Cooper's arms makes me feel like a teenager again.

"Damn, you two are fucking hot," Alexa howls, fanning herself.

"It seems hot at first, but you'll get sick of it soon." Brody's eyes roll to the back of his head. "Real soon."

A waiter walks by and Cooper grabs me a drink, and another, as we continue to dance. I'm feeling the full effects of all the drinks I've poured down my throat; somewhere between wanting to pass out and ready for a marathon.

"I'm so glad I came to Vegas," I say into Cooper's ear and then chomp down on his lobe.

"Me too. To think I almost didn't come out tonight."

It's destiny, I'm sure of it.

"I'm going to slow it down for a minute." The DJ's voice booms over the speakers. "Cooper, Violet this one is for you, from Brody." We both glance over at the DJ stand. Brody is up there with Alexa and Julie, the three of them wearing mischievous smiles.

The opening to "My Everything" vibrates through the sound system. All the couples around us, start to sway as Cooper's smooth voice begins to sing the lyrics, I know by heart.

"I used to be told dreams never come true
And I shouldn't believe in the make-believe.
I almost believed it - 'till I saw you
My everything
You were standing in the crowd, your eyes on me.
I dreamed you would be mine.
You quickly became my dream come true
When you told me you loved me too
My undying love is for you
For only you
'Cause you're everything to me."

"I love this song. It's one of my favorites," I muse, letting the lyrics absorb into my heart and soul like they always do.

"I'm glad to hear that...because I wrote it about you," he whispers in my ear.

"You did?" I say, pretending to be shocked. The lyrics were always clear as day; it was our story, but then there was a part of me that would think maybe someone else claimed his heart along the way.

I would fall asleep thinking Cooper was beside me singing this song.

He brushes his hand down my face, and pushes a loose strand of hair back. "Of course I did. You're my muse, Ace. Most of my songs are about you."

"I was always afraid to admit to myself they were." The tears slip from my eyes. "I never stopped loving you Cooper…" My words slur.

"And I never stopped loving you, Violet." He bends down and kisses me, our bodies no longer moving and our tongues doing the dancing instead. The two of us are in our own little world, our mouths desperate to make up for lost time.

Somehow, we manage to separate as the song fades. His forehead rests on mine, and his hungry eyes search mine.

"I don't want to lose you, Violet. I wouldn't be able to go on if I let you slip through my fingers again. I need you in my life—everyday."

"I'm not going anywhere." There's no other place I want to be but with him.

A look of panic and worry crosses his face. I'm not sure what caused the sudden change, then he blurts out, "We should get married."

My heart jumps into my throat and I try to swallow it down. Did he say, get married? My head is spinning from the words and the liquor running through my veins. Me? Mrs. Cooper Reid?

"Married? You mean me and you?" I wave my finger between us, giggling like a nut. I'm not really sure why I asked. I might be slightly dizzy and inebriated, but I knew he meant us, it just all sounds insane.

"Yes, me and you, goofy. We're in the perfect place. We should do it. Now," he pushes, excitement spinning in his blue eyes.

"Married? Now?" I ask again, to confirm the craziness that's about to go down. The words of my promise from the last time we saw each other circle in my head, a promise I swore I would keep if I had the chance...

"I love you too, Violet. I always will. You're my girl. My only girl and one day I swear I'm going to marry you."

"And I promise to say yes."

"Say yes, Vi. I never want to let you go again. Marry me, *please*."

"Yes…"

TWO

OCTOBER 5th, 1999

Violet

I'm walking down the halls of Riverside High that are littered with Halloween decorations and posters asking to vote for your homecoming queen and king. I've just gotten out of a meeting with the yearbook committee, a club I only joined because my friend Kayla told me how fun it would be. I'm always game for anything, so I joined. It hasn't been too bad; tomorrow I'm going to be taking pictures around the school.

Before I leave, I stop at my locker to grab my calculus book. The halls are quiet, almost everyone has gone home from their after-school activities.

"Well, well, well, you're looking fine today, Violet."

My blood runs cold at the voice that's been stalking me and my nightmares for the last two months. And no matter how much I complain, nobody seems to care. His family is part of the high society and his dad is the superintendent of schools.

Thomas Ryan can do no wrong in their eyes.

I slowly close my locker, gulping down the panic that rises from my stomach. Turning around, I come face to face with the beady eyes of a sick monster.

"What do you want, Thomas?" I try to act put off by his presence, but it doesn't work when my voice shakes. His haunting, brown eyes roam over my body, and he steps closer to me.

"I think you know just what I want." He licks his lips and lunges for me. I try to make a break for it, letting my backpack fall to the ground, but I don't get far when he grabs ahold of my wrist.

"You're not going anywhere." He twists my wrist, and searing pain lances through it. He grabs the other one, then slams me roughly into the wall of lockers. My head makes direct contact with the metal doors causing my ears to ring and my vision to go momentarily fuzzy.

"I'm so glad I finally have you alone. We need to talk, honey," he whispers into my ear.

"GET OFF OF ME!" I yell at him, trying to kick and push him away from my body.

He grabs me by my neck and squeezes "Shut up, bitch. I'm finally going to get what is mine."

"HELP!" I squeak out, and he proceeds to hold my neck tighter.

Where is everyone?

"This will be so much easier if you don't fight me, baby." His hot breath burns my skin and when he licks behind my ear the wetness is like acid.

I'm doing everything in my power to get out of his hold. He puts his hand up my shirt and I freeze. My mind goes into overdrive remembering the letters he'd written to me describing in deep, disgusting detail the things he wants to do to my body. The letters, written in black ink, which seem invisible to other people's eyes.

Tears run down my face when he snaps my bra strap, the elastic stinging my back briefly. Thomas cackles like a madman as his hand inches closer to my breast.

No. I can't let him win today.

"Stop!" I manage to kick him in the shin and he

curses under his breath. It's enough to get him to remove his hand from under my shirt, but his grip tightens around my neck instead.

"Shut up, whore. You know you want this," he growls in my ear.

"No!" I try to scream again, but my voice is silent. I'm lightheaded and I close my eyes, feeling the darkness coming on. I think I'm still trying to kick at him, though I can't be too sure.

The tightness around my throat suddenly disappears, and oxygen fills my lungs again. There's a loud grunt and my eyes flicker open, knowing I need to get away.

Though when I take in the scene in front of me; it's not what I expected.

Thomas is on the floor, and a boy with wavy blond hair is laying punch after punch into Thomas' face.

My savior.

"She said no, motherfucker," the boy seethes, still laying punches to the monster's face.

Once I finally get my breath and equilibrium back, I approach the blond, putting my hand on his shoulder trying to grab his attention. As much as I hate Thomas, he'd never get away with it being self-defense if he killed him.

With one last punch to Thomas' jaw, my white knight turns to face me, a fire burning in his dark blue eyes. Once our eyes meet the fire extinguishes and concern washes over his features.

"You okay?" he asks me, looking me over, shaking off his hand.

My neck throbs and I can still feel Thomas fingers around my throat. I rub my hand across the pending bruises and look towards the ground in relief. "Yeah, thanks to you." Thomas is moaning on the floor, not moving, and his face is bleeding like crazy. With my attacker detained, I let out the long breath I was holding in.

I have no idea what would've happened if he hadn't come to my rescue.

My hero gives me a small smile, exposing a dimple on his right cheek. I don't get time to process how cute he is, or why he looks so familiar when he grabs my hand.

"We need to get out of here." He grabs my fallen backpack and slings it over his shoulder.

We run down the hallway and out of the school to safety. The cool breeze hits my face, easing me and my heated skin for only a second. I glance back to the school doors, wondering what's going to happen to the bloody boy on the floor and the boy holding my hand.

"Shouldn't we tell someone about him and what he did?" I ask him, though I don't know why, no one would believe it anyway.

"He got what he deserved, Violet," he spits.

Goosebumps prickle on my skin as a chill runs up my spine once again.

"How do you know my name?" I stop in the middle of the sidewalk, yanking my hand from his. He looks at me confused, his eyebrows knitting together.

He's a sexy son of a bitch, but I don't need another stalker on my hands.

"Everyone knows who you are…and it's not like I could ever forget the name of the most beautiful girl in the world." He smiles, showing off his dimple again.

I blush. I'm not popular by any means, but I get along with mostly anyone I run into. I look over the almost six-foot guy, whose arms bulge every time they flex, and try to figure out where I know him from. I know I've probably seen him in the halls, but there's another memory in my mind attached to his face. With everything that just happened, my mind is in a fog.

"I wish I could say the same, but I'm afraid I don't know yours?"

I FOUND YOU   **October 5th, 1999**

"Cooper…Cooper Reid."

"That sounds familiar." I've heard the name before, but it's not clicking.

"Have you heard of X-rated?"

Then it hits me like a ton of bricks. Though, the last time I saw him was from the stage of a full club. I never got a clear look at him, with the array of colorful lights on the stage, but now it's coming back to me. Along with the sound of his honey voice.

"You're the lead singer. I saw you play at Sonic Boom last weekend. You're amazing."

"Thank you. I saw you too, and I had to ask about you."

He saw me? How the hell did he see me?

"Really? Me?"

He stifles a laugh. "Yes, you. I saw you in the crowd dancing around, then later when I passed you in the hallway of the bathrooms. You were laughing with someone, and wearing a skin-tight dress, looking sexy as hell." He shakes his head. "My guitar player, John, has English with you and told me about you. He mentioned you joined yearbook and I was waiting to talk to you. When you didn't come out with everyone else, I asked Kayla and she said you went to your locker." His hand meets my cheek and I lean into the smooth, warm skin of his palm. "There's something about you…"

I giggle nervously at his compliment and don't know what to say. I notice his free hand, and it's cut up and bleeding. I pick it up and exam it, his left hand falling from my face. "We should get some ice on this. It's starting to swell."

We walk the block to my house and since my mom isn't home, nobody can ask any questions about what happened. I grab an icepack from the freezer and we sit on the couch.

"This should help." I take his beat-up hand and place the icepack over it.

"I think you need one for yourself," he mutters, his free hand touching my neck.

"I'll be okay. It doesn't hurt as much as it did a little while ago." I wave it off. It's true it doesn't hurt that bad, but I also don't want a freezing icepack on my neck.

"You sure, because I'm not sure if I believe you?"

I nod. "I am. My throat does hurt a little, but I'll be fine. I swear. I can breathe again, that's what counts," I reassure him. "You saved me from that animal. Who knows what he would have done if you didn't."

"I was told he's been giving you problems."

Everybody knows, yet he still roams the halls like he owns the place. I wouldn't be surprised if he cornered me in the open like he did because he thought he was invincible and would get away with it. I can only hope that Cooper's fist has taught him a lesson.

"Yeah, but nobody seems to believe me...not even my mom." I frown and look down at my lap, wondering if now they'll believe me?

"After today, you shouldn't have to worry about it anymore." His arm wraps around my shoulder and I instinctively rest my head on his shoulder. It oddly feels right. He smells of aftershave with just a hint of sweat. Surprisingly, it's intoxicating.

I never liked the way a boy smelled before.

This is new and I like it. I inhale deeply.

His fingers brush through my hair and I turn my face to his. Our noses touch, and his warm breath tickles my lips. His deep blue's gleam, and I don't allow myself to think before grabbing the sides of his face and pressing my lips to his. His mouth parts, his tongue slips through my lips, brushing with mine. My arms move around his shoulders and he pulls me closer to him.

I've never been kissed like this before. It's freakin' amazing.

I break away from him slightly, our lips only millimeters apart. "More," he murmurs, and he kisses me again, not allowing me to reply.

When we are both panting for breath he pulls away.

"Go out with me," he breathes, his eyes searching mine.

"What?" I swallow, not sure if I heard him right.

"You heard me. Go out with me. Be my girlfriend."

Girlfriend?

My head spins; that happened fast.

But, shit, why not? He's hot and an amazing kisser, the lead singer in a band—what do I have to lose?

"Yes…"

He pulls me back to him, his hand roaming up and down my back, kissing me intently. I was only attacked an hour ago, I shouldn't feel so relaxed, but being held in his arms makes me feel safe. The affection, the sweetness of someone caring for me is overpowering and melts the shit away from earlier, making it feel like a distant past.

There are fireworks and unicorns jumping over rainbows. I'm elated to feel so wanted by someone.

"VIOLET HARPER SPENCER!" my mother bellows, causing Cooper and me to jump apart.

Cooper slides to the other side of the couch like I'm on fire. I try to fix myself, but what's the use? My lips are swollen from his kisses. I touch them, missing the connection already.

"Hi, mom," I say cheerfully, pretending I wasn't seconds away from letting Cooper defile me on the family couch.

Maybe I should be an actress.

"What do you think you are doing?" she asks me with her hands on her hips. "Who the hell is this?" She points over to Cooper, whose eyes go wide. Welcome to the Wrath of Amber Spencer.

"Mom, this is the milkman...he said we can buy the cow and save on delivery fees," I tease, trying to lighten her mood, but fail. At least I got a chuckle out of Cooper.

Come on mom, not even a crack of a smile?

"This is Cooper...He's my boyfriend." I take his hand.

"Boyfriend?" she scoffs. "I don't care who he is. Do you think it's appropriate for you to be doing that on my couch?"

"No, ma'am." I frown and look towards the dining room, however, inside I'm laughing.

"He needs to go. Now!" She points her manicured finger towards the front door.

Cooper stands, bowing his head, and walks to the door. I rise to my feet and quickly follow him out. Once we are safely to the sidewalk, I grab a hold of his arm. "Sorry about that."

I'm embarrassed and hope this doesn't change anything that happened between us. His head pops up from its bowed position, his winning smile back.

"It's okay. I can't blame her. You're her daughter and I was kissing the fuck out of you. Can I see you tomorrow to finish?" He wiggles his eyebrows, making my cheeks redden.

I nibble on my lower lip, glancing up at him shyly. "Yeah, of course."

His lips press gently against my cheek, and my heart flutters.

"I'll see you later, baby." He winks at me and I can't help the giggle that escapes my throat. I wave him off and watch as he walks down the road.

I turn around, facing my front door, and my stomach

I FOUND YOU **October 5th,1999**

twists as I prepare myself for a lecture. I feel there's no point of telling my mother about Thomas and how he gave me the bruises on my neck. She didn't believe me about his letters and she saw those too.

With my mother it's like talking to a wall. I can never do anything right. The only thing I do is disappoint her.

It aches all over that she can't just be a mom, tell me she believes me, hold me, and tell me it will be okay.

At least something came out of this horrible day; a white knight saved my life, swept me off my feet, and now I get to call him my boyfriend.

A person who will *hug me and tell me it will be okay.*

May 19th, 2006

Violet

"Say yes, Violet. I never want to let you go again..."

"Yes..."

I just told him yes…Didn't I? Because yes, yes, yes, always.

Before I can wrap my head around it, I'm in Cooper's arms and our mouths are absorbed in a kiss so hot and cosmic my foggy, alcoholic brain has cut off all sense of my reality.

I was single only hours ago and now I'm getting married. If it wasn't for the deep throb between my legs I would say all of this was a dream.

"I love you. I'm going to make you so happy, Ace. I'm never..." He's cut off when Brody grabs his shoulder making Cooper stumble backwards out of my arms.

"What the fuck, man?" Cooper punches Brody in the arm.

Alexa and Julie giggle like little school girls beside him.

"Sorry, I thought I would save Vi from you sucking her face off. So, I'm guessing this means you two are back together?" He flicks his finger between us.

"We're getting married!" I shout over the loud music. I'm giddy, jumping and clapping like a child on a sugar high.

"What?" Alexa and Julie both yell, their eyes wide

I FOUND YOU **May 19th, 2006**

and jaws hanging down to the ground like cartoon characters.

"Violet and I are getting married, and we're going to do it *now*." Cooper grabs my hand and pulls me flush to his body. "So, if you want to come along, get your stuff because we're leaving."

"Holy shit, Cooper" Brody claps his hands together. "I'm so there. I've been waiting for this for six years."

Brody used to believe by the time Cooper and I were nineteen we would be married and have a kid or two. That might have been true if I never left. I guess we'll never know, but we're catching up now.

"Just you three. I don't need everyone following us. Can you inform Collin? Let him and the others know we're going to "The Little Chapel" down the street. Tell him to bring Tucker as well for back up."

"Will do." Brody dashes over to them. I laugh at the departing man who might be happier than I am about my impending nuptials.

"Vi?" Alexa grabs my face and has me look at her. "This is what you really want to do?"

Wow! I don't remember there being two Alexa's.

I smile at my best friend when my vision focuses and she becomes one again. I nod. "I'm sure," I chirp. She lets go of my face and looks at Cooper, then back to me.

"You sure, you're sure?" she says more forcefully, double checking with me.

She's always been more of the mama bear between the three of us.

And even if I never dated Cooper before, who in their right mind would turn down a proposal from Cooper Reid? Julie would be all over this like a bad rash.

"Of course, this is what I want to do. I love him!" I tell her, wrapping my arms around Cooper, kissing his stubbly cheek. My man grins from ear to ear. "And if you've seen the size of his *you know what*, you would

51

snatch him up too."

"Violet!" Cooper shakes his head at me, fighting back his embarrassment.

"Yeah, Vi! Nobody here needs a visual," Brody groans as he comes walking back over, dramatically putting his hands over his eyes.

"Don't be jealous, Brody!" I stick my tongue out at him and he does it back to me. I really have missed our brother-sister relationship. Hell, now we're really going to be brother and sister. Vegas is playing out for me.

"Come on, let's gooooooo! I'm not getting any younger," I yell to the four most important people in my life.

This girl is getting married. I don't have a white dress, but I suppose this cocktail dress will do. I look hot. It's enough to get the man putting the ring on my finger to drool.

"Let's get you married, girl!" Alexa cheers. "I can't believe this happening."

"Well, there go my dreams of ever being Mrs. Reid," Julie tells me with a playful pout before jumping up and down. "I'm so happy for you... if anyone else should have the title it should be you." She gives me a hug and squeals in my ear.

"Does that mean you'll take that picture of my husband off your wall now?" I stare at her pointedly and put my hands on my hips, playfully.

Julie blushes, looking shyly towards my man. "Umm... maybe...?" I have a feeling it's not going anywhere. "Come on girl, let's get you married. WOOO!"

"We just need to make a quick pit stop first. I need something shiny for your finger." Cooper grabs my left hand and rubs his thumb over my naked ring finger. "Come, fiancée."

Fiancée!

I'm floating on the clouds next to a tiny angel, as my

I FOUND 𝓎𝓸𝓾   **May 19ᵗʰ, 2006**

future husband yanks me from the bar.

This girl is getting married.

The five of us, plus two Jolly Green Giants, make our first stop at a high-end jewelry shop on the strip. I don't think I should even be allowed to walk in here. All the jewels shine brightly, all worth millions I can't afford.

Violet don't touch anything; you break it, you buy it. And you'll be paying forever out of your ass if you do break something.

"Pick something," Cooper whispers into my ear while I'm blinded by all the sparkly, pretty stuff.

"What?" I gasp in surprise. Isn't this every girl's dream? A guy telling her to pick whatever they want from a display of jewels?

Somebody pinch me.

Wait, don't. I never want to wake up from this dream.

"Pick something. You're going to need an engagement ring and a wedding band. I want you to pick whatever you want. Sky's the limit, baby."

"Shouldn't you do that or should we be somewhere less, *umm,* fancy? Maybe a Zale's or something?"

"I want you to have the best. I can afford it, trust me."

Oh yeah, he's a superstar. How could I forget that?

Because to me, he's just Cooper. My Cooper.

"I know, it's just—"

He places a finger to my lips, cutting me off. "What if I pick out your engagement ring and we pick out your wedding band together?"

We could be here all day if I had to pick my ring

because I'll spend too much time debating about price and style. I just want to hurry up and get married.

"How about you pick out both of my rings and I pick out yours instead?" I counter, and he squints his eyes at me.

"I see you still have to debate *everything*."

"It's what I do best," I tease, a cheeky smile rising on my lips.

He grabs my chin and kisses the corner of my mouth. "Since I don't want to argue about this all night. I'll let you win. This time." He releases my chin then gives me a hard smack on the ass. I yelp in response and rub my now sore behind. "There will be a lot more of those coming later, don't you worry." He winks, a cocky grin playing on his lips.

"I'm not worried." I return his wink and move to the display boxes.

The man behind the counter pulls out a bunch of rings for me to see. There's so many to choose from and I need to make sure it's perfect. Cooper will be wearing it for the rest of his life.

Talk about pressure.

After what seems like an eternity, we pick out our rings, and take the short journey to the "Little Chapel."

Outside two large white doors—doors once we enter, we'll become one—Cooper grabs my hand, halting me from pushing them open.

"Ace, one more thing before we go in."

"What?" I gaze down at the man who I've loved since I was fifteen, as he takes both of my hands and falls to one knee, giving me an honest to goodness proposal. Out of the corner of my eye, I catch our friends with their phones capturing the moment.

"Violet, I've loved you forever. I remember the first time I saw you dancing at my show, you were stunning, but it was your eyes that captivated me, and I found

I FOUND YOU   **May 19th, 2006**

myself desperate to talk to you. Then once we kissed, I knew you were going to be the only girl for me. I became who I am because you believed in me, encouraged me, and kept me in line with your smart mouth. I love how adventurous you are because you always kept life exciting. I love how you love everyone, especially me and give second chances. There was never a moment you didn't have my heart even when we were apart. It will always be yours and I promise I'm never letting you go again. Here, today, I want to make an everlasting commitment to you because you'll always be my number one girl. You're my forever. So, Ace, will you marry me and be mine for as long as we both shall live?"

He pulls the velvet box from his inside pocket and presents it to me. Between the cushions is the largest diamond I've ever seen. The man is nuts; I'm going to tip over wearing that. Maybe I should've picked it out.

But it is so pretty. Look how the moonlight hits it.

"Violet? Don't leave me hanging…"

My eyes pop to his and I realize I got selfish staring at the ring that will tell everyone I'm his and he's all mine.

Our souls were really always meant to be together and tangled in sheets.

"Sorry. Yes, yes of course I'll marry you."

He slips the ring on my hand and kisses me ever so softly, while our friends clap for us.

"Let's do this thing." He clasps my hand and pushes open the large white doors.

Entering the chapel, we are met with red carpets, hundreds of different kinds of multi-colored flowers, which makes the smell of the place almost nauseating. There are golden figurines of Elvis and what might be Michelangelo standing in the corner. It's tacky as hell, but I love it. This is where I'm getting married. Plus, in a way, this is me and Cooper: spontaneous and not giving a damn where and what we're doing as long as we are doing it together.

We walk to the desk and from around the corner come out Frank Sinatra and Marilyn Monroe.

Only in Vegas.

They both smile at us and I think Marilyn's pupils turn into twinkling stars as she stares at Cooper with her mouth gaping open. I think it's safe to say someone is a fan.

"What can we do for you guys this evening?" Frank asks, looking between us, his voice sounding nothing like Mr. Sinatra's.

Aren't you supposed to try a little? Hope he's not singing at the reception.

"We would like to get married. So, whatever we have to do to make that happen," Cooper tells him wrapping his arm around my shoulder.

"Oh my god, you're..." Marilyn stutters finding her voice. "You're...Cooper Reid...Holy shit...I love all your stuff."

"Thank you." He beams sweetly at his fan and I think she's about to expire. Her chest heaves and her face reddens to the color of the carpets.

"Can I have your autograph?" She frantically scavenges for a piece of paper he can sign. "I'd be happy to—if you can promise to get us married ASAP afterward."

"Yeah, no problem." She shakes off her starry eyes and looks between us with a sincere smile. "Thank you and Congratulations."

Oh, I was sorta waiting for her to scratch my eyes out once she realized *he* was here to get hitched.

Marilyn finally finds an acceptable blank sheet of paper, and hands it over to Cooper. She thanks him repeatedly as he signs his name with a flourish. *We have a fangirl for life here.*

After we sign all the required paperwork, including

I FOUND YOU   **May 19th, 2006**

our marriage license, we are ushered into the ceremony room. It isn't any different than the lounge area, except for the white floral arch and Elvis standing beneath it; a pot-bellied Elvis, dressed in a sequined suit, with the perfect lip action going on. I break into a fit of giggles.

"What?" Cooper looks down at me, smiling. Probably wondering what's going on with his nut of a future bride.

"We're getting married by Elvis. I swear we had this conversation before."

"We did when we were sixteen. You said if we ever had to run off to get married you would want Elvis to do the ceremony," he tells me kissing the top of my head. "I make dreams come true, baby," he teases me and I shove his shoulder.

"I was kidding, but this works. I don't care who marries us, as long as we're together." I wrap my arms around his neck and kiss his cheek.

"I should've worn my sequin boots and jacket!" Brody moves to stand next to Cooper. "So I'm the best man, right?"

"Sure. Why the hell not? I can let you be best at something for once."

"If you weren't getting married and need your junk tonight, I kick you in the nuts, asshole."

I roll my eyes at them, wondering if they'll ever grow up.

Alexa cheers beside me, "Julie and me are the best girls, then." She throws her arms around my shoulders, hugging me tightly.

"Wait, you'll need this." Julie places a veil on my head and fluffs my hair a bit. "Now you're a bride."

"Who's wearing a cocktail dress," I say, suddenly unsure of my attire, and look at my reflection in one of the shiny statues against the wall.

"You look amazing," Julie assures me.

"She's right, baby." Cooper pushes my hair out of the way as his lips travel down to my ear. "Plus you're not going to be wearing this for much longer." He bites down on my earlobe and it sends delicious shivers down my spine.

Can we just skip to the I do's?

"Let's do this. Get you two lovebirds married, uh-huh," Elvis says interrupting our chatter.

"Yes, let's!" Cooper twines our elbows together while Elvis grabs the papers we signed moments ago, to look for our names, I'm sure.

Alexa and Julie come to stand at my side, and Brody at Cooper's. I look at the back to see Collin, and Tucker, standing guard at the door.

Elvis starts the ceremony, babbling about love, bliss, and commitment, but the only thing I can make out clearly are the uh-huh's after every sentence.

Cooper and I stare at each other, not only do I see his love for me shining in his blue orbs, but he's also biting the inside of his cheek, like I am, to stop from laughing.

"Do you, Cooper, take Violet to be your lawful wedded wife...*uh-huh?*"

"I do," Cooper says staring at me with the brightest, dimpled smile I've ever seen on his face.

"And do you, Violet, take Cooper to be your lawful wedded husband... *Uh-huh?*"

"Uh-huh..." I burst out laughing, no longer able to hold back after the fiftieth uh-huh.

"Hey, that's my line," Elvis says, falling momentarily out of character.

Don't mess with the King, Violet.

"Sorry," I say sheepishly but can't control my laughter. Cooper is also laughing hysterically. My sides are beginning to hurt.

Oh, this is great.

Elvis sighs, annoyed, and stomps his foot like my

father did when I was a kid, when he was waiting impatiently for me to do something. "So? Do you?" he urges.

"I do!" I scream out, my arms pumping the air, like a cheerleader asking for a 'Y'.

Elvis rolls his eyes, but quickly gets back into character and twitches his pelvis. "With the power vested in me by the State of Nevada, I now pronounce you man and wife. You may kiss your bride."

"Uh-huh!" Cooper and I say at the same time, still in a fit of hysterics.

Cooper grabs a handful of my ass and sliding his other hand through my hair, eagerly pulls my lips to his. My arms curl around his neck to keep myself upright for this over powerful-fourth-of-July like kiss.

Elvis begins singing "Love Me Tender" but I can barely hear anything with the fireworks going off in my brain as Cooper's tongue dances with mine.

I've missed this man and the way his kisses make my toes curl. He moans against me as our bodies merge closer together. How I just want to jump on him right here.

Cooper's lips rip from mine violently. Brody pulls Cooper off me and I guess I should thank him for stopping us from putting on a free show. We might be in Vegas, but they don't tolerate that on this side of town.

"Come on you two, break it up. There's other's waiting."

"There's no one else here, moron," Cooper growls at him smacking him in the chest.

"Fine, then take it back to the room. I've seen enough of you two go at it to last a lifetime."

"Sounds like a plan to me." Cooper grins at me. I have to fan myself because now I'm picturing what his tongue was just doing to my mouth, *down there.*

We walk out of the chapel to the noisy streets of Vegas. Cooper pulls me flush to his chest and runs his hand down my face. "I love you, wife."

I beam, "I love you, husband."

We're married! Holy crap!

Cooper bends down and gives me a searing kiss. The white double doors where he just proposed as our backdrop. My heart soars, knowing I'm back in the arms of my white knight, who once again swept me off my feet. I'm wanted, loved, and feel whole in these strong arms. This is where I belong.

I vaguely hear Brody yelling for us to get a room, but we ignore him, our lips not ready to disconnect.

I don't want this moment to end.

Tonight is the start of our second chance. Our new forever.

THREE

October 5th, 1999

Cooper

I leave Violet's house with an extra bounce in my step. I have myself a girlfriend; a girl who actually likes this angry kid. A voluptuous babe, with legs that go on for miles, and an amazing pair of perky tits. When I spotted her out in the crowd at Sonic Boom, I felt instantly drawn to her. I couldn't stop watching her dance around. Her amazing blue eyes captured me, and I had to figure out who she was. I knew she went to my school because she was standing next to three people I have a class with.

Thankfully, John knew her and gave me the low down. I thanked the lord above that she was unattached. However, I couldn't work up the nerve to talk to her right away. She was always surrounded by her girlfriends and if she were to turn me down, I wanted it done in private, so I waited after school for my chance.

I'm grateful I did.

Everyone knows Thomas Ryan. He's the kid who gets away with everything because no one is willing to stop him. His dad is superintendent of schools and loaded. He has a lot of weight in this town, making teachers fear for their jobs and students fear for their academic standing if they dare say something.

Everyone knew he was stalking some girl in our class, but nobody did anything. I just didn't know it was Violet.

When she didn't come out of yearbook with everyone else, I went in to look for her. I heard the strangled screams and rushed down the hall. Rage tinted my vision when I saw Thomas' hands around her neck. Like a man possessed, I stormed over to them and grabbed the asshole by his collar. I laid punch after punch into his pompous face, giving him everything he deserved for laying his filthy hands on her.

I kept hitting him 'till I felt Violet touch my shoulder, causing me to stop. If she didn't, I'm not sure if I would've stopped 'till the meathead was brutally tenderized and stopped moving.

I shake it off, the images still circling in my head, not wanting to think what could've happened if I didn't get to her in time.

When she kissed me and I got a taste of her sweet-honey lips, I knew right then I had to make her mine.

And I did.

I spot two cop cars outside my house as I approach. My gut twists, knowing this has everything to do with Thomas-fucking-Ryan.

I walk into the house, the door closing behind me, announcing my presence. My parents and the officers' heads snap to look at me. I gulp nervously when one of the officers approaches me.

"Cooper Reid?"

"Yeah?"

"You're under arrest for the assault of Thomas Ryan," he says roughly and reads me my rights while putting my hands behind my back, slapping cuffs on my wrist.

I FOUND YOU *October 5th, 1999*

"It was self-defense. I was protecting a girl from being attacked by him," I tell them, pleading my case, looking towards my parents for guidance. My mom is crying with her hand over her mouth and my father is still talking to another officer.

"You'll have your chance to talk down at the station. Your parents will meet us there."

"You gotta be kidding me."

I can't believe the stupid fucker called the cops on me. I saved a girl, and now I'm the one who is going to be punished for it.

"Mom, Dad…" I plead for them to do anything.

"We'll meet you there, Cooper. Don't say anything 'till I get there," my dad says firmly, taking off his dad hat and replacing it with his lawyer one.

This is a load of shit.

I arrive at the station and immediately get shoved into an interrogation room. Shortly after, my dad joins me. Never thought I would ever consider myself lucky for having a dad as a lawyer.

"What happened?"

"There's this girl, Violet." A smile tugs at my lips, her name bringing me a moment's peace to this awful situation. "I was waiting for her after school to talk to her, but when she didn't show up with the others, I went to look for her. When I found her, Thomas had her in a chokehold. I acted quickly and pulled him off her. I then punched him a couple times to make sure he stayed down and off her." I pause and look at my dad who is staring back at me, pursing his lips.

If he doesn't trust what I'm saying who will?

"You believe me, don't you? I know I don't have the best track record, but this time this punk really fucking deserved my fist to his face."

"I didn't say that. I'm familiar with the Ryans' and their son's issues." He clenches his jaw and my stomach

sinks knowing his family has outranked my father before. "They have deep pockets and know many people." He lets out an aggravated sigh, pushing his hands through his graying hair.

I guess money really can buy you anything. Another reason why politics and big business hold no interest to me; I'd never let assholes like the Ryans' get away with this shit. Why bother trying to find justice when you're not even the one in control anyways?

"Do you have this girl's information?"

"Yeah."

"Alright, write it down for me. And I will try to get you out of here in the morning."

"The morning?" I say, aggravated, standing. "I have to stay in this stink hole 'till morning?"

No wonder nobody helps anyone anymore. The law turns on you and somehow gets the good Samaritan in trouble. This is fucking bullshit.

"They're going to end up booking you for the night. You beat him up really good, and until we can get this girl's statement, it's out of my hands. The kid has a broken jaw and nose, and you have a few cuts on your hand. I'm sorry, Cooper. I will work something out." My dad pats my shoulder. "Just hang tight and it'll be alright. I'm sure I can keep all this off your record and it won't affect your future to Princeton." I silently stew at my father's final words. Like I give a flying fuck about Princeton. I've done nothing wrong and just want to get the hell out of here. It should be Thomas Ryan in here, not me.

Hours later, I'm processed and put into the detention center at the jail. Luckily, I don't have to share a room with anyone.

I lay down on the concrete slab they call a bed and try to get some sleep. I pray that I will be out of here in the morning.

I FOUND YOU October 5th, 1999

For now, I'll dream of the strawberry blonde, blue-eyed beauty I get to call my girlfriend.

I'm startled the next morning by the large metal door opening.

"Reid!" A large man, with arms bigger than my head yells at me. I jump up, my back aching, as I walk over to the detention officer.

"You're being released. Let's go."

Thank fucking god.

I collect my stuff for the clerk and walk out to the cement block lobby to meet my dad.

He puts his arm around my shoulder to walk outside telling me my mother is waiting in the car. The smell of exhaust and pollen hit my nose, and a car horn blares as it drives by. I sigh in relief at the smells and sounds of my freedom.

"Thomas Ryan and his dad dropped the charges. Violet claimed you did save her and the bruises on her neck were enough proof of the attack," my dad tells me.

"Tell me Thomas is going to pay for what he did," I growl.

My dad doesn't say anything, and glances off behind me. The bastard is going to get away with this.

"Dad, he could've killed her and he gets to walk around free?" My teeth clench down so hard, I think they might shatter.

What the fuck?

"Part of the deal of him dropping charges against you was to let this incident go. Thomas' father promised to have him stay away from Violet and get some anger management classes."

"What about her? Could she press charges?"

"Her mother wouldn't let her. It's over now, let's get you home. You still have school today."

Unbelievable.

Erica Marselas

I notice Violet by her locker right before lunch. I wish I had talked to her before yesterday. She's smoking hot and all I've been thinking about this week. I hope even after the mess yesterday, she's still my girlfriend.

She tucks a strand of her strawberry hair behind her ear as I approach her, and closes her locker. Her shoulders slump and she stares at the red door, unmoving. I tap her on her shoulder wanting to grab her attention from her mindless staring. As soon as my finger makes connect with his shoulder, she jumps with a loud shriek.

Fuck that was stupid, Reid; just come up behind her at the scene of the attack.

"It's me," I say gently. Her trembling body sags with a deep breath before she turns around to look at me. The panic quickly vanishes from her eyes when she looks me over and a bright smile lights up her face.

"Cooper! Thank god." She wraps her arms around my neck, pushing her body flush with mine as she hugs me tight. "I'm so glad you're alright. I was so worried."

"I'm fine. Thomas dropped the charges. How come you didn't press charges? You have the proof written on your neck." I gently outline her bruise on her neck.

She moves away from me and looks down at her feet. I'm already missing her touch.

"My mom didn't want me to. I saw her talking to Thomas' father and I think she made some private deal with him."

"That's bullshit!"

"What's even worse is my mom wants me to stay away from you." She frowns, crossing her arms tightly around her body.

"Why?"

What the hell did I do? I saved her and now I have to stay away?

"She was talking with your mom or something. She thinks you would be nothing but trouble," she mutters sadly. My heart races and my palms sweat, wondering if she's going to tell me it's already over. Though, I'm quickly put at ease when she wraps her arms around my waist, resting her head on my chest. "I guess your mom said something about this not being your first fight. Then your mom said something about me causing trouble for you and they thought it would be best to stay away from each other."

My mother is behind this? I fight for the right reason and now I'm being punished for it? Who the hell did I piss off up there? Well, I'm not going to stand for it; I've never been one to listen to rules.

"Do you agree?"

She snorts and squeezes me a little harder. "No. You're my white knight. If it wasn't for you I don't know what he would have done. You're my hero. I'm not letting you go."

If that doesn't make my heart swell, what will? What is this girl doing to me?

"So, you'll still be mine?"

"Yours," *she whispers into my chest.*

Erica Marselas

May 20th, 2006

Cooper

My Violet is tangled in my arms, naked, with her head on my chest. The sounds of her steady breathing and little breathy moans as she sleeps harmonize in my ears. I bury my nose in her hair and inhale the sweet scent of vanilla and coconut, a smell I've missed so much. Her skin is as soft as it is warm, like all those years ago, and it's hard to believe I finally got her back. I didn't think it was ever going to happen. When I saw her at the bar last night, I thought I was seeing things. I had to kiss her, to make sure she wasn't some figment of my imagination.

Once our lips touched, my heart—that had stopped beating after she left— started pumping again. She was my everything, and without her, I had only been going through the motions. I was only ever truly alive because of her.

I remember those letters Amber had sent me of Violet and *her 'boyfriend'*. I didn't want to believe it. I wanted to hear from her we were over. Before graduation, I'd made the trip to Arizona. Her mom answered the door telling me to go away, but I waited in my car for her to come home. When I saw her with *that* guy, laughing, and he had his grimy hands all over her, I had to walk away. It fucking hurt to let her go and I cried like a fucking wimp over my steering wheel, when instead I should've fought for her. After my visit, Amber ended up calling my mom

I FOUND YOU **May 20th, 2006**

and dad demanding, yet again, I leave her daughter alone; she'd moved on and was doing better because I wasn't around.

It was the final nail in the coffin, and I left shortly after for L.A.

Amber Spencer had hated me since day one. Honestly, I didn't like her either and I sure as hell didn't care what she thought about me. In my eyes, she treated Violet like shit and couldn't care less about what made her happy. The two were always fighting—mostly about me—but even I could tell Vi didn't have much love lost for her mother.

Hell, I didn't even care what my own parents thought of us together. The only person's opinion that mattered to me was Violet's.

I knew part of Amber's dislike for me was because I was known to fight all the time. But what most people didn't know was what started my reputation as a 'bad boy'; I had to protect Brody from bullies. He'd suffered from leukemia when he was younger and was always getting picked on because it had made him an easy target. He couldn't defend himself, so I did it for him. Some people learned quickly not to mess with us Reid's, others didn't. Later on, it became a game for douchebags to want to piss me off just so I would fight them. I guess getting a black eye from me back then was like a badge of honor, and I was willing to give it to them. But once I started dating Violet, the fights stopped, and people left me alone when I was with her.

Or maybe it was because I had been the one to take care of Thomas finally.

Whatever the reason, Violet was the one to bring me calm and light a spark in me. She was the only one besides Brody who believed in my music career. They pushed and inspired me to keep going no matter what my parents thought. That it was my life and I should make my own choices.

My dream was always to be a singer. When I was thirteen my uncle gave me a guitar, and I taught myself how to play. Freshman year, my music teacher was impressed with my voice and being able to write my own music. She would take time with me after school to teach me new things to help me excel. It was she who told me to start a band, and I should make sure people see my talent. Now everything I had hoped for came true.

I'm famous, and I have the girl I've always loved back in my arms.

I knew I had to act fast last night, I always did when it came to her. I couldn't risk losing the best part of me again. Sure, I've had my share of one-night stands, but they meant nothing. I kept hoping it would fill this void inside of me.

It never worked.

Despite both of us being drunk, I had no doubt asking her to marry me was the right thing to do, and I wasn't surprised in the least when she said yes.

She did promise me all those years ago she would.

Who would have thought both of our improvised visits to Vegas would be what connected us again. I'm glad I listened to Brody about needing the escape to loosen up a bit.

Violet stirs in my arms as my phone rings beside me. There's only one person it could be this early in the morning and I'm not ready to deal with that. I ignore it because right now, the only thing that matters is my wife.

Her left hand is splayed out on my chest, the diamond sitting proudly on her ring finger, telling the world she belongs to me.

Mrs. Violet Reid.

My Ace, my number one girl, finally shares my name.

Nothing can tear us apart now. Not even meddling mothers.

I FOUND YOU **May 20ᵗʰ, 2006**

My hand traces down her naked arm, causing little goosebumps to appear on her heated skin. Her eyes peel open giving me a sleepy crooked smile.

"Good morning, baby." I lay a kiss on her lips, which are still swollen from last night's activities. Visions of her plump lips wrapped around my dick quickly come to the forefront of my mind.

"Morning…shouldn't you answer that?" She points to my phone which is still ringing obnoxiously on the nightstand.

"No, it's probably just my PR agent." I wave off and she stares at me confused.

"Why would they be calling this early?"

"Oh, maybe because there's a bunch of questions that need to be answered. Starting with them asking about who you are." Taking her hand, I press my lips to her wedding bands, and her eyes grow wide at the sight of her new jewelry.

She jolts up, retracting her hand from my hold to stare at her ring then back at me, a nervous giggle leaving her throat. "I thought—I thought it was all a dream. Holy cow. We're married."

"It was no dream, baby. You are now my wife, *Mrs. Reid.*"

"And you're my husband, Mr. Reid."

Vi moves to straddle my lap and runs her nails through my scalp before kissing me. When she pulls back she gives me a witty grin. "Do you hear that?"

I shake my head and try to listen for what she's hearing. The room is dead silent. "No?"

"It's the sound of teenybopper hearts breaking everywhere because you're all mine forever."

I grab a handful of her ass and latch my mouth around her pert nipple. She moans trying to brush her hips against my aching morning wood.

"I want you," she whispers and I release her breast

with a pop.

"You want more already do you? I expected you to be sore. I mean, we did fuck over almost every inch of this room for hours and hours *and* hours." I wiggle my eyebrows at her. Her teeth sink into her lip and I watch as she surveys the destroyed room. There's clothes, blankets, and a bunch of papers thrown everywhere. A framed picture has fallen from the wall and even the desk is upside down. The two of us were always wild and all over the place when we fucked, but the mess we made last night is pretty epic.

Her eyes meet mine again and I feel her arousal coat my dick. I wonder if she's remembering all the things we did last night.

"I am pretty sore, but it's never stopped me before." She shrugs and crashes her lips to mine.

I tighten my grip on her ass, my dick rubbing at her entrance waiting to enter his home in her tight heat. "God, I love you." I hiss out between our violent tongue war. "I can't wait to get you back in my own bed…"

Her body freezes and she pushes herself away from me.

What the hell?

Her eyes fall to our laps and she closes her eyes as if she's pained. "What's wrong?"

She takes a deep breath and looks back up at me with worried blue eyes. "How will this work? We live in two different states. We both have totally different lives."

"You'll come live with me," I say simply, figuring it's a no-brainer. Plus, there's no way in hell I would live in a ten-mile radius of her mother.

"But Cooper, I have a life in Arizona…"

Her comment throws me for a fucking loop.

Does she really think we are going to live apart now that we're married? Fuck That.

Even if we didn't get married, I never want to be apart

from her again. Now that I've found her, I'm never letting her go.

"That's not what you were telling me last night. You said you just broke up with some asswipe and you haven't found a job yet. So what's holding you back, Violet?" I do my best to keep the anger out of my voice, but fail.

I refuse to be separated from her again. This woman is my obsession. My muse. My everything. I'm dragging this girl wherever I go now, whether she likes it or not. I'll handcuff her to me if I have to.

"Friends?" she says meekly.

I understand her not wanting to be far from her friends, but it's *me.*

"Don't you want to be with me?" I brush my hand up and down her shoulder, and put on my best pout, making my whole bottom lip pucker. A pout which used to always work like a charm back in high school. Not only did it get what I wanted but it also always worked for getting into her pants.

The Cooper Charm, she used to call it.

"Of course, I do. I just wasn't expecting us to get married after seeing each other for the first time in so many years." She laughs nervously. "Everything changed in an instant. I haven't had a chance to think anything over."

"Do you regret it?" I ask her, needing to know if I messed everything up for us.

"Only that we didn't do this sooner." She smiles and bats her eyes seductively.

Thank God.

I lunge for her, pushing her down to the mattress, needing to show her all over again how much she means to me.

We fall back on the bed in a sweaty heap. I push her matted, strawberry hair away from her glowing face. She's still panting slightly as her hand snakes up my chest to my face.

"How much time will you need to move out to L.A. with me?" The quicker she moves into my house the better.

She shrugs. "I don't have a whole lot. I'm sure you could help me set up a moving company for my furniture. The rest is just clothes and knickknacks."

"We can make a pit stop there first if you want."

"You're not wasting any time, are you? No chances to say goodbye to my friends?" She smirks, and although I know she's being sarcastic, I can see the worry behind her baby blues.

"I don't have to be anywhere for a while. I'll stay with you 'till you're ready to go if you want," I offer and I see some of the tension she was holding in roll off her shoulders.

"I would like that."

My hand runs down her face. "I know this is a big change for you and no matter how much I want and need you with me, I want you to be happy…"

Her fingers push against my lips to silence me. "My home has always been with you, Cooper. It is a huge change, but it's what I want. The only thing I worry about is breaking the news to Julie and Alexa. We've been through everything together and I feel bad about leaving them behind with my part of the rent."

"I'll handle that, don't worry." I'm not going to leave her two best friends in a lurch. I'll buy the house if I have too.

"I wasn't asking you to cover the rent. It's just they didn't really get a fair notice that I'm leaving."

"I understand, but I can afford it. They're part of your life and they mean a lot to you, so I'll do what I can. Don't over think it."

"Anyways," she mutters, "we can discuss that later." She pulls the sheet around her chest, sits up, and rests back against the headboard. "Hopefully L.A. will be a nice change of pace and I'll have better luck there with the job hunting."

"You could always come work with me?" I offer. It had always been part of our original plan for us to work together.

"Doing what?" Her forehead wrinkles as she eyes me curiously.

"If I remember correctly, you were supposed to be my team. Whip me into shape and tell me what to do. It just so happens, Brody is looking for someone to help him. My record company gave me full permission to hire anyone I want."

"Why doesn't Brody have help now?"

I clench my jaw thinking about the ignoramus we recently let go. "We had someone, but he got fired for being a moron and fucking up tour dates. It was a mess. Brody vowed to work alone rather than trust another idiot."

Brody is not only my brother but my best friend. Like Violet, I trust him with everything when it comes to my career and my livelihood. Without his help, I wouldn't be where I am now. We annoy the shit out of each other, and still beat each other up when we're pissed, but it's what all brothers do.

"So, what makes you think he'll want my help? I don't know anything about tour management and scheduling live appearances, or any of that."

"I think you know more than you let on. You have a degree in business management." I raise my eyebrow at her and she glances away to look at the television. "You and Brody used to book shows all the time for me in high school."

"But that was high school." She throws herself back into the headboard, her hands flopping down to the mattress. "This is the big time. Roadies, dealing with record companies, venues that *aren't* bowling alleys. I would be totally lost."

"But if anybody could figure it all out, it'll be you. Just think about it. I'm sure Brody will give you a crash course."

She purses her lips and nods. "I'll think about it, but I make no promises to anything."

"I don't want to be away from you for long periods of time. Hell, you don't even have to work if you don't want to." I raise my finger to stop her when her mouth pops open to protest, and she instantly snaps it shut. "But I know you want to. You didn't get that degree for nothing, right?"

She nods.

"I need to go get some clothes from my room," Violet tells me, dropping the conversation.

"You going to come back here afterward?"

"Considering you're my husband, I'd say you're kind of stuck with me now. I just need to get my clothes, and I owe Julie and Alexa an explanation. Give me an hour or so to get my story out."

"How about I call Brody and we can go get some food?" I don't need her answer, though, because her stomach rumbles, answering for her.

Her cheeks heat and she rubs her stomach. "Food sounds amazing right now. I'll be back shortly." She moves in to kiss my cheek, but I need more. Pulling her into my lap, my lips mold with hers, trying to show her how much she means to me. I try to project every ounce of my love, and my need for her into my kiss.

A moan comes from deep in her throat and her hips wiggle against my growing crotch. I break away from her because if I don't she'll never get her stuff and we might end up starving to death.

"I love you, Mrs. Reid."

Violet rubs her nose against mine. "I love you too, Mr. Reid."

After a quick shower, she leaves, and I decide to call my PR agent, Louie, back. I am sure I'm about to get an earful about my quickie Vegas wedding. Brody probably called him to give him a heads up.

After the third ring, he answers, irritated. "Cooper, I have been trying to reach you all morning. What is this about you getting married last night? Please tell me this is a hoax. Please tell me there is another explanation for these pictures."

"I did get married, Louie," I say proudly, looking at the silver tungsten ring Violet picked out.

"To who? I never pictured you as the guy to get drunk and married in Vegas." I hear the sounds of shuffling papers. "Your dad has been calling me nonstop, talking about annulments and muting the press. He's giving me a headache, even though he has a point. Just tell me it's not a stripper or a prostitute or something."

I inwardly laugh at his panic and figure I should put him out of his misery. "It's Violet. I married Violet Spencer."

The line goes silent. I think I stunned him. "Violet? *The* Violet? I thought you hadn't seen her in years. What the hell man?" Leather squeaks through the phone and I'm certain he's fallen into his chair.

Anyone who is close to me know about my feelings for Violet. It wasn't something I could hide. I wear my devotion to her like a bright neon sign hanging over my head. Almost every hit song I've had is written about her. I also tend to be a sentimental drunk, and she's all I'd talked about after about three shots of whiskey.

"Yes, *the* Violet."

"Wow. Man." He blows out a large breath. "Congratulations, but how did this happen?"

"We ran into each other at the club last night, and one thing led to another. I asked her to marry me and she said yes."

"I never believed in fate before, but damn. Alright, I'll spin this somehow, so it doesn't look like a Reid drunken adventure in Vegas." I hear keys start to click on a keyboard as he gets to work.

My phone beeps, telling me I'm getting another call. "Thanks man. Hey, I'm getting another call. Talk later."

"Sure man. Good luck, and I can't wait to finally meet the little lady."

We hang up and I answer the call waiting, hoping it's Vi. Unfortunately, it's not.

It's my mother.

"Cooper Michael Reid!" she shouts in my ear, her shrill voice doing nothing to help my hangover.

"Hello mother," I say with all the sugary sweetness I can muster.

"What is this I'm hearing about you getting married last night? Do you even know who this girl is? Your father is doing everything for you to quickly get an annulment and hopefully, it won't cost you anything." The words spill out of her mouth so fast, they leave my head spinning. I pinch the bridge of my nose wondering if Evelyn Reid can ever say anything about my life without amping it up to ten on the extreme-freak out meter.

I sigh heavily and know this is going to take every ounce out of me. My fantastic day is about to plummet. "Listen you don't need to worry about an annulment because the girl I married is someone I know…"

I FOUND YOU   **May 20th, 2006**

"You never bring any girls home. Who is she Cooper?" The volume of her voice continues to escalate.

"Well, if you let me finish mom, I could tell you it's Violet."

"Violet…" All the air leaves her lungs and I enjoy the second of silence from her dismay. "That *girl* you dated in high school?" she hisses with all the bitterness she can muster.

Some things never change.

"One and the same."

"I don't believe this," she huffs

"Well, believe it, mother." I run my hand through my hair and yank on it in frustration.

"And let me guess, she's going to be moving in with you and you're going to be supporting her."

"Of course she's going to be moving in. She's my wife. You know how I always felt about her," I say, raising my voice; this conversation is pissing me off.

Why can't she just be happy for me? She knows how much I loved Violet, even though she didn't like it. It's like my happiness always takes a back seat because it isn't the life she envisioned for me.

"Seems convenient," she scoffs and it's the final straw.

"Mom, I don't have time for this. I need to get ready for brunch with my *wife.*" I hang up and toss the phone across the room.

I fight the urge to scream. Why can't she just say congratulations, son?

Instead of yelling, I manage to get out of bed and throw on a pair of sweats. Glancing around the destroyed room, I smile with pride remembering taking Violet over every inch of it. Though the wedding was rushed, the consummation wasn't.

Plus, who needs a big lavish affair? Elvis was fitting, and I'll be loving her tender for the rest of her life.

Uh-huh.

An inspiring rhythm pops into my head, my muse on full blast. I grab my guitar, to write down the lyrics and chords before I forget.

> *You went away*
> *I was lost*
> *Lost without you*
> *Our parents thought we were wrong*
> *Never happy with our young love*
> *Thought our love wasn't strong enough to survive.*
> *They ripped us apart*
> *When you went away*
> *But you remained in my heart.*

I hum out a tune, but the rest of the lyrics aren't there yet. The chorus quickly comes to mind, thinking of my bride in front of a fake Elvis, his pelvis gyrating, and curling his lip.

> *I found you*
> *Made you my wife*
> *I found you*
> *To have, to hold, for the rest of my life.*
> *Uh-huh,*
> *We'll prove to them*
> *They'll never win*
> *You're mine forever*

I'm in mid-erase of a d-minor chord when a pounding echoes against the doors of my suite.

"Motherfucker, open the door," Brody's obnoxious voice bellows and I place my guitar on the bed. I pick up the sheet music and hide it in my bag, not wanting my Violet to see it quite yet.

Grabbing a shirt, I pull it over my head and swing

open the door. Brody is mid-knock when I come face to face with him. A cocky grin pulls at the corners of his mouth and he walks into my room like he owns the place.

"Where's the missus?" His eyes dart around the room before they land back on me. "Did you manage to scare her away already?"

I growl and sock him in the arm. "Not funny, jackass."

"Oh lighten up. But seriously, is Violet here?"

"No, she went back to her room to get the other girls and a change of clothes. What do you want?" I glance down at the papers he has curled in his right hand.

"You and Violet made the front page of every newspaper." He throws the newspapers on the table, displaying said front pages.

"Cooper Reid, HITCHED"

The headline screams from the Las Vegas Sun, and below the large, bold print there is a five by eight a picture of Violet and I kissing outside the 'Little Chapel.' There's a close up of her left hand, which is in my hair, with a red circle around her wedding rings. I pick the paper up and read the article.

Cooper Reid was spotted outside of The Little White Chapel in an intense lip lock with a blonde beauty. The wedding was spontaneous according to sources. The two were only spotted hours before at the Bellagio, drinking, and dancing. Reid has no prior relationships known to the public. So, who is this mysterious woman who was able to convince the long-term bachelor into marriage? We have reached out to Reid's publicists for answers.

Will this quickie marriage be quick or will it be one to last forever? Stay tuned.

The other papers say much of the same thing. I smile again at the picture of us outside the chapel and look back up at my brother. "I might have to frame this. But this explains how Louie and Mom found out so fast." I lay the paper back down on the table.

"I should also warn you, there is a large crowd outside the hotel. Photographers, crazy fans, you know, the works. Collin and Tucker have gotten a couple more of the hotel guards to help out with crowd control."

Collin and Tucker have been my bodyguards since I found I couldn't go anywhere without a camera in my face or a fan chasing me down. I consider them family, but they made it clear their jobs come before friendship.

"Should I have someone get Vi?"

"Probably. If they figure out who she is, I'm sure many of the broken hearts will want to rip out her hair."

I snort in reply. I love my fans, but sometimes they scare me. There are days when I'm ambushed by them and I don't know how I make it out alive with my clothes still intact. "So much for staying under the radar this weekend."

"*Buutttt—*" he extends the word out and grins, "you're married. How does it feel?"

"I'm still processing it a bit, but fuck, I'm over the moon. I owe you for bringing me here. What the fuck were the chances of running into her, you know?"

"It was destiny," he says in a mocking, singsong voice. "You should've tracked her down years ago like I told you instead of believing Amber. I also don't care what you think you saw, if you didn't let that woman into your head…" Brody shakes his own head and slips into one of the lounge chairs. "Though the good news for me is, I was able to hook up with Alexa. She was," he whistles through his teeth, "dynamite in the sack."

"Well, that's great. Oh, and I don't know if you want to sit there…" I point to his chair, the same chair I was sitting in hours ago while Vi sucked my dick.

Brody jumps from his seat and groans, "Fuck man. I'm going to have to fucking carry around the sanitizer again."

"I would say sorry, but you know I'm not…better get used to it," I quip. Me and Vi fucking when we're in the same room together is inevitable.

"Fucker," he growls, "then where can I sit?"

I look around the suite and scratch the back of my neck. "Um you might be better off standing."

FOUR

October 23rd, 2001

Cooper

I'm twirling my keys on my finger, getting ready to go pick up Violet for our trip to San Diego to visit her dad. He lives on the Naval Base there, but next month he is getting deployed to Afghanistan.

Violet was devastated when she found out, and now is trying to spend as much time with him before he ventures out as she can. Today is the perfect time to ask him for his daughter's hand in marriage. I don't know how long he'll be gone, and even though I don't have the proposal planned, I want to have his permission just in case he's not back by the time I do.

I know Vi is worried about everything that could happen to him overseas, especially in these times. The dark thoughts of possibly losing him have plagued her mind all the time since she found out he was leaving. She idolizes her father and he supports her in everything.

If anything happened to her dad, I don't think Vi could handle it. We're both still trying to recover from the miscarriage, a loss which weighs heavy on both our hearts. The bad days were getting further apart, up until two weeks ago when we both broke down, realizing the date. The date in which we should've been holding our

I FOUND you **October 23rd, 2001**

baby in our arms...

My stomach twists and I do my best to shake off the ever-depressing thoughts. I can't think of them today. No, today, I need to be strong and keep being the man she needs me to be. I'll do everything in my power to keep her smiling because I hate seeing her cry. I know we'll start a family one day—as soon as we're married.

I'm almost out the door to freedom, when my mom stops me. I spin around, putting on my winning smile, knowing I'm going to have to face her familiar wrath over my girlfriend.

"And where do you think you're going now, young man?" she scolds, her hands on her hips.

"I told you, Violet and I are going to visit her father for the weekend."

"I just think you could do so much better than her, Cooper. She's leading you down—"

"The wrong path...and destroying my future," I say, cutting her off. "Yeah, yeah, you've said it all before, but you have it all wrong and you know it. Violet is on my side and wants my dreams to come true. I don't want what you and dad want, and eventually, you'll have to understand that." I'm exhausted from this same fucking fight anytime I go anywhere.

Almost every day for the last two years.

Two years, I've spent listening to her talk down about my relationship with Violet, and my career choice. What's so wrong with wanting to be a singer and songwriter?

Every now and again she does back off. Today is not that day. Dad is even to the point where he just nods but agrees without saying a word.

She's going to have to get over it though because I'm going to marry Violet one day. We'll have more kids, a house —the whole shabang—and she'll just have to live with it.

"It's bad enough you're dragging Brody into your bad choices too. I mean he's studying music management," she continues her rant. "Thankfully, you haven't gotten to Dustin, yet."

My little brother Dustin is twelve and has his head in the clouds. Video games and Pokémon are the only things he cares about. Just how he should be at that age.

"That's because Brody has faith in my career. If he can't be my manager one day, he'll do it for someone else, and he will be great. I need to go." I open the door and slam it behind me.

I arrive at Violet's house and she comes out the door in a short, pink sundress, her ponytail swaying back and forth as she bounces over, showing off just enough cleavage to make me want to nuzzle my nose in her chest.

She swings open the door and throws her bag into the backseat. "Hey." She leans over the console and gives me a kiss.

"Hey. Did you get some sleep last night?"

Last night, we celebrated Violet's seventeenth birthday. Her best-friend, Kayla, threw her a huge party at her house, inviting everyone from our Senior class to join. It was just the thing we both needed to clear our heads and try to be okay. Though, I think we both ended up drinking too much to do so—but we had fun.

It's probably another reason my mom wasn't too happy about my adventures with Violet; I had stumbled into the house at three a.m. smelling like beer and Vi.

"Yeah, after the romp in the car, how could I not fall asleep?" She says cheekily and I glance towards the backseat where I'd had her withering under me and had made her come twice. She buckles her seatbelt and we set off onto the road.

I FOUND YOU   *October 23rd, 2001*

I'm not sure how we made it to her father's house two hours later, but we did. Violet had leaned over the console to suck my dick while I drove, making me think it was my birthday, considering how long her mouth bobbed up and down my shaft. I don't know how I managed to drive straight, or not have semi-truck drivers get distracted with our show. Her ass had been pointing out the window, in a very short dress. At least the windows are lightly tinted, but I love how wild and spontaneous she is, and my dick is in agreement.

I park in front of her father's house and kill the engine. She moves to grab the door handle when my hand reaches behind her neck, pulling her to me, our lips millimeters apart.

"You know one day you're going to have us killed because of that mouth of yours."

"I guess that would be one way to go," she pants, and I take the opportunity with her lips parted to slip my tongue into her mouth. I can taste my saltiness on her tongue along with the lingering flavor of her mint toothpaste. She moans, her nails digging into my shoulders, and I can feel the indents she's making in my skin. Out of the corner of my eye, I see her dad's front door open, and I break away from her lips.

"We should get out before your dad makes good on one of his threats."

"No, we wouldn't want that," She giggles, giving me one last peck before getting out of the car.

Ron is standing at the front door and Violet goes flying into his arms, causing him to stumble back.

"Daddy, I've missed you."

"I've missed you too. Happy birthday, sweetie." He continues to hug her tightly. When he sees me approach, he pulls back from Violet, putting his hand out for me to shake.

"Cooper, my boy, it's good to see you."

"It's good to see you too, Ron. Caught anything good this year?"

"A 50-pounder catfish just last week," he says proudly, rocking on his heels.

I stare at him in amazement. I have no idea how he's able to catch these monster fish. The best I can get is a 10-pounder, anything.

"And let me guess…that's what we're having for dinner," Violet says with disgust. The girl can't stand any kind of fish.

"Maybe for Cooper and me, but I have your favorite for dinner," he tells her. *"It is your birthday."*

"Lasagna?" Her eyes light up and she claps her hands together in excitement.

"Mayyybe." He extends the word out and her enthusiasm wanes.

"Wait, who made it?" She squints at him. *"It better have been Beth. If it was from Morgan, I'll pass."* She sticks out her tongue, *"Blah."*

Beth and Morgan are Navy wives on base. When they heard Violet was coming over last time, they had cooked for her. Both of them have known her since she was little, but last time Morgan cooked, I was there, and her meat pie was food poisoning R' Us. I shudder at the memory.

"Maybe I should say it was Morgan, just so you'll eat my fish." He puts his arm around her shoulder and pulls her into the house. *"Let's get you two settled in and we can go for that hike you wanted to go on."*

After a five-mile hike, leaving my calves burning from all the hills, we arrive back at the house. Violet is supposed to be upstairs taking a shower, but more than likely she passed out on the bed. I'm standing in the kitchen with Ron helping him grill up the catfish.

"Ron, I was wondering if I could talk to you about something before Violet gets back." I pull on my collar nervously. It's suddenly very hot in here, and sweat is forming on my brow.

"What is it, son?" He turns to me, pointing the knife at me, the fish guts hanging off it.

I gulp, hoping after I ask, I come out better than the fish.

"I know Violet and I are young, and I'm not saying I want to do it now. I mean, I would if we could." I shift from foot to foot, my heart beating out of my chest.

"Spill it son. This fish isn't going to cook and season itself."

"Okay, what I'm trying to say is, when the time is right, I was hoping I could get your permission to marry your daughter…"

I look away from him, anxiously awaiting his answer—or my death. He surprises me when he laughs deep from in his belly. My head spins back and he places the knife back on the cutting board.

"Well, I have to say I'm impressed, son. I'm glad you actually have the guts to ask me. I agree with you two being too young right now, but when you find that perfect moment to ask her, you have my permission. God knows you won't get it from Amber." He shakes his head. The waves of residual bitterness about his ex-wife roll off his shoulders.

I snort. "That's the truth."

"Just promise me that if you do become some big star, don't push her aside and make her feel any less than she is. You'll get busy, surrounded by women at every turn, and if you break her heart, I'll break you." He picks the knife back up, pointing it towards me, and I pale again. "Understand?"

"Very much, sir."

"You really should see your face," he chuckles, finding humor in my fear, "but good. Because from what Violet tells me, and the tracks I've heard, I think you do have what it takes to make it. And I'm not even big on the music these days."

His words make me realize how much his leaving affects me too. He always treats me like his own. Has faith I'll succeed, something I have yet to get from my own home.

Yeah, this next year is going to suck balls without him in Vi's and my corner.

"Thank you, Ron, it means a lot. I only wish my folks felt the same."

He pats my shoulder. "I'm sure they'll come around."

I'm not so sure of that.

"What's going on, you guys?" Violet asks, coming into the kitchen in a pair of sweats, my Spinal Tap shirt, and her hair wet from her shower.

"Oh, nothing," Ron and I say at the same time, both of us trying to play innocent.

"Uh-huh..." She looks between us perceptively, but doesn't say anything else before grabbing her water from the fridge.

That was a close one.

May 20th, 2006

Violet

I'm standing outside my room, knowing I'll have to face the music with Alexa and Julie. They're going to give me such hell for not telling them about Cooper, and more so because I'm coming back doing the walk of shame.

I should've stolen more than a spare pair of boxers from Cooper.

Entering the room, Alexa and Julie are sitting on the edge of the bed clicking through channels. Both look like they got hit by Mack Trucks filled with Tequila.

"Good morning," I say cheerfully.

"Well, well, well, if it isn't *Mrs.* Cooper Reid," Alexa snickers, giving me a slow clap. "You look like you must have consummated your marriage a couple of times."

Oh, I did. I didn't get this ache between my legs for nothing.

"Maybe just a little." I pinch my fingers together.

"Only a little? You look like you got hit by a bus," Julie giggles.

"Obviously you haven't looked in the mirror." I stick my tongue out at her and collapse on the bed. "I think we all need coffee."

I close my eyes for a second, exhaustion washing over me. "I can't believe I got married," I mumble to myself, throwing my hand over my eyes. The large, sparkling rock makes contact with my forehead.

Ow!

I better start remembering this glacier lives on my hand now.

Alexa and Julie crawl up the bed and lay down next to me on each side. Julie grabs my left hand and gawks at my rock.

"It's so pretty. I can't believe you didn't tell us you dated Cooper. You let me drool over your boyfriend-husband for years." She throws my hand back down and it hits my chest. I prop myself up, knowing I have a lot of explaining to do.

"Sorry. I told you it was too hard to talk about. I missed him so much and I don't know, maybe pretending he was a fantasy, kept it easier to deal with. I'm not sure. Maybe I didn't think you would believe it, or if you did, you'd force me to reach out." I shrug. I don't have a real reason why I didn't other than it twisted me up inside every time I would think he used to be mine.

"Watching you two last night," Alexa fans herself. "Whoo. I swear I thought you guys were going to fuck in the middle of the dance floor with the heat coming off you both. Nobody would ever believe that you haven't seen each other in years. Was it always like that with you two?"

My cheeks heat, remembering how intense Cooper and I always were. "Yeah. We were always pretty intense with each other. Like glued at the hip in love. I mean, that's normal, right?"

"What I want to know is how did you guys meet?" Julie asks. "You said last night about how you two dated for a couple of *years*," she stretches the word. "Now spill."

I go into a quick history of how we got together and him saving me from Thomas. They both stare at me with their fists under their chins.

"It was like after that we could never be apart. Our parents hated us together. Brody was our gatekeeper. We snuck out all the time and he would lie for us." I laugh at the memories. Poor Brody, I don't know how many stories the guy had to come up with to cover our asses. "His parents hated me because I pushed him to do his singing. They really wanted him to go to Princeton and become some hot shot lawyer or a congressman. They blamed the whole Thomas thing on me, convinced it was my fault Cooper got arrested. My mom thought he was some bad boy and was going to ruin my life. It was my mom's fault we didn't get back together sooner."

I should've known she would've stooped so low. Why didn't I question her more? Why the heck didn't I get my own burner phone? Why was I so stubborn not to go after him? Why did my mother want to destroy me forever?

"Why?" Alexa asks the same thing I'm musing about.

"I don't know. When we moved to Tucson, he and I would write each other and talk on the phone sometimes. Then one day it all stopped. I didn't know why he just gave up." My heart clenches thinking of the words of my final letter. "Last night, I come to find out she sent pictures of me and Mark from prom, telling Cooper I had moved on. There's more to the story, I'm sure. When I see her again, you bet I'm going to drag it out of her." I picture the catfight between me and my mother. I'm so mad at her, maybe more pissed then when she made me move for a marriage that ended up only lasting six months.

"Well, you're together now and that's all that matters." Julie nudges me with her shoulder. "I mean let's be honest for a second. Do you know how many women, mainly once me, would love to be in your shoes?" Julie gasps, a large 'o' shaping her lips along with her wide eyes. "Think of all the shoes you can buy now."

I laugh at my nutty friend and shake my head. "You're crazy. I'm going to miss you guys." I frown. "I feel so bad leaving you guys so suddenly."

"Hey, turn that frown upside down." Alexa grabs my face and squishes my cheeks together, forcing my lips out. I'm giggling through my mushed smile. "It's fine. We'll visit all the time. Who knows? Maybe things will go well with Brody and me then we can all be family."

She finally lets go of my lips and my jaw drops. "You hooked up with Brody?"

Her lips purse into a self-satisfied smirk and she shrugs her shoulders. "Yeah, you guys kind of left us to go fuck after the wedding, so the rest of us went to get more drinks. Me and Brody hit it off and one thing led to another."

"Oh my god, I can't believe this." I gape in shock that Alexa hooked up with the one person I always considered a brother. If there's anyone I would want as a future sister in law it would be Alexa.

I mean, if anything comes out of this one night.

"Believe it…he did this thing…"

My hand quickly covers her mouth and I'm shaking my head wildly at her. "No, no, no. You can do whatever you want with Brody, but *please* spare me the full details though." I do not want to hear in length about, well, Brody's length.

"Hey, I wasn't the only one in on the action. Our girl over here hooked up with Tucker." Alexa shoves Julie, who blushes deeply.

"Tucker? Who's Tucker?" I ask, confused, looking between them.

"One of Cooper's bodyguards. The one with the jet black hair, built like the Hulk, piercing green eyes with a hazel ring around them?" Julie swoons, daydreaming with glassy eyes about the man I suppose took her to "oh, my god" town.

"Well, I'm happy for both of you. I guess we're all in debt to your dad now for the hotel vouchers."

I FOUND you **May 20th, 2006**

"He'll be mad he didn't get a wedding invitation." Alexa pauses and takes my hand. "You're happy, right? I know you have a past and he's a big superstar now, but if we need to bolt you out of this hotel away from him, you'll have to tell us now."

"I am." I know these two loony birds would kidnap me in my duffle bag out of the hotel if I just said the words. "I really am happy. Cooper is...amazing."

I'm sure I have stars in my eyes from how hard I've been hit in the head with the love stick.

Julie wipes her finger along the corner of my mouth. "Sorry. You had a little drool."

"Shut up!" I smack her with a pillow, the three of us falling into a fit of laughter.

The suite phone rings on the nightstand, and we all sit up to look at it before bursting into another round of giggles.

"Bet it's lover boy," Julie muses as the phone continues to ring.

I reach over and pick up the headset. "Hello?"

"Hello, wife." Cooper's honey voice sings through the speaker and my cheeks are instantly on fire.

"Hello, husband," I reply back, giddy at how calling him that makes me feel like I'm flying.

Alexa and Julie stick their fingers down their throat, making loud gagging noises. I throw them both evil looks and they only snicker in return.

"There's been a change in plans with brunch. There's a bunch of reporters outside the hotel waiting for us. If the girls didn't tell you, we were spotted outside the chapel last night by the paparazzi."

"Wonderful," I breathe. "Does that mean our parents probably know?"

"Yeah, I've already had my call from my mother."

I'm glad I missed that conversation.

"Let me guess, she was *thrilled*?".

95

"Oh yeah, thrilled. As always when it comes to us," he mutters sarcastically. "Don't worry. I've put her in her place for now."

"Okay," I say meekly. The one thing I'm not ready to do is face Evelyn Reid and her permanent bitter face every time she sees me.

"What about yours?"

"No, nothing yet. I also turned off my cell when we got here. I didn't want to pay the roaming fees." Finally, my crap phone is good for something. Poor service keeping the mother hen away.

"Smart. Anyways, we're going to have to have brunch in our room. Whenever you girls are ready. Brody and Tucker will be here too. If that helps them get a move on." I can hear Brody in the background telling me it's a must for me to bring the girls. He's babbling about something else when Cooper tells him to shut up.

"Tell him I'll drag their hungover asses with me. We'll see you in a little bit. I still need to change."

"Alright, I love you, Ace." He says my nickname seductively, sending tingles to my core.

"I love you, too."

"AWWWW." The cooing comes from Alexa and Julie with their fists folded on their cheeks, eyes fluttering. I swear I see little hearts over their heads like cartoon characters when they're in love.

"I see you have your own peanut gallery," he says with an amused chuckle. Well, that's one way of saying it.

"Yeah. There just full of themselves today. I'll see you soon, babe."

"Soon. I miss you already."

We both hang up and I move off the bed to throw all my stuff into my bag. I grab a pair of cut off shorts and a long ivory cami.

"I'm going to change. We're having brunch upstairs

in Cooper's room. Your men should be there as well."

"Great, now what am I going to wear?" Alexa ruffles through her luggage, and I leave to get ready.

When the three of us open the door to our room to head up to Cooper's suite, Tucker is standing there, waiting for us. He informs me he'll be following me around 'till we leave Vegas because of the crowds; something Cooper forgot to tell me about. Looking at this huge burly man as he walks in front of me makes me quickly see how much my life has changed by being with Cooper again. It's going take some getting used to; always having someone follow me around. Though, I guess it's better safe than sorry. I'm sure there's a bunch of crazed women waiting to rip me to shreds for stealing their man.

Tucker lets us into the room since I didn't grab an extra key on my way out. Cooper and Brody both stand from the couch as we walk in.

"Wow, this suite is awesome," Alexa muses taking in the sights.

Cooper scoops me into his arms and kisses me gently. "Hey baby," he whispers against my lips.

"Hey." My heart flutters; I'm not sure this feeling of euphoria of being his arms again will ever pass.

His eyes dart behind me and he hooks his arm around my waist looking towards my friends. "It's good to see you guys again, welcome."

"Thanks for having us," Julie answers. Alexa is already busy flirting with Brody.

"Shall we?" Cooper gestures to the large dining room table. My eyes grow large remembering some of last night's activities, some which took place on that very table. I grab his arm, stopping him while everyone goes and sits down.

"Should we be eating on this table?" I whisper.

His eyes glint humorously and he kisses my forehead.

"I had it cleaned. No worries. But what do you say later today we reenact what we did last night and maybe what we did in the pool?"

I squeeze my legs tight at the delicious thought. "I look forward to it, husband."

Cooper growls and grabs my face, kissing me forcefully, making it hard for me to breathe. My legs wobble under the intensity of the kiss. I moan into his mouth, pushing myself further into his hardened body, ready to wrap myself around him, not wanting to wait for tonight.

"Will you two cut that shit out, we're going to eat!" Brody barks from the table.

My arms clamp on Cooper's shoulders pushing myself away, and my cheeks heat when we turn to see three pairs of eyes staring at us. Cooper moves behind me, and his hand caresses my ass as he tries to adjust himself.

We sit down at the table and there's everything under the sunset on this table. Pancakes, eggs, sausage, bacon, crepes, salmon, steak, pitchers of orange juice, and coffee. I'm starving, but I do think this is overkill. Then as I look around the table at the three men, plating up their food, making mountains out of pancakes and steak, I quickly change my mind about it being too much.

A phone rings, and Julie pulls hers from her pocket and groans. She waits for it to stop, then turns the Nokia device off.

"It was your mother. I'm not playing middleman for her," she says before she shoves a piece of bacon in her mouth. "Fuck, this the best bacon, I've ever had." She hums in delight.

"You can't handle the wicked witch either?" Cooper asks once she's done moaning over the brown sugar bourbon pork.

"Uh…no. I'm just glad Violet has Ron!"

"Oh, no, Dad!" I shout, slapping my hand on the table.

"Oh, you better run Cooper…" Brody roars with laughter. "He's going to come after you with a shotgun. You married his little Violet, and you didn't ask for her hand."

"I'm not worried. Ron always liked me, unlike the wicked witch of the west." Cooper snorts.

"Will you stop, she's still my mother." I smack his arm jokingly. She is a freakin' wicked witch.

"Thankfully you ended up more like Ron then her," he says, rubbing his arm, pretending it hurt.

"Me too," I scoff. "I better call him. It's a good thing he's not into reading entertainment news."

"I'll go with you." Cooper takes my hand and helps me from my chair.

"Oops, dead man walking here folks." Brody hums the funeral march as we walk to the bedroom.

My dad adored Cooper like a son. I know he'll be more disappointed because he didn't get to walk me down the aisle then the fact I got married on a whim.

"You know Brody's right. He's going to give you lip that you didn't ask for my hand in marriage. You know how old fashioned he is," I tease Cooper, who sits on the edge of the bed with a huge grin on his face. I eye him curiously. "What?"

"I kind of did."

"When?"

"When we went to see him for your seventeenth birthday, shortly before he left."

"You really asked his permission?" I curl myself into

his lap, surprised that he had asked my father for my hand. At seventeen.

"Yeah. I told you I wanted to marry you. I didn't have a plan, but I had hoped when we turned eighteen it would happen, and I knew I would need permission from the big guy." He kisses my cheek.

"You surprise me at every corner, you know that."

"Got to keep you on your toes, Mrs. Reid." His hand brushes my hair back and nibbles on the side of my ear, sending signals straight to my core.

I push him down on the bed, locking my lips to his and rubbing myself on his ever-present boner.

God, I want him.

He pulls me up, while my hands continue to claw at his shirt.

"I would *so* love to do this with you. But we have a room full of people, and you still need to call your dad."

Oh, yeah.

I sigh dramatically and hop off him. "I *guess* you have a point. Promise me a rain check."

"Oh, you bet your sweet ass!" he tells me.

Cooper offers me his phone and I dial one of the two numbers I know by heart. I remember when he came back from Afghanistan—after extending his tour—and how stunned he had been to hear Coop went AWOL. He had gone to visit me in Arizona, to convince me to go back to California with him, to see if I could get in touch with Cooper, but I passed. My heart had been broken enough by his sudden desertion. It didn't matter anyway, because by the time my dad came back he was already a superstar. At the time, I thought he would be untouchable.

Even after everything I told my dad, he never spoke badly about Cooper.

The line rings twice before my father's gruff voice answers, probably thinking I'm a telemarketer. "Hello?"

"Hi, daddy," I say cheerfully.

I FOUND you May 20th, 2006

"Violet, I was wondering when I was going to hear from you, young lady." His voice is hard and stern. A tone I know well enough from when I would get in trouble. I still with sudden panic and glance at Cooper.

"You heard?" I swallow the sudden nervous lump in my throat.

"I think the whole world heard." He laughs and I release the breath I was holding as the knot in my stomach unties. *He's not mad, thank god.* "It's made national news, little one. I was turning on the news this morning and there's my daughter, outside a Vegas chapel, with *some* famous singer," he chortles. "How did this happen? I thought you two hadn't spoken in years."

"We kind of ran into each other last night, and one thing led to another. I know it's kind of rushed. But…I do love him, daddy."

"I know you do, Vi. If you're happy, then I'm happy. I'm only bummed I couldn't walk you down the aisle."

I knew he was going to say that.

"Thank you, daddy!"

"Now, you just need to promise to come see me soon. I assume Cooper is living in L.A. these days? Or has he bought his own island?"

"He's in L.A."

"And I'm guessing you'll be moving with him."

"Uh-huh," I say, sounding like Elvis from last night.

"What about Alexa and Julie?"

"They both know. It's going to be a big change for all of us, you know. Luckily, I haven't found a job yet, so I don't have any commitments down there."

"Do you think you'll find something for you to do in L.A.? It might seem like an easy place to get a job, but it's harder than you think."

"I'll start looking when I get there. I got lucky and found a guy that can support me 'till I do," I joke. He shakes his head with a smile and pulls me back into his lap.

"I'll always support you, baby," he whispers in my ear.

I know it's true. He wouldn't care if I worked or not, as long as he was being sexed all the time. Also, I'm sure he'll still do everything to talk me into working with him. It's what I used to want to do, but it makes me nervous. I don't want to mess anything up when it comes to what Brody has done or Coop's career.

"Alright, as long as you're happy, Vi. Does your mom know?"

"Probably, but I'm not going to call her. I have nothing to say to her," I snip much harsher then I intended to. But I'm pissed because no matter how many times I try with my mother she always does something else to disappointment again. I don't think there's any coming back now after what I learned last night.

"What did she do now?" My dad groans and I picture him pitching his nose.

"She sent Cooper letters and pictures for him to stay away from me"

"She did what?" he roars, and I think he's more upset then I was by the news of my mother's deceit. I'm sure the man wants any reason to burn the woman at the stake.

Much like my husband now.

"She's the one that kept us apart all these years. She told him I was with someone else." I brush away the sudden loose tear that has slipped from my eye. "I'm so mad at her, dad. I'm not sure if I'll be able to forgive her."

"I don't blame you. I guess it'll get better now since you're getting away from her and finally fully venturing out on your own. Now let me talk to *that* boy."

"*Daddy*..." I stretch out his name, coming out more as a whine.

"I have to give him my speech," he argues, and I roll my eyes.

"I think he knows your speech. You gave it to him every time you talked to him for two years."

"Well, it's been a while and he needs a good reminder. It'll be a little bit different now that he's your husband."

Do all dads with daughters do this? Maybe I should make a questionnaire.

I pull the phone away and hold my hand over the mouthpiece. "My dad wants to talk to you and threaten you with his gun…*again*."

"Wouldn't expect anything else from Ron Spencer."

Cooper takes the phone from me and removes me from his lap. "Hello, Mr. Spencer…uh-huh." He laughs with a shake of his head. "Yes, Ron."

Standing from the bed, Cooper's grin reassures me he'll be fine, and I decide to join the others and give them some privacy.

When I sit back down at the table, they all look at me as if I just left the gallows.

"So, how did your dad take it?" Alexa asks.

"He was fine. Supposedly Cooper asked him to marry me back when we were seventeen." I can't contain the smile that breaks out on my face.

Can we say swoon?

"Really? Wow!" Julie exclaims. "That's like the sweetest thing I've ever heard."

"I know, right?"

Another brownie point to Cooper Reid

"I knew he did. He was sweating like crazy for a week, and I caught him talking in his mirror preparing the words to say," Brody chirps in. "Where is he now?"

"Getting his '*If you ever hurt my daughter, I'll hunt you down and you'll wish you never lived,*' speech." I smile, thinking back to all the times my husband has had to endure that speech.

"Oh, boy. I wonder if the speech is any more detailed

now, something like '*I'll rip you apart limb by limb if you hurt my little jellybean.*" Brody imitates my father's voice, wiggling his finger.

"Jellybean?" Alexa chirps. "I didn't know your dad called you jellybean."

"He doesn't. Brody calls me that to drive Coop crazy," I tell her before taking a bite of a ripe strawberry.

"Oh," Alexa's mouth makes a little 'o' and her eyes light up.

"Don't even think about it…"

She puts up her hands defensively but mutters the word jellybean under her breath.

Her and Brody might actually be perfect for one another.

The bedroom door creaks open and I look over as Cooper walks out with a smile on his face. He gives me a kiss on the cheek and sits back down beside me.

"You survived?" I tease.

"Of course I did. The man adores me. But this time, instead of the gun, it was doing 'unspeakable things to my vocal cords and hands,' if I ever hurt his little Violet Harper." Cooper throws his arm around me and nuzzles his face in my neck. I giggle, the prickles from his light stubble tickling me.

"He's always so over dramatic for someone that he likes." I shove Cooper's head away, and he puts his hand on my cheek.

"I know where he's coming from. When we have a daughter, I'll be saying the same things to her boyfriend." He swings his arm over my shoulder and pops a blueberry into his mouth. He laughs at something Brody says, but I don't hear it, thinking of the words he just uttered.

When we have a daughter?

My heart beats erratically in my chest and I nervously pick at the food on my plate. He seems so sure we will have one and if I'm honest, getting pregnant again scares the shit out of me. The miscarriage we suffered in high school is a burden I continue to carry around every day. Though as the years went by, I didn't think of it as much as before, but it lingers in my mind when I would see pregnant women or even children around the age our baby would've been. It still hurts and I know now that we're married he's going to want a family. I do too, but I just don't know if I could handle another loss.

"We're leaving tomorrow," Cooper tells me, pulling me from my darkening thoughts. I turn to look up at him and he brushes my hair off my shoulder. "You okay?" his eyebrows knit together as he looks me over curiously.

"Yeah…yeah…" I give him a small smile.

"You sure? You seemed kind of zoned out there"

"I'm fine. So, how are we getting back?"

"I chartered a jet, it'll take us to Arizona, and we can stay for however long you need before heading home to L.A."

I nod. My new home. Exciting, scary, and nerve-wracking as shit.

"Oh, Violet you get to go home on a private jet? Nice. You'll have to join the mile high club on your honeymoon. Hope you got one with a bed, Coop. Just don't rock the plane too much or stain the sheets. Not that you can't afford to have them replaced," Brody rambles on and the girls laugh. Alexa's laugh much louder, as her eyes flutter and she touches his arm flirtatiously.

"Shut up, Brody!" Cooper tells him, throwing a roll at his head. Cooper then leans down to whisper in my ear. "He's right though, I do want to join the mile-high club with you."

"Have you ever been a part of that club?" I choke out.

I don't want to think about some other dirty whore sharing something *special* like that. Maybe I'm being selfish, hoping I'm all still all of his firsts, no matter how many he's had after me.

Let's not think in numbers, *Violet.*

"Never, I only want that milestone with you." He kisses me gently on the lips.

Thank god.

"How about we go to the Stratosphere and go ride the rides? I always wanted to do that," I say changing the topic so I can stop thinking about the midflight hors d'oeuvre I'm going to make out of my husband.

"Are you nuts?" Julie exclaims. "What's fun about Rollercoasters eighty million feet in the air?" She shakes her head, terror written all over her pretty face, while her hands wave around like an air traffic controller. "No way."

"Come on, you only live once. They're safe."

"Yeah, okay. No. I'll keep my feet on the ground while you crazy people do that and probably fall to your untimely deaths."

"Well, I'm down." Brody claps his hands and Alexa nods her head with a smile. She's the most like me and will try about anything once.

Tucker clears his throat. "I'll need to make some arrangements and talk to Collin before you guys do that. I'm sure you remember the crowds' downstairs. Also, we need to make sure the area is secure."

"Oh, yeah, I forgot." I take a deep breath, knowing this is my life now and it's going to take a lot of getting used too.

Cooper's fingers trace around my ear as he sticks a piece of hair behind it. His warm breath tickles as he leans in to whisper in my ear. "When we get back, I'm going to make good on my promise about re-doing our wedding night."

His delicious threat heats my belly and makes my skin prickle.

I turn to him, so our noses touch. "Bring in on, Mr.

Reid. But if I can walk in the morning I'll be disappointed."

His eyes darken and they're primal looking. I can only wonder what he has in store for me.

"Oh, I like the challenge, Mrs. Reid."

May 21st, 2006
Violet

Walking up to the porch of my house in Tucson, I feel like we arrived on horseback and not by private jet. Cooper made good on his promise, recreating our wedding night, and making sure I couldn't walk straight. Then we joined the mile high club together. There was no bed, but we made good use of the leather lounge chairs. My core is sore, but the good kind because I'm aching for more.

Alexa and Julie stayed behind in Vegas for an extra day and so did Brody. He and Alexa seemed to have hit it off while Julie made her mark with Tucker.

I'm glad I'm not the only one to have a love connection in Vegas.

"So, this is home?" Cooper asks looking around the outside of the townhouse with blue siding.

"This is it." It's going to be weird not living here anymore with Alexa and Jules. Now, instead of them jumping in my bed to harass me, it's going to be Cooper.

I smile and remember all the good times we had here. "I'm going to miss it; lots of good memories here."

With my house key gripped in my hand, I line it up to the keyhole when Cooper stops me, putting his hand over mine. I look at him curiously and his free hand brushes down my face.

"I promise to make new memories with you in L.A., and we can come back and visit whenever you want."

"I would like that. Thank you." I reach up and peck a kiss on his lips. I'm about to open the door when it swings open and my mother is standing on the other side. With her hands on her hips, she glares at us through the narrow slits of her eyes.

Well, I guess there's no denying she heard the news.

"Mother, what are you doing here?" I ask, annoyed as hell because I was seconds away from showing Cooper how bouncy my bed is.

Why did I ever give this woman a key? Oh, that's right I didn't have a choice if I wanted help with the deposit.

The anger I felt towards my mother after she made me move always lingered. Even still, I did my best to want to try and repair our broken relationship. She's my mother; I was born to love her. I wanted to love her the way I was supposed to. Yet, all the energy I put into trying to dispel the anger and the hurt I felt just never worked. She didn't give back the same effort and never became the mother I needed. Now as she stands in front of me, knowing she's the cause of so much of our extra heartache only fuels my temper. I'm not sure I want to keep trying with her. Mother or not.

"Waiting for you to come home. We need to talk." She addresses only me, not even looking at Cooper.

"Hello, Ms. I have no idea what your last name is now…" Cooper greets her in his best smart-ass voice. I can't help but giggle.

"It's *Ms. Winston*," she hisses harshly, her evil eyes now glowering at him. I see him bite the inside of his cheek to keep from laughing.

"My mistake. Hello, Ms. Winston, it's been a long time."

"Not long enough," she snaps, and glares back at me, "How could you, Vi?"

"How could I what?" I put my hands on my hips, imitating her.

"Cut the crap, Violet. How could you marry this boy? I thought I took care of that problem years ago. And aren't you dating Darren?"

"Ugh, Darren and I broke up weeks ago. He was an arrogant asshole. I just happened to get very lucky running into Cooper in Vegas…" My hands roam over Cooper's firm chest, his right dimple well defined in the cocky grin spreading across his face, "and well, one thing led to another. So, if you don't mind. I need to pack up a few things so I can go move in with my husband."

I shoulder past her and walk into *my* house, pulling Cooper along with me.

"You can't do this, Violet. Your life is here."

The cackle rises in my throat and escapes, making me sound like the wicked witch the west.

"You're one to talk, mother. You of all people know about sudden marriages and uprooting lives," I growl. "I only had a life here because I was forced to. I grew into it, but now the only place for me is with Cooper. I'm twenty-one now and thank the lord you have no control over what I do."

"Violet, I'm still your mother. I know what's best for you."

I snort, "Best for me? You wouldn't know what that was if it bit you in the ass! I would've married him a long time ago if you hadn't interfered. I know all about the letters and photos you sent him at the end of senior year."

"I have no idea what you're talking about." She places her hand on her chest, pretending to act put out. Cooper snorts at her blatant lie.

"You know exactly what you did. Don't try to lie to me now, mother," I spit out. The harshness in my voice hits her like a slap in the face.

"I did what I did for your own wellbeing. He was going to drag you down. You wouldn't have gone to college. What would you have done? Followed him on the road, while he cheated on you night after night!"

"I can assure you, *Ms. Winston, that* would have never happened then, and it's not going to happen now," Cooper says.

"Oh, please." She rolls her eyes.

I FOUND you **May 21st, 2006**

"It doesn't matter what you think. You can't assume what would have happened. Did you think just because Jeremy cheated on you and left you, Cooper would too?" Like a light bulb turning on, the timeline of that jerkoff leaving suddenly fits the same timeline when she sent Coop the pictures. "Is that why you sent the pictures, mom? Because the bastard cheated on you, you thought it would be fair for me to be unhappy as well? Because if I ran off with Cooper you would've been all alone 'till number three came along?"

"Don't be silly, Violet. Cooper has never been any good for you. His own parents agreed. I was trying to help you and now—" I raise my hand to stop her and thankfully her mouth clamps shut.

"Mom, you're just going to have to accept that Cooper and I are married now and get over it. Now, if you excuse me I have some packing to do."

I grasp Cooper's hand and yank him to my room, leaving my mother huffing and puffing in her place. Locking the door behind me, I scream out in frustration. Loud enough it shakes the walls, making the pictures rattle.

I never thought I could hate my own mother, but right now, I do. Hearing her admit in her own words she's the one who split us apart is like a sword ripping through my heart. Why does she not want me to be happy? Cooper pulls me into his arms, pushing my head to his chest, holding me tight as angry tears roll down my cheeks.

"Why can't she be happy for me?" My voice croaks and I nuzzle my face into his chest, inhaling his cologne, reminding myself it's going to be alright now.

I found him again. He's here with me. It'll be okay. He's mine.

"I swear she wants to ruin my life so I'll end up as miserable as her. It hurts. She's supposed to love me, let me make my own mistakes sometimes, but she's out to control me."

Lifting my head from Cooper's now wet shirt, I rub my face, pushing away the burning tears, and try to shake it off.

"I know, but you have me now and we're not going to let her win." I smile at his words and nod. He's right. The first thing I need to do is get out of Arizona and away from my mother. Though, when I quickly glance around my room, doing a quick survey of all the things I have to pack, it gives me a headache.

I didn't think I had this much crap.

My eyes dart back to Cooper, who is looking at me, concerned. A wicked idea pops into my head, sure to piss my mother off.

"Cooper…" I take a step closer to him and rub my hands up and down his chest. "I want you to fuck me. Fuck me hard, so hard, I scream this whole place down." His lips curl mischievously, and my hand rubs over his hardened dick. "Do you think you can handle such a task, Mr. Reid?" I purr.

"Oh, Mrs. Reid. I think I'm *just* the person to handle such a task."

***

"I hope she got the hint and left," I mutter as I put on a bra and a lace thong.

"Hopefully. You were *insanely* loud." Cooper smirks deviously and slips on a pair of boxers.

"Who, me?" I flutter my eyes innocently. My vocal cords are a little scraped from calling out '*Oh Cooper*' a lot more than I needed to. I wanted to make sure she heard who was claiming me. The other sounds were all the same, just a pinch or two beyond the normal level.

"Yes, you…" He kisses me lightly on my swollen lips.

"Oops," I bite my finger, playing innocent. "*Well, you enjoyed it and were just as loud as me. Though, yelling, "Oh fuck Ace, your pussy is so tight, I've missed how it felt wrapped around my cock,"* might have been overkill," I tease.

He grins widely, looking oh so pleased with himself. "You liked it," he returns my sentiment.

I reach out my hand. "Come, I'm hungry. Let's see if we can scrounge something up to eat."

We both pad our way to the kitchen. It's quiet as we approach and breathe a sigh of relief that my mother seems to have left. I find some frozen chicken and vegetables in the freezer. Pulling the rice out from the cupboard, I figure we can make some chicken fried rice. It's easy and quick enough. I throw the chicken in the microwave and pull out a cutting board to chop it up.

Arms wrap around my waist, and light kisses trace my neck, Cooper's five o'clock shadow tickling me in their wake. I squirm in his arms, enjoying the feeling. The microwave beeps, announcing the chicken is thawed. Though it's the last thing on my mind when Cooper nips on the bottom of my earlobe and his honey voice rings through my eardrums.

"I can totally get used to watching this every day. You mostly naked, standing in my kitchen, making us dinner. This reality is so much better than I ever dreamed."

"This is really nice," I murmur turning myself around in his arms. I'm no longer hungry for food. My arms skate around his neck, and I capture his bottom lip with my mouth and suck on it.

His eyes darken and my butt gets pushed into the counter. "You need me again, Vi?" he growls before taking a bite of my bottom lip. I thrust my hips against his growing dick, giving him my answer.

"I think you both have had enough for one afternoon and I certainly don't need to hear you again," my mother's shrill voice surges into the room, causing Cooper and I to break apart.

Where the fuck did she come from?

"And why don't you put on some clothes?"

My jaw tightens and my temper races through my veins, making me feel as if my head is about to explode. "It's my house. I'll walk around half naked if I want. And why are you even still here?" I grit out.

Cooper's arm slides around me again, pulling me towards him, putting a calming presence on my sudden volcanic anger.

Though it doesn't last when my mom opens her mouth again. "We weren't done talking." She crosses her arms, looking at me, then at Cooper, and back to me.

"There's nothing to talk about. I'm married, and you're interrupting our private time. If you don't want to hear or see, I suggest you leave and take your opinions with you," I hiss. My chest heaves, my vision getting fuzzy as my anger escalates to rage.

Cooper places his lips to my temple. "Ace, relax…breathe, baby," he whispers, his hand running up and down my shoulder. I close my eyes tightly, still seeing red. I take a couple deep breaths and the red starts to fade.

"This is what I'm talking about, Violet. You haven't talked like this to me in years. The only time you did is when you're with this boy. He's no good for you."

The fire instantly surges back and when I open my eye again, I swear I can see the fireballs shooting out of them towards her.

Doesn't she see he's trying to calm me down instead of helping me unleash my fury? He's the last person I know who would want me to go off on my mother no matter how much she deserves it right now.

"You're the person who makes this part of me come out. Because I wouldn't act like this if for once in your life you supported me and the choices I make. You've been too blind by your vile loathing, to truly see how good he is for me, how happy he always made me."

"You're still so young and back then even younger. It's my job to try and help you. If anyone was blind it was you, Violet. If you didn't meet him, you would've kept your grades up, wouldn't have started drinking, and been gone for days doing who knows what," she argues. She doesn't even have the nerve to look at me.

I rub my hands down my face. "Or I could've done all that stuff because I was a teenager and trying to have fun. My grades were fine, I got mostly B's and the occasional C. I was never a straight-A student, so don't lay that shit on me. Hell, I think my first D was when we moved here. So, my poor grades were your fault."

I'm seething and Cooper holds me tighter. I have so many years of aggression built up and it's ready to be unleashed. I'm feeling vengeful and refuse to let her make me cry. She's caused enough tears.

"You act like you're so perfect," I yell again, stabbing my finger in her direction, wanting to make my point clear. "You've made so many fucked up decisions in your life, done a hundred things wrong. For once, let me live and stop trying to control my life. I'm happy right now. So fucking happy, so let me enjoy it."

My breathing is ragged, the volcano finally erupted, and now I feel lighter. I'm fully engulfed in Cooper's arms now, breathing in his scent, calming the lava flow of my explosion.

"You need to go now, *Ms. Winston*. You're not welcome in my wife's home," Cooper seethes, and I can see the fire now lighting up in his eyes.

"Alright," I glance over at her and she has her hands

up, "I can see there's no reasoning with you. I'll let you *enjoy* yourself for now, and we can talk another day."

I don't say anything. Instead, I bury my face in Cooper's chest. There's nothing left to say. 'Till she can accept Cooper is back in my life, there's no point. I refuse to deal with it all again.

Once I hear the front door close, Cooper lifts my chin, kissing me forcefully and eagerly, knowing what I need, without saying the words. He hoists me up in his arms and lays me down onto the kitchen table. His mouth meets mine again with the same rough intensity, making me forget everything that was troubling me moments ago.

FIVE

December 10th, 1999

Cooper

Today was supposed to be my chance at the big time. I should be in the middle of signing papers for a record deal, not about to be belittled by my mother. Along with Violet, Brody, and my bandmates, Billy and John, we skipped out of school before lunch to drive almost two hours to L.A. to play at Club Skye, where they're holding the final Battle of the Bands.

X-Rated was chosen to perform here after six rounds of competition. If you won the final round you had a chance to be signed to a record deal. There was also a chance if you didn't, one of the record executives might take a chance with you.

It was my chance. My chance to prove to everyone I had what it took.

I came so close, only to have my mother snatch it away from me, to snatch it away from my friends.

We were halfway through our set, when out of the corner of my eye I saw Violet talking wildly to my mother, trying to stop her from charging onstage. As hard as she tried to stop her, my mother ripped the cord from my amp and pulled me off stage, all while yelling at me.

It had to be one of the most embarrassing moments of my teenage life. I'm only fifteen, and if she could do this to me today, I can't imagine what's to come.

The crowd's hysterical laughter pinged in my ears as we left the stage.

I'm glad they found the moment funny.

My mom made Billy and John leave so we could talk alone. They promptly ran off, scared of the death rays shooting from my mother's eyes. She tried to get Violet to go, but Violet refused and wrapped herself around my arm. I'm a little shocked, but maybe this is her way of protecting me.

This girl, whom I've only been dating for two months, has more faith in my ability to succeed than my own mother.

"I told you and told you that you weren't allowed to come to this. Then I get a call from the school telling me you didn't show up to your last two classes of the day." She wags her finger at me and then points to Brody, "and I can't believe you helped them do it."

Brody rolls his eyes. "Mom, it was one day, and I think it's dumb you didn't let him." My brother was the first to see my talent, pushed me to form a band, and got me my first gig. He also doesn't understand mom and dad's pushback. They didn't even give him a lot of grief when he decided to go to UCR instead of Yale, where he was expected to go.

I asked him once why he wanted to help me so much, and his response was simple: "It's what brothers do." He did follow that up with the condition that when I got famous I wasn't to forget about him. That I was to buy him a car— preferably a cherry-red Lamborghini.

"I don't care if you think it's dumb. It's not for you to decide," my mother bellows, her face turning dark red from her anger. "I raised you boys better than this. You shouldn't be skipping school and hanging out with certain

people *who will only bring you down."* She sneers and looks dead center at my girlfriend.

"Why don't you understand? I told you this could be my chance mom. My chance to be something. I've been working my butt off, practicing like crazy with the guys. I was going to prove to you, to the world, how good I am."

I grind my teeth, a combination of anger and dejection swirling in my veins. I'll never understand why she wouldn't be proud of my success.

Violet rubs her hand over my chest doing her best to calm me.

"This is a pipe dream, Cooper. I hate seeing you throw your life away for this fantasy you know could possibly never come true." She places her hands on her hips, annoyed.

What's wrong with having dreams?

"How can you say that my dream will never come true, mom? You've never even heard me sing. And we had a chance 'till you came barging onstage. I don't get why you don't support me? Or at least why you didn't wait to yell at me when we got home and destroy my life?"

"Being some singer will never get you anywhere in life, Cooper. Plus, if you keep hanging out with this *girl you really won't make it."*

I look down at Violet and whose jaw has fallen slack.

"What have I done?" Violet asks. *"All I've done is love and support your son. He's an amazing singer. You won't even give him a chance."*

Did she just say…?

"You love me?" I gape at her, and a blush creeps up on her cheeks, as she gives me the smallest nod.

She loves me.

Well, if that didn't pick up my spirits…

She fiddles with her fingers and looks away from me. "Yeah…" she whispers, her eyes still unable to focus on mine. *"I know it's early, you don't have to say it back."*

Erica Marselas

I lift her chin, so she'll finally look at me. She bites down on her lip, and I know she's worried about what I might say. I'm trying to form the words as my heart beats a mile a minute, and my ears continue to ring with the words she told me. My palms are sweaty, and I swallow the large, nervous bundle piled in my throat.

This is the best news I've had all week.

There's only one thing to say, and I better say it fast before her little bunny nose wrinkles more in worry.

"Babe, I love you too…" I kiss her lightly on the lips.

"About time," Brody mumbles from beside us. I whip my head over and narrow my eyes at him, silently telling him to shut up. He mouths the word 'What?', then points his finger to mom—who now sounds like a fire-breathing dragon.

I forgot she was here.

"Cooper! You are way too young to understand what love is. Now go get in the car! Brody, we will talk more at home!"

"No, mom. I'm going home with everyone else. You have the right to be pissed because we skipped school, but I think you punished us all enough by ruining the night. And I love Violet, and you're just going to have to deal with it. Come on, let's go help the guys pack."

I take Violet's hand and lead her out the door. The last thing I hear is my mom shouting my name.

May 24th, 2006
Cooper

Violet and I arrive back in L.A. after spending two days at her place. We took our time getting packed, taking the important things with us. The moving truck will bring the rest tomorrow morning, but most of the big things stayed with Alexa and Julie.

Amber thankfully stayed clear of the house and hasn't tried calling. Violet is hurt about her mother's disapproval and, even more, her betrayal, no matter how much she tries to tell me she's fine.

When we land at LAX, Collin is at the gate to guide us to the car. There's always Paparazzi waiting for celebs to get off flights, so Collin is essential if we hope to make it out alive.

Paparazzi is part of my life now. I'm *almost* used it. Most times they're cool, just doing their job. Other days, they're dogs with a bone trying to get the next big story to put on the front of a tabloid.

This week, I'm still the big story. Cooper Reid, singer and once confirmed bachelor, now has a bride. Actually, it's not me they want—it's her: the girl who tied me down and managed to get a ring on my finger.

Louie had given a statement about our history, but it didn't matter; the roaches are never satisfied 'till they capture it all on camera.

Violet's eyes dart nervously as we come down the escalator to the sea of photographers.

"Just stay at my side and listen to Collin. He'll get us through before the flashes blind us," I joke, trying to ease her jitters.

She looks up at me and gives me a weak smile before nodding her head.

I wrap my arm around her shoulder and pull her closer to me as we hit the ground floor. Collin is in front of us keeping the flood of paparazzi back, along with the airport security.

They shout questions at us and I can't make out any of them as they all ask simultaneously.

We make it to the town car unscathed and, once safely in the back seat, Collin slides into the passenger seat. The camera flashes still come through the heavily tinted windows.

"You okay?" I take her hand in mine as we pull out onto the road.

"Yeah, I'm fine. It's going to take some getting used to." She shrugs, biting on her finger anxiously.

"After a while, it tends to be just one or two of them trying to get a shot of you. Like why is me going to the store so exciting?" I mutter sarcastically.

Who knew something so basic as buying food would be big enough to publish in *US Weekly?*

Cooper Reid buys frozen pizzas.
See what brand he bought and be just like him.

"I found it exciting. I liked to stalk you every once in a while. I have to say you make grocery shopping look very sexy," she says with a sultry voice and runs her hand up and down my chest.

"You stalked me, huh? I didn't know any of this before I married you. Should I be worried?" I slide closer to her and tangle my hand around the ponytail she's sporting.

"Maybe a little." She pinches her fingers together. "I am your biggest fan after all." She winks at me and leans in to kiss my cheek.

"So, are you like Julie and have a picture of me on your wall? Because I didn't see it."

Violet took great pride in showing me Julie's room and pointing out the picture of me she had pinned up. It's one I did for GQ and I'm standing in only my underwear.

"But I wasn't paying close enough attention either," I kiss the spot behind her ear and she noticeably shivers. The only thing I noticed was her, naked, spread out on her bed.

"I didn't need it. I have you ingrained in my memory. If I needed to, I would go stare at Julie's wall," she teases, and I crush my lips to hers.

My tongue invades her mouth and she moans against me, her nails clawing at my scalp. The seat belts are lost and she moves to sit on my lap. Letting my hand creep up her skirt, I reach the straps of her thong and snap them.

She pulls back, panting, her eyes glowing lustfully. God, I want her—now, but my eyes dart to the front seat where the driver and Collin are seated, and there's no way they're getting a free show.

She leans back into me and I stop her, placing my hand against her mouth. "What?" she looks at me warily.

"We need to wait 'till we get home."

"But I don't wanna," she pouts grinding her hips into me. "You started this…and I need you to finish it."

Pinching her chin, I pull her face closer to mine, kissing her gently. Her eyes stare into mine and I kiss her again, and again, 'till we're back in a passionate embrace, and I'm saying fuck it.

She's rocking her hips against my crotch and her hands fall to my lap to work over my belt. She manages to get the hooks undone when the car comes to a sudden stop. Collin clears his throat, obnoxiously, and we separate immediately.

Glancing to the right, we're stopped outside my gates in Bel Air. "We're home," I tell her and manage to move her off my lap.

She's looking out the window as the gates open up to the driveway, letting out a large puff of air. "It's so big," she mumbles.

"Thank you," I wiggle my eyebrows and grab my junk. Her head snaps over to me and her eyes drop to my lap. She quirks an eyebrow before slapping me in the chest.

"Smartass. I mean the house. For a bachelor, it's a lot of square footage."

She's right. The property I bought is way too big for one person.

It has seven bedrooms, twelve baths, and almost fifteen thousand square feet. Large, automatic glass doors that open fully to the canyon, city, and ocean views. It's like your inside and outside all at the same time. The house has a home theater, bar-party area, and a spa. My favorite part, and what sold me, was the infinity pool, BBQ area, and the putting greens.

I don't even use 90% of the house. I have the rooms I've made my own, and the rest are for guests or family. Everyone thought I was crazy when I first bought it, but it was a great investment. Though I should admit I was always waiting *for her.*

"Do you like it?" I ask as I help her out of the car.

"The outside is nice." She smiles up at me. "As long as you have a bed, water, and food, I'm sure I'll like it."

I fling the front door open and swoop her into my arms. She giggles wildly from deep in her chest. "What are you doing?"

"Carrying my bride over the threshold of *our* home."

"Our home. I really do like the sound of it. Can we get a mat out front that says *the Reid's* to greet our guests?

I FOUND you   **May 24th, 2006**

I always wanted one of those." She grins, and I'm not sure if she's serious or not. First I'm hearing about it.

"Whatever you want, Ace. This is your home too."

I carry her through the foyer and place her back down on her feet in the massive living area. There's a large, gas fireplace to the right, massive light gray couches against crème colored walls, and a large chandelier hanging from the ceiling. The whole house is painted in earth tones and every room except my bedroom and the music room was decorated by an interior designer.

"Feel free to change anything you want. I want you to feel comfortable here."

"I wouldn't know the first thing to do. It's already nicely done, though I'm not sure I would want to sit or eat in any of these rooms. I wouldn't want to get them dirty or leave *butt prints.*" Giving me a cheeky smile, she walks back and wraps her arms around my waist.

"Do you want the tour?"

"Yeah, to your bedroom?" She chews down her lower lip and bats her innocent, doe eyes.

"It's our bedroom now. Let me show you around our place and we can end the tour there and break in the bed." With her still cuddled into my side, I lead her around the house. I show her an empty room next to my office that I offer to have turned into her own home office.

"What would I need an office for?"

"When you need your own place to work as my assistant tour manager," I say pointedly. She hasn't agreed to take the job yet, and I feel like she's leaving me hanging on purpose. Waiting for me to get down on my hands and knees to beg.

Maybe I could get Brody to do it.

"I haven't said yes, though I guess I will need it once I lock down a job."

Gripping her shoulders, I pull her to my chest, resting my forehead on hers. "Why won't you take the job?"

She exhales deeply and pushes me back. She walks to the large double windows, where a single blue loveseat sits and draws her finger over the soft fabric. "I just want to think about it a little longer. I'm not sure if it's something I know how to do. I told you that."

"Well, if you don't want that one. I do have an opening for a private masseuse. Especially one who is really good at happy endings."

Her head pops up and she looks at me wearing a wicked smirk, and a familiar glint in her eyes. "What do you know, I happen to be very good at giving happy endings…"

She charges for me and leaps into my arms, knocking me backward. I stumble, but am able to keep a hold of her.

"Where's. Your. Bedroom?" she growls and yanks my hair, causing my head to snap back. I laugh. I've missed these moments with her, where we're able to stop an uncomfortable situation and end up goofing around instead.

"Changing the subject on me, baby?" I groan when her luscious lips latches onto my neck, sucking hard enough to leave a mark.

"Yes," she hisses and bites me lightly where she was once sucking. I'm hard as a rock, but there's one more room I desperately want to show her. A room I have pictured fucking her in countless times. More so than in my bed.

"One more room. The place I spend most of my time, where you'll usually find me when you *need* me."

"Fine." She blows a puff of air out. "But you have to carry me there, so I can…" she doesn't have to finish the sentence as her lips attach to my earlobe.

I haul her ass to my music room with her wrapped around me, nibbling at the exposed skin on my neck. Pushing open the double doors, I tell her we're here. She releases her mouth from my neck and her head swings around to examine the room, a surprised gasp leaving her lips.

Maybe it's the large portrait of her on my wall, or it may be the couple of pictures of us that rest on the piano that have her astonished.

So, maybe I'm a little bit like Julie when it comes to gawking at the person I admire most.

"Wow. This is *unexpected*." She squirms, wanting out of my hold and I put her down. Her eyes dart around the room in wonder before they shift back to me.

"I told you, you're my muse." I thread my fingers through her hair above her ear and my thumb caresses her cheek.

"Is this why Collin finally realized who I was? He stared me down for a minute after I said my name."

"Probably." I grin, unembarrassed by my infatuation. "I like to talk about you and show you off. Does it freak you out?"

"No. It's sweet." She leans her head into my palm. "But you didn't tell me how obsessed you were before we got married. Should I be worried?" She smiles slyly throwing my earlier comment back at me.

"*Very*." I lean in and kiss her nose, making her giggle.

"Good thing I always knew you were crazy." She darts around me to the piano where a few framed pictures sit. She picks up one of us with the guys from my old band, X-rated, and Brody.

"I remember when this picture was taken. It was the day we all snuck out of school early and Brody drove us up to L.A. Your mom found out and drove to the club, ending the show early." Violet clenches her jaw at the memory.

"I remember the day too. I thought everything was lost." I frown deeply. I thought it was going to ruin all my chances of playing another show ever again.

"She embarrassed the hell out of you all instead of just letting you finish. It still irks me to this day." The acidity rolls off her tongue.

"It was pretty embarrassing, *but* I remember the day turned out good in the end. We said we loved each other, in front of her. I thought her head was going to explode." I laugh, remembering how red my mother's face had gotten and the lecture I received when we got home. She went on about being too young to be in love and how I didn't even know the girl, forgetting all about me skipping school. I still ended up grounded for a month.

And for all those thirty days I snuck out of the house to see Vi.

"It did turn out really good." She gleams back down at the picture before putting it back in its spot.

"Do you know the kicker of it all? Max Young was there that night, and when he saw me again in L.A., he remembered who I was. I made an impression on him that night. He said he's never seen someone's mother come and stop a show before. He wanted to sign me then, but we had already left, and, well, now the rest is history."

"I guess in a way your mom helped you, without even trying." Her arms wrap around my neck and she kisses my chin.

"Yeah, I guess she did."

"I love you," she says wistfully.

"I love you, too, always." I kiss her with everything I have, sucking her in.

Her erect nipples poke into my chest as she molds herself to my body, making us one. We step backward, and I'm not sure where we're going 'till my ass hits the piano keys, making an obnoxious noise of the minor keys.

Our lips part and I move away from the keys as a satisfied smile tugs on the corner of my lips. I glance at the grand piano, thinking of all the dreams I've had of her

I FOUND YOU   **May 24th, 2006**

on top of it. Naked.

"You know there is always something I wanted to do with you and I think of it every time I come in here." My hands grip her ass and nip at the side of her neck.

"Yeah…and what would that be?" she purrs, tilting her neck to give me better access.

"Fucking you on top of this piano," I growl into her ear and thrust her into my waiting erection.

She bites her lower lip and glances at the piano. "Yes, please," she begs.

"Get naked," I command her and push her off me so she can strip out of her clothes.

Her arm reaches behind her back for the zipper, and she takes her time pulling it down. Inch by agonizing inch the skirt lowers exposing her flawless body, and finally pools at her feet. Slowly, she unhooks the buttons of her blouse, letting it join her skirt on the floor. My eyes roam her entire body, drinking her in, looking insanely hot standing before me in black lace panties and a matching bra. I'm quickly picturing each position I want to take her in for the rest of the night.

I'm pulled out of my thoughts of twisting her around like a pretzel when her bra goes flying passed my face. My dick twitches painfully, watching her as she slips her panties down her long-tanned legs. I groan loudly, at her flawless naked form, as the black garment dangles off the end of her finger. I twirl my finger, silently asking her to turn around. She does as asked.

She's so fucking hot and I'm one lucky son of a bitch to call her my wife.

When she's done with her 360 presentation of herself, she looks at me with a wicked glint in her eyes before her panties come hurtling for my head.

I catch them mid-air, roll them into a ball, and press them to my nose to inhale her heavenly scent. A scent only made for me. "Perfection," I growl.

Stuffing the black thong into my back pocket, I stalk towards her like she's my prey, ready to consume her. I inch closer, and she steps back closer to the black and white keys, but makes no real attempt to run. I catch her in my arms and my hands grab her ass, lifting her into my arms. She squeals when I plop her onto the cool top of the piano.

Her legs dangle over the keys and I sit down on the bench to just admire her; perched on the object that has helped me write so many songs, mainly about her.

Yep, this is better than I could've ever imagined.

I spread her legs, opening her to me, and dip my head into her hot, dripping core. My tongue darts into her heat, exploring every inch of her tight slit, devouring her arousal. She moans, and her body sags causing her feet to hit the keys making a discordant noise.

She *always* tastes fucking amazing, like strawberries, and I don't think I'll ever get enough her. I'm not sure how I even went without this for so long.

Two fingers ease into her while my tongue flicks and sucks her swollen clit. She's mewing, wiggling like crazy as my fingers make a come-hither motion inside her.

"You like this, Ace?"

"Yess…" she hisses and I insert another finger inside of her, pushing them past my knuckles.

I've mastered the way to play her body like a fiddle and I've never forgotten. She collapses back on her elbows as her hips buck towards me, begging for more. The sounds of sweet ecstasy leave her lips.

That's it, baby.

I nibble on her hardened clit, my fingers moving faster inside of her, and with a loud call of my name, she convulses around them. Her sweet juices pour into my waiting mouth. I suck up all of her lasting flavors, and my dick aches, no longer wanting to wait to get inside of her.

Once she's done quivering, I remove my fingers

I FOUND you **May 24th, 2006**

from her and I place them in my mouth. My taste buds going insane from the strawberry overload.

"So fucking good," I moan and kick the bench away.

My clothes quickly disappear and I grab my throbbing dick in my hand, pumping it, eager to get inside of my girl, my wife.

This motherfucking dream is finally coming true.

She scooches back on the piano and I crawl on top of her. My lips mold the side of her neck and she squirms below me. "God, do you know how beautiful you are? Laying naked on my piano?" My mouth works its way to her breast and I nibble on her pink nipples.

"Mmm." She moans and her hands make their way into my hair, yanking me back to her face. My eyes meet hers, which glow with deep heated lust and love that match my own, and I slowly sink myself into her soaked core.

"Ahhh," I groan as I fill her completely and she grips me like a vise. She's so fucking tight right now. "Fuck, yes, baby. You feel so fucking good."

"Coop..." She pulls my hair and relaxes enough to allow me to plunge into her, hard. Her ass and my knees squeak against the laminate of the piano with each punishing stroke.

Resting my body weight on my elbows, my mouth latches back to the side of her neck. I love kissing her here. Her whole body breaks out in goosebumps, no matter how many times I do it, and her sweet scent is the strongest here, where all I want to do is inhale her.

Her arms wrap around my back, pulling me deeper inside of her. Our mouths meet once again, and she moans into my mouth, her hips matching my thrusts.

"God, Cooper," she calls, not parting from my mouth; the cries of her ecstasy vibrating down my throat. My pace picks up, my knees are sore from the hard surface, but I don't care.

I know she can't be comfortable either, but the way she's writhing under me, I can't really tell.

Piano, bed, whatever. It's all fucking amazing.

My hand moves under her head, to make the surface softer, as I ram into her faster. Her nails dig into my shoulder and her pussy hugs my cock. She screams and her orgasm takes complete control of her body.

I still inside of her letting her ride out her orgasm, enjoying the feeling of her pulsating around me.

"Cooper! Move!" she mutters as she comes down from her high. I move my hips again and I'm relentless with my pace. I need to consume her, absorb her, feel her every inch.

I'm fucking her so hard, her body is squeaking loudly against the hardcover. I wrap her in my arms, lifting her and pushing her chest against mine, kissing her feverishly. With a final few pumps, I come deep inside of her.

"Come, let me show you our bedroom," I say as I slip off the piano. She doesn't move, laid out, and spent on my grand piano. Her strawberry hair is haloed around her, one leg propped up, making her look like an erotic model.

I trace my finger around her chest. "Are you not going to get up?" She moans and shakes her head. "Tired?" I ask, rolling her nipple between my fingers. Her eyes finally meet mine, and she blinks, but still doesn't give me an answer. "Do you want me to carry you?"

She nods.

Lifting her back into my arms, I carry her bridal style back to our room. Her head lolls onto my shoulder, and a content sigh leaves her lips.

I FOUND you May 24th, 2006

When we make it upstairs to our bedroom, I lay her down on the bed and she immediately cuddles into the pillows.

"This is nice," she moans, finally finding her voice again. "Are these like a million thread count sheets?"

"I have no clue," I crawl in next to her and pull her into my arms.

Her hand reaches out to touch my face. "Glad to see my face is not gracing the walls in this room. But I guess it would scare the girls away," she says humorously. But even though she's trying to play it off I can still make out the tint of hurt in her eyes.

I know the feeling. The thought of someone else holding her, giving her pleasure, kissing her, irritates the fuck out of me. As I look at her now, I only wish I hadn't done what I did with other women. They meant nothing to me and they were only strings of one-night stands. Sex only filled a void and I never dated anyone. No one piqued my interest.

No one could ever come close to Vi.

I wanted her even though I didn't think I could have her again.

Placing my hand over hers, I pull it to my lips. "I've never had a girl in here before…or in this house, except for the ones that work with me. As for pictures, I have my own special collection of you hidden somewhere." I wink.

The collection of '*dirty*' pictures we took in high school is kept in a locked box. I like having them at arm's reach for when I need some '*self-comforting.*'

She flushes. "I have mine too. I kept them under my bed; the reason I didn't need a photo of you hanging on my wall. I had the good stuff."

My hand works its way down her stomach, aiming to make its way between her legs when the phone rings. I groan, moving my hand away.

"Ignore it," she pants, reaching for my hand.

I should. I really should, but since I don't have my cell on me it could be important. "I have to, just in case something is going down."

Rolling away from the warmth of my wife, while she pouts, I sit up and grab the headset from my dresser.

"Hello?"

"Cooper. I've been trying to reach you," my mother's voice comes booming through the phone, "but I'm glad to see you're home now."

"Yep, I'm home. With Violet," I state firmly, feeling the need to remind her of my new wife.

"Oh, that's wonderful," she spills out sweetly, and I'm shocked at her accepting words.

Violet's arms snake around my neck, "Who is it?"

"My mother," I answer softly, still confused by my mom's change of personality. Violet's arms quickly fall from my shoulders and she plops back onto the bed.

"Did you need something?"

"Yes, I've been thinking, since we couldn't be at your wedding, I want to throw you a party to celebrate your marriage. I've been trying to plan for days, but you wouldn't answer. So, what do you say?"

I shake my head and wonder what parallel universe I've just fallen into. I don't mind this one if this is what things will stay like.

"You want to throw us a party?" I question, saying each word slowly. "I thought you were against this whole thing."

"Well, it's done now, and I'm trying. I thought this would also be a good chance for everyone to meet her."

My eyes roll to the sky, trying to keep my sudden temper at bay. "You know most of the family has met her. You just did a good job making everyone dislike her. I'm not sure I need her walking into a firing squad."

Besides my grandfather, Brody, and Dustin, everyone else in my family had their ears filled with

I FOUND YOU **May 24th, 2006**

Evelyn Reid's poisonous opinions of my girlfriend.

"She won't be. Everyone can't believe you got married. They want to meet her, and it will be the party you deserve. Maybe we can have a real priest give you a ceremony; we could give you a real wedding," she offers, meddling once again.

"We had a real wedding, mother. It might not be the high society wedding you'd have thrown, but it was ours." I refuse to let her downplay the best day of my life.

"You're right. You're right, I'm sorry. Just the party then."

Closing my eyes, I take a deep breath. Maybe she is trying. I have to take every moment and hope we're leaving the past in the past. I cover the phone with my hand and turn to Violet. "My mom wants to throw us a party."

"Your mom?" She snorts. "Evelyn? You're kidding."

I nod and her eyes go wide in disbelief.

Yeah, I know the feeling. I don't quite believe it either.

"What do you think?"

"I mean, I guess." She shrugs. "Whatever you want to do, but can you hurry with your call? I *really* want you again." Her eyes glaze over as she moves her hand down her body, between her legs. Her fingers meet the goal I had been going for earlier and dip inside her glistening core.

Fuck!

I lick my lips. I need to smother my face between her thighs again.

"Cooper?" My mom's voice pulls me back.

"Mom, whatever you want to do is fine. I need to go." I hang up, throwing the phone to the floor, and crawl over to my wife and bury my face into her needy center.

Erica Marselas

May 27th, 2006
Cooper

After two full days of steamy passion, locked up in our mansion, Vi and I have been forced to my mom and dad's place in Riverside. I don't know why I agreed to this madness.

Leave it to my mother to go to the extreme. I don't know why I thought it would be a simple gathering of some family and friends. Our birthday parties were always three-ring circuses as well.

This place looks more like a Hollywood movie premiere, than a wedding reception. There are bright lights, streamers, huge tents set up out back, and a DJ. Hell, there's even a red carpet.

Who the hell did she invite to this thing?

Violet grabs my arm, halting us from going further into the insanity of the backyard.

"Holy crap, Cooper! How many people are here?" She looks up at me nervously, and I pull her to me.

"I have no idea. And I bet I don't know half these people. We can go back home. I know there are other things I'd rather do." I wiggle my eyebrows. Fuck this party. I was enjoying being away from the lights of Hollywood for a few weeks.

"We have to at least make an appearance or we'll never hear the end of it," she groans, and unfortunately, she has a point.

"If at any time you want to leave, tell me, and we'll rip out of this place like a tornado."

"I'll let you know, I promise."

I lean down to kiss her soft, pink lips, and I'm drawn back to this morning when they were wrapped around me. She looks irresistible tonight, wearing a sexy, black dress

I FOUND YOU **May 27ᵗʰ, 2006**

that makes her legs look like they go on for miles. The dress is backless except for a few straps, and I don't know how I'm going to keep my hands off her. Around her neck is the double heart necklace I gave her years ago for her birthday, which dangles between her breasts.

Okay, let's not get me started on how great her tits look in this dress.

"Coop? Did I lose you there?" Vi teases, waving her hand in front of my face.

"Sorry, I was thinking how stunning you look tonight. I'm not sure if I told you."

"You did, about fifty times already," she quips, "but I won't get sick of hearing it. Thank you." She reaches up to kiss my cheek. "Shall we?"

"We shall." I take her hand in mine, feeling like we're headed to the gallows—the high-end gallows with flashy lights and glitter.

Following the red carpet to the large, white tent, the first person to greet us is Brody, with alcohol. He hands us each a glass of champagne and Violet downs it in seconds.

Brody laughs at her. He grabs another glass from one of the passing waiters, and hands it to Vi. "I had a feeling the two of you were going to need those. Did you really tell mom she could do whatever?"

"I might have, but I got kind of sidetracked." I nudge Violet's hip and she giggles.

"Oops, my bad." Her giggles cease as she looks around the bustling tent. "Do I know anyone here?"

"I saw Billy and John floating around somewhere, other than that I don't think so. I barely know anyone other than family," Brody answers, and Violet throws her other drink back.

"Wonderful," I mutter, and can't help but wonder if my mother hired people to try and make Violet uncomfortable.

"Was my dad invited?"

"I don't think so, jellybean. Sorry," Brody tells her.

"It's fine. Kind of expected it."

I'll have to remind myself to ask my mother about *that*. Speaking of my mother, when I look up, she's making a bee-line for us, smiling brightly.

I wonder if she needs to be tested for split personalities.

"Violet! It's been so long, dear." My mom opens her arms and pulls my wife into a hug. Violet keeps her hands to her sides, shocked by the affection. She glances to me, begging for help.

"Yeah, it has? How are you?" she mutters and my mom pulls away.

"I've been good. Quite a turn out, huh?" my mom gushes, her hand waving around the tent.

"Yeah. Who are these people?" I ask, perturbed.

"Just family and friends," she answers simply, and I think she's leaving out the random people she met at the check-out line in Bloomingdales. "I tried to call you for a guest list, but you weren't answering your phone."

Violet and I smirk at each other, knowing why we weren't answering. The two of us spent days christening every room of our house and completely ignored the outside world.

We have four years of making up to do. I have no idea how my baby is walking straight.

"We were busy," I say with a shrug and Brody snorts as he walks away to talk to someone. He has the right idea. "I guess we should go and mingle." I pull Violet away, heading straight for the bar to get us another drink.

It is going to be a long night.

After we get a good buzz, we finally feel brave enough to greet the guests who have come for us. The first person we conquer is my grandfather. He always had a soft spot for Violet. At least someone besides my brothers sees what an angel she truly is.

"I'm so glad you're back, sweetie," my grandfather, Charles, says pulling her into a hug, and kissing her cheek. "How are you?"

"I'm great. It's good to see you again, Bud," Violet says, using my grandfather's nickname. My mother wasn't too happy about him allowing her to; it supposedly took her years to get his permission.

Only his friends and his wife call him Bud

"I couldn't tell you how happy I was to learn you were my grandson's bride. I always knew you two would find each other again." He slaps me on the shoulder. "Hold onto her this time."

"That's the plan. It's why I weighed her down with that ring so she couldn't run far," I joke and Violet elbows me in side.

"I have two left feet, I'm not running anywhere. You're stuck with me anyways, babe."

As my grandfather and Violet continue to catch up, making jokes at my expense, my dad and Dustin walk over to join us.

"Oh, my god, Dustin…" Violet pulls my little brother into a hug.

"Hey, *Ace.*" The little bastard knows how I feel about anyone else calling her that, and I hit him upside the head. "Not cool, butthead." He growls and rubs his head.

"Well, don't call her that."

"Whatever."

"Okay, enough." Violet pushes me away so she can look over my brother. "You've grown up so much. I've missed you, squirt."

"*Violet,*" he whines and I know she called him that on purpose. He always hated when we called him that, but the once shorty is now almost six-feet tall.

"I'm sorry. Now we're all even. How have you been?"

"I've been awesome. I just got my license, but mom and dad won't let me drive the Benz." He rolls her eyes, looking over at dad, who's shaking his head as if to say, 'it's never going to happen.'

"He can drive anything else, but," my dad says. "Be happy you get anything or I'll make you take the bus again."

"Yeah, yeah," Dustin mutters.

"But that's awesome, Dust. You can drive my car if you want."

His eyes light up and he beams at her offer. I bite my cheek, trying to contain my amusement, knowing what's to come.

"Really? What is it?"

"No clue. I don't have one yet, *but,*" Dustin's face drops instantly and she turns to me with a devilish grin, "your brother has a pretty cool Jag. And since you know we're married and all…it's mine, and you can take it for a spin."

"Violet!" I growl, and she breaks into a fit of laughter. At least she's smiling, so I'll take it, but no way Dustin is touching my Jag.

"What? Have some trust in the boy. You drove fine at sixteen."

"And it's not like you couldn't buy another one." Dustin shoves my arm.

"Alright, Alright. I haven't gotten my 'hi' yet," my dad interrupts the bickering. Good thing because it could last hours.

"It's good to see you, Violet." My dad pulls her into a hug, but unlike with my mother, she hugs him back.

By the end, my dad had become a little bit more lenient about my relationship with Violet, even if he did side with my mother.

"It's good to see you too, Mr. Reid," she greets with a lopsided smile.

I FOUND YOU May 27th, 2006

"I think you can call me Andrew now. We're family," he tells her sincerely.

Biting down on her lower lip she glances at me, unsure, as she utters my dad's first name for the first time. "Okay, Andrew."

"Come with me, I want to introduce you to some people." He puts his arm around her shoulder and looks back at me. "You don't mind, do you son?"

Yes!

"No, Violet?"

"No, I guess not." She shrugs, knowing she's going to have to suffer.

"Good." My dad chuckles and leads her out to the sea of people.

"Don't worry, Cooper. Dad was actually happy to hear about you and Violet, once he knew you didn't marry some random chick. Mom on the other hand..." Dustin waves his hand. "I'm not quite sure which way she's really flowing these days. She's all over the place, but I'm happy for you. I know how you two really felt about each other. It was sickening."

"Thank you, Dustin"

"Hey, hey..." Brody yells, jumping in the middle of our brotherly bonding moment. Beside him are Billy and John.

"Where's the little woman?" Billy asks, looking around the room. "It's like a high school reunion tonight." Dustin slaps my shoulder, telling me he'll talk to me later, and walks away to say hi to one of our cousins.

"My dad kidnapped her to show her off." I point in the direction they had walked off in. My dad is now introducing Violet to his brother Rodger.

"Damn!" John exclaims. "How is it possible she got even hotter?" He looks back to me, clucking his tongue and wiggling his eyebrows at *my girl.*

"Fucker, stop eyeing my woman." I punch him in the

arm and he punches me right back in my shoulder, shifting me back.

"It was a compliment!" he guffaws. I'm about to hit him again when Brody interrupts us.

"Oh, fuck!"

"What?"

Brody points over to the bar and there stands Ainsley Green.

What the hell is she doing here?

She sees me looking and comes walking over with exaggerated sway in her hips. Her emerald lace dress leaves nothing to the imagination. Her breasts are seconds away from spilling out, and if she bent over she'd give the party a view of her nasty goods. It doesn't look good on her and I'm repulsed, knowing she probably wore it to get my attention.

Ainsley and I had a one night stand a couple years back; huge mistake on my part, and every time she sees me, she thinks we should hook up again. Never going to happen. However, my mom likes to think we're perfect for each other. She's the daughter of one of her closest friends. I never liked her, but one day, at one of my lowest points, I caved.

I look at the three guys beside me as they flinch in disgust and I know they've all taken a drunken ride on this tricycle.

"Cooper, it's so good to see you," she purrs and puts her hand on my arm.

I shrug it away. "Ainsley," I say curtly and take an extra step back.

"How you been? I haven't heard from you."

There's a reason for that. Fuck off.

"I'm good. Actually better than good. I'm married and couldn't be happier."

"Yeah, I heard about your rushed marriage." She laughs and flings her black hair back. "What about me and you have one last fling?" Her tongue darts out of her mouth and she licks her lips. It isn't sexy and she reminds me of a giraffe. She takes a step forward and reaches for me again.

Her hand is slapped away by a delicate tiny hand wearing a large diamond on her finger.

"Excuse me?" Violet's voice thunders through her clenched teeth. "Who the hell do you think you are?" She moves to my side and snakes her arm around my waist.

Brody, Billy, and John are stifling their laughter beside us. I'm glad those fuckfaces are finding this funny.

"I'm Ainsley. Who the hell are you?"

"I'm his wife. I'll ask again, who the fuck are you?" My baby sneers back. Ainsley cackles and I swear I see Vi's claws coming out to tear the she-bitch apart.

And well, I'm not going to stop her if she does.

She puts her hand on her chest as her sick laughter calms. "Really Cooper? Her? Over me?" Her hand moves up and down her body. "I don't believe it."

"Believe it. She's *my everything,*" I say.

Ainsley noticeably flinches at the familiar lyrics, realizing my most popular song was for my bride and not for her. I'm sure with her twisted personality she thought the song was actually for her. I pull Violet to me and kiss her forehead.

Ainsley shakes off her disappointment and sneers towards my wife. "*Please.* Did he tell you, honey? We hooked up…a lot."

"*So?* Am I supposed to care?" Violet cocks her head to the side.

"Girl, are you blind? I'm sure we'll be hooking up again. Especially, when he goes back on tour. You do know he has a side piece in every state, right?" Ainsley cocks her head to the opposite side of Vi's, trying to not seem put off—but she is, I can read it all over her.

Bitch, you're not going to win against my Ace.

Erica Marselas

"You mean he *did!* And it's all fine and dandy since we weren't married at the time. Plus, he's going to have a hard time when I'm on tour with him. You know being his assistant tour manager and all."

"Oh, fucking hallelujah!" Brody cheers, clapping his hands. He's only been begging me for a year to hire him some help. Now he has it, with probably the only person he'll be able to work with.

"You're going to take the job?" I turn to her, holding her by the shoulders. She's finally saying she'll do this. I want to pump my fist in the air; my girl always by my side, the way we always dreamed.

"Yeah. I thought about it last night after we talked. I would have been doing something like that for you anyways. It was the original plan. I was just scared I'd fuck up. The music industry is a bit different from what I was learning," she says quietly.

"Oh, baby." I hug her tightly, never wanting to let go. My success is in part thanks to her, and I need her to keep it going now. "You don't know how happy you've made me."

"Oh and me too," Brody adds.

"Hello?" Ainsley's obnoxious voice interrupts our moment. Violet pulls away and cocks an eyebrow at her.

"Good-bye." Violet waves her hand, then pulls me to walk away. The other three follow behind us.

I hear a high-pitched squeal and I know it's Ainsley stomping her foot, like the stuck-up brat she is.

We make it outside the tent, and the fresh air hits my face, as well as a feeling of peace from all the craziness.

"You hooked up with *that*?" Violet waves her hand towards the tent, twisting her lips in disgust.

"Mistake years ago. I swear. One time." I hold up a finger, my eyes pleading with her—I fucked up.

"Still promise you're clean?" Violet looks me up and down, wrinkling her nose.

"Damn! That's harsh," John hoots and I glare over at him.

"Do you guys mind?"

"Not at all," Billy pipes in, laughing.

Violet reaches up on her tippy toes and kisses my cheek. "If you don't mind, I need to say hi to some people." Violet goes and hugs Billy and John. "I've missed you guys."

SIX

August 29th, 2003

Violet

I've started my second year of college and I'm renting a house with my best friends, Alexa and Julie. I needed my mom's help with a deposit but I've never been happier to be out of her home. She divorced Jeremy six months after we moved here. He was the whole reason we made the move in the first place, the reason she ruined my life, and she couldn't hang on for a year? She changed her whole life for the asshole—yet for some reason me being with Cooper was all wrong.

Maybe she was right, though. He stopped writing me and didn't have the guts to tell me we were over. I wrote my final letter to him a couple months ago. When it came back unanswered, I knew we were over.

I had hoped after so long he would say something—anything—to put me at peace, but he left me broken hearted instead.

Yet, I still love him. I can't let go of it. There's something not right about it all.

I fiddle with the necklace around my neck that Cooper gave me for my sixteenth birthday. It's two gold hearts linked together, with tiny diamonds around them.

I hate how much I miss him. I grip it in my hand and

I FOUND you　　　　　　　　**August 29th, 2003**

hold the jewelry tight in my palm. Telling myself I should yank it off, let the pain sear through me as it snaps apart from my neck. But I relent.

My door flies open and Julie comes marching in, flopping on my bed.

"I think I'm in love," she says dreamily, kicking her leg back like a lovesick teenager who subscribes to Teen Beat Magazine. This girl, I swear, falls in love with some new celebrity every month.

I laugh. "Okay, who is it this week?"

"Oh my god, he's this amazing singer, super-hot and his voice is out of this world."

"Okay?"

Nothing new.

"I'm now in love with Cooper Reid."

My heart stops. The blood in my veins ceases to flow and I think I'm dead on the floor. There's no way his name just left her lips.

No, I'm hearing things lost in my own daydream.

"What did you say?"

"His name is Cooper Reid, and he's so dreamy. You need to listen to his new CD." She sits up on my bed. "He's got this song called, "My Everything" and whoever it's about is one lucky girl."

"Yeah, I bet." I smile weakly.

"Do you want to listen?" I nod, but I'm not sure if actually do.

"Okay, let me grab the CD." She springs off my bed and rushes out of my room, eager to show me her new idol.

I pick up my phone, dialing a number I know won't work.

"The number you are trying to reach has been disconnected."

Slamming the handset down, I wonder if he changed his number to get away from me, or is it because now he's some star.

Julie comes back in and hands me the CD. It's called 'Blue Skies' and on the cover is the face of the man who stars in my dreams every night. He finally did it. I'm so proud of him, yet mad that he didn't tell me.

Me.

I was always there for him when his parents weren't. I believed in him more than anyone. Together or not, I would think he'd share that with me, knowing no matter what I would always want the best for him.

Maybe it's time to move on. Even though it's the last thing I want. I wonder if he still thinks of me.

Why would he though? He never called, remember.

"Vi, are you ok?"

"Yeah, I'm fine." *I wave her off, not sure how to tell her.* "I'll listen to this later if it's okay?"

"Yeah, of course. But listen, there's no way you'll be able to resist his vocals."

Nope. There's not. His honey baritone voice always made me wet, but it was when he would whisper in my ear...

Julie pats my leg, grabbing my attention back again. "So, you ready for tonight?"

Julie, Alexa, and I are going on blind dates. Well, I'm going on the blind date; their boyfriends are bringing one of their friends for me. I'm so overjoyed—not.

"Yeah, I guess." *I shrug, unenthusiastic.*

I need to get back out there and try to meet someone new. I'm sure Cooper is. The thought makes my heart sink, thinking of other women with him. God knows he probably has all kinds of women throwing themselves at him and nothing to stop him from saying no.

It sure isn't me.

"Come to my room, let me find you something to wear." *Julie drags me to her room, and I notice right away the picture of Cooper gracing her wall.*

I FOUND YOU　　　　　　　　　　**August 29ᵗʰ, 2003**

I stand in front of it, looking over every inch of his body. He's been working out. His abs and arms are bigger than the last time I saw him. My fingers brush over my left hip bone, where his name is etched permanently and I frown when I don't see his.

Maybe they airbrushed it off.

Or he's moved on from you Violet and got rid of it.

"He's fine, isn't he?" Julie asks me, pulling me out of my thoughts...again.

I turn away from the poster and mumble, "Yeah."

"Come on, let's get you ready."

Hours later, I'm standing at a round table inside Club 99. They have a 'teen night', so there are no alcoholic beverages, but there is a dance floor with a pretty good DJ spinning tunes. Alexa and Julie's dates just arrived and I'm introduced to their friend Austin. He's a good-looking guy, but he has nothing on Cooper.

You need to stop thinking about him.

Austin is a nice enough guy, though I don't see this going anywhere past friendship. Alexa and Julie, along with their dates, have moved to the dance floor, leaving me alone with him.

We're both watching our friends dance, not saying anything. The song changes and all the couples pull each other close. It's a slow guitar melody and when the vocals start, it's a voice I would know anywhere—my blood runs cold.

It's like he's haunting me tonight.

"Do you wanna dance?" Austin offers and I shake my head.

"No thank you." My eyes close letting the lyrics sink into my soul.

"It was you who made me complete.
You believed in me when no one else could
Gave me the hope to keep on going

Erica Marselas

Even after you were gone
You're my everything, my one and only,
My reason for breathing, my only reason for living
And I only started living when you were ripped from me"

I couldn't dance with anyone to this song. It feels wrong. In a way, I feel like the lyrics are calling out to me. As much as I would like to think he wrote this about me, I'm sure he didn't. It's been over a year and a half, there's no way I'm his everything anymore.

If this song was really about me, and he wanted me, he has the means to come and find me now.

"Who is he?" Austin asks, with no malice in his voice and my head snaps up. I quickly wipe away the fallen tear that has made the great escape from my eyes.

"What?" I whisper, trying to feign confusion.

"I can tell you're still hung up on someone, Violet. It's okay. I just got out of a long-term relationship, too. So, I know the feeling. I came tonight to get Craig and Will off my back. They keep saying I need to move on."

"I'm sorry. Alexa and Julie feel the same way. They think I'm some dating hermit." I sigh regretfully, knowing it's my own fault they pushed me into dating. "They mean well, and they don't know about him*, so they don't understand I'm not ready yet."*

They think I'm some little virgin who's afraid of men, and I let them believe it.

"Still in love?" he asks with no judgment.

"Yeah, even though I try not to be, I'm sure I will always be," I admit, and my shoulders sag, realizing I can't lie to myself about it. Even if I date again, I know nobody will compare or make me feel the way he did.

Damn it, Cooper Reid, you've ruined me for everyone.

"We kind of lost touch and there was never a

breakup."

I have no idea why I'm spilling my guts to this guy. Maybe it's because I don't know him, or he's able to relate. "You?"

"Yeah, her dad was in the army, so they had to move to Japan. We decided it would be better to part ways."

"I'm sorry." I frown and rest my hand on his shoulder.

"It's okay. Maybe me and you can be friends?" he offers, and I smile my first real smile of the night.

"I would like that."

May 27th, 2006
Violet

After catching up with Billy and John I excuse myself to the bathroom. The night is going better than I thought it would. Everyone has been friendly and accepts me as Cooper's wife. Well, except Ainsley.

Evelyn has been tolerable and I wonder if she's turning over a new leaf. Although, as I come back out of the bathroom, she stands in front of me with her arms crossed, snarling at me.

Yeah, I knew I was just kidding myself.

"Hi, Mrs. Reid," I greet her cheerfully, trying to go around her, but she moves into my path.

"I didn't want to say anything in front of anyone else, but now that we're alone, I had expected you not to come to my house dressed like a whore."

"Excuse me?" My skin prickles with my sudden, rising anger.

What the hell?

I glance down at my dress and see nothing wrong with it. The dress has an open back with criss-cross straps, and the neckline shows off a bit of my cleavage, but it's more of a semi-formal summer dress. When I'd picked it out, I had thought this would be a family gathering, not a Hollywood wedding reception. I shake it off, knowing I can't let her affect me.

And she has no right to call me a whore, no matter how I'm dressed, especially with Ainsley walking around with her breasts practically falling out.

"Have you seen what Ainsley's wearing?" I remark, crossing my arms over my chest and cocking my head to the side.

"She's not my issue. I know the only reason you've come back after all these years is because Cooper is famous and raking in the money. I mean there must be at least a couple million dollars on your finger."

Holy shit, really?

My eyes fall to the glacier on my hand. I knew it wasn't cheap, but I didn't expect it to be millions. Maybe I should've helped pick it out.

"I find it funny how you two ended up in Vegas at the same time and got married. How did you do it, Violet?" She glares at me.

Did she really just ask me that?

I squint at her. "I drugged him and dragged him to the altar. The bodyguards thought it was funny so they let me," I bite out sarcastically. "Give me a break. For one, I always knew Coop would be a huge success and it was you who always tried to drag him down. So, maybe it's you who is only supporting him now because of all the money. I for one couldn't care less about his fortune or his fame because I loved him and have always loved him before he had a dime to his name. You know as much as anyone else I'm not some fling he just picked up and married. If you could just open your eyes and see how much we love each other, how much we care for each other, maybe you could start being happy for us. But you refuse, don't you?" I seethe, and she has the nerve to look annoyed.

She looks away like I'm wasting *her* time. "Are you done?"

Closing my eyes, I count to ten, trying to calm down. I'm not done, but I need to breathe before I go Jackie Chan on her.

"No, I'm not. As for 'getting' Cooper to marry me, it's called fate. It was finally on our side. And so you know, it was *your* son who asked me to marry him. He picked out these rings. I have no idea what they're worth, nor do I care. All they mean to me is Cooper and I are joined together in *matrimony*. Now, if you'll excuse me, I need to go find my husband."

I storm pass her, making her swallow whatever else she has to say.

So much for Evelyn's new leaf.

I'm not ready to see Cooper, and instead make my way over to the bar, asking for the strongest thing they can make me. The bartender obliges and pours a Long Island, doubling the liquor.

Bless his heart. I suck it down quickly, letting the burn soothe my anger, and help me de-stress. It doesn't last long when I see Evelyn come in; she spots me, and just when I think there's going to be round two, she beelines for Coop.

"I'll get you another," the bartender says from beside me. He seems to notice the tension tightening my back and shoulders.

"Thanks." I give him a grateful smile and he mixes me another drink.

A hand lands on my shoulder and I come face to face with the kind brown eyes of the youngest Reid. "Hey, Vi. You okay?"

I shrug my shoulders and his hand falls away. "Yeah, just a long day."

"You don't have to lie. I heard what my mom was saying to you. Just so you know, I'm on your side."

"Thanks, Dust. But can you keep it between us?"

"Why?" He scrunches his face in confusion.

Taking a deep breath, I glance down at my drink. "Because I don't want to upset Coop. I'm sure he's questioning your mother's sanity already, but I think it's easier to imagine she's trying then see the reality. I know personally how much it stings when all you want is good and..." I trail off, realizing I'm laying my feelings on a sixteen-year-old's shoulders. "Sorry," I mumble.

"No, I get it. I love mom. But she has her moments where I wonder what she's doing. But Vi..."

I hold my hand up. "It's fine and you made my point. You love her, so does Coop, despite those *moments*. I can handle her, don't worry. So *please,* keep this between me and you," I beg, seconds away from offering money or even finding a way to sneak Cooper's cars keys to him.

"Fine," he relents, "Just don't let her win and I'll have dad check on her meds," he jokes, with a little chuckle.

"Well, make sure they double them," I tease back and the bartender gives me my drink.

"I want you two together..."

I really want us together too. I muse inwardly as he continues.

"I was in the middle of teaching you how to capture a 'Spearow' when you left. I probably have to re-teach you the game now though."

I laugh outright, remembering how he tried to teach me and Cooper how to do play Pokémon cards. Cooper figured it out easily, but I had no idea what I was doing.

"Well, now that I'm around again, maybe you could teach me something new."

"Sure thing. I'm really into Madden now."

I pale. I'd rather go back to Pokémon.

Finishing half my drink, I set it back down on the bar and leave the guy a twenty for the tip.

Dustin and I walk over to where Cooper and Evelyn are standing. I slip my arm around his waist and snuggle into him, placing my left hand on his chest. Giving a full display of my ring to Evelyn. Dustin snickers and Evelyn clears her throat, glaring at me. I don't think Coop notices since he's too busy staring down at me.

"Husband, would you dance with me?" I purr, and rub my hand in circles on his chest.

"I would love to, wife."

"Oh, good you guys need your first dance as man and wife," Evelyn says, and somehow manages to keep the sourness out of her sickeningly sweet voice.

Why is she acting so two-faced? Everyone knows you hate me, lady. Stop playing games.

"Have the DJ play 'Have You Ever Really Loved A Woman' by Bryan Adams," Cooper tells her and leads me out to the dance floor.

Our song.

"I'm glad you remembered, Mr. Reid." I brush my hand across his cheek.

"I could never forget, Mrs. Reid. Winter Formal, 2000. We got in trouble for PDA in the middle of the dance floor." He grins cheekily at the memory.

"Mmm…I think it was more because we were dry humping as well."

"Can I have everyone's attention?" The DJ's voice booms through the speakers. "Will everyone huddle around the dance floor for the newlyweds' first dance?"

All the guests circle around us as Cooper pulls me into his arms. The song starts to play and the two of us sway as the romantic lyrics croon through the sound system.

I nuzzle my head into Cooper's chest, feeling suddenly shy with everyone watching us dance.

This song didn't only become ours because of the intense make-out session, and being our first slow dance together. It was the lyrics. When Bryan Adams sings of seeing your unborn children in her eyes, Cooper also had sung the words into my ear. The chills it had given me, thinking about being his forever, one day carrying his babies, having a family with him, had sparked and ignited something through my whole body. We had only been together for four months and I'd known then he was my future.

All the same feelings are still there, and as he sings into my ear softly, there's a different kind of fire burning inside of me.

When the song ends, he cups my face in his hands, taking my lips into a feverish kiss that isn't at all PG rated for this event. The crowd around us erupts with clapping and cheers, making us break apart. "I love you," he whispers against my parted lips

"I love you too."

Once the cheers die down, Elvis' 'Can't Help Falling in Love' comes on next and we both break into a fit of giggles.

I glance over at Evelyn, who is standing by the DJ stand, grinning wickedly, and I'm guessing she requested this song on purpose.

Does she really think Cooper or I care that we got married by Elvis, or that we care who knows? It was a blast and will always be the best day of my life.

Cooper twirls me around the dance floor and it's like we're the only two people out here. We are the only ones that matter.

He pulls me flush to his chest and runs his hand down my face, pushing the loose tendrils out of the way.

"Do you take me to be your lawful wedded husband…*uh-huh*?" he says in his best Elvis impersonation, grinning like crazy.

"*Uh-huh*. Do you take me to be your lawful wedded wife?" I ask through my bubbles of laughter. My impression of Elvis is horrible.

"Uh-huh…" He dips me to the floor and kisses me just like when we said, 'I do' over a week ago.

When he lifts me, I wrap my arms tightly around his neck, resting my head on his shoulders, another song now strumming through.

My eyes dart around the room and land back to Evelyn who is now standing with Ainsley. They both look like they swallowed a wasp, considering how pained their expressions are.

I nuzzle my head into Cooper's neck. He's the only person I need to worry about today. Cooper glances back to where I was looking, and when he turns back to me he lifts my head, his dark blues staring into me intently.

"Did something happen with you and my mom?"

My lips press into a hard line, quickly debating whether or not I should tell him. "Why do you ask?"

"She mentioned you two had some sort of disagreement and that you took what she said the wrong way."

I took it the wrong way? Ha! "Pfft. I bet she did."

"What happened?" he urges, but I'm not in the mood for Evelyn to ruin this perfect moment.

"Listen, your mom and I aren't ever going to see eye to eye. Just like you and my mom won't. It's a given, and I'd rather let it go for now."

"So, you're not going to tell me what she said?"

"Not right now. I want to enjoy my time with you tonight. I mean this party is for us. We should keep it that way."

He purses his lips and I know he wants to push the issue more.

"Please," I beg, fluttering my eyes sweetly.

"Alright," he relents, thankfully letting it go for now. I nuzzle myself back into his arms and we sway together again. His hand moves down my bare back and lands on the swell of my ass, pulling me into his erection.

I love the feeling of his hard dick poking me in the belly. His warm breath tickles my ear as he leans in to whisper, "I'm thinking of hightailing it out of here soon. I want this dress on the floor, you splayed out naked on our bed, with me deep inside of you."

"Well, we could always sneak out to the pool house or your old room," I suggest, needing him as much as he does me.

"Oh, I think it can be arranged, baby. You know, anything for you." He grabs my hand and rushes us off the dance floor. On the way out of the tent, we pass Brody. "Cover for us, I need to be alone with my wife."

"I always do. Go." Brody dismissively waves us off.

We rush out of the tent and across the lawn to the pool house. Once inside, our clothes go flying off in every direction, and Cooper bends me over the couch, plunging deep into me. All the tension rolls off my body with each of his powerful thrusts.

It's not long before I'm screaming his name so loud, I'm sure they hear me in the tent over the drunken rendition of "Y.M.C.A."

But I don't care, what better way to say 'fuck you' to Evelyn and that bitchy Ainsley girl.

Cooper pulls out of me, while I'm still a shaky mess, my hand moving to my clit, needing to extend my orgasm.

"I want you to ride me," he growls, twisting me around and lifting me up in his arm. He falls to sit on the couch, and I straddle his lap, sliding down his waiting shaft. I bounce on his dick, each bounce filling me to the hilt. His mouth locks around one nipple, suckling it 'till it's long and hard before moving to the next one. The musky smell of our lovemaking fills my nose. I inhale deeply.

God, our arousals smell good mixed together.

With my nails digging into his shoulders, I bounce faster, feeling every ripple of his cock as it bangs inside of me, my pussy begging for the ache it will feel when we're done.

"Damn, baby…" Cooper hisses through his teeth, his hands gripping my ass so hard, I'm sure he's going to leave bruised fingerprints in their wake. "You feel so fucking good. I love you so much, Ace," he says through strangled breaths.

"I love you too," I pant.

Cooper's large hand moves behind my head, pulling me forward. Our tongues dance to the music from outside. My whole body tightens, my orgasm hanging on a thread.

"Ah, fuck..." Cooper groans, his mouth releasing from mine. He grabs a hold of my hips and pulls me down hard on his cock. He does it once more and we both explode together.

~~*~*

After we catch our breath, we lie down on the couch, and I cuddle myself on top of him. This brings back so many memories of when we used to sneak in here to fool around.

Cooper's arm lazily moves up and down my body, his fingers occasionally rubbing over my tattoo of his name. The party is still going on, and I'm sure everyone is unaware the honorary guests are missing.

"Can I ask you something?" His voice comes out in a hoarse whisper. I'm instantly worried about what's on his mind.

"Of course." My head pops up to look him in the eye.

He scrubs his hand down his face, and I can see the internal conflict in his eyes. "Do you wish that we were still each other's one and only?"

Okay. Not what I was expecting him to ask.

"What do you mean?" My eyebrows knit together, not sure what he's really trying to ask me. But I have a sick feeling swirling in my belly it has to with the trashy one night stand outside.

"The four years we were separated, do you have any regrets about sleeping with other people? I mean if I could, I would take it all back. Especially Ainsley." He cringes.

I pinch the bridge of my nose, annoyed, thinking he couldn't have been this disgusted when he was balls deep inside of her. The thought alone makes me want to heave. I want to say, 'I wish you didn't sleep with that bitch either,' but I refrain. There's nothing I can do about it now. It's in the past. We did what we did to keep moving forward with life.

"We had no idea we would see each other again, Cooper. I can't blame you for trying to move on, especially since you thought I did. I just wish you had more faith in me. But I get why now." I sigh and lay my head back down in the crook of his neck. I don't want to talk or think about this.

"I'm sorry," he says, the soft tone of his voice laced in pain. My head pops up again and I press a kiss on his lips, conveying to him it's alright.

"It's okay. It's in the past." We both grow silent as we stare into each other's eyes.

I see the wheels turning in his head, the next words he blurts out take me by surprise. "How many have there been since me?"

Why is he trying to kick himself down, and kick me down by asking such a stupid question? I'm pissed and move off his body.

"Are you going to tell me how many you've been with? I mean you are a big star now, I can imagine it's more than both hands can count," I snap, and bend down to find my underwear.

"Vi…" He stands up, reaching for me, but I take a step back.

No, since he wants to be stupid, let's get this over with now. Let's shatter each other's hearts because it's the only way to go forward now without it continually circling around us like a vulture.

I had waited over two years before I tried again. I had gone on a blind date and couldn't enjoy my time because he was all I thought of. I eventually found someone to try and have *something* with, but it could never be more because it hadn't been *him*.

"You really want to know?" I pull my dress over my head and straighten it out.

"Yeah," he says softly.

You're an idiot, Reid. Well, fine here you go.

"Three...happy now?"

"No," he mutters and drops his head.

Yeah, that's what I thought.

"And what about you hot shot? What's your number because we know it's bigger than mine. Thirty? Forty? *One-hundred*?" I roar out the last number so loud it causes my throat to ache and my abs to hurt.

Is he like the guy from KISS who slept with all those women?

Gross!

"Violet..." he reaches for my hand and I pull it back.

I'm not ready for him to touch me. He should've known this is what this question was going to do to us.

"Is it more than that? Who are you, *Gene Simmons*?" I hiss.

"No, Vi..." His voice cracks and my eyes close, needing to calm myself.

The question is now deep rooted in my brain. He needs to answer me so we can put it to rest. But I'm fearful of the number that might roll off his tongue.

"Then how many?" My voice softens, but I refuse to look at him. "You had to know, then so do I, right?"

"Ten," he mumbles.

The number hits me like a slap in the face but it's not even close to the number I was imagining. Though, the bitch's nasally voice echoes in my ear about a girl in every state. So, did he fuck these girls every time he saw them? Does it matter?

"Including, the crazy chick out there?" My finger

points towards the tents.

"Yes."

"And are we going to run into any of these women on tour hoping to suck your dick again?"

Better prepare myself for the extra crazy ones I'm sure are going to go after my blood and my man's dick.

"They were all one-night stands. They meant nothing to me, and you won't run into them. I promise. Well, besides Ainsley."

"It wouldn't matter if you had relationships with all of them, but it was better to stay naive." My body sags, exhaustion washing over me. "I want to go back to the party or go home."

"I'm sorry. I don't even know why I brought it up. It's just sometimes I wish I went after you, kept you as only mine. The jealousy gets to me sometimes because it should've always been me loving you and not someone else." He approaches me cautiously wearing his signature pout. His arms open wide around me and I allow him to engulf me.

There's no doubt I feel the same way too.

But it's done and over with. Can't fix it now.

"I get it, Coop, I do. The thought of other girls with you destroys me. Especially, when I meet them. But right now, I don't want to talk about it anymore. Like I said, it's in the past and I want to leave it there."

"I should've come after you," he murmurs into my hair.

"You can't beat yourself up over it. Sometimes everything happens for a reason."

There's a loud synchronized knock on the door, and we know right away it's Brody. It was his code for letting us know his mom and dad were close by.

I give Cooper a quick kiss on the lips and step out of his arms. "I like what we have now and it's all that matters. Come dance with me again after you get dressed. I'm going to go see what Brody wants."

I walk away from him to the door, still trying to wrap my mind around what just transpired. I'm surprised he didn't ask how many guys shared my air.

The jealous ape of a man, but I wouldn't have him any other way.

I open the door, to greet Brody's sly smirk. I step out of the pool house, and close the door behind me. Nobody gets to see Cooper's bare ass but me from now on.

"Thank you for the lookout, Brody."

"It's what big brothers are for. Mom was looking for you both. She wants you to cut the cake."

"Really? I didn't know we got a cake."

The cake might make this all worth it. Though, what are the chances Evelyn poisoned my piece?

"She wants you to have your dream wedding. She can't believe her little boy would elope; he needs to have his big wedding. I mean he is *The Cooper Reid.*" He impersonates his mother with a high-pitched voice and fluttery eyes.

"Doesn't she know we would have eloped four years ago if we were still together?" I pinch my nose, "Gotta love how supportive she is of him now."

"I know. I don't get it. Anyways, wait 'till she finds out she's not going to the Grammys and he's taking you."

"The Grammys?"

"Yeah. It's a lot of fun. It's in two weeks."

How come I know nothing about it? And what the heck do you wear to that type of event?

"I know nothing about it…" I trail off when I hear Cooper coming up behind us.

"That's because I haven't had a chance to ask you." He slings his arm around my waist and looks down at me with all seriousness in his eyes. "So, Ace will you be my date to the Grammys?"

I tap my finger with my chin. "Hmm, well, I can't

have you go with your mommy. She's embarrassing enough as is. So, *sure*, why not?"

"That was one year. One. Louie thought it would be good for my image since I never brought a date to one of those things. They thought if I brought mom it would bring out this soft side of me. I guess girls dig that type of thing."

"Sure, with other mothers," I grumble and both brothers laugh.

"Brody agreed with him."

"Oh, I know, but I agreed because I knew it would be torture for you." Brody slaps him on the back. "Now let's get you two back before she sends out a search party."

The three of us walk back to the lavish affair, and we're not even a foot inside the tent when Evelyn demands that we cut the cake. Now. Cooper and I are led to the center of the room where a three-tier wedding cake is presented to us. It's covered in white icing, with purple and pink flowers draped down the tiers. A plastic bride and groom stand on top holding hands, with painted on happy smiles. I'm surprised Evelyn didn't get the one of the bride dragging the groom to the altar by his collar. I mean, it's what she thinks I did.

Cooper is handed the knife and my hand lays over his and we pose for pictures. Sinking the knife into the bottom layer together, we each cut a slice and place them on a plate. I'm expecting to see something vile flavored, like lemon or a rum cake, but it's chocolate.

Thank god.

Someone calls out from the crowd to feed each other and I glance down at the plate with an idea. An idea sure to ruin my hair, makeup, and dress.

But you only live once.

I pick up my slice of cake holding it out for him to take a bite. He opens his mouth and I smash the whole slice into his face. Icing and crumbs hang from his chiseled chin and nose. I break out laughing so hard I snort. The cameras click away at the pop star covered in cake.

He swipes his finger across his face, looking like he's about to eat it when he runs it across my cheeks. Seconds later his slice is smashed into my face.

"How dare you?" I tease in mock outrage.

"Me? You started it." There's a twinkle in his eye, telling me he's up to no good, much like myself. I lick my lips seductively, tasting the vanilla icing, and to keep him focused on my mouth while my hand reaches for more the cake. I manage to pull off a piece and smoosh it into the side of his face.

"You little..." he growls and does the same thing.

Soon, both of us are covered in cake, spreading it around each other's faces. Some guests are laughing with us, watching our display, while others gasp in disgust.

Well, you can't please everyone.

"Did you two really have to do that?" Evelyn scoffs. She glares at me, and I bite down on my cheek to keep myself from falling over in hysterics.

It's just a little food fight, *mom,* I muse inwardly.

"Here clean up." She waves a couple of rags at us.

"I have a better way to do that." Cooper winks at me, grabs my face, and runs his tongue over my cheek to lick up the icing. "Mmm. I think it tastes better coming off you." He gives my right cheek a slow lick before his tongue is entwined with mine.

"Cooper!" Evelyn barks sternly, "that's enough." We don't stop though and I'm vaguely aware of Andrew's voice telling her to leave us alone.

"Evelyn, let them be," Grandpa Bud agrees. "They're newlyweds. This is what they're supposed to do."

We should be naked doing this.

I FOUND YOU   **May 27th, 2006**

Cooper finally pulls away from me, with one final lick to my chin. "Delicious. Best cake I've ever had."

I'm glad no one can see how red I am under this icing.

After we clean as much icing as we can out of our hair and clothes, Cooper and I return to the dance floor.

"I want to take you somewhere for a couple of days. A mini honeymoon," he says, his forehead pressed to mine. "Then maybe later, we can really go on one, anywhere you want."

"I'll be happy with whatever you give me, Coop. Plus, I get to go around the world with you on tour. I'm with you, which is all I care about."

"What do you say we blow this joint?"

"I'd say, I would like that very much." My feet are achy and I still have some icing in my hair I need to wash out.

"Cooper, honey," Evelyn's voice interrupts our conversation. She's another reason I want to get the hell out of here.

"Yes, mother?" he smiles through clenched teeth.

"I was hoping you and Violet would join us for brunch tomorrow morning."

Why, so you can insult me more? No thanks.

"We can't. Vi and I will be going on a little honeymoon." Coop kisses my forehead and I sigh in relief.

Thank God.

"Oh? Where are you going?"

"It's a surprise for Vi, mom."

"Yes, of course. How sweet." She gives us a fake, toothy smile, but inside I know she's boiling, like a tea kettle ready to blow.

I bury my head in my husband's chest, wanting to avoid her gaze now.

"Are you sure you two won't consider redoing your vows?" she asks for the millionth time tonight. "I know everyone would be so happy to see you exchange them."

"And I've already told you, mom, Violet and I are more than happy with how we got married and the vows we made," he says sternly, and his body tenses up.

"Very, well." She brushes it off, but I know she's mad that her baby boy didn't have a huge wedding that included her. Hell, who am I kidding? It's because he married me, and has nothing to do with eloping or with an Elvis impersonator officiating our wedding.

"I think we are going to head out, thank you again for the party."

"Oh, it was a pleasure, sweetheart." Evelyn pushes me aside to hug her son. Thankfully Andrew and Grandpa Bud come over and give me a hug goodbye, telling me they enjoyed seeing me again.

At least someone likes me.

SEVEN

August 5th, 2000

Cooper

Violet and I are in San Diego visiting her father for the weekend. This is the third time I've met him since Vi and I started dating and he seems to like me.

I mean, the man is allowing me to borrow his boat to take his daughter out, alone. He trusts me not to wreck the boat or lose his daughter in the middle of the bay. Okay, so when I called him I had to work him over a bit; give a blood sample, sacrifice my left kidney, listen to a long lecture on responsibility, and had to fax over a copy of my boat license.

All but two of those is true, but it felt like I gave a piece of me away for the keys.

My dad, on the other hand, told me there was no way in hell I was taking his boat out by myself, and to keep dreaming. Though my dad's boat is a huge yacht, worth triple to Ron's, but the point is Ron trusts me and my dad doesn't.

But dad has an onboard cabin, so I will keep dreaming.

"Now, not only am I trusting you today with my daughter, but also my other pride in joy," Ron says,

dangling the keys to his jet around his finger. Taunting me.

"Gee, glad to know I'm above a boat, dad." *Violet rolls her eyes.*

"Only some days..." *Ron chuckles, and I bite my tongue trying not to laugh as well.*

"Humph." *Miss smarty pants crosses her arms and stomps her foot. I can't hold it in and snort my laughter out. She turns her head, glaring at me, playfully.* "Don't encourage him."

"As I was saying before I was rudely interrupted," *he squints at Violet,* "you take good care of it. I don't want to see a scratch on her."

"Yeah, no scratching me, Coop." *Violet nudges me.*

It'll be you who is scratching me, baby.

"I'm talking about the boat..." *Ron shakes his head frustrated.* "I give you a lot of credit for putting up with her sometimes."

"I'm going to go wait by the truck... I see how much I'm wanted around here. And don't worry he'll have your other baby home by eleven," *she huffs dramatically, and strides over to the truck.*

Ron shakes his head as his daughter moves to lean against the truck, and slips on her sunglasses.

"She's really on today, isn't she?"

"Yeah," *I mumble.*

"What happened?" *he asks me seriously.*

In the almost year I've been with Vi, I learned she covers up her hurt, by making smart jokes. Right now, she's really affected by the fight with her mother. When I came to pick her up today, they were still yelling at each other, and she got into my car crying. She's been doing her best to cheer up, but in the process, she becomes a smart ass.

"Our mothers. Amber didn't want her coming here with me; they had a huge fight. Then my mother didn't

I FOUND YOU **August 5th, 2000**

want me coming here either. It's just getting old."

Ron knows the score with his crazy ex-wife. Violet calls him all the time complaining.

"I don't understand. I tried talking to Amber, but I think I would've gotten more response from a brick wall." He stares at his daughter who's kicking around a couple of stones, and shakes his head. "How did you finally convince them?"

"My mom caved, and Violet just hopped in my car mid-fight. I'm just glad I got my driver's license on my birthday and my grandfather gave me the car. Makes for easier escapes."

My mother protested me getting a car, knowing it was going to make it easier for me escape and see Vi. But when my grandfather handed me the keys to a Dodge Ram, there was no going back. My grandfather loves Violet and supports my music. The truck is perfect for hauling equipment, so I knew he was sticking it to them as much as I was.

"They need to let you guys just live your lives. You make her happy, and treat her well, that makes you okay in my book."

"Thank—" He holds up his finger to stop me from finishing.

"But if you hurt the boat, you have another thing coming to you," he says gruffly and crosses his arms.

It's easy to see where Violet gets her smart mouth from.

"Thank you for this, Ron," I tell him sincerely.

"And I expect at least one fish to be caught," he adds, narrowing his eyes at me. "I'm not asking for a lot."

Is that code for 'don't spend all your time screwing my daughter?' I'm not sure.

"Yes, sir."

The wind whips our hair around as we cruise out into the ocean. It's about ninety but the ocean breeze keeps the air cool. The sky is blue and there's not a single cloud in the sky, making today the perfect day to be out on the water.

Mission Bay is great for zipping around and has a channel leading out into the ocean; the first place I want to give the Yamaha Jet Boat a test run; crashing over waves at 30 knots and letting the water splash on our faces. Next time we'll have to bring the jet skis.

Once we finish whizzing around the Pacific, we take a break, anchoring in the middle of the bay. There aren't many boats around. Violet throws off her lifejacket and pulls off her shorts and shirt. Her strawberry hair whips in the wind, making her look like an angel in a pink bikini. A very tiny, pink bikini. The little triangles she's trying to pass off as a top barely cover her nipples, and the bottoms are really a thong, her perfect ass almost fully exposed.

"*What are you wearing?*" *I gulp at the scorching temptress standing in front of me. My dick turns to granite and I think I might be drooling a bit. My eyes dart around the open water, not wanting anyone else to see her like this.* She's mine.

"*Don't you like it?*" *She spins around giving me a 360 view of her.* "*I bought it just for today.*"

"*I hope so. I'll be very mad if you parade around in this for anyone else.*" *I reach out grabbing her hand, yanking her down to straddle my lap.* "*Do you feel what you do to me, baby?*" *I thrust my hardened dick into her and she wiggles her hips in reply.*

"*Mmm, I do...*" *she moans, pushing her hands*

I FOUND YOU August 5th, 2000

through my wind-blown hair.

My hand comes down sharply on her bare ass, making a loud whack. She yelps and pulls on my hair in reply. "What was that for?"

"Teasing me."

"Me? I would never do that." Placing her hand on her chest, she scoffs pretending to look shocked. She pushes away from me and moves out of my lap.

"Where are you going?"

"I need to cool down…" She hops over the seats to the swim platform and jumps into the water.

I thought we were going to fuck.

I climb over and stand on the platform, watching her float around. Sometimes I wonder how I got so lucky to find her. Before I started my freshman year, I thought my high school years would be filled with countless girls dying to fuck the lead singer of a band. Well, I had girls after me, but none of them caught my attention, none I ever wanted, 'till I saw her. The fantasy of endless women went out the window, and she was all I saw. She's the only one I ever want to be with. The sex with her is on fire and I don't think anyone would compare. Nor do I want to find out.

She's my Ace of hearts.

"The water is perfect, Cooper. Aren't you going to join me?" she calls to me.

I waste no time and jump in the water to join her.

We swim around for a while, and Vi keeps trying to dunk me under the water any chance she gets. After about the seventh failed attempt, I allow myself to go under. But as I come back up, I grab her legs, lifting her above the water before tossing her back in. When she comes back up, she comes back after me, laughing her gorgeous head off.

I'm glad after the fight with her mom this morning, she's back to her normal self. I was worried it wouldn't happen.

I come across a sandbar by a tiny island and figure this spot could be perfect for a little fun. There's no one around us, and I can stand perfectly here.

"Come here." I wave Violet over. She looks smug, I'm sure reading the expression on my face. She swims over and wraps her arms around my neck. "Want to have some fun?"

She nods vigorously. "Is that really a question?"

"You do know if we're caught we are going to be in so much trouble," I whisper against her lips.

"It would be worth it."

Her legs wrap around my waist, and the cool water covers my shoulders. Hopefully it only looks like we're cuddling to any passersby. Pushing the tiny fabric from between her legs aside, I slowly ease my way inside her silky center. Her lower lip is trapped between her teeth, keeping herself from moaning loudly, as I fill her completely. There's no better feeling in the world than being encased inside her warmth.

My lips mesh with hers as I rock gently into her, not wanting to cause a lot of splashing or waves. Her walls clamp around my dick, sucking me deeper into her. She does it again and again, each time tighter and pulling me in further. Hell, I think I'll bust a nut just like this.

"You feel so good, Vi. So fucking good. Squeeze my dick again, baby," I groan, and she does it again.

With her head tilted back, I latch my lips to suck the salty skin of her neck. She's moaning like crazy, no longer caring who hears us.

"Oh, Coop, I'm so close..." Her fingers push through my scalp and her eyes glaze over.

I love watching her unravel and she's right there.

"Look at me!" I demand.

Her eyes instantly land on mine. Her lips are parted, releasing heavy pants, ready to fall apart in my arms.

I FOUND you **August 5th, 2000**

She's so fucking sexy when she's about to come. I don't know what it is, but something about her changes—maybe it's her flushed skin or the darkening of her blue eyes, but whatever it is, this look is special. Mine. Only I make her look and feel this way.

Gripping her juicy ass in my hands, I slam her down on my dick, hard, and her body convulses with her orgasm. She's whimpering and her pussy is gripping my dick so tight, I'm seconds away from bursting. With one final thrust, I come deep inside her, calling her name to everyone on Mission Bay.

Her body sags and her head falls to my shoulder as we both catch our breath.

"Will it always be like this?" she coos.

"I hope so, Ace."

She pulls back and looks at me inquisitively. "Ace?"

I grin. "Yeah. You're my number one girl and you have my heart."

Her cheeks flush a dark pink. "That's so sweet," she whispers, resting her head on mine, kissing the side of my neck.

"Wait until you hear the song." I wink, causing her to giggle.

"I get a song too? You spoil me, you know."

"Always. Now, let's get back on the boat and have some lunch. I just worked up an appetite."

It's a little after ten when we pull into Ron's driveway. We spent the rest of the day swimming, and me writing a new song for my girl...which ended with me getting laid again.

We get into the house and Ron is standing in the kitchen, with a Miller Lite in his hand, dressed in plaid sweats and a blue undershirt, no doubt waiting up for us. I place the cooler down on the kitchen table.

"*There's not a single scratch on me or the boat, daddy.*" *Violet hands her dad back the keys.* "*Thank you for letting him take me out.*" *She gives her dad a hug and kisses his cheek before going to the fridge for a drink.*

"*You're welcome, sweetie. I'm glad you had fun.*" *He moves to the cooler and opens it, then looks between the both of us.*

"*So, where's my fish?*"

Oops…

May 28th, 2006
Cooper

A flock of seagulls' squall overhead as Violet and I walk through Marina Del Rey marina to my boat. I've been nervous, wondering if she'll like the surprise I'm about to show her.
"Which one is it?" she asks, gripping my hand as we pass a long row of docked ships.

"It's the one straight ahead." I point out to the short distance ahead of us, where my boat bobs alone in the water, at the end of the rows.

"Wow, Cooper it's beautiful." Violet ooh's and ahh's at my shiny white catamaran. It's an Antares 44i, a 44-foot yacht with all the bells and whistles. It's the perfect boat for long distance cruising. I bought it last summer and haven't had much time between tours to use it. Once we make it to the dock, she stops, looking wide-eyed at the name I gave the vessel.

"Ace of Hearts"

"You named your boat after me?" she gasps, gaping at the gold script on the stern.

"If I gave it your first name, I would've appeared extra obsessed with you," She spins to look at me with her mouth still hanging open. "Do you like it? Because this boat is yours now...I want you to be happy with the name."

"I—" She turns back to the boat, then back to me. "I

love it. It's just I'm still getting used to everything. I mean just the fact you could afford to buy *this*." She waves her hand to the boat. "Do you get out much?"

"I don't get to use it as much, but it's nice to be able to tell my dad he'll only be able to drive it in his dreams."

"That's mean. I'm actually liking your dad now. So, it's time to forgive. You wouldn't let our child do it either at sixteen."

A smile splits across my face when she mentions children without paling. I know the hurt from losing our baby all those years ago still affects her. It gnaws away at me every time I think about it as well, and I always think of the life we could have had with our potential son or daughter. But I also want to try again, and I know I'm going to have to figure out how to ask soon.

"You're probably right." I kiss her cheek and grab her hand to help her climb aboard.

"This is so much better than the boat my dad had. It finally saw its last days. This time around he bought a simple fishing boat."

"Hey, we had some good times on that little boat."

"We sure did," she hums as she kisses my lips. "Remember how upset he was when we didn't bring him home a fish that one time?"

I laugh, remembering how disappointed he was when we didn't catch him his next night's dinner. He ended up taking us out the next day, saying we weren't going anywhere 'till we caught one. Though, it was supposed to be a 'punishment' we ended up waterskiing the whole time instead. The man drove the boat like a maniac.

No fish were caught that day either.

"I totally forgot about it because someone distracted me with the scraps of bathing suit they were wearing."

"You should see the one I have on today." Her hands run up my chest and around my neck. "I'll give you a hint, it's purple."

I FOUND YOU **May 28th, 2006**

"Well, if you're going to torture me, wait 'till we're out to sea. I don't need anyone getting a picture of me fucking you on the port."

Her face turns white and her eyes dart around the marina nervously. "I thought you said no one knows we would be here."

"They don't. Only Brody and Collin know my route, but that doesn't mean people won't get lucky. Don't worry your pretty little head about it. Now come, you can help me set up the sail."

We spend the next hours sailing down the coast, finally anchoring outside Long Beach for the afternoon. I forgot how much I enjoy coming out into the water. It's freeing with the sea breeze in your face, the smell of the salty air, and no one to bother you for miles.

Peace.

My wife's arms slip around my waist and she places a kiss on the center of my back. "This is nice. It's been a long time since I went out on the water." I spin around and hold her in my arms, admiring her.

She's pulled her cover off and stands before me in a purple bikini. It's not as tiny as the pink one she had which is ingrained in my memory forever, but it's close enough. No matter what she wears she looks amazing.

Her hand reaches out for my hip, her thumb tracing over my tattoo of her name. "I can't tell you how horny this makes me every time I see it. Especially with your board shorts hanging down like this…" She hisses through her teeth. "This fucking 'v' shape you have…" A lustful glint dances in her eyes as her hand travels to the top of my shorts, working their way in.

"Are you wet?"

"Very," she purrs, licking her lips.

My fingers lace through her wind-blown hair and I pull her roughly to my body. My lips latch to the side of her neck and I suck, hard, wanting to leave my mark. Her skin tastes of the sea air and coconuts.

She's a fucking tropical paradise.

Her little moans and groans are driving me wild, my cock is dying to escape its confines and dive into her.

"Coop," she says my name like a prayer, clawing her nails into any available skin.

"Yeah baby," I slip my hand into her bikini bottoms, grabbing a hold of her bare ass, and pull her harder into my aching dick. I can feel how soaked she is through my shorts.

"I want—" she murmurs against my lips. In the distance, there's the sound of an incoming boat motor. I'm not too worried about the approaching noise because they'll just drive by. Though it's enough to grab Vi's attention and she pulls away from me. Her head snaps to the left at the engine idling from the boat now sits beside us.

"Fuck," I hiss and yank my hand out of Violet's bottoms.

On the boat are two men in jeans, with cameras attached to their faces, clicking away at us. I don't think I've ever gone soft so quickly.

How did these mother fuckers find us?

"Is this your honeymoon?" One of them has the nerve to call out while they continue to click away. "What was the real reason for your quick nuptials? Are you pregnant?"

I grab Violet's hand and move her towards the cabin.

"Come on Cooper, we came for the show…" the asshole yells as I fling the door open and flip him off.

"I thought you said nobody knew we were here." Violet wraps her arms around herself and sits down. She's shaking, her eyes darting all around the cabin, and I know she has to be frightened.

We've had our run-in with paparazzi this last week, but this is the kicker. We were supposed to be safe out here. This was supposed be our time alone and these motherfuckers went and ruined it all.

Follow me to the fucking store, but *god-damn it.*

"FUCK!" I roar, frustrated as hell, ready to rip my hair out. "Can't I ever just get a moment of peace?"

"How do you think they found us?" she whispers, her body still trembling. I grab a blanket from the lounger and wrap it around her shoulders.

"I don't know. Are you okay, though?" I kneel in front of her, taking her hand in mine.

She nods, and a small giggle suddenly leaves her lips. "Yeah, good thing they came when they did. Another minute, you would have hoisted me in the captain's chair and had your way with me."

"Or bent over it," I interject, taking the moment to find the humor in it.

"I wouldn't have minded." She smirks. "But if there's going to be a sex tape, I'd rather have the creative control than those two doofuses outside. No way he would've gotten my good side."

I shake my head and kiss her nose. "All your sides are good, Ace."

Her smirk falls from her face and she wraps the blanket around her tighter. "What do we do now?" she whispers, all humor gone from her voice.

"I don't know." I stand and grab the satellite phone located on the counter.

Once booted up, I call Collin. He's going to have to meet us back at the docks and take us somewhere else. There's no way we can stay here tonight.

"Cooper?" he answers, surprised after the second ring. "Is everything alright?"

"The paps found us. Any idea how that could've happened?"

"Are you fucking kidding me?" he growls and cusses a couple times. I hear him radio Tucker in the background. "My guess is they either followed you or someone said your boat was missing from the Harbor. I'll call Louie and see if he and his team can figure out the leak."

"Hey, could you also do me a big favor and book us a room somewhere...nice? I need something quick because I'm not staying out here with these assholes floating around." I look out the porthole to see them still out there—waiting.

"I can do that. I'll meet you at the marina to take you there."

"Thank you, Collin."

Even if we're followed out of the marina, Collin can lose anyone.

"Before you hang up, I have other news."

"What?" I blow out a large puff of air, wondering what it could be now. Violet stands and walks over to me. She wraps her blanket covered arms around me and rests her head on my chest.

"An Amber Adams came to the front gates of your estate asking to see Violet."

"Oh, this just gets better and better," I grumble. Violet looks up at me with a raised eyebrow. "Your mother is in town," I say bitterly. Another thing to ruin this trip.

"Are you flipping kidding me?" She pushes off my chest, her face turning red as a tomato, while she paces the small area. "What does she want?"

"She refused to leave, demanding to see her daughter. She wouldn't leave the property, so the cops were called. They made her leave, but she mentioned she would be back," Collin answers.

"Great. Thanks, Collin. I'll call you when we're five miles out."

We say our goodbyes and I hang up. Violet has moved to the bedroom and is sprawled out on the bed on her back, the blanket discarded on the floor. She's staring up at the ceiling, her chest rising and falling rapidly, and her face still rosy.

I lie down beside her and turn her to face me. She gives me a small smile before kissing me on the lips several times. The heaving of her chest calms and we both enjoy the moment of peace.

My hand runs down her arm and I watch as the goosebumps rise on her skin. "I'm so sorry, baby. I really wanted this to be special. I'll find a way to make it up to you."

"It was special. I always kind of knew what I was going to get into if you became a famous singer. Plus, it's when they stop hounding you, you have to worry." She snuggles closer into me and kisses the side of my neck. "Besides the end, I had a great day and I know there's more to come. You don't have to make up for anything."

"Well, I'm going to try and save this weekend. We're going to get a hotel room and I plan to cherish every inch of your body before I fuck you raw, Mrs. Reid."

Her skin flames with her arousal. "Yes, please." She pants, throwing her leg over mine, and running her core into my stiff dick. "Can we start now?" Her lips hover mine, her baby blues begging me to show her a preview.

There's no way in hell I can say no to those eyes. I push my tongue into her mouth, accepting her request, and rolling her into the mattress. Screw the parasites outside. This is my honeymoon and I'm making love to my wife. If they get it on camera, at least everyone will know Violet Harper Reid is mine.

The people on the boat follow us back to the docks, but Collin meets us as promised, blocking the two assholes from getting any good shots. It doesn't stop them from asking their moronic questions though.

"Is it true there isn't a prenup?"

"Violet, Violet, is the reason you broke up because you cheated on him?"

"Violet, is the only reason you sought him out again because he's a big star now?"

"How do you feel about all the women who came after you broke up?"

Collin manages to get us into the back of the car before I punched their lights out. Couldn't they just taken their pictures and be done.

"I don't remember the other reporters being this harsh." Violet snuggles into me as Collin's leaves the assholes with their flashing cameras.

"Most aren't, but sometimes you get the ones who try to provoke you to do something and try to sue you, or twist your words around and put you in the cover of *Star* magazine. Those are bottom feeders looking for a story." I put my arm around her, burying my nose in her hair, needing to breathe her in.

"It reminds me of our mothers. Annoying as fuck."

Fair assumption.

I FOUND YOU   **May 28th, 2006**

Violet

We arrive at Hotel Casa del Mar in Santa Monica just as the sun disappears fully into the ocean. Leave it to Cooper to get the best room and his only words are, 'Don't complain, it's our honeymoon.'

I won't.

The two-bedroom suite looks out to the pier and the purple and white lights from the Ferris Wheel shine in the large windows. The palm trees sway in the breeze as the waves crash into the sand. I have a sudden urge to stick my feet in the cool sand. Though, my plan to run outside is ruined, when my cell rings, and my mother's name lights up on the screen.

Why won't anyone leave us alone?

"How did she get my number?" Cooper only got me a new phone a couple days ago, unless she managed to get it from Julie or Alexa.

But they wouldn't do that.

"No clue. You want me to tell her to get lost?" The phone stops ringing, but a second later it rings again with another incoming call.

"Yes, but she'll only keep bugging us." My shoulders slump, defeated. "I'll talk to her." Coop hands me the phone and I hit the green button accepting my doom. I already know this isn't going to go well and plop onto the fluffy cushions. "Hello, mother."

"Violet, I've been trying to get in touch with you. Where have you been? They called the cops when I came to your place to visit," she yammers, and my head starts to throb with an oncoming headache.

"That's because people can't just walk up to the house and demand to get in. Plus, Cooper and I are *trying* to take a honeymoon. How did you even get this number, or know where we live?"

"*If you must know* I got it from his mother," she grumbles, as if I have no right to ask. "I tried to get here in time for your little *party,* but my flight got delayed."

"You were invited?"

And Dad wasn't...Rude.

"Yes, of course. Why wouldn't I be?" she says smugly and I bite down on my tongue trying to contain my growl.

I wonder when my mother and Evelyn came to be on such great terms. They had always hated each other. Now they're buddies?

"Why would you come to a party to celebrate my marriage, if you're not even happy about it?"

"I figured being here would show you I was trying. I only wish you could understand from my point of view why I didn't want you two together. I mean the first time I met Cooper, he was getting thrown in jail hours later for almost beating that poor boy to death..."

Did she really call Thomas Ryan a poor boy? The words shock me to my core; rage bubbles inside of me, and like a can of soda, shaken one too many times, I explode.

"POOR BOY!" I scream into the phone and jump to my feet. Cooper is by my side in a second, taking my clenched fist in his hand. "He was no poor boy, *mother*. The bastard stalked me for *months,* then attacked me, and would've killed me if Cooper didn't come in and save me. You saw the damn marks on my neck. Why the fuck did you never let me press charges? That had nothing to do with Cooper..."

"We're still on this?" she groans and it only serves to piss me off more.

"Yes, we are. You brought it up, you called him a poor boy. He should've gotten in trouble."

"There was no point." My eyes go wide as I look at Cooper. His eyes match mine, as he listens to this drivel.

I FOUND you **May 28th, 2006**

"No point?" I hiss. "No point? Of course, there was a point! He needed to pay for what he did! God knows what else he's done to other people!"

I watch as Cooper pulls out his phone and starts typing away. I have no idea what he's doing, as I go back to listening to my mother's antagonizing voice.

"Listen, Violet, there were a lot of politics involved. Thomas had a bright future ahead of him. Plus, his father made him change schools shortly after, so you were safe. I'm sure he's very successful now. Made amends."

"Made amends? For trying to rape me? I never got an I'm sorry letter." I shake my head as something dawns on me. "Did he pay you off?"

"Vi, why are we talking about something that happened forever ago?"

"HOW MUCH? How much did his dad give you to drop the charges?" I bellow into the phone. I'm sure my words are ringing in her ear.

She doesn't say anything and I'm grateful for the sudden quiet to cool down. Cooper hands me his phone and points to the screen.

The words instantly repulse me as I read the 'bright future' Thomas had. In college, he was arrested for raping a couple of girls. He only served a couple of months for each crime. I snort, loving how great our judicial system works. I scroll down further and have to laugh. It seems karma works though.

The bastard died of a heroin overdose shortly after getting out of jail. Bright future, my ass.

"You seem speechless mother? Are you not going to tell me? I'm sure I can figure it out. Maybe Evelyn knows. She was there that night. She thought I was always money hungry, like my mom."

"Violet—"

"No. Don't talk. Do you want to know about Thomas' bright future? Since you didn't let me press charges, it appears the fucker thought he was invincible and raped a bunch of girls in college. Then, he finally met his own demise. So, how much was this bastards freedom worth? Because your hush money ended up costing more girls getting hurt a lot worse than me. How does that make you feel?" I sneer. She ruined other people's lives when she took a bribe instead of doing the right thing. She didn't do the right thing for me

Hell, I'm partly to blame for rolling over so easily. For listening to her.

"Just think. I did it for the boy too. Mr. Ryan dropped the charges against him remember."

"I do remember, but if Cooper didn't save me that day, you would be singing a different tune. You should be thanking him. You didn't have to bury your daughter that year, or if I'd survived you didn't have to deal with my physical and emotional scars that would have lasted for the rest of my life." I choke back the tears, the memory of that day coming back to me in flashes. Cooper's arms are instantly around me, holding me tight.

"Oh Vi, you're being dramatic. Maybe we should get breakfast. Talk over mimosas."

Is she for fucking real right now?

"I'm not being dramatic. I'm saying all the things I needed to say for years, some I've said before, but you don't seem to want to listen. It hurt me, it hurt others, and it's probably the catalyst to the Reid's hatred of me. I want to know how much it was worth to you."

"Violet."

"NO! HOW MUCH?" I yell again, this time scratching my vocal cords. Cooper's grip around me tightens, and he presses his lips to my forehead

"Twenty thousand," she says softly, but I hear every word.

My life is only worth twenty grand to her.

"As a mom, you want what's best for your kids. At

the time, it seemed right. I needed it then, and everything turned out fine. It's over now, in the past," she rambles.

What the actual fuck? She's insane.

"It's not in the past because it still affects me." I inhale a shuddering breath and my body suddenly droops, my anger exhausting me. Cooper scoops me into his arms, reading my body's signals, and sits me in his lap on the couch.

"Vi, I'm here all week. We should get together. Talk."

"I'm done talking, and I'll be busy all week doing honeymoon things with *my* husband." I click the end button and momentarily wish I was on a landline so I could've slammed the phone down.

"If I never talk to her again, I would be okay with it. I can't believe she took a payout, and thought it was a 'misunderstanding.' AHHHH!" I scream through my cries, burying my face into the crook of Cooper's neck.

It hurts deep in my soul knowing she won't allow me to live my life and be happy. If she could just come around and love me again like she did when I was little, everything would be okay. I take a shuddering breath, knowing I'm only kidding myself once again with the thought. It's too late for us. I can't let her hurt me anymore. It's like every day she slices the open wound more, to the point it can never heal.

I know in this moment, I've lost my mother because there's no point in trying to fix something that's permanently broken.

Once my tears finally ease, I'm lifted back into the arms of the man I love who carries me to bed. He lies beside me, cradling me in his arms. I feel safe, loved, calm. His soft, warm lips gently kiss my face, kissing away the leftover tears, as he whispers how much he loves me, how much I mean to him, and that he'll never let me go.

When he kisses me it makes me forget all the bad we faced in our past. I know there's more to come. My mom isn't going away without a fight, but with Cooper, I know we can make it through this time.

It would just be easier if our mothers would stop conspiring against us.

Even if only for a day.

EIGHT

April 26th, 2000

Violet

We've been staying at a hotel in San Diego for the last two nights and Brody, John, and Billy are staying in the room next to ours.

X-Rated is competing in a Battle of the Bands contest. I'd seen an ad in the Herald about the competition and entered them. If they win, they get to play at the Del Mar Music Festival. It will be huge for them and I know they have what it takes to win. So far they are in second place and tonight is the final round. Hopefully, this time Evelyn won't ruin it all.

One day Cooper is going to make it big, and they will eat crow.

Since I stayed with my dad for spring break he allowed me to stay at the hotel with Cooper and our friends. It's nice to be trusted and be a teenager without walking on eggshells. My mother doesn't know I'm here, thank god.

As for Cooper, he had to lie and tell them he and Brody were going on a "Road Trip" to spend some quality 'bro time' together. Once they mentioned I wouldn't be around, they gave in.

I stretch, my body stiff and sore from standing, dancing, and all the wild sex. When my arm lands with a soft thud on the mattress, I realize my boyfriend is missing. I faintly hear the shower running and perk up.

Shower sex sounds wonderful right now.

Rolling out of the bed, wearing only Cooper's t-shirt, I head for the bathroom. When I get to the door I hear Cooper's voice, but I'm not sure what he's saying.

Who the hell is he talking to?

I crack open the bathroom door and spot Cooper in front on the sink, butt naked, talking to himself in the mirror. I lick my lips, admiring his firm ass, and toned back. He's been working out this summer and he's bulked up—a lot.

I'm brought back to his monologue when his voice goes deep, sounding like James Earl Jones, announcing the winner of 'band of the year.'

"*I would like to thank the people that helped me with my record so I could earn this award. My producer, my manager, all my fans...*"

I break into a fit of giggles, unable to control myself. This is so flipping cute. If only he was talking into a hairbrush it would be even better.

Cooper's eyes meet mine through the mirror and he spins around. His eyes roam up and down my body, and a seductive grin spreads across his face, replacing the fleeting embarrassment.

"*I would most of all like to thank the girl just standing in my shirt today, looking sexy as ever....*" *He strolls over to me and lifts my chin with his index finger.* "*You spying on me?*"

"No. I heard the shower and thought I would join you."

"Is that so?"

"Mmm-hmm. You know one day you will make that speech."

I FOUND *you*   **April 26th, 2000**

He shrugs and grabs the hem of my shirt, pulling it over my head. Wet kisses trail down the side of my neck, his hands gripping my ass before lifting me into his arms. I wrap myself around him as he carries me into the shower.

Later that night, Brody and I are standing in front of the stage watching X-Rated perform. They are on point today and this is the best show they've had this week.

Next to me are a couple of girls, totally drooling over my man.

"God, he's a dream..." one of them swoons. She's licking her lips and batting her eyes as Cooper hops around the stage.

"How I would like to be under that..." The other one purrs, and I swear she's seconds away from flashing him her boobs.

"Better get used to that." Brody nudges me, drawing my attention away from the drool piles next to me.

"They can look all they want, as long as they don't touch," I say simply and go back to dancing.

The music changes and it's one of the songs he wrote for me, called "Desire." It's sweet, but sexual. I almost didn't want him to share it, but its beat is so catchy, it couldn't be passed on.

Cooper bends down in front of me, giving me a wink, singing the next verses to only me.

"I want to keep you up all night
having my way with you.
In the morning,

I'll taste you on my tongue
And I'll be begging you for more
because you're what I desire."

He kisses me forcefully before standing back up. I love the way he tells everyone he's mine. The girls next to me are boring holes into the side of my face with their laser stares.

"What?" I shrug with a smirk, doing my best not to laugh. "He's mine."

Only mine.

They both take the hint and push away from the front of the stage, pouting all the way to the back of the club.

"I swear, I can't take you two anywhere," Brody groans beside me.

After their set, the guys come and join us in the audience as we wait for the results of the winner.

"The results are in! In third place, we have 'Expo!'" The crowd claps as the band walks up on stage. "In second is 'Defiant!'" The crowd goes wild again as the band takes the stage, but immediately silences, everyone anticipating who won. "And in first place.... the band who will be opening up for the Del Mar Music Festival is... X-Rated!"

Cooper grabs me around the waist, giving me an all-consuming kiss on the lips, making my head spin. "I couldn't have done this without you, baby."

"Yes, you could've. This is just your beginning Coop. Now go." I shove him away and he grabs my hands kissing me swiftly on the cheek. Everyone is still going crazy around us and John comes over and grabs Cooper's arm yanking him away.

"Come on dude, give your woman a break..."

"That's never going to fucking happen..." he winks at me before moving to the stage.

I FOUND YOU   *June 2nd, 2006*

June 2nd, 2006
Violet

My back is pressed against Cooper's chest, his arms tightly around me. One hand plays with my nipple and the other rubs my clit. My leg is thrown over his as he slowly works in and out of me.

His lips hover over my ear, whispering all the perfect things: how much he loves me, how he'll never get enough of me, and will never let me go.

Out of all the times Cooper and I have had sex, this is one of those times I feel the closest to him, truly feeling every ounce of love and heated passion he has for me. There is just something special and magical about this moment. We've been at this for the last hour—or god knows how long—and I don't want the never-ending pleasure to end.

My head turns so I can capture his lips with mine. His tongue swirls around mine, hungrily, making my head spin.

"I love you, Cooper..." I moan.

"I love you too baby, so much." His slow pace is torturing, but oh so good. My stomach tightens and my core tingles with another impending eruption of euphoria. I've already had countless orgasms and I'm about to come again.

"Let it go, baby. I love the feeling of you coming

around me." He pinches my clit and I cry out his name, tumbling over the edge.

I push my ass back, my body still convulsing, feeling his dick swell and I know he's almost there.

"Fuck, Vi" He groans and grabs my hip, holding me still as he spills into me.

His teeth sink into my shoulder, tweaking my nipple, starting his sweet torture of thrusting into me again.

This man is a fucking machine today.

"I don't think I can get enough of you today, Violet. I just want to stay inside of you all day."

"I want you to stay inside of me too." I pant. It's true; I could live the rest of my life in this man's arms.

He slips out of me and before I can ask what he's doing he rolls me on my back, my body instinctively wrapping around him. Resting his forehead on mine, his eyes shine with his adoration for me, as she slowly sinks back into me.

"I love it, even more, when I can see you because when you come your irresistible."

There's a loud bang on our bedroom door snapping us out of our fervent embrace. "Hey, bro. We're here!" Brody's voice comes booming into our room.

I try to push Cooper away, knowing our door isn't locked, but he grabs my wrists and pins them above my head. He shakes his head, mouthing to me that I'm not going anywhere.

"Fuck off, Brody. We're busy," Cooper growls, continuing to pump into me with his eyes locked on me, consuming me once again.

Brody guffaws, "I'm sure you are, but we have rehearsal, and Violet is going dress shopping with Alexa."

"Give us five minutes."

"That's all? I'm disappointed brother." His final words echo through the room before we finally hear him walk away.

I FOUND YOU   **June 2nd, 2006**

"I have to remind myself why I gave him the codes. I think after today I'm going to change them." He leans down and kisses me. "You think you can come again, start this day on top?"

"Oh, it's already started on top."
I'm practically flying.

We walk into the living room with our arms wrapped around each other, showered, dressed and totally content.

"Well, hello lovebirds," Brody greets us. "It's about time you come out. We're already running late."

"I'm here now," Cooper says, annoyed.

"Oh, Violet, this is going to be so much fun." Alexa stands up from the couch, pulling me into a hug.

Alexa came into town yesterday to be with Brody and to go shopping with me for the award show. The two of them have been doing the long-distance relationship thing, and it seems to be working—while Cooper and I were on honeymoon he drove down to stay with her.

Julie and Tucker have fizzled, though. Julie says she's fine; that they had their fun but she knew it would never last.

"You know how badly I've always wanted to play dress up with you. I'm going to make you the prettiest girl at the ball," she says in a sing-song voice, pushing my hair back, pretending I'm Cinderella.

"Ugh, do I have to go, fairy godmother? I'd rather hang with the rats." I flutter my eyes and put on my best pout. I hate shopping, but I guess I'm not allowed to wear jeans to the Grammys.

"Well, you married a Prince so you're going to have

to deal." She wags her finger at me.

"I'm going to grab my bag and then we can go, Brody." Cooper grabs my hand. "You come with me for a second."

He leads me to the music room and I still haven't gotten used to my *large* face on the wall. It's like going into a time warp because the portrait is from my sixteenth birthday when we went hiking with my dad. I'm sitting on a large rock that looked over the city, the sun at my back makes me look like I'm glowing, while I smile at the camera.

"You're as stunning as the day I took that," he coos in my ear, causing a shiver to run down my back. It's crazy how this man can still cause me to blush.

He reaches into his back pocket to pull out his wallet. Slipping out a credit card, he hands it to me. "I want you to use this and get whatever you want." I look down at the card and realize it's his black Amex. The credit card Julie would call endless amount of fun with its non-existent spending limit.

"Coop, I can buy my own dress. I don't need *this*." I thrust it back at him and he pushes my hand back.

"Violet, don't argue. I have a feeling the dresses you will be looking at will cost more than what you have."

I snort. "I'll go to Kohl's then."

Why do I need a dress that costs twenty grand?

"Violet Reid!" he exclaims grabbing my shoulders, I'm sure fighting the urge to shake the defiance out of me. "We're married now. What's mine is yours. What's yours is mine. Plus, think of it as an advance on your paycheck." He smirks, placing a light kiss on my lips.

"Fine." I reluctantly slip the card in my purse. No point in arguing about it. I won't ever win.

Gathering me in his arms, he pulls me tight to him. "I know you're still getting used to all this, but I'm glad you are finally able to share it with me. You're a big part of why I'm so successful, so please don't worry about whose is whose, okay?"

I nuzzle my head into his chest and nod. "Thank you."

He lifts my chin, rubbing his thumb over my lips. "You're welcome, and have fun. I shouldn't be out too late. And remember, Tucker will accompany you and Alexa. I don't trust anyone not to try and get close to you again."

"I understand. I love you."

"I love you too, baby."

Alexa and I are searching the racks at a high-end dress shop in Beverly Hills. I feel out of place dressed in a flowing pink summer dress, but I do have to admit the clothes here are breathtaking.

Maybe this could be fun.

"I'm guessing everything is *real* good with you and Cooper?" Alexa wiggles her eyebrows at me.

"It's been amazing," I croon, remembering how last week we stayed at the hotel in Santa Monica. We locked ourselves in the suite, tucked away from the outside world, and we were finally able to get some peace and quiet. Before we came home though, we visited my dad. When I told him what my mom had done, he praised me for standing my ground, and didn't blame me for not wanting to talk to her anymore. She hasn't tried calling me either, and Julie told me she was back in Arizona. Thank god.

"How about you and Brody?" I ask Alexa.

"It's been good. We talk all the time when we're not

in the same state. He makes me feel cherished. I've never had that with anyone before, even though we're far apart. And the sex," she whistles through her teeth, "is hands down the best I've ever had."

"I guess that means a lot coming from you." I nudge her shoulder, laughing.

"Oh, and like you can't say that about Cooper?"

"Cooper has always been the best, but now it's even better. I don't know how to describe it, I mean this morning..." I clamp my mouth down, realizing I'm about to say too much in the middle of a store, with who knows listening around us. The last thing Cooper and I need is someone eavesdropping and transcribing our sex life word for word to the press.

"Oh, me and Brody heard this morning." Her cheeks redden. "I'm glad you're happy. You deserve it."

"Same back at you sister. Now come on, you're supposed to be helping me find a dress." I drag her to the back and let her use me as a life size Barbie to play dress up with.

Forty-five minutes later, I'm standing in the dressing room surrounded by about twenty different dresses, all different styles and colors. I'm so overwhelmed.

My phone buzzes in my pocket and I pull it out to see my husband's face along with a new text.

Coop: **I LOVE YOU. HAVE FUN**

Oh, I'll have some fun alright.

I slip out of my dress, leaving me only in my panties. I cover my arm over my breasts and take a picture. I double check the number before I send it to him.

The first dress I try on is an extremely short, prison orange, cocktail dress with sequins. Alexa thought I should have it for all the upcoming clubbing I might do—or whatever.

I FOUND YOU June 2nd, 2006

I check myself out in the mirror; it's not awful, but I kind of look like a pumpkin. For the fun of it, I take a picture and send it to Cooper to ask his thoughts before stepping out of the dressing room. If Alexa likes this I'm going to think she's lost her marbles.

Instead of Alexa waiting outside the room, I'm startled to find Ainsley staring at me with her arms crossed. She doesn't seem the least bit surprised to see me as I am her.

Wonderful.

...And my day started out so well.

She looks me over with her raggedy eyebrow raised at the sky and laughs. "Wow. You look hideous."

"Well, it's a good thing nobody asked you," I hiss.

"I just don't understand what he sees in you. I mean, he had me and then goes back to you. What? Did you have to drug him?" She cackles, thinking she's funny.

"No, but I question the beer goggles he was wearing the day he slept with you."

"It must kill you to know he had me, doesn't it?" she retorts, using the only ammo she has against me.

Too bad it won't work.

"Nope." I tell her popping the 'p'. "He's told me about his mistake, I think the term he used was 'she-bitch.' Now, if you don't mind…" I turn around heading back to my dressing room, wanting to get away from her, when her mouth opens again to spew her trash.

"You'll never keep him satisfied, remember that. You're nothing but a poor little girl from the wrong side of the tracks. He'll find someone so much better. And then where will you be?"

I close my eyes to steady my temper. What I really want to do is punch her in her motherfreakin' face, but it would mean letting her know she got to me. Her words don't bother me, it's her damn presence.

"You seem to forget, I have the ring on my finger…"

I hold up my hand, showing off my wedding bands. "He married me! He comes home to me! I sleep in his bed every night! And we have crazy monkey sex all the time, everywhere! I'm his everything, his ace of hearts," I spit the song titles at her, and she pales. "You know it too, so if you don't mind, I have things to do." Marching into the dressing room, I slam the door in her face.

Fucking Psycho bitch.

And what the hell is she doing here? Doesn't she live in Riverside?

Once I calm down, I pick up my phone and see a message from Cooper.

Coop: I'd much rather see that dress on the ground. And you naked with your legs wrapped around my ears.

Yep, no worries for this girl. I have no doubt he loves me and *only me.*

After trying on countless dresses, I finally pick two I really like. The price tag makes me sick though: five thousand dollars for some fabric. The other is a steal at two thousand.

"What's wrong?" Alexa asks me, placing her hand on my shoulder as I set my dresses on the counter to pay.

"I'm still getting used to it. I don't think being married to a pop star has hit me yet." Everything is still new and we're in this honeymoon stage where it's only us. He's still just Cooper to me. I don't think it'll hit me 'till we go on tour and it's in my face.

"Try not to over think it. I know it's different, but it's kind of your life now."

"I know." I exhale heavily, trying to own up to my new life.

The cashier tells me the total and informs me they will be delivered to the house after they make a few alterations to the length. I give her the address and hand her Cooper's card. It's the first time I really looked at it and it has my name imprinted on the front.

The sneaky bastard.

"I see you don't have any trouble spending my son's money," a voice sneers from behind me belonging to the one and only Mrs. Evelyn Reid.

Lord, why are you punishing me?

I turn around and see she's standing next to sour face Ainsley. I should've known they were together.

"Hello, Mrs. Reid. Fancy seeing you in these parts." I plaster on my best, sickly sweet smile. "How are you?"

"I will be a lot better once you and my son are apart."

My false smile drops and I wonder how much longer this is going to go on. "So, we're back on this merry-go-round. When will you understand that we will always be together?" I turn back around to the cashier, who hands me back my card. Her expression is neutral, and I wonder how many cat fights she's seen in this place to not even blink an eye.

"As soon as you were out of the picture, he finally started doing better in school, stopped late night partying, and coming home drunk. Now he's all over the tabloids with his floozy wife making a fool out of him."

I rub the sudden hammering in my temples with my index fingers.

"Are you okay? "Alexa whispers in my ear, looking at the interfering witches standing behind us.

"Yeah, I'm used to this," I sigh, and turn back around.

"Listen, Evelyn, we're married now. Don't you think it's time to move on?" I glance out the window to where Tucker is standing. I think I'm going to need him for what I might do if she doesn't get out of my face soon.

Our eyes meet and I nudge my head for him to come inside.

"Ainsley tells me you're going to be working as a manager on his tour. So, you just swoop in and take over Cooper's life, but also take Brody's place," she says, totally ignoring my question.

I look at Ainsley who has her nose stuck up in the air like the spoiled bitch she is.

"Well, I think you were misinformed. Cooper had to beg me to take the job, and as for Brody, I'm helping him. I'm only his assistant. If anything, it's going to make his job a little easier. You do know if it wasn't for you and my mother's meddling it would have all happened this way in the first place. You need to get over yourself. He's twenty-one, don't you think it's time you let go of the reins?"

Tucker walks into the store and comes to stand next to me. Beside me, Alexa watches the verbal tennis match, I'm sure having no idea what to do.

"I see you still have a mouth on you," Evelyn scoffs. "I hope the dress you picked for the *Granting Hope Ball* is tasteful. There will be children there, and I would hate for you to embarrass my son again like you did at the reception."

"How did I embarrass him? He happened to like what I was wearing, thank you," I spit.

"You looked like a two-bit whore," Ainsley's big mouth butts in, "and that orange jumpsuit you were trying to pass as a dress didn't help the whore factor. Poor Cooper. Does he know how bad your taste is?"

I step forward about to slap the bitch when Tucker grabs my shoulder. I'm pleased when the little wench flinches.

"Violet?"

"What?" I snap, whipping my head to Tucker.

"We should go," he says calmly, instantly bringing me down a peg. I did bring him in to stop me from doing something stupid.

"Yeah, Violet. You can't let them get to you." Alexa wraps her arm around me.

"He gave you a bodyguard too? Really? You're nothing important," Ainsley scoffs.

"Listen, Bitch, you need to shut your mouth," Alexa snaps at Ainsley.

"And who do you think you are?"

"Her best friend. I also happen to be dating Brody. I've heard things, but I really didn't think you were this bad, Mrs. Reid. Shouldn't you just be happy for them?"

"She will never be good enough for my son. And now I need to have a talk with Brody." Evelyn's beady eyes rake over my best friend. Oh no, she can be a bitch to me, but leave my friends out of it.

"Wow! You're such a special lady, aren't you? I have no idea how you managed to raise such good kids when they had you as a mother…" The venom flows from my lips. I hope my words sting.

"Let's go, Violet," Tucker urges pulling me out of the store to lead us to the car.

"Freakin' Bitch!" I scream, and a bunch of people turn their heads to look at me. Slightly embarrassed by my outburst, I hop into the back seat of the town car.

"Brody wasn't kidding when he said she didn't like you," Alexa mutters. "All because she doesn't think you're good enough?"

"Basically. I mean even Andrew got over what happened in high school. And for some reason, she thinks Ainsley would be better." I snort, and look up to see Tucker on the phone. "I need a drink! Do you want to go back to the house with me? I plan on getting drunk."

"Sounds like a plan."

We're halfway home when Cooper calls me on my cell.

"Hi," I answer meekly.

"Tucker told Collin you had a run in with my mother

and Ainsley. What happened?" I groan inwardly, I'm so sick and tired of almost every conversation we have together is about our mothers. I swear they're the third and fourth people in our relationship.

"Your mother is just making it clear to me again how much she doesn't approve of us. How I'm not good enough for you. Oh, and I'm the reason you were such a drunk party animal. You know same old, same old. I'm surprised she doesn't have it in playback to save her breath."

"Baby, I'll talk to her."

Yeah, because that would do anything.

"Don't worry about it, Cooper. I can deal with it."

"But you shouldn't have to." He exhales heavily, and I picture him running his hands down his face.

"She's not going to tell you the truth and you know it. Just like at our reception party. When she told you about our 'misunderstanding'?"

"You still haven't told me either."

"It doesn't matter now. She's still your mother and at least she didn't sell you down the road for money." My eyes close tightly, choking down the sudden lump in my throat. Everything in me is screaming to tell him, to divulge everything she's said and done, but I can't. I know he would kick Evelyn to the curb if I just said the words, but it's not what I want. It'll cause a tidal wave of ramifications between his brothers and his father. The last thing I want is for another family to fall apart because they feel they might have to pick sides. They still love her and they need her a hell of a lot more then I need my mother.

"I can deal with it because I'm not going to try to come in the middle of it all. I know how you feel about me, and I can only hope she doesn't change your mind." Alexa rubs my back trying to console me.

Violet, don't cry, don't cry.

"She's never been able to before, she isn't going to

now. I love you, baby." His smooth voice tells me sincerely, and it soothes my heart.

"I love you too." I wipe away the tears welled in the corner of eyes and take a deep breath. I'm not going to let Evelyn ruin the rest of my day. I have him, we love each other, and it's all that matters. "Alexa and I are going to go back to the house. We might be a little inebriated when you get back."

He chuckles softly, I'm sure thinking about how crazy horny I get after a couple of glasses of wine. "Well, I guess we'll have to play catch up when we get back. Just don't get too wild and crazy. Did you at least get a dress?"

"Yes, I found two, for both events. I do have to say you're a sneaky bastard giving me my own card."

"I have no idea what you're talking about." I can hear him smirking over the phone. "But you know I take care of what's mine."

"Yours," I say seductively.

"Oh, god. Please don't start doing that now. I'm sitting right here," Alexa moans.

"We should be done shortly, baby. I'll see you soon."

"Bye." I hang up the phone.

June 11th, 2006
Violet

Tonight is the Grammys. I'm getting excited about the event and no longer breaking out into a cold sweat knowing I'm going to be surrounded by some of the best musicians in the world. This fangirl might pass out, but it won't be because of my husband; especially if Usher or Adam Levine are there.

Cooper's tour starts in two weeks, so after tonight our lives are going to get hectic. Cooper is putting the finishing touches on his record and then rehearsals with the band will start. Brody and I have already buckled down on the roles I will take over for him.

The poor guy really did have everything on his shoulders.

I wonder how different life is going to be on the road. I'm eager to travel the world with my husband and see up close the life he's been living the last two years. To see him onstage, in his element, and his adoring fans cheering for him.

If anything, it's what I look forward to the most.

Cooper is on the phone with someone from the recording studio, and I've just finished getting my hair done. I make my way to my closet to check out my dresses which finally arrived today. They should've been here days ago, but there was some sort of delay with the alterations. I unzip the bag and when I open it up, my heart pumps rapidly out of my chest, my body tingles, and my vision blurs. I feel as though I'm having some sort of anxiety attack at the sight of the monstrosity in front of me.

What the ever-living fuck?

The dress in front of me is *NOT* the one I picked out. It's a purple, peacock looking dress, complete with huge colorful feathers. I don't believe this.

And the first thought that pops into my head is that Evelyn Reid is, without a doubt, behind this. Cooper did end up calling her after the 'dress store showdown' and he told me she *apologized.* We both knew it wasn't genuine—the truth always comes out; this time in the form of a hideous dress.

"Is that the dress you picked?" Cooper asks walking into the closet. He's wearing a pair of black slacks and nothing else. And I can't even be bothered to think about how sexy he looks when I'm about to look like Barney at the Grammys. "Doesn't seem like your…*color*."

His face pinches in disgust, not even trying to play it off just in case it is the one I picked out.

"That's because it's not the one I picked. I can't wear this Cooper…" Tears slip from my eyes. This is a disaster. The whole night is ruined. There's no way Cooper should be on my arm when I make the worst dress list.

"Baby," he murmurs and collects me in his arms, "I can fix this. Don't worry. This isn't that big of a deal."

"How? We have to leave in two hours! Cooper, maybe you should go without me."

"That's not going to happen." He grabs my chin and kisses me on the lips, his thumbs wiping away my tears. Picking me up he carries me to our bed, and sits me down on his lap. His lips are instantly back on mine, his tongue softly massaging mine. My body relaxes from its panic and I turn to jelly in his arms. He breaks away, his fingers running down my face. "No more crying, baby. Everything will be fine. I promise." I nod and lay my head on his shoulder. I'm so glad I haven't done my make up yet because runny mascara doesn't even go with the purple peacock dress.

"Did you finish your speech?" I ask, trying to changing the subject.

"I think so, but I might just wing it."

"I guess you've had a lot of practice talking to mirrors over the years." I giggle seeing his cheeks pinken.

"You were never supposed to hear that. Now come on, finish getting ready and I'll go deal with your dress."

I slide off Cooper's lap, and he stands, pulling his cellphone out of his pocket. With a final kiss on my cheek, he leaves the room. Running my hands down my face, I have no idea how this is going to work out. I move back to the closet and have a stare down with the ugly purple intruder.

Can I really keep dealing with Evelyn?

Between trying to tear me down, making me jealous, and now maybe trying to make me a laughing stock, how much more can I take?

Is my mom also a part of the things Evelyn is doing to try to destroy my spirit? It's clear they're talking, but how much?

I scream with all the nagging questions running through my mind and collapse into the lounger I have in my closet.

I wanna believe I have thick skin from all this. That they can do whatever they want because nothing is going to make me leave Cooper. But today is one of those days, I just want to cry, and wonder if it would be easier without him.

I don't deserve this hurt. I deserve a mother who loves me and a mother in law who likes me. I should be able to go to family events without being accosted or being told '*oh, you guys aren't right for each other*'. And for once not worry about if the next thing our mothers do will be the thing to break us up.

I FOUND *You*   **June 11th, 2006**

My mom succeeded once. Why wouldn't they again?

I bury my head in my hands and try to push away those thoughts. Instead, I remind myself how much I love Cooper and how much he loves me. We share a special bond only we know about and being together doesn't make that piece of us seem so *lost.* That even now with all the meddling, we support and complete each other. And most of all I don't want to live without him again.

I lift my head and wipe my face. The only thing I can do is keep weathering through this storm and show them they can't win. Just because she wants to break us up, doesn't mean I too want to break their relationship up.

Why am I trying to be the bigger person here again? Oh, maybe because Daddy at least raised me right?

Rising to my feet I move to the bathroom. I'm going tonight, even if I have no idea what I'm going to wear. Anything will be better than that purple monster.

~~*

I'm finishing putting on lipstick when I see Cooper walk into the bathroom through the mirror. "Hey." I put the lid back on the stick and turn around to face my husband. He looks handsome and debonair in a Tom Ford tux.

His eyes roam my body and he licks his lips. My cheeks heat, feeling suddenly shy with how his eyes are undressing me out of my bra and panties. "It's too bad you'll have to cover yourself with a dress now." He walks over to me and puts a hand on my hip and the other goes to play with the clips of my strapless bra. "Actually, maybe we should just stay home, and I can have my dirty way with you."

"I wouldn't mind," I say breathlessly, his lips moving to hover mine. I'm begging for him to kiss me.

Instead, he unhooks my bra and throws it across the room. He cups my breast and I wonder for a second if we're really going to say screw the Grammy's and stay home. Which is all I want to do right now.

"I don't think you'll need it for the dress I got you." His thumbs run over my nipples perking them up, and then his hands run down my stomach.

"You got a dress? That was quick…" I really didn't think he would pull it off and I'd have to wear something out of my closet.

"It's good to know people." He winks. "Come. I hope you like it…" Grabbing my hand, he pulls me out of the bathroom to my closet where a gold dress bag is hanging, with Elie Saab written in black lettering.

I unzip the bag, revealing a gorgeous silver gown, layered with flapper style fringing. It has a plunging neckline, so Cooper was right about me not needing a bra. "This is…" I shake my head, my eyes roaming over the dress still in a state of disbelief. Spinning back around, I wrap my arms around my husband and kiss his cheek. "It's perfect. Thank you."

I finally feel like I can breathe and maybe this night won't be all bad.

"You're welcome, Ace."

"Did you ever find out what happened to my other one?" I ask, trying to be casual. Maybe the dress shop will throw Evelyn under the bus and I won't have too.

"They think one of the girls who just quit mixed up orders. They're going to look into it."

"Oh." I turn to look at my dress, not believing a word of it. I wonder if Evelyn paid for them to keep quiet. "I hope they don't mess up the one I picked for the ball." My eyes close tightly and I only hope Evelyn doesn't try to destroy that night for me too.

"They promised to bring it over Monday. Any problems we will have time to fix." He takes my chin forcing me to look at him, his eyes shining down at me affectionately, "No more thinking about this. You're going to wow them tonight. I promise."

"Wait, shouldn't I be saying that to you?" I stifle a laugh.

He shrugs. "When they see you, they'll forget about me."

Yeah right.

"Now get dressed, the limo will be here shortly." He places a quick kiss on my lips and then without another word leaves me to it.

You can do this Vi. You will survive.

~~*

We pull up to the red carpet, behind another limo, waiting our turn to get out. Even through the darkened windows, I can see all the cameras flashing. I can also hear all the screaming from the awaiting fans. I grip Cooper's hand, my insecurities getting the best of me again, remembering his mother's words from the dress shop:

'Now he's all over the tabloids with his floozy wife making a fool out of him.'

"Vi, what's wrong?"

I bite my lip and look at him. "I won't embarrass you, will I?"

He snorts, looking at me like I'm crazy.

Maybe I am by letting Evelyn get in my head today.

"Are you kidding? You look amazing. I told you that. And I'm glad to have you on my arm tonight." His fingers brush over my cheek. I nod, still feeling unsure. "Where is this coming from?"

I shrug and look out the window as the limo pulls forward.

"Is this because of the whole dress thing?"

I pinch my lips and turn back to him. "No. This is our first big event together and I'm just nervous. I mean look at all these people. What if I do or say something stupid?"

He takes my hand and presses my knuckles to his lips. "You won't. I know this all new for you and no doubt it's fucking terrifying the first time around. But you got this and I'll be beside you the whole time." I nod and take a deep breath, as the limo stops in front of the red carpet.

My heart hammers out of my chest as the door opens to the screaming crowd.

Cooper slides out first and then he reaches in to help me out. I take his hand, and as soon as I'm standing his arm is around my waist. He kisses me ever so gently and it relaxes my nerves. This kiss, yet simple, not only conveys his love for me, but gives me the confidence boost I've been needing all day.

Okay, maybe the confidence boost is from the hundreds of cameras clicking away capturing the moment and knowing Evelyn will see them in the morning.

What better way than to say 'forget you,' than seeing me in a stunning dress and kissing her son.

After we walk the red carpet, and Cooper is interviewed by a bunch of media outlets, we take our seats inside the Staple Center. Cooper puts his arm around me and leans into me. "How are you holding up, baby?"

"Great, this is actually a lot of fun." I smile brightly.

Cooper introduced me to a bunch of other singers and musicians. I am thankful when I don't stutter talking to any of them and that my palms aren't sweaty when I shake their hands. Actually, everyone I meet seems so normal. Everything that happened earlier now seems like a distant memory.

"I'm glad I could be a part of this with you." I kiss his cheek over his dimple I love so much. "Thank you for bringing me."

"Of course. I wouldn't be here without you, Ace."

Hours later, after speeches and musical performances, we are finally at Album of the Year. The presenters for the award go over the list of nominations and when they say Cooper's name his handsome face appears on the huge screen onstage. I take his hand and

I FOUND YOU June 11th, 2006

squeeze it. He's already won 'Best Male Pop Vocal Performance' tonight, and he was surprised about being up against some big names like Rob Thomas and Seal.

"And the winner is…*15* - Cooper Reid…"

The crowd cheers loudly around us as an announcer lists the names of the producers and engineers who worked on the record. Cooper kisses me before making his way up to the stage. He's handed his golden gramophone award and shakes hands with the presenters. Everyone that worked on the album gathers behind him as he takes the mic.

"Wow. This is amazing, thank you. I have to thank everyone behind me: Mike, Arnold, John, and Ramone. There's so many of you to name and I promise to thank you tomorrow in person. I know I wasn't always the easiest to work with, but I couldn't have done any of it without you. Also, thanks to my brother Brody for dealing with my ass for the last seven years. To my fans, I couldn't be here without you. And also, my wife, Violet."

His eyes meet mine and I sink a little into my seat as heads turn to look at me.

"You stood by me and always believed in me when no one else did. You never had any doubts that one day I would make it. You were always pushing me to take every gig I could get. Even the one at the bowling alley where we got paid in hotdogs and free games. You've always been my inspiration, my muse. I'm so glad we found each other again. I love you Ace; this is for you too."

My eyes flutter open and there's a slight hammering behind them from my hangover. After the Grammy's we hit up a couple after parties, and the both of us drank to the point I wonder how we got back home. The partying we did back in high school has nothing on how celebrities do it. But now I'm paying for it.

I snuggle my face into Cooper's chest, hoping his scent will cure the pounding in my head. He's already awake on his phone, while his free hand runs up and down my shoulder.

"Afternoon…" He kisses my forehead.

"Afternoon. How long have you been awake?"

"About twenty minutes. Louie called me; we made the news again." He hands me his phone with a video slowly buffering on the screen.

I sit up to see better, and before me, in black and white, is Cooper and I in the elevator of this hotel, making out. It was right after the show and we were coming to change for the after parties. Collin and Tucker are standing to the side, as Cooper and I are all hands, mouth, and teeth. There's an article and couple of pictures under the video as well.

> **Cooper Reid wins for Best Pop Male Vocal Performance and Album of the Year for '15'. During his speech for Album of the Year, he thanked his wife for being his inspiration. We knew most of the songs were about someone, but we were never told who. Cooper's song "My Everything" won last year for Song of the Year, and it appears it's now safe to say the song was about the new Mrs. Reid.**
>
> **If you look above at the video, it's clear as day these two are crazy about each other. They're so lost in each other, they don't even care that their**

> bodyguards are in the same space as them. However, it seems maybe the two guards are used to this type of affection from the couple.
>
> Cooper posted a picture on his website last night of his new wife holding his winning Grammy awards with his arms around her. (See Below) He captioned the picture: "This is just the beginning. With her by my side, I can win, and do anything. She's my everything." Also posted was a picture of the two at one of the after parties.
>
> All we have to say is we're happy for the couple, who found their way back to each other. Congratulations to Cooper on his Grammy wins.

My phone rings on the nightstand and the caller ID lights up with my mother's name. I send the call to voicemail. She calls several more times before I turn off my phone. She hasn't called me in weeks and I don't want to hear anything she has to say.

I know it has everything to do with the article and nothing to do with congratulations.

Cooper's phone rings next, and he groans. "It's *my* mother."

Bet she's going to say how un-classy the video of us in the elevator is, or maybe ask what happened to the Peacock-Barney dress.

Whatever it is, neither of us need to deal with it.

"Just turn it off, and let me show you again how proud I am of you…"

Erica Marselas

NINE

May 30th, 2002

Cooper

It's been six months since she left. I haven't been the same since the day she said goodbye—the last time I saw her face. The letters and the phones calls aren't nearly enough to keep me going. I need to hold her, kiss her, touch her, love her. Once she turned eighteen I was hoping to run off with her, marry her, giving our families the big fuck you. Then four days ago everything came to a screeching halt.

Sitting in my mailbox was a letter, not from Vi, but from her mother. Amber sent me pictures of some guys scrawny arm wrapped around *my Violet*. She went to prom with the fucker and didn't even tell me.

Amber attached a letter with the pictures telling me she'd moved on and I wasn't to contact her anymore, per Violet's wishes. I read the letter a hundred times, not wanting to believe the words on the paper. I tried calling her, wanting to hear it from her lips that it was truly over, but I got nothing but voicemails. I left message after message hoping she would give in and call me.

Then yesterday, my mom told me Amber called her, reinforcing I was to stop calling their house. Vi no longer has a cell phone because her mom didn't want to pay the

I FOUND you   **May 30th, 2002**

bill, which makes getting in touch with her even harder.
   But I can't, I won't believe it 'till I hear it from her.
She loves me. This is going to work. I know it.
   Which brings me here, outside her house in Arizona. I woke up early this morning and drove the six-plus hour drive to see her. My mother has no clue I drove out here. I wouldn't hear the end of it if she knew. Turning off the car, I grab the lavender and violet roses I bought from a flower shop I found along the way. The colors of the roses are cliché as fuck, but they're her favorite.
   I make my way up the porch, pushing my shoulders back, ready just in case her witch of a mother answers the door. I ring the doorbell twice before I see the doorknob twist.
   The door flings open and I come face to face with Amber's beady brown eyes. "What the heck are you doing here? Didn't you get the hint that she doesn't want to see you?" she sneers.
   I try to stand taller, holding my ground. "I want to hear it from her. I'm owed that."
   "You are owed nothing. She made me do it for a reason. She's in love with someone else."
   Like a dagger jabbed straight through my heart, the words suck the life from me, and I stumble backward.
In love? With someone else? No.
   I shake it off, and plant my feet to steady myself. "I won't believe it 'till I hear it from her. I'll wait all night 'till she comes back."
   "You need to leave. She doesn't want you anymore."
   "Come on," I plead, "you know what it's like to love someone. If it was over with your new husband, I'm sure you would want to hear it from him rather than in a letter from his mother."
   Her eyes darken and narrow at me, her own pain hinting through. Maybe I got to her, but when she opens her mouth again, she snarls, "You need to go, Cooper.

Move on. Goodbye." She moves back in the house and slams the door in my face.

Fucking Bitch.

I bang my fist on the door, heartbroken and frustrated, before trudging back to my car. I'm going to wait 'till she comes home, even if I have to wait out here all night. I'm going to talk to her.

Hours tick by when a maroon sedan pulls into the driveway. The headlights turn off and Violet hops out of the passenger side. She looks beautiful, wearing a pair of cutoff jeans and a tank top. Her strawberry hair is slightly longer and it falls down her back in a ponytail. I hear her laugh, and watch someone step out of the driver's side.

The guy from the prom photos.

He says something to her as he comes around the car and she throws her head back humored by whatever the fucker is saying. The pictures are now live action playing out right in front of me.

She's moved on. Without me.

My eyes close painfully as they walk to the house with his hand on her back. He's touching my girl. I'm doing everything in my power not to bust out of this car, beat up the limp dick, and demand answers.

I need to know why. I want to know how she could give up on me.

Though when he goes into the house with her, something I was never allowed to do unless Amber wasn't there, my heart shatters into a million pieces.

It's over.

My biggest fear has come true. I came here needing to hear her tell me to my face it was over, but now I don't think I could handle the words. I was really hoping this whole thing would have a completely opposite turn out and we would go run off to L.A. like we were always supposed to.

Now, I feel like I've been kicked in the balls and

I FOUND YOU   **May 30th, 2002**

stabbed in the heart.

I should've come sooner, visited her more—letters and phone calls weren't enough to save us.

Maybe if we were eighteen I would kidnap her and force her to marry me. Remind her how good we were together. She's mine—always.

And she promised she would say yes.

But if she's happy without me, I have to let her go. Her happiness is more important than my own.

It makes my heart twist and my gut clench knowing I'm not the guy to make her smile or make her laugh again. A deep lamentation comes from my chest, from the agonizing pain retching through me. Before I know it, my cheeks are wet, and I'm crying like a giant sissy.

I've only cried like this one other time, and it was after we lost the baby.

The tears rain down on my steering wheel to my lap. I feel like a complete loser crying like this. Guys aren't supposed to fucking cry. But that's bullshit, especially if their heart had just been ripped from their chest, and they'd lost everything good in life.

She was that.
My everything.
And now she's gone.
.

June 17th, 2006
Violet

One week after the Grammys, Cooper and I walk hand in hand inside Vibiana where the charity event, *Granting Hope,* is being held. The charity grants dreams to kids who are in long-term hospital care. Tonight's theme for the event is 'A Very Fairytale Ball'. To go with the theme, I'm wearing a floor length, pale pink princess gown with a corset back. The front of the lace appliqué is ruffled to my left hip with stunning embellishments that sparkle in the light. I truly feel like a princess here, and on Cooper's arm. Who happens to look dashing dressed as Prince Eric from the Little Mermaid.

They delivered the dress I picked out with no hitches this time.

"I feel like we're going to prom." I brush my finger along the fringe of Cooper's epaulettes attached to his white tailcoat.

"If we were going to prom in a Disney movie, *sure.*" Cooper snorts. "I think mom over did it this year." His eyes dart around all the scenery.

"I think it's kind of perfect in here." I admire the ballroom which looks like a fairytale come to life. Flowers of all different kinds dangle from the ceiling and walls. There's even a huge wooden castle on the stage for the kids to play in.

Evelyn Reid had started this charity twenty years earlier with fellow Pediatric doctors. It began small, with only the ability to fund dreams at Riverside Children's hospital, but expanded over time. Now it's a countrywide charity organization. Cooper is a sponsor and uses his name to help drive people to donate.

I'm glad to see Evelyn giving back to a good cause. I only wish someone who could do something so kind could cut me—her son's wife—some slack.

"It's not a prom unless someone is losing their virginity or getting punched," Brody retorts from behind us dressed like Prince Charming. On his arm is Alexa wearing a strapless, baby blue, princess gown. I worry about what's going to happen with Alexa and Brody when the tour starts and they won't be able to see each other as easily. They're all smiles and kissy faces now, but I know distance can be a killer.

"Can I get a picture Cooper?" a man from of the media outlets covering the event asks us, his camera ready to click away.

Brody and Alexa tell us they'll see us in a bit and wander off to the bar.

"Sure. What's another picture in the paper, right?" Cooper pulls me closer to him.

Since the video and the picture's Cooper posted after the Grammys were published, the paparazzi have been going insane, more than before. It seems people are nuts about our second chance romance. I guess it's normal for fans and media alike to go ga-ga over celebrity love, but is it really that exciting?

While the man takes a couple shots of us, I spot in the distance my mother dressed in a black ball gown wrapped with floral lace sleeves.

The wicked witch has arrived. I better warn the kids.

Dustin had called Cooper letting him know his mom invited my mom to tonight's event. If that's not a screaming neon sign that the two are up to something, I don't know what is.

I wish they would just give up and get a clue. There's nothing they can do that will tear us apart again.

But I do wish Dustin was going to be here. I need all the Reid's I can get on my side.

"She's here," I grit out grabbing Cooper's attention away from the photographer.

His eyes dart around the room and I spot my mom who is now walking over to talk to some older white-haired lady in a crème dress.

"Fucking-A," Cooper mutters and places his hand on my face concerned.

"Thanks guys," the photographer says, but we pay him no mind as he walks away with however many hundreds of photos he took of us.

"Just stay close to me tonight. I won't let her near you." He places a kiss on my forehead.

"I wasn't planning on leaving your side anyways. I don't know a single soul in this place."

"Well let's change that. Plus, it gives me a chance to show you off to the people who run this. You'll like them." He clasps my hand and we stride over to where Brody and Alexa went.

"Wait. Do you think we can get a drink first? Or fifty?"

After what seemed like hours of walking around and shaking hands, I'm beat. Though the people I've met have been amazing. The doctors who run this non-profit never pull the funds for these events away from the charity. Everything I'm looking at is donated and supplied by the supporters, from the food to the decorations, to the bands. The costumes for the kids were also donated and or made. And those supporters *still* donated the same amount of money in every year.

I'm glad Cooper is a part of this and I really want to do my share. Well, if I don't have to work with Evelyn. We have a lavish dinner served for Royalty; chicken, steak with wine sauce, potatoes au gratin, and some kind of risotto. The kids, of course, got hot dogs, hamburgers, pizza, or specialty dinners made for their diets.

I'm stuffed.

The dance music has started again and the lights dim while colorful strobe lights display Disney characters on the floor and ceiling.

Two little girls run past us towards the dance floor in princess dresses and crowns, giggling. They're about five or so and have the biggest smiles on their faces. My heart constricts watching their happy, little faces, knowing it's about how old our child would have been now.

Cooper's arm wraps around my shoulder and he kisses my temple. "You okay?"

My eyes drift away from the kids and turn to the curious eyes of my husband. "Yeah, I was thinking how cute all these kids are and how much fun they're having," I lie, not wanting to ruin tonight with unpleasant thoughts.

Cooper looks at me skeptically. He's about to ask me something when thankfully Andrew comes along and claps his son's shoulder, drawing Cooper away from questioning me.

"Hey Coop, come with me to get a drink."

"Do you want to come with me?" Cooper asks, no doubt not wanting to leave me alone.

"No, I'm good. My mom has stayed in her corner all night."

"You sure?"

"Yeah, I'll be fine. You haven't had a chance to talk to your dad tonight." I kiss his cheek and he stares at me an extra second before heading to the bar with his dad.

Alexa excuses herself to the bathroom while Brody and I remain at the table. Across the way I see Evelyn looking at me as if I was gum on her shoe. I give her a wave with a fake smile before she turns her head away. I'm thankful I didn't have to share my meal with that attitude.

Brody catches where I'm looking and shakes his head.

"Aren't you guys best friends yet?" he teases, picking up his glass of water and chugging it down.

I snort, "It would be so much easier if we were. I'm trying to ignore and deal with her because I'm not in the mood to come between your mother and Cooper, or you for that matter."

"He knows how she is. We all do."

"I know, but she's still your mother." I pick up my champagne and drink down the last sip. "You love her, she loves you.

"Yeah, but…"

"No buts. I think of it this way: I now consider myself out a parent and I really don't want that for Coop. He shouldn't have to pick sides, and if he did it would affect you, Dustin, and your dad. I don't want that."

Brody gives me a small smile. "He'd choose you in a heartbeat, but I get what you're saying. Hell, I was hoping his speech, *the one heard around the world*, would make her lighten up, but…" he trails off and his eyes go wide looking at whoever is behind me. "Shit…"

I spin my head and see my mother coming towards me. I guess I should've gone to the bar with Cooper after all. But I didn't think she would approach with Brody here.

"Violet!" my mother's voice grates on my nerves.

"Hello, Mother," I grit through clenched teeth. "Glad they could valet the broom for you."

"Don't be smart. I've been trying to get in touch with you for weeks." She sits down in the chair Cooper had just vacated, pretending to look poised.

"Do you want me to get Coop, Vi?" Brody asks, eyeing my mother.

"No, I'm fine. Could you give us a second though?"

I FOUND you June 17th, 2006

He turns to look at me and I know he's tempted to say no. I just need to say my peace *again,* and pray afterwards she'll leave me the heck alone.

"You sure?" I nod. "Alright. No bloodshed, okay?" He gestures at the children. "Little eyes." He gives me a wink before getting up from the table.

"Why are you here, Mother? Did you decide to give the hush money to a good cause after all these years? Oh, I guess you couldn't since you've spent it all now," I hiss quietly, trying not to draw attention to myself.

"I came to see you. You won't return my calls and I'm your mother, we should talk."

"Some mother." I roll my eyes at her persistence. "The only thing we have to talk about is you getting a clue that I *don't* want to talk to you. You've done nothing but hurt me—over and over again."

"Violet, come on. Everything was fine with us *until* he came back in your life." I bite the inside of my cheek, pissed that she could even think we were *fine*. "I did what I thought was right at the time. Was it a mistake to take the money? Yes, but it's over now. Time to move on."

"You know it's not just the money, Mother. How about the fact it seemed you stopped caring about me after you and Daddy divorced. You shitted on my relationship every chance you got, then took me away from Cooper for a man who ended up being a creep. You didn't care how much I hated Arizona, and the only way I survived was because I had my friends. You're meddling caused me a broken heart and instead of doing right—whether or not you agreed with us being together—you could have healed it. I tried over and over again with you. Wanting to do everything I could just to get along with you because you were my mother. I needed you, though you seemed to never care about me. You played games with my broken heart to try and prove to me you were right all along. I think that sums up just some of the scars you made,

Mother." I collapse back in my chair feeling winded. She stares at me blankly, my words not even grazing the outer layer of her cold heart.

"You're overreacting. What I did with Cooper was so you would open your damn eyes. You were always so damn blind when it came to that boy. You needed to see how easy he would give up on you. Which he did, and he'll only do it again, Violet."

I shake my head and wrap my arms around myself. I'm trying not to cry, but my head feels like it's about to explode from the pain she keeps trying to inflict on me.

Why do I keep letting her make me feel this way?

"That's because you broke his heart. We were teenagers. Neither of us could rationalize it then. You won for a little while, but now it's over. We're married and happy. Let me be happy, damn it."

Her eyes glance behind me and an evil smirk pulls at the corner of her mouth. "Look at him, Violet." She points behind me and I turn around to see Cooper at the bar now talking to some woman, his father no longer in sight. "He sure looks cozy with her, doesn't he? You need to see he'll eventually break your heart. If not cheating, one way or another, I'm sure."

I snort, very un-princess-like, and spin back to my mother. I've had enough of this for a lifetime. I stand and rest my fist on the table staring my mother down.

"I don't know what you and Evelyn are up too, but if it's trying to make it look like Coop would cheat, I'm not falling for it. Because you know what I see?" I stab my finger over back in Cooper's direction, demanding she take a good look at him, as he shifts on his feet uneasily.

"What I see is a very uncomfortable man, doing his best not to be rude." I snap my head back to her, my blood boiling. "I'm done with you."

"Vi…"

"No! You listen to me now. I've given you so many

chances because my brain tells me I should love you no matter what. But you see, Daddy always told me I should listen to my heart first. And you know what my heart is saying? The heart you have shattered so many times to the point it can't be mended, is telling me to tell you to fuck off." Finally, it seems my venomous words get to her and she flinches.

Lifting my dress off the floor, I turn around and head for Cooper.

Let me show you just how much he loves me, and I won't be falling for your damn shit.

As I approach the bar, Cooper turns around to grab his drink from the ledge. The girl is still flapping her lips. "We can talk about working together, maybe over coffee or something. I swear you wouldn't be disappointed in what I have to offer." The double innuendo is evident when she raises her hand up to touch him.

She's inches from his chest when I come between them, my puffy dress knocking her out of the way. My arms wrap around his neck and I kiss him, which he accepts by pushing his tongue between my parted lips. He enfolds me in his arms pulling me as close as he can with all the fluff in the way.

"Dance with me?" I say breathless, when our lips part.

"I'd much rather go do something else." He pushes himself into me, with a wicked gleam in his eye.

"Come…" I take his hand and lead him out to the dance floor. Glancing back I see the girl looking crestfallen. She grabs her drink and walks off.

Once in the center of the dance floor, surrounded by all the other couples, some cuter and smaller than others, we wrap around each other and sway to the music.

"Everything okay?" he asks, his forehead pressed to mine.

"My mother approached me wanting to *talk*. Nothing

new besides her trying to make me jealous."

"Of what?"

I raise my eyebrow at his confusion and answer slowly. "Of you and the girl you were talking to?"

His mouth forms an 'o' shape in realization. "Oh. Yeah, my mom brought her over, asking me to listen to one of her tapes. She works in the peds unit with my mom."

Hmm. I'm surprised she didn't use Ainsley. Though I'm glad not to see the tramp here tonight. Did she get a clue?

"Are you going to listen to her tapes?" My interest is piqued, but Cooper instantly snorts at the idea.

"No. I have no control over people getting signed. Sure I can suggest, but I wasn't going to. As soon as my mom left she started gushing over me and my work. That's when you came in and saved me." He kisses my nose.

"You did look uncomfortable."

"I was." His hand runs down my face. "You know I only want you."

"I know. I wasn't worried." Snuggling into him, I rest my head on his shoulder. From across the crowded dance floor, I spot our mothers talking to each other. The uneasiness is back in my stomach as they both glance our way.

Cooper is unaware of what is taking place in my line of vision as he sings the words of "A Whole New World" in my ear. This is one of my favorite Disney songs, and leave it to our mothers to ruin it.

My hand dances around his neck and I turn my attention away from the pair. "Cooper?"

The lyrics stop cooing in my ear, his eyes now looking at me. "Yeah?"

"Promise me we won't let our mothers come between us again." His eyebrows knit together in worry.

"Just promise."

"I promise, baby. Nothing will ever come between us."

While we dance, a sweet, little girl wearing a Princess Jasmine costume approaches us, and asks Cooper for a dance. She said her name is Teresa, she's seven years old, and Cooper's biggest fan—ever—stretching her hands out as far as she could to show the size of her love. Cooper happily agrees to a dance with the tiny princess. I watch as he spins her around and she giggles gleefully, making my heart soar.

He's going to be such a good dad one day.

One day, when we're ready.

Though the tiny voice in my head is screaming out that Cooper might be ready now, while I'm still hesitant. I really don't know what I want. I'm back and forth sometimes, knowing we're still young, and traveling all the time. Though sometimes I think having a child would be nice, we'd be happy, and they would be loved.

Suddenly, the air gets thick and I'm choking once again on my biggest fear. Is having a baby something I can do? My eyes close and I remember back to that night in February, all the blood, and the overwhelming heartache I felt when they told me I lost the baby. What if I have another miscarriage? What if I can't have kids? Is it something I could handle?

But I won't know unless I try.

My hand travels to my stomach, the what if's keep popping up in my head like a game of whack-a-mole, and I keep trying to smash each one down.

Suddenly, Cooper is surrounded by a bunch of other, tiny, adoring fans, and they're dancing crazily to "Footloose."

"Oh no, he's doing it all wrong…" Brody teases, watching his brother cut loose.

"Why don't you go show him, honey?" Alexa nudges his shoulder, pushing him out to the floor.

"Yeah, I should. These kids need to know who the cooler Reid is." Brody slides over to the dance floor getting in the middle of the fan group and breaks down with the sprinkler dance moves.

Only Brody.

"There's your man in a nutshell. I hope you know that," I giggle at Alexa. She doesn't look at me, fluttering her eyes at the goofball in the middle of the floor.

"Oh, I know."

After two more songs and a myriad of crazy dance moves the music fades and all the kids are asked to come to the front of the stage for a show: One shoe, One Prince, Only one Cinderella.

Cooper, along with about ten other men walk up to the stage, gather around a large bin. Next to the bin Evelyn stands with two of her co-workers. She looks over at me, and gives me an evil grin that makes her look like Cruella De Vil.

Why can't she just leave me alone?

At least my mother thankfully took the hint and without another word to me, exited the ball, taking her broomstick with her. I hate myself for still holding onto a sliver of hope she'd come around. That maybe the years and years of heartache could be washed away, but it's naive thinking. There's only so much a person can take and I've taken enough hits from her, so I know I'm doing the right thing by cutting her out of my life.

"Do you know what's going on?" I ask Brody, who sits down next to me, a sheen of sweat glistening on his head.

"Oh, how it was explained to me was the ladies donate money to raffle their shoes for a dance with one of the guys. They each pick a shoe and have to match it to one of the ladies. Whoever's shoe fits gets a dance with said *Prince.* Mom tried to convince me to get in on it, but I told her *hell* no."

Why didn't he tell me about this?

"Would've been nice to know. I would've donated…" I mumble. Even if I didn't win the dance I would've liked to help.

"Next up is the event of the night," the MC announces from the stage. "Now, I'm sure you know the story of Cinderella. She goes to the ball and dances with the Prince, but at the stroke of midnight runs off, leaving her slipper behind. The next day the Prince scours the village looking for the fair maiden who would fit the slipper."

Fifty ladies walk on the stage and sit in the fold-out chairs. They're all in full ball gowns, but their bare feet peek from underneath the taffeta. One by one a guy is handed a shoe from the bin by Evelyn. Each 'Prince' tries the shoe on one the ladies, as the MC continues a playful story for the kids.

When the first Prince finds his Princess the kids and the crowd clap. They step aside, waiting for the others.

I watch as Cooper is handed a stiletto from Evelyn and walks to the first awaiting lady. "Prince Cooper Reid is looking for his fair maiden. This princess will be sure to be his everything, when he slips the slipper on her foot." I bite the sides of my cheek at the MC statement. I suddenly feel very possessive. It's bad enough I have to deal with Ainsley and her warped mind. I don't need someone planting the wrong idea it into one of these girls head also.

Cooper looks over his shoulder at the crowd and I

know he's looking for me. When our eyes finally meet, he gives me a wink, easing me just a little bit. The next 'princess' Cooper approaches I recognize right away as the woman he was talking to earlier at the bar. I glance at Evelyn as the shoe slips on the woman's foot, and she looks back at me slyly.

"The shoe fits!" the MC yells.

I'm stewing as Cooper helps her from her chair and walks her to the other side to wait for the other princesses to be claimed. I knew something like this was coming, but I wasn't prepared for how angry it would make me feel.

"Vi, your head looks like it's going to explode," Alexa whispers in my ear.

"Because it is," I hiss, and I'm stomping my foot waiting for the dance to start so I can find a reason to pull the other wicked witch aside and throw her in the fountain outside.

And pray she melts.

"Violet," Andrew's voice pulls me from my stare down with Evelyn, even though I'm the only one staring. She's clapping and looking at the next couple making a shoe connection. "You have nothing to worry about. This is just for charity."

Oh, god he thinks I'm jealous. That's not going to help me with the brownie points I've earned with him.

I do my best to put on an Academy Award smile, but I can't tell if it's lopsided or not. "I know, Mr. Reid. I actually have a headache. All the fancy food."

But it's really your pain in the ass wife giving me the migraine.

"Andrew, sweetie." He gives me a sweet smile and turns his attention to the final Cinderella couple. I'm unsure if he fell for my excuse or not.

Everyone claps as the couples are announced. "Can you Feel the Love Tonight" from The Lion King fills the room and the new *Princes and Princesses* make their way to the dance floor. I have no doubt Evelyn selected this song to push my buttons. Cooper pulls the girl into his arms and keeps her at a comfortable distance. She's talking up a storm while Coop mutely nods, his eyes darting around the room.

I spot Evelyn and she's walking towards the garden. I stand and Brody grabs my arm.

"Where are you going?"

"The bathroom. I trust him, but it doesn't mean I want to watch."

"Do you want me to come with you?" Alexa offers and I shake my head. This is something I have to do on my own and with the least amount of witnesses.

I make my escape out of the ballroom and into the garden. There are only a few people out here in the crisp night, standing around high top tables wrapped in white lights. It doesn't take me long to find her staring up at the sky.

"Evelyn," I growl.

Her head drops, looking at me disapprovingly through the slits of her eyes. "I came out here for a moment of peace and quiet."

"Well, too bad. I think it's finally time we chatted, don't you? Lay it all on the line so we can move on?"

"Oh, like you have moved on with your mother?" She crosses her arms and narrows her eyes at me.

"My mother has nothing to do with this. This is between me and you, so I ask, why do you hate me so much?"

"Do you really think it's appropriate to be getting into this now?" she says, looking contrite.

She might be right, but I couldn't care less right now.

"Maybe not, but I've had enough of you trying to come between me and Cooper. All your snide remarks, the dance raffle, the mix up with the dress, Ainsley, and pretty much every comment that comes out of your mouth at me. Why? Tell me!" I demand, my voice raised to a shrill for my final two words.

"Because you will never be good enough for him." She points her manicured finger at me. "He needs someone who meets his standard. You caused him to lose focus on what was really important. He was starting to turn around about going to Princeton, 'till you came along. Sure, he got lucky, but what happens after the hits stop coming, hmm? Now he has no college degree and some hussy of a wife who in the end will take every last penny he has. I mean you made sure you got married so quickly there's no prenup. What now, trap him down with a baby, is that your next goal? I'm actually surprised you didn't do it years ago," she spits out.

Unexplainable rage and hurt pours out of me. I grab a glass of wine sitting on a table and toss the contents at her, the red wine splashing her face and green silk gown. The wine drips off her as she stares at me wide eyed and mouth gaping, in total disbelief.

Holy crap. Did I just do that? And why did it feel so good?

I mean she had it coming, right? She's lucky I didn't slap her.

She wipes her face with her hand, but remains staring at me in shock. I shakily put the glass back down on the table. "I—um," I mumble.

Why isn't she saying anything? Her silence is unnerving me.

My eyes glance around me, lucky no one saw the display.

"Well, you've gone and done it now haven't you…" she finally speaks before angerly turning on her heel and walks back towards the ballroom.

My elbows fall to the table and I hide my head in my hands. I have no idea how I'm going to talk myself out of this. I should have never confronted Evelyn today after dealing with my mother. Will Cooper be mad? Will he understand?

I jump with a screech, startled when someone grabs my shoulders. I'm spun around to face my husband who actually looks worried. His hand runs down my face and I take a moment to lean into his touch. "What's wrong?"

I should tell him, confess everything that occurred because there's no way Evelyn had enough time to say anything to him. But for some reason, I chicken out. All I want to do right now is go home, crawl under my covers and deal with it tomorrow with a clearer head.

"Can we go home?" I whisper, at a loss.

"Why? I thought you were having fun?"

"I am. I'm just tired and my feet hurt…" I look down at my feet and nibble on my lower lip.

"Ace, I can tell something is wrong…Does this have anything to do with your mother?"

"Yes." Not a total lie.

He looks up and over my shoulder. I glance back and see Evelyn with a couple of napkins still wiping off her dress.

"What happened?" Cooper asks curiously looking over at his mother. Cooper has his arm around my waist keeping me close by.

She's silent for a moment looking between us. I put my head on Cooper's shoulder, not ready for the showdown. "I—I tripped and spilled my glass of wine all over me. It went up instead of down." She laughs softly, and my head pops up in disbelief.

Did I hear her right? Did I enter an alternate dimension?

This was her chance to tell Cooper how crazy I am, anything her imagination could come up with and she doesn't take it?

I stare at her, trying to get a tell on the game she's playing. The first thing I notice is her eyes have softened from the angry orbs she glared at me with when I first came out here. The second thing are the waves of hostility I usually feel when we're in the same room seem to have vanished.

Maybe the wine took the demon out of her?

Cooper looks between us, and all I want is to get out of here before she changes her mind.

"Thank goodness I always have a change of clothes in the car," she adds, smiling sweetly before walking away to the gates where a couple guards stand to lead her out.

What just happened?

I've never been more confused in my entire life.

Could this be the start of something good or is this the beginning of something worse to come?

I'm hoping—praying—for the better.

"I have a feeling I'm missing something…" Cooper grabs my chin staring down at me. I give him a small shrug.

"No clue. I didn't see it happen." I lie and he narrows his eyes at me. If Evelyn can keep what happened a secret, well, so can I. "Hey, why didn't you tell me about the Cinderella dance?" I change the subject and his face drops, his hand falling from my chin.

"Shit…" he mumbles, "I meant too. She asked me while I was at the bar with that girl. Then everything else happened…" he trails off. "I'm sorry."

"It's okay, but can you take me home now?" I rub my hands up and down his chest. "I have a few things I would like to do to you."

"Oh yeah?" He raises an eyebrow, wearing a cheeky smile. "And what would those things be?"

"I want to ride your dick, hard and fast," I purr, licking my lips. My hand traveling south to his crotch.

Yep, he's rock hard.

"How hard?"

"Hard enough I'll feel you for the rest of the week and I'll walk like I just got off a horse. *Please.*"

"Who am I to say no?"

TEN

February 10th, 2001

Cooper

Desperate to spend some much needed alone time with my girlfriend, I rented a room for us in San Bernardino to celebrate Valentine's day weekend. Vi and I both had to lie to our parents about our whereabouts and frankly, it's getting old. Though I'm sure not many parents would agree to teenagers spending the night alone in a hotel room, regardless if they were happy with their children's relationship.

But how would I know? My parents never agree with anything I do anyway.

Violet has been in the bathroom for twenty minutes now. I don't know what's she's doing since she bolted in there as soon as the motel door was unlocked. Okay, I do know what she might *be doing. She had promised when we got here she was going to change into my Valentine's Day gift.*

I can't wait.

I've been picturing every type of sexy lingerie known to man since we started this adventure. I grab my growing dick knowing my baby would look scorching in anything she wears. Her in only stockings and a garter belt is a

I FOUND YOU **February 10th, 2001**

personal favorite of mine ingrained forever in my memory.

"Coop?" she yells, her voice radiating agony. "I need you…"

I rush to the bathroom and without a second thought I bust open the door.

My eyes grow wide as I find her sitting on the toilet, hunched over. Laying on the floor at her feet are the panties I know she was wearing earlier, only they're covered in blood. Lots of blood. Her blood. Everything in me is telling me to freak the fuck out, but Vi needs me. I take a deep breath trying to calm my nervous shaking body.

"Ace, what's wrong?"

"I— I don't know." she cries turning her head to me, her cheeks wet from the tears tracking down.

"What?" I'm at a loss for words at the scene that is unfolding in front of me. Violet is extremely pale. There isn't a hint of her naturally rosy cheeks. Her strawberry hair is matted to her face from sweat and tears.

"I was having cramps I thought it was my period, but I'm bleeding…a lot. I don't ever bleed like this, and it hurts so bad." She's rocking back and forth, a never-ending stream of tears continuing to flood her beautiful face.

I've never had a fear of blood—my mom's a doctor—I've seen a lot in my young life. The only difference right now is this is my girlfriend, and I have no idea what to do.

Somehow my legs figure out they need to move and I kneel next to her. I touch her face, causing her to jump. Her watery eyes meet mine and I brush her hair and tears away, doing my best to comfort her. "What do you need me to do?"

"Pads. I think I have some extra in my purse. Also, grab me a pair of my least sexy underwear," she manages to gasp out before she hunches over again.

"You sure you don't um...have to, you know...shit?" I question and her head snaps to me, glaring fiery daggers at me.

"Since when does having to shit cause bleeding? Think before you talk, Coop!" she snaps, and I flinch. Yeah, that was a fucking stupid thing to say, but I'm fucking scared.

And maybe I'm hoping this isn't as bad as it seems.

"You know, it's embarrassing enough to be like this in front of you, can you not try to be a smart ass?"

I put my hands up defensively. "Sorry." I kiss her cheek. "And just so you know, you have nothing to be embarrassed about. I love you. It'll be okay..."

Three hours later, we find out she isn't really okay. The cramps and the heavy bleeding are the effects of a miscarriage. They think she was about eight weeks along. The news comes as a shock, and I'm not sure once we're told we know how to process it all.

She was pregnant.

And now she isn't.

We lost our baby.

Brody is the one and only person we trust enough to tell about our loss. We decide there is no way we can tell our parents; they'd use it as ammunition against us later on. And after all this, I'm not sure Vi could survive that.

Violet goes quiet for weeks, speaking only when she has to. The loss eats her up inside; I can see it in her eyes every time I look at her. She rarely smiles, and is a shadow of her former self. She's closed herself off, always wanting to stay in and she avoids our friends. She's lost, blaming

I FOUND YOU **February 10th, 2001**

herself, no matter how many times I tell her it isn't her fault. She hadn't even gotten drunk in the weeks she would've been pregnant. If anything, it was like she knew, but even then, it wasn't enough. I really wish she could see it was out of her control.

Holding her is the only thing I can do, the only thing she lets me do. I don't know what to say, but having her in my arms is enough to help me begin to heal, for her to heal. We still have each other. It's what matters the most to me.

The only thing is, I never knew I could miss something—someone—so much. It was stripped away from us and sometimes I question if I'm allowed to miss what I never had a chance to know.

I can't deny losing the baby hurt like crazy. There is a piece of me missing, the baby was a piece of us.

Our future.

A future I don't think either one of us knew we truly wanted 'till it slipped from our fingers without warning. A special treasured bond we made together, and he or she was gone in an instant. I feel attached to this baby I never met or got to see.

The hardest thing about this whole situation is we don't have anyone to really *talk to about it. Brody had to go back to school and talking about it over the phone just doesn't work. If I'm honest, too, these are feelings I don't know how to put into words. All I know is that it sucks our baby is gone. We'll never get to hold them or watch them grow.*

"I've been doing a lot of thinking, with this whole thing," Violet whispers. She's curled up in a ball on my lap, her arms lazily wrapped around my neck. We're sitting on a blanket, both of us staring out into the distance at White Park.

"Yeah?"

"They say everything happens for a reason, and as

hard as it is to admit, I don't think we would've been ready for a baby. I mean, look at us. We're sixteen, neither of our parents would have helped us, neither one of us is responsible enough, and we don't have jobs. It wasn't our time."

Her voice is soft, but the regret and hurt in her words shout at me as if they're coming through a bullhorn. She doesn't look up at me, but I know she's on the verge of tears. We've already cried so much, and I wish I could stop them for her.

"Maybe, but you know I would've done anything in this world to make it work." I lift her chin to look at me, and I was right; her eyes are clouded with unshed tears.

"I know," she chokes out. I release her chin and kiss her. My lips linger and neither of us move to deepen it. We don't need to, every kiss means all the same. "You would have been an awesome daddy. It's just, I keep thinking... and maybe it's to make myself feel better, I don't know..." She drifts off and stares back at the sky.

"Go on," I urge, knowing she needs to get it out, placing a lingering kiss in her hair.

"If it happened now, you might not have a chance to be the superstar you want to be. We'd have to get jobs and wouldn't have time for gigs. Our life would be dirty diapers and sleepless nights, instead of guitars and singing. Dreams might shatter, and we could end up growing to hate each other." She rambles, but finally looks back at me. "Like I said, there's a reason and it might not be any of those as to why it happened. But we're young and it'll happen one day."

"Yes, you're right. One day..." I echo her words, and pull her back tightly into my arms, kissing every inch of her exposed skin.

"I love you," she purrs, as I suck on her ear. We can't do anything because she's still healing, but it's not going to stop me from fooling around to show her I care

about her, and love her. I want to hold her in my arms and never let go.

"I love you too, Ace. Forever. No matter what!"

Erica Marselas

July 2nd, 2006
Cooper

Life has been hectic since the *Granting Hopes* Ball, sometimes making me wonder which way is up. In two days we leave to go on tour; four months of traveling the states, and afterward we'll take a small break before another three months of overseas dates in Australia, Europe, and Japan.

Today, my family is throwing a BBQ party for Brody and me. This is the first time in weeks I've been able to relax and spend a full day with my wife. Between my rehearsals, putting the finishing touches on the new record, and Violet working with Brody to finish coordinating the rest of the tour, we only see each other at night.

Brody tells me she's mastered all the things she has to do. It's a huge laundry list of responsibilities and every time I see the daily 'to do list' I feel as if my head might explode.

Not only is she going to be an asset to helping Brody on this tour, but she'll also be with me the entire time. I'm not sure I could survive not seeing her daily, even if it's only for a little bit.

Violet and I arrived early and I currently have her wrapped in my arms between my legs on a lounger outside on the patio, enjoying the peace and quiet.

My gaze falls to the lawn in front of us. There, my cousin, Richie, is cradling his infant daughter, swaying around, and smiling down at her happily.

I FOUND YOU　　　　　　　　　　　　**July 2nd, 2006**

I want that.

Only last week, Ron came over and started asking about when he'd be expecting some grandchildren. We both laughed it off, not giving him an answer. There was no way we would have that conversation in front of her father.

It is something I want, sooner rather than later. I keep telling myself I'm going to wait until she brings it up, but I can't hold it in any longer. I really want to start a family with her. I know we're still young, but ever since the miscarriage I've always wondered what life would be like with a child. Fill the hole we've been missing. I want to see her round, carrying my child, knowing how beautiful she would look.

"Ace?" I whisper.

She turns her head, and our eyes meet. "Yeah, babe?"

"How would you feel about starting a family?" I blurt out the words quickly thinking they'll burn me if I don't push them out fast enough.

"You mean, like, now?" she asks confused. Sitting up she twists her body so her legs hang over mine, her shoulder now pressed into my chest.

"Maybe, or maybe when we get back from the tour, or maybe we could start trying on tour." I push my hand through her hair and she stiffens under my touch. Her teeth sink into her lip and her eyes drop to her lap.

"I don't know if I'm ready yet, Cooper. We're so young and we've only been married for a month and half. I mean you're always so crazy busy, traveling, and it would mean I'd be left alone at home, raising a child on my own."

"No, I would take a break if I needed to, but we can bring a baby wherever we go. People do it all the time."

She nods, but I know I'm not convincing her. Instead, she's shutting me down. "Could we wait a little bit longer? I just—" her hand twists in her lap, "I'm not ready yet, I want more time with you. We've spent so much time apart and I haven't been on the road yet, to know what it's like or if we can handle it being together all the time or..."

"Or what, Vi?" I rake my hands through my hair, trying to control the feelings of disappointment-anger-defeat running through my brain.

She stands to her feet and wraps her arms around herself. "Or I don't know," she whispers and looks out towards the lawn. "What's so wrong with letting me get used to this new life? You know what being on the road is like, but you haven't done it with me yet. It changes things. Maybe not in a big way, but it will. Let us adapt first. Please."

My heart breaks seeing how much she's pushing back, but I get where she's coming from. I don't know what is making me want a baby so badly lately.

All I know is that I do.

I stand from the lounger and encircle her with my arms. "You're right. I'm sorry." I kiss her head and she cuddles into me. "Can we talk about this after the tour?"

"Of course."

Violet has left my side to go and talk with my grandfather and one of my cousins. I'm heading for the kitchen when my mom stops me.

"Cooper, could I talk to you for a minute?" She gives me a small smile, her eyes filled with genuine concern. I glance behind me and watch Vi laugh at something my grandfather said. I can give my mother a minute to hear what she has to say.

I FOUND YOU   July 2nd, 2006

One.

"Yeah, sure." I follow her into my father's office and sit down in one of the chairs. I've spent many days of my youth in this office, getting yelled at. But when I was really little I would go through all his books that are lined up in the wall and color in them. My father always got so mad, but he keeps the books holding my masterpieces.

Bet he could get a mint for those on eBay.

"What's up?"

She leans across the desk and moves a red folder closer to her. She sighs dramatically, staring at the folder as if it's giving her the meaning of life.

"Is everything alright?" I ask slowly and her eyes pop to mine. She sighs again, giving me another weak smile.

"I don't mean to pry, but I overheard your conversation with your wife earlier. About a baby?"

Great. "Mom, this isn't something I want to talk to *you* about." I stand from my seat and head towards the door. It's none of her business.

"Cooper, stop." I pause for a second, my hand on the doorknob ready to make my escape. I should go, but I'm also curious to know what she has to say. "I wanted to tell you I support your decision to want to have a baby with Violet."

I shake my head, trying to clean out my ears because I'm sure I didn't hear her right. "What?"

"I think it's great you two want to start a family. *You'll* be a great father."

"Thanks?" I'm still unsure what is going on.

"The thing is, I just hate she's making these decisions about a baby on her own *again,* without taking what *you* really want to heart." My mother sniffs and she wipes away a fallen tear. Her eyes dart to the folder again.

"What are you talking about?"

I'm so fucking confused and what the hell is in that

folder?

"I wasn't going to tell you, but seeing as though she still hasn't told you, since she's your wife now, I couldn't sit idly by and watch her make another decision that impacts the both of you."

I run my hands down my face, exasperated. "Tell me what, Mother?"

"I talked to Amber a few days after the ball. She was upset with her daughter as you know, and figured I had the right to know why she took Violet away."

"She took Violet so she could be with her new husband, Mother," I grit through my teeth. I've told her this until I was blue in the face when it all went down. She knows why Vi left.

"That was part of it, but there's something else."

"Then spill it already," I snap at her. *Stop dancing around and get on with it.*

"It'll be better to show you." She picks up the red folder and hands it to me.

"I rather you tell me," I growl and flip open the file anyways. From the inside, a picture falls to the ground at my feet. When I pick it up, my eyes grow large as I come face to face with a sonogram. My eyes flit back up to my mothers. "What's this?"

"Amber had gotten a call from a clinic where Violet was going to have the abortion done. After she found out, she wanted Violet away from you so she couldn't make any more mistakes. Think about how fast she left. Overnight, wasn't it? You had zero warning. Along with the new husband, Violet knew the move was because of the abortion. She was never going to tell you because according to Amber she didn't want to upset you."

"You're lying. She wouldn't do this."

She wouldn't. Not after everything we had been through.

My eyes scan the piece of paper in front of me, the

words: *women's clinic, abortion, seven weeks pregnant*, glare at me as if they are bold and highlighted. On the sonogram, it has Violet's name and the date. The time stamp is two weeks after she left.

No, she wouldn't.

My mom grabs my shoulder. "I didn't want to believe it either, but it's there in black and white. I thought maybe she did tell you, but after your conversation today, I knew she didn't. I'm telling you because if you two are going to start to have kids together you should know why she might not be able to have them or why she might have issues. To me, it sounded like she was going to keep pushing back for as long as she could."

"I don't believe you!" My voice cracks and I shove her hand off me. I don't want to be touched right now. My heart is racing in a panic as I keep staring at the words, which are starting to blur.

"I'm sorry Cooper. I—" Her words trail off and she raises my chin to look away from the paper. "Cooper? You should talk to her." She sounds worried, but she's the one that just threw this on my lap.

"She wouldn't," I gasp.

After the miscarriage, why would she even think of doing *this*? The pain we both felt at the time. How many times did she say we weren't ready? That it would mess with my career if we had a baby too soon? But she knew I would have done anything for her if she got pregnant again. I wanted a family with her.

We could've stayed together.

"It's all there, Cooper. Amber said Violet wasn't ready to be a mom. The timing was all wrong and she was too young. Maybe it's the only nice thing she did for you because she didn't want to tie you down."

I wanted to be tied down.

"She—" Words escape me. There's a piece of me not wanting to believe this, but the proof is staring me in the face. Now, all I can think is, how could she do this?

Is this why she's against trying to have one now? Will she ever want a child with me?

Pregnant, Abortion, Gone. *Are the only words spinning in my head.*

There's only one person that can give me all the answers.

I storm out of the office and spot Violet walking towards me. She smiles brightly, but it's fuzzy looking through my fury.

"What's wrong?" she asks.

I grab her elbow and pull her upstairs. "We need to talk," I growl. The fuzziness turning a cloudy red.

"What the hell, Cooper? You're hurting me."

I push open the door to my old room and lock the door behind us. I release her, making her stumble back a bit. With the folder still clenched in my hand, I pace the length of my room.

"What in the world is going on, Cooper?"

"Were you ever going to tell me?" I slam the folder down on the desk next to her. She flinches at my tone, but I don't give a fuck right now.

Answers. I need answers.

"Tell you? Tell you what?" She looks down at the folder then back to me. Her eyes glaze over in confusion.

"About the baby."

"The *baby?*" she says softly, her eyes never leaving mine. "Coop…"

I hold my hand up to stop her from talking. "Yes, Vi, the baby!" I hiss and she takes a step back from me, shaking her head. "An innocent baby you took away from me."

Her mouth drops open and tears fall from her eyes. I have the sudden urge to hold her in my arms, but I step back instead, needing the extra space.

She shouldn't be crying, anyway. She's the one who made the choice to do what she did.

"You know what happened to the baby." Her voice shakes, barely above a whisper.

"Don't play fucking games with me. You never told me anything. It sure was never in any letter you ever sent me. I have it here in black and white, oh and even a photo memory of what you did, Violet." I can feel the vein in my neck pulsate from my rage as I scream at her.

Her eyes finally look down at the folder and she opens it up. She looks over the words on her chart and picks up the sonogram. Her eyes widen, and she covers her mouth with her hand.

"Coop..." she glances up at me, "this isn't—"

"Just don't, Vi." I cut her off, not wanting to listen to her excuses. *Yeah, you were caught. You can't get out of this, sweetheart.* "I thought there were no secrets between us. How could you do this? To me? To *us*? I should've known there was something else fishy about your mom moving you so quickly."

"That isn't mine, Cooper. I never had an abortion. I wouldn't—" Her voice cracks and the sonogram falls from her fingers. "Who gave you this?"

"Doesn't matter because it has your name written all over it. Violet. Harper. Spencer." I point to her name on the paper, showing she can't lie about this.

"It does matter. Because. This. *Isn't*. Mine," she growls back at me stabbing her finger on the paperwork like I did seconds ago. "Now tell me who gave this to you?"

"Your mother gave it to my mother. Told her how

you've been keeping this from me and thought she had a right to know, I guess. After my mom overheard us talking about a family and you turning me down, she told me."

Though even as I say the words, they leave a funny taste in my mouth and an unsettling feeling in my stomach.

"My mom told her? And you're believing this after everything that has happened to us." She snorts, her tears drying on her face, and she stands a little taller.

I open my mouth and she stops me, poking her finger in my chest. "No, you had your chance to piss all over me. It's my turn."

I cross my arms, pretending I don't give a shit about what she has to say, but I'm actually worried about the words she's going to unleash on me. There's a fire in her eyes I've never seen before.

"So, let me ask you something. Do you think after what happened when we were sixteen, I would *willingly* have an abortion? After how much it hurt to lose our baby, after you saw what it did to me, what it *still* does to me, you think I would do it on purpose?"

"You're the one who said you weren't ready back then, and thought it could ruin me from being a star, remember? So instead of dealing with *me*, you were selfish and got rid of it." I can't control the words as they spill from my mouth. I don't think Violet would lie to me, but the proof is here, staring at me as if it were a brightly lit theater promenade. It's not only that; it's the miserable feeling I have from her telling me today she wasn't ready, to the miscarriage years ago, to seeing those papers. It's overriding all rationality.

"I wouldn't have hidden this from you. God, if I was pregnant we could have gotten married."

My eyes glance to the papers again. The proof she's not telling me the truth is glaring at me, mocking me.

I FOUND YOU   **July 2ⁿᵈ, 2006**

It says it there. Why can't she admit to me?

The anger is back and the devil on my shoulder is encouraging me to keep going with it.

"There's proof you did hide it from me. Papers which have insurance information and your social on it. Don't deny it. You fucked up, you fucking did this to us. You killed our baby."

She stumbles back as if I slapped her in the face. Though I guess in a way, I did. She chokes on her sobs and the tears pour from her face. She tries to wipe them away but they're falling too fast. I move to her because no matter what, I still love her, and seeing her like this, kills me.

But you caused it dipshit.

"You're right. I did kill our baby when we were sixteen…I failed. I fucked up because I did something wrong and I'll never forgive myself for it," she howls mournfully from deep within her chest, the sound hitting me like a dagger to the heart. It's the dagger I needed to open my eyes because I was too blind to see what I was doing to her. Now it's slicing through to my soul, leaving me open and bleeding.

"I'm sorry I failed…" Her shaky words continue to stab me.

No, No, No.

I'm yelling out to her. That's not what I think, I know she had no control over it. I thought she knew that. "Vi…you didn't," I step to her and she backs away again, fearfully. Disgusted.

Her blue eyes turn icy and I feel the temperature of the room drop dramatically.

Everything is crashing around us.

"No," she screeches, "don't touch me."

"I'm sorry…"

"You're sorry?" she scoffs, the tears still rolling down her rosy cheeks. "Why? Because you choose to believe bullshit from our mothers? Your mother, the woman who has always hated me. Who thinks I'm some slut, has no trouble calling me one at our reception or in the middle of a dress store. She thinks I'm only after your money and planning to trap you with a baby to get more of it! Then you have my mother; her name should've been a red flag to anything that was happening. I mean it's in her nature to lie. I mean she's only done it to us countless of times. Oh, and it's not like she didn't use to *work* as a medical assistant, and would know how to write up this shit." I cringe realizing I forgot about that, but I don't think it would've mattered at the time. "But no, you choose to believe them. Sure, you have a piece of paper spilling of their shit, but it shouldn't matter! You should've come to me calmly with what you had. Instead, you grabbed my arm and stepped all over me without trying to explain what was going on, so I would understand. You didn't give me a chance, you weren't willing to hear me out. You came in here *not* wanting to believe me."

"Ace—" I beg, trying to move to her, but she slides past me heading for the door.

"No, don't fucking *Ace* me right now. We promised to stand together against our mothers. Yet, here you are believing everything. I guess maybe they won again...." She trails off, unlocking the door. When she looks at me all I see is defeat in her eyes. She doesn't say anything else before she's out the door.

I'm left standing alone as the door closes in my face. My feet feel glued to the carpet, unable to move.

I got my answer, but now I'm left with more questions.

Did I just lose her?
Will she forgive me?
Why would our mothers go this low to tear us apart?
And last of all, why did I let them?

I FOUND you   July 2nd, 2006

Collecting myself, I grab the folder, and I rush down the stairs to go after her. When I make it to the bottom I come face to face with a pissed off Brody.

"What the fuck did you do to her?" he growls at me.

"Brody, get out of my way." I try to shove him out of the way, but he shoves me back.

"Not 'till you tell me what the hell is going on. Violet came down here in tears and when I asked her what happened she said *they won* before running out the door."

"I'll explain later. I need to stop her," I say urgently, pushing my way past him, but he grabs my shoulder stopping me.

"I think she needs a minute, and you do too."

"What the hell? Get the fuck out of my way."

"No, fucker. Tell me, so I can fucking help you." He pulls me roughly into dad's office. "I get you two had a fight, and you're chasing after her with your tail between your legs. But I feel like I've always been the third wheel with you two and know your relationship pretty damn well. Almost too fucking well for my own fucking sanity, but I've never seen her like that. She looked—*broken*."

My heart falls from my chest and shatters at my feet.

"Broken?" I gulp.

"Yeah, much like you do right now, which tells me you know you were being a dumb fuck." He jabs his finger at me.

"I know," I mumble.

Listen it's clear you need someone to talk to. Just tell me. I'm guessing this had something to do with Mom."

"How you guess that?" I snort and fall into one of dad's chairs. My body no longer has the strength to stand.

"Oh, I don't know…the way Mom treats her and the '*they won*' comment, but I want to know what she did."

The words quickly stumble out of my mouth as I tell him what took place. I show him the papers and his eyes widen, horrified. "And you just went to her guns blazing?"

"Yeah, when I asked if she was going to tell me about the baby, she kept saying she did. It didn't click right away she was talking about the miscarriage because I was too hung up on the papers. Brody, they look so fucking real."

He runs his hands through his hair. "I get it, but still man, I was *there* when you lost the baby. It destroyed both of you. Did she ever see anyone to talk about it?" I shake my head. "And you had no idea how much she was hurting."

"I knew she thought about it, but it's been six years. I didn't know she was still blaming herself for it. She only uttered those words to me once and that was right after it happened. So, no, I didn't know the extent."

My head drops to my hands, and I'm at a total loss. "It was just this morning I was asking about having a baby, and she wanted to wait. It's all I've been thinking about lately and it sucked when she told me she wanted to wait. I guess I took it harder than I thought…" I rise to my feet, "I need to go—"

"What's going on in here?" Our mother walks in with our father behind her.

"Like you don't fucking know, Mother," I growl so loudly she takes a step back in shock. "You started this shit. Who knows, maybe you finally got what you wanted."

"Cooper…" My dad starts and I immediately cut him off.

"No, Dad." I spit. "Did she tell you she gave me a file and told me Violet had an abortion as soon as she got to Arizona? That she got this file from her mother who hates me and wants us apart?"

Picking the folder off my dad's desk, I thrust it into his hands.

I'm so fucking angry; at my mom, sure, but more at myself. I let her get into my head, just like Amber did all those years ago. I assumed the worst and once again, instead of listening to Violet and getting her side, I let the evil words haunt me.

My dad's eyes scan the papers and the sonogram. He turns to his wife, confused. "What is this, Evelyn?"

"Amber gave it to me and told me it's why she hightailed it out of Riverside. Violet wanted the abortion but didn't want to tell Cooper. So, she moved her out, helped her get it done, and that way she couldn't make the mistake again. You had the right to know, Cooper. I didn't expect you to handle it here."

"But you did. Like perfect timing right before a tour to fuck it all up for us. You took the knowledge I wanted kids and exploited it."

"That's not true. I really wasn't going to tell you, and then I heard you talking today. It's not like I could have made this up in the time frame of today. I had no idea you wanted kids, and hearing what was being said, it concerned me, knowing what I knew! She was going to break your heart, Cooper. You needed to have this out. She did something wrong. You missed this chance because she took it away from you."

"She didn't take anything away from me, Mother. She didn't have it done because she wasn't pregnant then," I bellow and step forward to get in her face, but my dad puts his hand out to stop me.

"Yes, she did. She's trying to protect herself. It's there in black, white, *and gray,* Cooper. She took your chance away from being a father. Sure, there's no way I would have been thrilled about you having a kid so young, but I would have helped. She could've given it to you and not been so selfish." Her voice is clipped, and raised, pointing her fingers at the vile, red folder.

"She's not being selfish, Mom," I yell back, begging for her to listen to what I'm saying. Much like Violet was trying to do to me.

Beside me, Brody runs his hands through his hair, his eyes darting between our verbal volley.

"I know she didn't do this. I'm the one who fucked up by accusing her, because I believed something you said. I trusted you more than you deserve. Hell, I even gave Amber fucking way too much trust."

"So, you're just taking her word? Even when it's in front of you?"

"Didn't you hear me? It came from Amber. I don't know when you two suddenly became all buddy-buddy, but her word is as good as shit. I can admit, you had me fooled, and it looks fucking real. The thing is you have no idea—" A large lump collects in my throat. I'm about to admit to her something only two other people know. "The thing is you have no idea what we went through before. I should've never even believed for a *millisecond* she could do it." I shake my head and find myself crying, falling back into the chair. "She wouldn't have because she knows how it feels. I know how it feels—"

The moment of when I found her in that bathroom surrounded by blood, to rushing her to the hospital, and all the tears we shed together flash through my mind. How many times back then did I see she was always trying to convince herself it would be alright, to convince me, so we could survive it? The thing is: do you survive it *or* learn to live with it?

"Cooper?" My dad kneels in front of my chair, placing his hand on my knee.

I sniffle and wipe away my running nose and tears. "What do you mean you know how it feels?"

"When we were sixteen, Vi had a miscarriage." I hear my mother gasp as my dad's stares at me in disbelief. "We were away, together for Valentine's. We didn't know she was and I found her in the bathroom, bleeding and in pain. We thought maybe it was a bad period, but it didn't stop and the pain got worse. So, I took her to the hospital and we found out she was having a miscarriage. For the longest time the Vi I knew vanished. It ate away at us both. I knew she thought about it…but…" My words fall off. The words of her blame hit me like a slap again.

"She had a miscarriage?" my mom whispers, and I finally look back over at her. Through my hazy eyes, I see the shocked look and her eyes watering.

"Yeah, she did. That's what makes this all worse," I sigh. "You know, I would tell myself it would be okay. That we could move on, but you don't. I still think about it, the what if, and the what could've been. Sometimes I wonder if you and Amber weren't so vengeful on breaking us—maybe it wouldn't have happened, or maybe we could've talked to you and you could have helped us. Tried to tell us it would be okay. *Especially* Vi."

I remember vividly Vi's sorrowful eyes she wore for months after it happened. She suffered the most and I was never enough to completely help her heal. What she needed and maybe what I needed was someone to talk to who wasn't so close and vent out the heartache it brought us.

My eyes glance to my mother who has tears in her eyes and my father's arm around her shoulder. Though, I wonder how she could be upset when she helped create that whole mess. Brody grips my shoulder, giving me his silent support.

No one says anything, waiting for me to continue.

"We couldn't tell you because we didn't want you to try to break us up over it when we needed each other the most. Imagine how easy it was for you today; could you picture how easy it would've been six years ago when we were pretty much defeated?" I stand and turn to get in my mother's face. "It's my fault today for fucking up with Vi. I should've known it was a scheme to break us. The thing is all of this could've been avoided if you'd just supported us in the first place." I point my finger in her face. "Why did you want to destroy her? Destroy what we have? How could you never see how happy she makes me?"

I see the confliction in my mother's eyes, but she remains quiet, which only makes me madder.

"WHY?" I scream so loud the wall shakes. All the veins in my neck pulsate with my anger.

Brody and my dad grab my shoulders pulling me away from my mother. I shove them off once I'm far enough away.

"Tell me! And not the bullshit stuff you told me in high school. A real reason!"

"Because I thought she would be like her mother," she whispers, and her body sags.

"What?"

"The night you went to jail for beating up that boy, I watched Amber take the bribe money without even blinking. I saw Violet's neck and all I could think was what mother would settle so quickly when her daughter had those nasty bruises. I confronted her and she turned it on you; made it *your* fault."

She's right about Amber, but I'm still failing to see how it falls on my wife.

"I didn't want you mixed up with a family like that, especially at the time when me and your father had great hopes for a prestigious future."

"Yeah, a future I didn't want," I hiss. "Vi, Brody, and Dustin were the only ones who had hopes for the future *I wanted.*"

Mom smoothes her dress and stares for too long at her shoes. "I get it now," she admits what I already knew. "Though at the time, I wanted you far away for that kind of trouble. One that could ruin your future. So, I mentioned your issues with fighting to Amber, hoping it would be enough to keep you away from her and suggested as well, it would be better to keep you two apart." She pinches the bridge of her nose and closes her eyes. "It didn't work, of course. When you two would go running off, getting drunk, it proved more to me you guys needed to not be together. Yes, you were happy, but you weren't—" A large sigh leaves her lips and she looks back at me sternly, and exasperated. A look I know well from getting in trouble all the time. "You weren't behaving. I really thought putting all your focus on music back then was a pipe dream. You had a chance at Princeton and I thought you were throwing it away for playing guitar at a coffee house. Sure, I was wrong, but at the time...I tried to let it go, but another thing would happen, like skipping school or coming into the house at three a.m. wasted. I thought it was because of her because when she left and you stopped all that."

"I did stop coming home late, but I was drinking in my room instead. How could you not notice how miserable I was without her? You saw, you watched how it fucking destroyed me when I thought she didn't want me…" I shake my head, remembering the hurt and my break down in front of her house that fateful day. "But why couldn't you let it go after we were married? Everyone in this house knew I still loved her. You've seen my house."

Brody snorts, and I turn to him glaring. "Sorry," he holds up his hands, "but it's a good point. You've seen his shrine, the mushy love songs that made him huge. I don't get how you can't see how helpless the boy is without her."

"I do—"

"Then why did you and Amber suddenly chum up to do this to us?"

My mother's head drops to her feet and she doesn't say anything, playing with her wedding rings. This isn't the same woman I've known who is ready to stand up for any fight and win.

"Evelyn?" My dad stands and moves to her, putting his hand on her shoulder. "What the hell did you do?"

"I thought I was doing the right thing for our son," she mumbles.

"By trying to destroy my marriage?" I growl, getting pissed all over again. I'm not playing this fucking game of dancing in circles.

"Yes," she mumbles, relenting, and moves to sit in a chair. "Amber called me early that morning after you got married. She was angry you had somehow weaseled yourself back into Violet's life. I was mad she had the nerve to say that, and I said it was her daughter trying to take your money. She agreed to disagree and asked if we could work together for what we both wanted this time."

"You can't compare Vi to her mother..."

"He's right," my dad interrupts. "If I had known this was your main reason I would've convinced you otherwise when they were kids. Instead, you convinced me she was making him lose focus, and yes, I also thought the music was a dead end, but not the way you saw it. I wanted him to be a Princeton man, to become a lawyer or politician like me." He turns to me and smiles. "You could argue yourself out of everything and I wanted you to put it to something good."

Yeah, I was pretty good at fighting for what I wanted, especially when it came to seeing Vi—no matter how much they fought, I did win.

Turning his attention back to my mother he moves in front of her and takes her hands in his. "But you knew also no matter what I would always stand by you. Violet is a wonderful girl and if you focus away from her mother's doing, you would have noticed even though he was staying out late and drinking, he stopped fighting and he was happy. They were only running off to be together, and you can't blame them. We were kids once and disobeyed our parents when they went against us. But now, since she came back, I don't know how you can't see how much happier he is. I was convinced the light in his eyes was gone forever, but Violet brought it back."

"I'm starting to see that. I saw it at the Ball when I kept trying to knock her down. The woman, Caroline, I admit was a setup between me and her mother to make Violet jealous and angry at you."

"Like you did with Ainsley?" I say her name with disdain. She *still* makes my skin crawl and my dick want to hide.

"Yes," she mumbles, "but after Violet went off on us, Ainsley had enough because you weren't worth your wife's ire. I would go to find that out myself..." She trails off and a small grin raises the corner of her lips.

"Find out how?" I ask curiously.

"I said things to her and she threw the wine at me at the ball…"

"Wait. Violet threw the wine at you?"

I had a gut feeling about it, but neither one had said anything. I figured if it was true one of them would've called out the other, so I let it go.

I should have pushed harder.

"Yes, and I deserved it. I said hurtful things, hurtful things which are now much worse in the light of tonight. I was tempted to go to you and make it her fault, but I noticed she didn't tell you what happened and thought better of it. It made me realize...she probably never told you everything going on. She probably didn't mention all I said at the reception or the dress shop, or blame me for the dress mix up."

I should've fucking known. Why didn't I know?!

"She had so many opportunities to turn you against me and she didn't. I didn't see it 'till I was covered in wine."

"She didn't want to turn me against you. I kept asking and she said it wasn't a big deal because at least my mother didn't sell me out for cash. But you sold me out another way, didn't you? You knew there was something off with the papers, and you still did it…"

"Yes, but I read the papers over twenty times. All of it seemed legit. The clinic and the doctor she saw were real, even the sonogram was realistic. I didn't plan on telling you, I figured you had to know, and there might have been a reason to why she had it done. But when I heard you guys talking about having kids and hearing her resistance, I thought she was being selfish like her mother and denying what you wanted. I let my own bitterness and heartache take over. I've had miscarriages and I couldn't imagine not carrying a baby. So thinking she didn't want to ever give you a child, thinking that she got rid of your child before, I caved and confronted you."

"But now I might never have the chance with her. Fuck!" I scream the obscenity and collapse to a chair.

"Cooper, I'm sor—"

"Are you?" I snap, cutting her off. "You should've never meddled in the first place. You saw what Amber was like and hooked up with her for your sick twisted games. Sure, I was stupid enough to believe what you were handing me, that's on me. I'll never forgive myself, but this could've all been avoided if you tried for me. If she doesn't forgive me..." My breathing becomes heavy and I feel the walls caving in around me. I can't breathe.

"Cooper you need to relax. Take deep breaths, man…" Brody's voice sounds distorted in my ears. His hand is on my shoulder and I try to take slow breaths. I can't see him through the fog because all I see is Violet leaving me, hating me.

I accused her of having an abortion. I didn't listen to her. I trusted the people who were always trying to tear us down.

What did I do?

I take out my phone and dial her number again and

again. All I get is voicemail. Everything is hazy, my cheeks are soaked, and my chest is heaving.

I need to get out of here.

"I need to go see her." I stand up and stumble backward. Brody catches me before I fall to the ground.

"You're in no shape to drive, I'll drive you."

I run into the house, calling for her, Brody hot on my heels. I run to our bedroom first. I yell her name like a crazed maniac, running towards her closet.

My panic rises to heart attack level when I see clothes scattered, a drawer hanging open, and clothes missing off hangers.

She's gone.

"NO!!" I bellow. "Fuck, no!" I grab the first thing I can and throw it at the wall and collapse into the cushioned bench.

"Cooper," Brody yells, gripping my shoulders. My head snaps up, tears running down my face. "It's okay,"

"Like fuck it is," I growl. "She left."

"Yes, but she went to her dad's."

"How do you know?"

"She left a note on the bed." He hands it to me and I read the hurried scribble.

I went to my dad's. I don't know when I'll be back, and as of now I can't go on tour with you. We made a promise, and the first chance you got, you broke it. I'll call Brody and I'll do what I can from dad's house. I'm not saying goodbye, but what you accused me of—what you thought I could do to our child—sliced through my very soul and I can't see you 'till it stops hurting so bad.

I crumble the note in my hands and let it fall to the floor. I fucked everything up.

Baby, I'm so sorry. Please forgive me.

ELEVEN

August 2nd, 2001

Cooper

I'm lying in bed wrapped around Violet's naked body, in some dingy motel with ripped floral wallpaper, twenty miles out of Riverside. X-Rated had a gig at the local bowling alley, which paid us only in hotdogs and free games. It doesn't matter where we play as long as my music is being heard.

Plus, I like hotdogs and bowling.

The upside was we sold a bunch of CD's which helped pay for this room so Violet and I can be alone. Her and her mom got into it yesterday over her mom's boyfriend. Vi thinks he's a creep and told her mom so. It escalated when her mom said it wasn't any of her business. She didn't understand how her mom could have so many opinions about our relationship, yet she gets none with hers.

That's what I made out through the hiccup cries.

It was a mess, which ended with me having to pick her up on the corner by her house around eleven. Her face was tear stained, her body was trembling, and her voice hoarse from yelling. There's nothing worse than seeing her cry, especially after these last six months. Vi was finally going back to her normal self after the miscarriage, the light was coming back in her eyes, and she was getting out, living again. Then her mother would bring her down and Vi would crumble inside all over again.

I had to sneak her into my room for the night because there was no way she was going back home when she needed me. I doubt her mom even knew she left. Which brings us here, now, avoiding going home for one more day.

With her father on a boat somewhere at sea, she didn't get to spend the summer with him and had no one to call who understands how 'truly crazy Mom really is'— her words. Violet didn't know how to share the news of our loss with her dad and was too afraid he'd be disappointed in her. In us. I urged her to, but didn't want to push it too hard.

I spent a lot of time online searching sites on how to help us cope. I stumbled on a bunch of parenting blogs where people wrote out their stories. It opened my eyes to know we aren't alone. The one story I related to the most was about remembering that they're always watching you from heaven. I've never been very religious, but it gave me hope, and inspired me to write a song for us to remember them. When I first sang it, the light in Violet's eyes flickered on again. I haven't sung it to her in a while, but I can tell she needs it.

My hand brushes down her shoulder, over her flat stomach, and I whisper the song into her ear.

"You were sent home to fly with the angels.
Made with so much love
You needed to share it with heavens.
You'll always be with us
And showed us our love had room to grow."

I FOUND *you*   **August 2nd 2001**

She turns around in my arms and wraps her arms around my neck. "Thank you." She kisses me softly. "Your singing always makes me feel better."

"What would you have done if I couldn't carry a tune?"

She purses her lips together and looks at the ceiling, before looking back at me with a humorous gleam in her eyes. "Um...hope you'd still have your writing skills and could read me poetry?"

"And if I sucked at that too?"

"Well, you're really good in bed and it trumps everything, so we'd be finnnne.*" She exaggerates the n's and rubs her core against my cock.*

Violet buries her face into the side of my neck, littering little kisses in her wake. When she reaches my lips she stops and looks at me seriously.

"You're going to still love me when you become a star right, Coop? Even if it's only on the bowling circuit."

"Of course. It's always going to be me and you. You'll be my manager or personal groupie."

She smacks me lightly in the chest, giggling. "I'd make a terrible manager," she jokes, and I push her into the mattress.

"Groupie it is then." I tickle her side and she falls into a fit of giggles. "I'll pay you only in hot dogs, too. If you know what I mean..." I wiggle my eyebrows, continuing to tickle her sides.

Between her uncontrollable laughter, she begs me to stop. I finally release her and she has tears running down her cheek from laughing so hard. The smile on her face lights up the whole room, and there's nothing more for me in this life; I love nothing more than making her smile.

I don't know if I could handle not being the one to make her smile anymore.

"Good thing I like your weenie." She giggle snorts at her little joke.

"I love you." I kiss her, as I sink into her again. *"You'll always be mine, Ace. Nothing will ever stand in our way."*

She moans, wrapping her legs around my back as I fill her completely. "You and me against the world. Forever."

July 7th, 2006

Violet

"Little Angel we never knew
You'll always be ours
Always in our hearts.
We'll never forget you though we never got to meet you.
You're a part of me, a part of her
Made of our love
Flying in heaven
one day we will finally meet
and wrap you in our wings.
Little Angel, fly.
Fly high with your wings
Know you'll always be loved
Soaring through our hearts
Where you stay with us
For always."

I whisper the lyrics to the song Cooper wrote all those years ago. When I was at my lowest, he would sing this to me, and I don't think he knew how much hearing it helped mend my broken heart. Our baby isn't here, but he is somewhere safe. Cooper never talked as much about how much he was hurting. I know he held it in to be strong for me, but the lyrics told me how emotionally attached he was to our loss. For him, the only way he could get those feelings out was through song. He had recorded it on a CD for me, and I would listen to it every time I felt *empty*.

Like now.

Life has felt empty these last five days. I'm surrounded by dark clouds and a monsoon of tears. My life has come to a halt, and I don't know how to get past this pain.

I miss *him*.

Though, no matter how much I miss him, I can't seem to get past this hurt he's inflicted upon me.

Cooper left on tour a couple days ago, and I haven't talked to him since our fight. Maybe I'm being stubborn; I always have been when it comes to arguments, but every time I think about it, my heart clenches in my chest. He looked at me as if he hated me.

I see that look every time I close my eyes.

He's been sending me messages and countless flowers, telling me how sorry he is. Though I know he's sorry, I can't escape this ache I have deep in my soul, caused by him.

You did this. You killed our baby.

The stinging words he said play in my head on a loop. I know he wasn't talking about our miscarriage, but the words sting all the same. The blame I've put on myself for years coming to life from the person I love the most. But in that moment, he really believed I would abort our child. Believing our mothers before me.

I don't care how real those papers looked. I thought he knew me better than that.

I look down at my wedding rings and think back to that night we got married. As much as I always loved him, maybe we shouldn't have gotten married after being apart for four years.

I don't regret it for a second, though, and would do it all over again. I love him, even if right now, I want to punch him in his perfect face.

I FOUND you   **July 7th, 2006**

Then there's poor Brody, who is always stuck between us. Though, I think this is the first major fight we've ever had where we have gone days without talking or seeing each other.

We were lovers, not fighters.

The thought makes me laugh for the first time in days.

Brody calls me every day, and I do what I can from this end, but it isn't the same. He says he understands, but he wants us to make up before he loses the rest of his sanity.

It's after eleven in the morning, and I'm still wrapped in my blankets in bed with my laptop to the side looking at concert pictures and articles from last night's show.

Cooper looks miserable, unshaven and like he hasn't slept all week.

Broken. Like me.

And no matter how pissed I am, I just want to hold him.

There's even an article about how he's acting differently on this tour and they're assuming his new marriage is on the rocks.

"Vi?" my dad calls through the door following a knock.

"Come in." I close my laptop, and wipe the tears I didn't realize were falling again.

"Hey, someone is here to talk to you," he says, walking fully into my room.

"Who?" It can't be Cooper he should be in Phoenix.

Maybe I should go see him while he's close by. He plays Tucson tomorrow. Also, I could see Julie and Alexa....

"Evelyn." My ears perk up and away from my thoughts. Evelyn? She's in my father's house?

"Wha—? Why is she here?" I can't keep the surprise out of my voice, wondering what she could want to say to me. Through Cooper's countless emails and voicemails, he mentioned having it out with his mother and telling her about the miscarriage. But even if she's feeling sorry now, that doesn't mean I want to talk to her.

"She came over to talk to me, filling me in on what she's done. She also showed me the file your mother gave her." He clenches his jaw trying to fight off his temper. "It was very convincing that's for sure…"

"Yeah, I know. Listen, I get why Evelyn believed it; it was Cooper who should've never believed it." The bitterness rolls off my tongue. I can't stop it every time I think about it. "We went through it together, he knew—" I close my eyes, trying to keep the damn tears at bay.

"I know." He sits down next to me on my bed and takes my hand. "I wish you told me, honey."

When I'd arrived at his house, I had cried into his arms and told him everything: the miscarriage and mom's handy work of trying to ruin my marriage, of trying to ruin me. He'd listened to me and before he could give me his fatherly advice I passed out. I haven't been able to talk more about it since.

"I just didn't want you to be disappointed or mad. Or maybe even end up killing Cooper."

"I wouldn't have been disappointed. I wasn't dumb, Vi. I knew what you two were doing. One of the reasons I continued to give the boy a hard time. I would have loved you through it, honey."

I nod my head, and the tears slip from my eyes. "Does it ever stop hurting? I know women go through this all the time and further along. I almost feel guilty for feeling this way when there are people suffering more."

My father puts his arm around me and pulls me closer. "I've never personally dealt with this before, but I can't imagine it's something you forget. I'm sure you hold it in your heart forever, no matter how far along you were, or if you knew or not, he or she was still your child. And your pain isn't measured by someone else's." My head falls against his shoulder. It feels good to finally talk to someone else about this. I've bottled it up for so long and this is a sweet release. "I believe, like any loss, you learn to keep moving and have to know it's okay to keep living your life. There's nothing wrong with that."

"I'm so scared to try again," I whisper.

"Have you told Cooper that?"

"No," I utter the word guiltily. "I always thought he knew, but I was wrong. He never mentioned wanting to try 'till the other day, but then he thought I could...I could have an abortion...after everything." My voice cracks and there's a dry ache in the back of my throat from all the tears I've shed.

"I know." His arm rubs my back consoling me. "She caught him at a vulnerable time, but you and Evelyn didn't know how much he was hurting. Like you, he didn't communicate his real feelings. He messed up, but he knows that. Maybe he does deserve the silent treatment, but it's not helping either of you. You're going to have to talk to him. I don't think this house can take another flower arrangement. If you want to save what you have and move on, you need to talk."

My heavy heart finally drops to my stomach. All the most recent pictures I've seen of him flash in my mind. He's a mess, I'm a mess. I told him it wasn't goodbye, but in his hundreds of email, I wonder if it's how he took it.

Should I have stayed and talked to him? He was crying when I walked out the door, but he believed them, when we promised we wouldn't.

"Stop that!" My dad hugs me to him, and his scent of sandalwood comforts me. "You did what you needed to for you. I couldn't tell you how many times I walked away from your mom or she did from me when we had enough. Now, we didn't make it, but it doesn't mean this is it for you. We had *much* bigger problems. This isn't good, but it's not the end."

I nod. "That doesn't mean I want to talk to Evelyn."

"I think you should. It'll help the healing process. You don't have to take her apology, but maybe it will be good to hear what she has to say. That way you can start to move forward without any more of her meddling. She's here. It's more than I can say for your *mother*."

I snort, this is true. I should call and scream at her, but I don't want to give her the satisfaction of thinking she won. Plus, it's not like she's tried reaching out to me. She can rot and I won't care if I never talk to her again. For all the things she has done to me, I don't want her. In my heart, she's no longer my mother.

"What did she tell you?"

"Everything, since the first time she knew about you at the police station 'till now. I gave her hell, don't you worry, but it's your turn. She's your mother in law." He pats my leg, chuckling. "Plus, you need to get out of this bed. You're starting to leave indents in the mattress from all your lying around. It's not healthy."

Throwing my hair into a messy bun, I take a minute to stare at the girl in the mirror. My face is pale, large dark circles hoop under my eyes from all the crying and lack of sleep. I need make-up, *stat*, to cover this disaster. I debate changing out of my sweatpants and Cooper's Spinal Tap T-shirt that I stole back in high school but decide, fuck it. I'm not glamming up for her; let her see what she did to me. If she's truly sorry, maybe she'll give a shit about my raggedy muffin appearance.

My cell phone buzzes with a text message on my dresser. I already know who it is before I open it.

Coop: I LOVE YOU

My fingers hover over the keyboard wondering if I should return the message.

Flipping the phone closed I decide I need to handle Evelyn first. Get that obstacle out of the way before me and Cooper finally talk. Tossing the phone back on the dresser, I make my way downstairs, preparing myself for the worst.

I find Evelyn and my dad on the couch. Both of them turn to me, and Evelyn gives me a genuine warm, yet sad smile. I've never seen her look at me like this before. It's kind of creepy, and makes me wonder what episode of the twilight zone I walked into.

"I'll leave you two." My dad stands and I try to will him with my eyes not to leave. "You'll be fine," he says answering my silent begging.

He moves to the kitchen as I plop on the couch in front of Evelyn. In the middle of the coffee table, I spot a shoebox with the name Louboutin etched across the top.

Did she come to bribe me with shoes? Because those sure don't go with my dad's attire.

"You wanted to talk?"

"I came here because I owe you an apology. Actually, I owe you more than that." I nod, telling her I'm listening and to continue. "You know the old adage, don't judge a book by its cover, well, I misjudged you and never gave you a chance, based on your mother's actions alone. Now, I'm not saying everything was her fault," she quickly adds, "I should've known better and seen around it—but I couldn't because I did truly believe you were helping push Cooper down the wrong path."

"I never pushed him down the wrong path, I only

encouraged him to do what he loved." I cross my arms.

I'm so sick of explaining myself.

"Yes, I know. I was blinded, but now I've seen what I was missing. I actually admire you, Violet." My mouth pops open and I suddenly have the urge to clean my ears. "You had so many times to throw me under the bus and turn my son against me. We both know my son would have done anything to make sure you were happy. Even if it meant cutting me off, but you didn't. My sons told me why you kept the burden of what I was doing to yourself for the sake of our relationships and I admire you for it. I know I couldn't have done the same if it was the other way around. I only wish it didn't take me so long to see how good you truly are."

I'm astonished by her heartfelt words. I'm not even sure what to make of them in this moment or know what to say. So instead, I stare at her blankly as she continues.

"I don't want to stand in your way anymore. I want you both to be happy. I'm not sure if I can make it up to you ever for what I did, but I'll keep trying to show you I've changed and support you two."

I pinch the bridge of my nose and take a deep breath.

Move forward. My dad's words echo in my ears. That's all I want. I want my husband back and to go back to the way we were. One less enemy is one less pain in the ass sticking their business where it doesn't belong.

"Okay, I have some questions."

"Anything."

"Why didn't you come to me when you got those papers from my mom? Or at least to both of us? You were willing to tear your son's heart out just to get rid of me?" My voice cracks and it's scary how much of this pain could've been avoided if Evelyn had used common sense.

Her shoulders sag. "Because at first, I wasn't going to say anything. I figured Cooper knew by now, but after I overheard you—" she looks to the front door, though I

I FOUND YOU   *July 7th, 2006*

don't miss the look of regret in her eyes. "Hearing you talk, and how you pushed back against the idea of kids, then thinking you had the abortion, I jumped to conclusions. Your mother said you would never tell him, and I thought he had the right to know because it was something he wanted. I was convinced you were taking it away from him."

"I would never, but despite the past, I'm only twenty-one. We're young and just married. Did that not occur to you? I get what my mother handed to you was very believable. I don't fault you for thinking it was real, but I do for you going to Cooper with it and not me. You used his pain against him on purpose to use against me. That's why I'm not sure if it's forgivable."

"I understand, because I'm not sure I could forgive myself," she says softly, reaching for her tea.

"Does my mother know you used her bait? Because what you did doesn't make you any better than her." I wonder if my mom knows how much damage she has caused.

Did she pour the celebratory champagne yet?

"No. I had told her I wasn't sure if I would say anything either. And I won't tell her now either. I've learned my lesson. She's been trying to call me, but I've sent all her calls to voicemail."

My hands push through my hair, confused about what to do. She seems sorry, my dad thinks she's sorry, but there's a part of me waiting for the other shoe to drop.

"Does Coop know you're here?"

"Brody knows. Cooper won't talk to me right now. I'm sure his brother told him. You know how they are."

I do. I roll my eyes thinking those two are worse than girls when keeping secrets from each other.

"Okay," I mutter. "I don't know what else to say or do."

"We don't have to iron out anything right now. I

know it'll take some time, and it's okay." I notice the tears swimming in her eyes. Honest to goodness tears. Something I've never seen her do or thought she was capable of. "I just want you to know, I really do wish I was smarter because knowing now what you guys suffered alone with your miscarriage tears me up inside. As a mother, no matter how young you both were, I should've been there, gotten you help. I had three before I had Dustin. It was hard, but I had support and someone to talk to. I should've seen how different he was—and maybe even you. I caught you a couple times together on my lawn crying but didn't think much of it. So, I'm sorry. I know it doesn't ever go away, but it'll get easier."

I swallow the lump in my throat and nod. "I know. I'm okay 'till I think about trying again and wondering if…" I snap my mouth shut and realize I don't want to purge my feelings to her.

"Don't let it stop you from *wanting* when you're ready. We never know what will happen and the what if's will crumble you more than the trying. Trust me. The best advice I got—and I know you don't want to hear it from me—is don't try, let it happen."

I let her words sink in and give her a small nod. "Okay."

"Oh, before I forget, I have something to give you." She changes the conversion and I wonder if she can feel my uneasiness. "Well, they're for Cooper, but I thought you might want to be the one to give them to him."

She picks up the brown shoe box and hands it to me. I peer at the box skeptically on my lap, knowing these aren't Louboutins before opening it.

My jaw drops when I see all the unopened envelopes that have Cooper's name and address written on them in my handwriting.

"You kept them," I whisper my disbelief, and look back up at my mother in law. "Why?"

I FOUND YOU   *July 7th, 2006*

Her eyes flick away from me with guilt. I really don't know who this woman is today. The shame, the admitting of wrongs, the kindness, is all a new look on her, and I can't help but wonder if this is who she truly is.

"After Cooper came back from seeing you, only days after your mother had called telling me you moved on, he was a mess. Crying and screaming that you had moved on. He locked himself in his room for days and wouldn't eat."

My already aching heart shreds a little bit more. Hearing of his pain, I swear if I see my mother again, I might rip her apart.

At least Evelyn is making an effort.

"He left a month later, got a record deal, yet your letters kept coming and I thought you were either trying to lead him on or going to break his heart again. But for some reason, I'm not even sure of, I didn't have the heart to get rid of them. I'm sorry, and I know it's too late for them."

"Thank you, I'll give these to him—" I frown, realizing I'm going to have to talk to him if I want to do that.

"I hope it's sooner than later. I'd like to see you both happy again, rubbing it in my face, and your moms face too. Because the both of you can't keep going on acting like zombies."

Shortly after Evelyn and I finished our talk, my dad came back into the room and offered lunch. Evelyn declined, wanting to get on her way, and saying she'd already taken up enough of our time.

I still haven't accepted her apology, but there might be some hope for that in the future. Especially, if Cooper and I ever have kids; I'd like them to have one grandma.

My mom won't even look at my children 'till she repents of all she's done, and that will be a cold, rainy ass day in hell, I'm sure. She was never one for 'I'm sorry's' unless they benefited her somehow.

I lay the shoebox down on my bed, letting my finger run over the white envelopes, wondering how life would be different if he'd gotten these. Glancing at my phone, I figure now is better than later to reach out to him. When I open my phone and I have a new email from him.

***

To: Violet Reid
Subject: I miss you
From: Cooper Reid

I know you won't reply, and I'm not sure if you're even reading these. I guess I still can't blame you.
I'm about to go onstage and wanted to tell you again I love you and miss you so much. I don't know if I'll ever say sorry enough. I kick myself every day for believing my mom and for not listening to you.
The pain of our loss still affects me more than I ever thought it could. She used ammunition against me she didn't even know she had. Then blend it with our conversation that afternoon. I was blinded and couldn't see reason.
But it's not an excuse. I should've never assumed, and no matter what given you a chance to talk and to listen.
I wish I could take it all back. I was an

idiot, I'm so sorry.
You not being here with me is killing me…but I can't blame you. I know you hate me now. I hate myself too.
I don't want to lose you.
I love you, Ace.
Sweet dreams,
Cooper.

I take a deep breath and decide to answer him after five long days.

Though I had every right to be mad and ignore him, my dad is right; only talking, will things start to work again. We're married now. This can't be the thing that breaks up apart. Regardless of how pissed I am, they can't win again.

To Cooper Reid
Subject: I miss you too
From: Violet Reid

I love you too. I promise we will talk soon.
I know you haven't been sleeping. I can tell by the pictures I've seen of you.
Promise me, tonight, you will get some rest.
I should have answered you sooner and I'm sorry I didn't.
I miss you too. I promise, I'm not going anywhere. We just need to talk.
Please get some sleep.
Love,
Violet x

I send the e-mail and I know it's not enough. There's only one thing I can do now.

I dial the familiar number and it rings. It's after six and they're probably in the middle of setting up the show, but I can't wait 'till later.

"Vi?" he yells over the loud music in the background.

"Brody, I need your help…"

The next morning, I'm standing in front of Room 1430 at the Desert Diamond Hotel. My wonderful brother in law picked me up at the airport at five a.m. half asleep. He caught me up on tonight's work, but told me that under no circumstances was I to come out of the room 'till me and Coop have made up.

Brody gave me his key to the room and I walk in closing the door quietly behind me. The room is bathed in darkness, but I hear the melody of a guitar playing from inside the suite's bedroom. I drop my bag and flick on the light, noticing right away the bottles of beer laying everywhere. Brody did mention he'd been drinking like a fish the last couple of days.

Yet, he's still not sleeping.

I follow the music into the bedroom. There's my husband, sitting on the edge of the bed, playing his guitar to a tune I've never heard before. I smile, wondering if this is something new he has written, because the melody is new to my ears, and also somewhat depressing.

He's only wearing a pair of gray sweatpants, the five-o'clock shadow he usually has is now heavy and in desperate need of a shave, and his blond, wavy hair falls

I FOUND YOU   *July 8th, 2006*

over his closed eyes. He hasn't noticed me as he finishes playing, and sets his guitar down behind him on the bed.

"What song were you playing?" His head snaps to mine. He rises from the bed and walks over to me, but stops feet away. The heavy bags under his eyes match mine, and I resist the urge to jump into his arms, to tell him it'll be okay.

His glazed over blue irises stare at me, as if he's waiting for me to disappear.

"I thought I told you to get some rest." I tilt my head and look at him, giving him a small smile.

"I tried. I—" he trails off. "You're here."

I giggle softly, "That, I am."

"I'm so sorry, baby," he blurts out and inches closer to me.

"I know." I sigh. "I would have talked to you sooner, but you hurt me. The way you looked at me *alone*, was enough to slice me open. The words were just the final cut. It kills me you think I would— especially after knowing the information came from my mother."

He bows his head. "It wasn't until I started saying them out loud that I was hearing how it all sounded. I didn't want to believe it at first, but those papers…" he trails off.

"They were realistic, but you knew they wanted us apart. They haven't stopped once since we said 'I do' and I can't help but wonder what you will think if some tabloid makes up some crazy story about me. Will you believe them, too, before me?"

He shakes his head back and forth, his tired body caves, sitting heavily on the bed. "No. I won't. I promise. *I swear.*" He looks up me, his eyes swimming with the tears he's holding back, begging for me to believe him. "I'm so sorry. I don't think I should get your forgiveness, but I love you, and I will do anything to make it up to you."

He looks like such a lost boy right now. I sit down next to him, wrap my arm around his back, and lay my head on his shoulder.

"The words in that file taunted me. I went back and forth between not wanting to believe, to the word abortion screaming in my ear," he whispers, and his body shakes under my arm. "Everything fit together, down to the dates. I think your confusion about what I was saying threw me too. I'm sorry. I should've stopped before I went after you." He pauses, trying to steady his breathing. "Though, I think I figured out why I wanted a baby so bad. One of the Roadies, Big Frank."

I giggle. Leave it to me to giggle and find a joke in a serious ass moment. But it eases the tension in the room.

Maybe that's why we don't fight much? Always cracking jokes. "Big Frank? Like a hot dog?"

Cooper looks at me, with a small smile, shaking his head. "This is why I love you. Your ability to find the humor at the worst time," he mumbles, "and no. He's fifty-something, and not very big. You'll see when you meet him."

"Sorry, continue."

"Anyways, he could tell something was wrong and I was tired of venting to Brody. I told him what happened and how I acted about wanting kids. He said he got it. He explained his wife had two miscarriages and all he wanted more afterward was a child. Like her, it was all he thought about. He wanted to fill the void. Wanting to have a child consumed my every thought. I wanted to have what we were missing." His face drops in his hands and groans, "I thought I was fine. I thought you were fine. But now I know we never had that chance to heal. I should have seen something wasn't right with how you were acting." He turns his head in his hands and looks at me. "I'm sorry."

"I know." My hands move into his hair, playing with the waves at the back of his head. "We held a lot in, so maybe our mothers did us a favor."

His head lifts up and eyes widen horrified. "Vi…" I press my fingers to his chapped lips, hushing him.

"They made us see what we've been hiding. It was due to explode. I mean maybe not *that* way, but it had to happen. I should've told you about how I was feeling about getting pregnant again, but I didn't know how. My fear always overpowered my rational thinking. Also, maybe I was hoping to have more time to wrap my mind around it before you asked. I'm sorry too, for not being more open to you about my feelings. But all we can do is move on. We still have things to talk about but for now, I think we both need to get some sleep."

"Are you staying?"

"Yes," I smile and touch his stubbly face. "I didn't come all the way to sleep in the lobby."

"Julie and Alexa are here. I'm sure you could…"

"Will you stop? We're trying to make up, and I'm too tired to think about anything else right now."

"Sorry. Sleep sounds good, actually. I think I can do it if your here." Before I can blink he's wrapped his arms around my body and buries his head in the crook of my neck. I hear him inhale deeply with his nose pressed against my skin. "I love you…"

"I love you too. There was never any question there. Now sleep. When we wake we can talk some more."

Cooper manages to untangle himself from my body and pulls back the covers. I lose my jeans, leaving me in an oversized t-shirt. His eyes roam up and down my body before I slip under the covers.

Even though I'm still be peeved at him, I can't help the way he ignites my skin with just a simple look.

Not yet.

Cooper pulls me into his arms, my back pressed against his stomach.

"I'm so glad you're here. I'm going to make it up to

you..." he murmurs softly, his voice laced with sleep. "I promise."

My eyes flutter open, and I'm met with Cooper's blues staring down at me. I had turned around in my sleep and I'm now nuzzled into his chest.

"Please tell me you slept." I yawn, stretching out my legs.

"*We* slept about six hours. It's almost two."

"Good." I plant a kiss on his chest, my lips tingling at the taste of his skin. "We both needed it."

"I'm so glad you are here," he tells me. "I had to pinch myself to make sure you were real. I should've never believed my mom. I don't know what the hell I was thinking at the time..." I place my finger on his lips to hush him.

"I know you're sorry. Listen, let's just put this to the side for now. I don't want to be upset or mad about this anymore. I really want to move on, and I know you regret what you said right away. Plus, if I see one more picture of you being pouty and depressed, well..." I wave my hand in the air. "I love you. That's all that matters. And Brody might have also told me if we didn't kiss and make up by tonight, he was going to kick both of our asses." I giggle, and for the first time in weeks, I do feel it's going to be okay. Being in his arms is where I belong, and this fight isn't a deal breaker, so why keep picking at it.

"God, I love you..." He slides his hand through my hair, gazing at me with so much admiration and love. Seeing the way he looks at me, I can feel my heart begin to stitch back together.

"Can I kiss you?" he whispers, his lips inches away from mine.

"Please…" I beg, desperate for his touch again.

Cooper rolls on top of me and his lips press against mine. His tongue dances with mine. The tension I felt in his body when I woke up, lightens. There's this familiar ease now circling around us, like we always used to have, and the hurt begins to melt away.

My sewn heart beats rapidly, as we connect again.

Has it really been five days since I kissed this man?

We are so lost in each other, I have no idea how much time has passed when my phone starts ringing.

"Ignore it," Cooper whispers against my lips, his hand gripping my ass tightly so I can't move.

"I can't. We probably need to get going." He groans and releases me. "Didn't I say no more pouting?" I push my finger to his lips, and he grins, pressing a kiss to my fingers.

I roll away to grab my phone off the nightstand. Brody's name appears across the screen as expected.

"Hey."

"Have you kids made up yet?" Brody voice booms over the phone.

"Yes, sir," I answer.

"*Oh*," he seems surprised, "*so* I probably interrupted something."

"Sorta, but you're fine."

"Sorta? If you haven't naked wrestled yet, then you haven't really made up… call me when you're done with that." He laughs. "Five minutes should be enough, right?"

"Shut up, Brody!" Cooper yells, causing his brother to laugh louder.

"Sorry, didn't mean to overestimate. Four then?"

"Did you need something?" I ask, giggling, hopping out of the bed so Coop can't take my phone and yell at his brother.

"Yes, for you to tell the ugly fucker to get ready and come down for stage rehearsal. You know, sound check and all that jazz. And also, come ready to work, I'm cracking the whip on ya now."

"We'll be down shortly." I hang up before we end up bantering for hours.

Once I'm out of the shower, feeling clean and rejuvenated, I go to get dressed, while Cooper finishes up.

Digging through my bag for some jeans and a comfortable shirt, I find the Louboutins shoebox Evelyn gave me. Placing it on the bed, I pick up one of the envelopes, tempted to open it.

"What you got there?" Cooper startles me, the white envelope falling from my hands, landing perfectly at his feet.

He bends down to pick it up, his tousled hair still wet from his shower and only a white towel wrapped around his waist. He flips the envelope around and looks at me curiously. "Fan mail?"

I shake my head. "No. Your mom gave them to me. They're from me. The ones you never got."

"Your letters?" he whispers in surprise. He stares back at the letter, I can tell he wants to open it, but I also note his hesitation. "You're telling me she kept them?"

I nod. "You don't have to read them,"

"Oh, I'm reading them…" He cuts me off and sits on the bed. He fingers through the almost fifty letters lined up in the fancy shoebox. "She had these all these fucking years and didn't give them to me," he says bitterly.

I sit down next to him and kiss his bare shoulder.

"She explained it to me. I kind of got it. She thought I moved on because *you* and my mom said so. She thought I was leading you on, but maybe with her keeping these, she didn't truly believe it?" I shrug. "I don't know. All that matters is she gave them to me to give to you to read."

"I should've read them fucking years ago. She had no fucking right." He places the letter I dropped back in the box and leans down to kiss me gently. "I don't know if I can forgive her," he mumbles. "I kept wanting to believe things would be better. I let myself be blind to her interfering." He pauses and stares into my eyes pointedly. "I wish you told me. The dress, the wine…I know why you didn't. You said why many times you didn't want to come between us, but you need to tell me this shit next time, Vi."

"I will. I promise. But also, the thing is I know you love your mother. Despite all the things she has done to you. I was the same with my mom. She'd had already done so much to me before she even broke us up, but I kept hoping we could repair our relationship. I didn't want you to lose her because I don't know any child who wants to lose their mother."

"Yeah, but when you found out the truth you cut her out. Like I should've." He closes his eyes, pained.

"Coop, what she did was wrong. Really wrong, and I'm not sure if I want to forgive her either, but…" I run my hands down my face, not sure what I'm going for. "I think if my mother put in as much effort as Evelyn seems to be, maybe one day I could let her back in. But you don't have to do it now. I didn't show you these for that reason. These are yours and maybe if you read, you'll see how much I always loved you."

"Too bad your mother didn't keep the ones I sent you. I sent you a couple, including some original lyrics to 'My Everything'. They could be worth a fortune you know, instead they're probably ash in a fireplace somewhere."

"Probably, but it is what it is. Now let's finish getting ready or we'll never hear the end of it from your brother."

The concert is going smoothly and though I'm exhausted, I'm invigorated by my first night of actual work. Nothing compares to actually being in the middle of it all and working with all the roadies and stagehands. I've also been dealing with more of the financial part of it, which I enjoy because I like working with numbers.

The crowd is going insane as Cooper finishes "15 Hours" and starts to introduce the band. He's been smiling and jumping around the stage, back to being 'The Cooper Reid.' He's shaven the heavy scruff and with the sleep he got the dark circles are gone.

"Thank fuckin' god," Brody says next to me. "I really was about to kick his ass. Not that I blame you for being mad. But thank the lord. You guys okay now?" He stops and looks at me with a raised eyebrow. "I mean you really are okay now, right?"

"I think so. We got some things to work out, but it's not the end of the world."

"Heard my mom came to talk to you too. You never told me how it went. She's still alive so I assume…?"

"Yeah. It might be a long while before I can forgive her; it's going to be one step at a time." I shake my head.

"Well, I know she's finally seeing the light."

"I just wish I could say the same thing about my mother. Although, I don't think I'm even going to try."

"Maybe one day, many moons from now…" His hand waves around dramatically.

I FOUND you   *July 8th, 2006*

Yeah, I won't be alive for all those moons.

"Where's Alexa and Julie?" I ask, changing the subject.

I haven't even seen my best friends yet. Between dealing with Cooper, and trying to help get the show ready after being a slacker, I've yet to say hi.

"Oh, Alexa went to go grab me a couple of tacos. I'm starving 'cuz I forgot to eat. You might not have been doing the naked tango for hours, but I sure was." He nudges me, clicking his tongue.

"The Naked Tango?"

That's a new one from him.

"Horizontal Hustle? Although, sometimes we were vertical."

"Alright, enough out of you. That's my best friend you're talking about. But it doesn't explain where Julie is."

"Oh, she ran into someone she knew and I got them in the front row. She said she'll meet up here later."

An hour later we are finally getting to the last song of the night. Big Frank, who really is only 5'7" and a rail with some arms, approaches me. I met him only hours ago and he's the nicest guy. He'd given me a hug and told me it would be alright.

"You're needed on stage…" he says, pointing to the stage.

"What are you talking about?" I'm confused as hell. Cooper is in the middle of his last song of the set.

"Coop just told me to bring you on stage for the last song." He nudges me to the stage.

"This is the last song…"

I look around for Brody and he's nowhere in sight.

"Bonus number. Now go…" He grabs my shoulders and pushes me past the large black curtains. The bright lights are instantly blinding and the crowd is deafening as he finishes the last chords of "Runaway", his latest song.

Cooper catches me as I slowly walk to the middle of stage and smiles. The bass player, Van, whispers for me to wait a second, putting his arm around me to stop me.

Or maybe keeps me from falling because I'm a shaky, nervous mess. I've never liked being in front of crowds.

"What's going on?" I whisper-yell to Van.

"You'll see." He winks.

"I have one more for you all tonight. This song has never been heard before because I was saving it for someone special. So, you guys are the first." The crowd roars as Cooper moves to sit at the piano.

Our eyes meet and he waves me over. Van has to shove me to go. Under the heavy lights, I walk towards him, and he pats the seat next to him. I sit down beside him and he kisses my cheek.

"As a lot of you know, I married this beautiful woman about three months ago. I have something I want to tell her, so bear with me while I do that, because she's the reason behind this song," he tells the crowd, and they cheer wildly.

I'm blushing so hard my face feels as if it's on fire. I just want the stage to swallow me up.

What is he doing?

"Baby, you are my life. I look back and I don't know where I would be without you. Every moment with you has been special. I know the last week has been hard, and we had some people in our lives who wanted to keep us apart. I hate to admit that it could've almost happened, but please know I will never let anyone try to come between us again. My life begins and ends with you. I spent four years without you, and that was four years too long. You're everything to me." He gives me his winning smile before turning to the crowd and if I could see, I would think the swooning girls are melting. "I've been working on this new song for a while and you all will be the first to hear it. It's called 'I Found You'."

I FOUND *you*   *July 8th, 2006*

He covers his mic, leaning in to whisper in my ear. "This is for you…even though you're the one who truly found me again, the meaning is all the same…I love you." He kisses me gently on the lips, and then moves his hands to start playing the black and ivory keys on the piano. His sexy voice fills my ears as he starts singing the lyrics…

"You went away
I was lost
Lost without you

Our parents thought we were wrong
Never happy with our young love
Thought our love wasn't strong enough to survive.
They ripped us apart
When you went away
But you remained in my heart.

Then, like six years ago
I saw you in the crowd.
Looking so hot
Our eyes met and you had to know
You'd always be mine
Our story is something divine.
So with a kiss
I let you know, you were missed.
And we finally became one.

I found you
Made you my wife
I found you
To have, to hold, for the rest of my life.
Uh-huh,"

Erica Marselas

He looks down at me with a wink. I can't help the giggle that escapes my lips at his perfect Elvis Uh-huh impersonation in the song.

"We'll prove to them
They'll never win
You're mine forever
Because I found you

Back then we were up to no good
Remember when
We did all we could
To be together
No one else wanted us whole
We stayed out late
Jumped from planes.
We got tattoos
Branding your name on me
Showing everyone you are mine
And me as yours.

Then like a bad dream
You had to go.
We stayed in touch
Dreaming for when we see each other again.
The darkest day was when
The letters stopped
And our parents won
Breaking us apart
Breaking us—
Untillllll

I found you.
I found you.
To have to hold, for the rest of my life.
Uh-huh

I FOUND YOU   *July 8th, 2006*

We'll keep proving them wrong
We won't let them win
This time we'll conquer all
Because our love is all we need
Love led me back to you.
I found you
Made you my wife
I found you
To have, to hold, for the rest of my life.
Uh-huh, your mine forever
Because I found you."

He finishes playing the song and tears pour down my cheeks. Grabbing my face, he kisses me tenderly before helping me stand up. Suddenly there's a bunch of violets and red roses being thrown up to the stage. Holding my hands over my eyes, I can make out Julie, Alexa, and Brody throwing them. The audience is still cheering at us. I can only picture this will be hitting every media outlet in a few minutes.

With his arm still wrapped around me, he turns back to the audience. "Good Night, Tucson. Thank you for being a wonderful audience!" he yells and we walk off stage.

Once away from the deafening noise and the blinding lights, Cooper grabs me and pushes me up against the wall, kissing me frantically, and I return it just as eagerly. His erection is pushing into my stomach and I only hope he isn't going to take me *here*.

Because that really will be front page news.

In the distance, I hear the shrills of my two best friends, and we break apart. Julie and Alexa come flying into my arms to hug me, pulling me out of Cooper's hold.

"No, we weren't busy or anything…" Cooper laughs, giving me a wink before walking over to Brody, Van, and the other members of the band.

"I'm guessing it's all good now," Alexa asks, and I nod.

I'd told them what happened a couple of days earlier, and they'd both been shocked by the events. They had given me their ears to bend and I realized how much I'd missed seeing them. I wish I could pack them up so they could come with me. I'm sure Brody would be happy about Alexa hitting the road with him.

"Yeah, it's good."

Nothing like your man confessing his love, and singing to you on stage in front of a thousand people to help you forgive and maybe forget a little.

"I guess it would have to be the way you guys were necking a minute ago," Julie hoots and I shake my head laughing at her comment.

"Did you really use the word, *necking*?"

She scoffs mockingly, and waves her hand, "Yeah, so? Grandma uses it all the time. Chill. I'll make it cool again."

I look over at Cooper and I can tell he's getting a hard time from the guys. Our eyes meet and he excuses himself to come over to me.

"Why don't me and you go somewhere private?"

I nod, and tell the girls I'll see them in a little bit. Cooper maneuvers me into the green room off stage and locks the door behind us.

Instantly I'm being pulled into his arms and his tongue is invading my mouth once again. I moan, clawing at the back of his neck wanting more. His hand cups under my chin, breaking us apart.

"I love you, baby. We never really finished talking, or really didn't even start."

I'm so tired of talking about the same shit.
I just want to go back to kissing.

"Just promise me you will start trusting me, above

I FOUND you   *July 8th, 2006*

our mothers, tabloids, and any other assholes who try to get in our way. I'm sure after tonight I've made some enemies," I joke to lighten the mood, thinking about all those poor girls who were swooning in the audience, wishing they were me.

"I promise baby. I'm so sorry." He pulls me tighter into his arms. "I have no problem waiting 'till you're ready to have a baby. I shouldn't have even said anything. God, what if I didn't maybe she wouldn't have done what she did."

"Cooper…" I try to stop him.

"But just the thought of you round with my child does things to me. Then when my mom showed me those papers, I just thought…" He shakes his head so vigorously his face looks like a blur. I jump when his fist connects with the wall with a loud bang. "I'm so stupid. I should've known right away you wouldn't have done that…" He rambles again, repeating everything he said earlier, giving me a headache.

"Cooper... Stop." He's not listening to me at all as he keeps going. "But I want you to know when you're ready I want to have a bunch of kids with you, and I promise to take time off from the road. If I must go I'll figure out an easy way to be together, all of us. And I promise to keep our moms away from our children…I've cut my mom out of my life. I just want you…"

"Cooper… SHUT UP!" I yell. He looks at me finally, confusion marring his handsome face. He steps back slightly.

"If you're still mad…" I place my finger on his lips.

"Coop. Shut the hell up." I wrap my arm around his neck and kiss him with everything I have, needing to silence his running mouth. When I break away and he gives me a shy smile. "For one, thank you for the song. It was perfect and I loved it. Second, I love you so much, Cooper and this will be okay, I promise. I think we've said everything we can about this for now."

"I love you too." He breathes and pulls me onto the couch to sit on his lap. We both talk mindlessly about the past few days and what is going on for tonight, when suddenly his eyes light up, spiking my curiosity.

"What? I know that look, which tells me you're up to something."

"Nothing bad. I've just been thinking about something and I think it'll help us move on. Do you want to do something a little crazy tonight?"

"*Crazier* than when we got married on a whim?"

"No, it's not really crazy, more spontaneous really. Something we've done in the past and always wanted to do again."

"Like what?"

His thumb runs over my left hip bone where his name lies. "Something we should've done years ago."

"Tattoos?" Julie squeals behind me, as we enter the tattoo parlor. The sound of buzzing fills the air as a woman with raven hair lays on her stomach to the left of us, getting a tramp stamp etched on her back. "I thought we were getting food?"

"We are, but after this. There's something me and Cooper have to do first." I grin at my husband who has his hand laced with mine.

Julie and Alexa look at me confused and I tell them to trust me.

It's almost like my wedding night all over again. My two best friends, and my brother in law standing by our sides as Cooper and I make a different kind of lifelong commitment together; all while Collin and Tucker stand back to guard our spontaneous asses.

There are two artists ready to take us right away. Cooper and I had talked about what we wanted and where we wanted it. Who would have thought, big Frank is also an artist and drew out the design for us.

I flinch at the buzzing sound of the pen when it starts, remembering the sting from the first time I got a tattoo.

"I don't know how you can—*ouch*." Julie cringes when the needle hits my skin. "I'm screaming in pain for you." Julie recoils and she covers her eyes with both hands.

"You don't have to watch, Jules. I know you hate needles."

"I'm fine," she gasps out, continuing to cover her eyes.

"What I want to know is how we never saw his name on your hip. You're full of secrets, Vi. How long have you had that?"

"Um, like six years. You did see it once, but you were wasted and wanted to know why I would have a mini Cooper on my hip. Next morning you asked about a car on my hip and I said you were crazy." I grin and she gives me a snarl in return.

"You could've told me."

"Sorry," I say innocently. "I love ya though, but you know why now."

"I know." She pauses when I hiss through my teeth when the tattoo artist hits my hip bone. "Well, I was thinking of getting one, but seeing that look on your face, I've changed my mind."

"It's not that..." I yelp when he hits the bone again, "*bad...*"

"Almost done." The burly tattoo guy laughs at the pain he's inflicting. I glance over at Cooper who looks relaxed, as if he's taking a Sunday drive and not having a needle buzzed into his skin.

An hour later, I watch as he makes the final leaf on the branch and then wipes away the excess ink off my sore irritated skin. Cooper comes and sits next to me, comparing his matching one to mine

"It's perfect." I smile down at the black ink tattoos. They're trees, which look sprouted from our individual names. They have four branches with tiny leaves hanging off them. Written between the first branches it says 'Our Angel' with little wings around the word Angel and a halo around the O. The other branches have gaps, which are *reserved* for who is yet to come. In the stumps it reads, 'my love for him/her grows and creates.'

TWELVE

August 11th, 2003

Cooper

I've finished my album, "Blue Skies", after being signed to Wild Records five months ago. I'll be going on tour in a couple of weeks to headline for "Jason Torness" a major pop-rock star right now. If this goes well, by next summer I could be headlining my own tour. Today I'm at a photo studio taking promotional pictures. Tomorrow I'm doing full TV and radio tours to promote the album and the first single, "My Everything."

The song I wrote for her.

My mind always wanders to Violet and I can't help wondering what she's doing right now. Has she heard the song on the radio? Is she thinking about me? Would she try to come see me on tour? Hell, is she still with that punk who had his hands all over her?

With a sudden urge to see her face, I pull out my wallet. Stuck between the plastic photo protector, her gorgeous face smiles at me. I miss her all the time. A month ago, I tried calling her and the house number had been changed. I have no idea if she tried calling me since that fateful day I last saw her. I had ended up washing my phone in the washer, forgetting to take it out in my rage.

Leave it to the phone company to not allow me to

have the same number since my dad made me get my own plan.

I sent her one last letter, with the lyrics to "My Everything" hoping she would respond, and when I got nothing in return, I knew at that moment that I really had to let go.

But I don't want to let go.

I can't let go. I'll carry a piece of her wherever I go forever. We share something together only we understand. She'll be stuck with me forever, no matter how much I want to let her go.

I only wish she was standing next to me right now.

"She would be proud of you right now, you know?" Brody tells me, pulling me out of the long dark tunnel of my thoughts.

"I know..." I shove my wallet back in my pocket, hating that I've been caught staring at her, again. I can't think of her right now. I have to stay focused, because now I have to go look pretty for the camera.

Twenty minutes later, I'm standing in front of a blue backdrop, my shirt is gone, and I'm only wearing a pair of torn jeans.

What this has to do with my album beats me.

The bright lights are blinding, along with each flash the photographer takes as he tells me how to pose; brooding, pouting, smile, and so on.

"Is that a tattoo?" the photographer yells out to me. He's pointing to my hip, where Violet's name proudly rests. Always

"Yeah?"

He turns to my PR agent, Louie, and they whisper something I can't hear. After some back and forth, Louie tells him to keep clicking, before looking at me. "We'll just have to airbrush it off afterwards...No worries," he tells me.

No worries? Who the fuck was worried?

I FOUND *you*   **August 11th, 2003**

"Why can't we keep it?" I yell back. I want Vi to see it, if she sees these, to know I still love her.

He doesn't answer me, and it ticks me off. I'm sure it has something to do with my image with my female fans. I decide to just shake it off and pose for the damn camera.

This will take some getting used to.

After a million and one *pictures, I put my clothes back on, ready to get the fuck out of here.*

"Coop!" Brody comes running over to me excitedly. He stops in front of me with a paper in his hand, waving it around in my face like a flag. "Fuck, guess what?"

"I don't know...what?" I'm trying to match whatever this excitement is, but I'm beat and annoyed as fuck.

"Guess who has the number one single on Billboard?" He hands me the paper which is a fax from the record company. I scan it over and there it is in black and white, my name next to my song, in the number one spot.

"You're fucking with me!"

"Nope. Max just sent this over. He got it early and wanted to tell ya. Congrats man." He pats my shoulder.

"Hey, this is much as you, Brody."

"Yeah, you owe me that car now." He punches my shoulder and I shake my head. His birthday is next week and I already ordered it. The cherry red Lamborghini he always wanted.

My car isn't even as nice, but I owe my brother almost everything for helping me get here.

And well...

Her.

"Do you think she's heard it?" The lovesick teenager I am comes spewing out of my mouth.

Brody narrows his eyes at me. "Are you for real? Unless she's started listening to heavy metal. She's heard it. I bet anytime she turns on the damn radio, she'll fucking hear it. Listen, why don't you..."

I hold up my hand to stop him. I know what he's going to say. "She stopped writing me first. I just want her happy, Brody, and if that's without me..."

"She never said those words, her mother did."

"I know what I saw. Come on, I have a few things to get ready for the tour and I need your help." *I want to drop the conversation.*

She'll always be mine, but I did have to set her free. If it's meant to be, we will find each other again. I know it.

October 5th, 2006
Cooper

The tour is on break for two days as we travel by bus to New York after finishing a show in Atlanta. I woke up early, not being able to go back to sleep despite the warm body next to me. I'm wired from singing ten straight shows.

I'm sitting in the front of the bus, reading through the letters Vi wrote me years ago. I can't believe my mother actually held onto all of these. I've been trying to read a couple a day, but I keep getting distracted. Or maybe it's because they get more heartbreaking the further I dig into them. Now, as I read the final one I can picture her pain as she wrote it. Each word is like a kick to the gut, and it's hard not to think of all the hurt that could've been avoided.

Dear Coop,

I hate that you won't answer me. Your phone is disconnected and it feels as though you threw me away without warning. Why couldn't you tell me it's over between us? Send a freakin' carrier pigeon for fuck's sake. Just <u>TELL</u> me.

I mean, didn't your parents ever tell you to use your words?

You know, for a while I kept thinking something horrible happened to you, then I got real, and knew you were just fine.

Fine without me, right?

I would call your house, but what's the point? You won't be there.

You're a big star now. As much as I'm happy for you, it hurts because now anytime I turn on the radio I hear your voice. It shatters me because I have this lingering 'what if' about us.

I had hoped after everything we've been through you would've dropped me a line telling me your dream came true.

To be honest, I don't know why I'm bothering writing you again. I stopped months ago when my heart finally ripped its final threads.

But I find myself not being able to get over you. No matter how many letters go unanswered or phone calls never connect, know I'll always love you, Cooper. I hope you know it even if you think I did something wrong... or even if you have moved on.

Maybe I'm hoping this will get tangled in your fan mail and you'll finally give me the answers I need. Tell me it's over so I have a chance to move past you.

It's bad enough I have your name inked on me so I'll always remember you. Because unlike you, we can't all get rid of it or the memory it holds.

This will be the last time I'll sign with the name which used to make me soar and the last time I write you.

Just know I wish you well. You have earned your success.

Bye.
(Your) Ace (or at least I used to be)

I fold the final letter back up and put it back in the box. I push my hands through my hair, and no matter how much I try not to let the words affect me, they do. Violet

I FOUND YOU   October 5th ,2006

told me to stop reading, but I think I'm a glutton for punishment. I stuff the shoebox back under the bench and try to remember they have no effect on us now what-so-ever.

We found each other again and got our second chance.

So, stop thinking about the past, Coop.

My phone rings with and Louie's name pops up on my caller ID. What the hell is he doing calling me at this hour?

"Hello?"

"Hey, Coop. Umm, I don't know if you noticed yet, but your wife made the tabloid news this morning?"

"My wife?" I question, wondering what the hell he's talking about? She's been with me all week, "When, and doing *what*?"

"Sometime last night it seems, maybe during the show? She was at a pharmacy. If you don't know you might want to see for yourself. Check TMZ."

"Is it bad?" I pull out my laptop from under one of the couch seats and plug it in. "It'll take me forever to get my computer loaded up and hooked up to the Wi-Fi hotspot."

"No. Listen if it isn't true, it'll go away. If it is, you might find yourself hounded a little more…"

"Can't you just spill? Geez, you're talking around in circles and I get that enough from fucking Brody." I groan as I type in my password to log into the Wi-Fi.

"When you see it you'll know why. But also, you might want to go talk to your wife," he adds firmly, sounding like my father. "Call me back if you need anything."

We say our goodbyes and I'm left scratching my head.

Once I get everything finally loaded I go to TMZ's website.

On the front page is a grainy picture of Violet in a store grabbing something off the shelf. Below, the headline knocks me backward.

IS VIOLET REID PREGNANT?

Violet Reid, wife of Cooper Reid, was seen inside an Atlanta Pharmacy, picking out—you guessed it— pregnancy tests. Not just one, but five different types. A customer captured the pictures above. The new wife of the Grammy Award Winner was by herself at the time, which makes us wonder if Reid knows about this nighttime adventure in the middle of his concert. I guess only time will tell if there's a little Reid on the way. TMZ is now on Baby Watch!

I click through another two big tabloid sites, saying the same things. I zoom in on the picture and indeed I'm looking at my wife reaching for a pregnancy test.

Why didn't she tell me? And why the fuck didn't she take Tucker with her?

I shut the laptop down and make my way to the back of the bus. Along the way, I pass Brody snoring like a freight train in his bunk. Violet is lying in bed with the covers up to her neck, looking peaceful. She told me she didn't feel good yesterday morning, but I would've never guessed it could have been morning sickness.

Why wouldn't she tell me she thought she could be pregnant?

After our *fight* and she joined me on tour, we found someone to talk to about our loss. It's helped a lot for both of us to get everything out at once. And last month we'd started trying. I didn't think it would happen *this* fast.

With a deep breath, I move to the bed and sit on the

I FOUND *you*   **October 5th ,2006**

edge beside her. I brush her hair back with my fingers and her eyes flutter open. A sweet sleepy smile spreads across her face. "Hi."

"Hey, we need to talk about something…"

"Now? Can't you come and snuggle in here with me? It's so early." She hums and reaches out her arm for me.

"Is there something you need to tell me?" I blurt out the words refusing to get distracted by the warmth and softness I'll find under those covers with her.

She looks at me curiously, her eyebrows knitting together. "No? I don't think?"

"Where did you go last night?" I try a different tactic and watch as she instantly pales.

"The pharmacy?" She sits up on the bed and wraps the blankets to her chest, chomping down on her lip.

I close my eyes and pinch the bridge of my nose, wondering why she's giving me the runaround. So, I'll do it for her. "Vi, you were all over the internet this morning buying pregnancy tests. Why the hell wouldn't you tell me?" The urgency in my voice bites a little rougher than I was expecting it too, causing her to flinch.

Okay, Coop, calm down. Take a deep breath.

Her head drops and she pulls the covers tighter. "Sorry. I was going to tell you."

I lean my forehead against hers, laying a kiss on her nose, trying to convey to her that I'm not mad. Her grip on the covers relaxes telling me she got the message.

"Why didn't you tell me when you went out and bought them?"

"Because I was scared. I went during the show just in case they came up negative. I didn't want to get your hopes up. Not after everything, and we've only started trying," she mumbles.

My heart drops, and I reach out to touch her face in a way to comfort us both. She's not screaming she's pregnant so it only means… "Were they?"

She shrugs, her glassy eyes dart to my face. "I don't know. I didn't take them. I was too scared they'll come up negative. When I noticed I missed my period, it was the first time I thought I *really* want this now and this was our time. I want a baby with you. And for once, the fear of what could happen doesn't freak me out as much. I think talking to someone finally helped."

Grabbing her face, I push my lips to hers, forcing my tongue into her mouth. She moans against my me, her fingers immediately finding my hair, to pull me closer, both of us expressing how we feel for one another through this heated, passionate, needy kiss.

I don't think there are enough words to express how elated I feel knowing she's ready for this next step. My wife, my baby, our family.

The way it was meant to always be.

I break away, leaving small pecks on her lips before I completely separate from her.

"Do you think we should, um, take them? Now?" she asks.

"Yes. And no matter what we can keep trying if they're not positive. It's half the fun, right?" I push a long strand of her hair behind her ear.

"Yeah, it is, but I still just want to wing it. No planning days or hanging by my feet to help it…trickle down to the egg."

I shake my head as I try not to laugh. *Trickle down?*

"Why don't we see what they say first? Then go from there before we worry about *that*?"

I stand outside the bathroom, waiting for Vi to take

one of the tests she bought. When I hear the toilet flush, a sweat breaks out on my forehead, anxiously awaiting the results. The door opens and she steps outside, holding the handle.

"So?" I step closer to her, my heart beating faster when her eyes say nothing. If it was yes she'd be shouting.

"It said to wait five minutes." She bites her finger and glances back at the test laying on the sink.

"Five?" That's a fucking lifetime.

"Yeah, I didn't want to stand there looking at them. You might have to tell me."

"Alright love birds, you don't need to canoodle by the bathroom." Brody brushes by us and removes Violet's hand from the handle.

"Do you mind?" I growl at him.

He turns back to me and flips me off. "I have to drain the fucking hose, bastard. Give me a minute." He steps into the bathroom and closes the door. I roll my eyes annoyed. At least we're waiting anyways.

Or I might have kicked his ass.

I take Violet's hand and pull her to my chest, my back leaning against the wall, to hold us steady. My hand travels down her face and she gives me a small smile.

"You okay?" I ask.

"Uh-huh. Nervous." She lays her head on my chest and takes a deep breath. "You're nervous too. Your heart is beating out of your chest."

"I am. But I have a good feeling. The only thing is, if you're pregnant, we can't go anywhere without Collin or Tucker." I pull her back and look her dead in the eye. "Actually even if you aren't it goes the same. They'll wonder for a while and I don't want to find out in a tabloid again."

She twists her lips annoyed. "Fine. If I have too." I bend down to kiss her when the bathroom door opens back up. Both of our heads turn to Brody who is smiling too wide for it to be simple relief from 'draining the hose'.

"Hey, do those two pink lines mean I'm going to be an uncle?" He points his thumb back towards the bathroom.

"There are...two…?" Violet stutters and Brody nods. She turns to me, squealing into my arms. "We're having a baby."

"We're having a baby." I hug her tight and lift her off the ground.

I stand her back up and take her face in my hands to kiss her. "You okay?" My eyes search hers. I know she's doing better, but I know it doesn't mean the *thoughts* and the *memory* don't peek in once in a while.

"Yeah. For right now, at least. This is—" She trails off and Brody clears his throat, drawing our attention to him.

"Um, you guys didn't already know?" He looks curiously between us.

"No, you shoved us out of the way you brute." Violet shoves his shoulder.

"Well, I had to pee and you were in the way." He shrugs. "*Butttt* congrats. Though you shouldn't be surprised with the way you two go at it. Eli says you two make the bus hard to drive because you're rocking it so damn much." Wiggling his eyebrows he slaps me on the shoulder. "This is gonna be awesome. I plan on teaching them *'Brody's Guide to Driving Their Parents Insane'*."

"Yeah, you have that mastered, you don't need the training guide." I roll my eyes and take Vi's hand. "Now if you don't mind, we're going to go rock the bus some more, so don't come a knocking."

"Oh my god." Violet groans, "Really? You had to add that to what he said."

"Um yeah? Now come, wife." I smack her ass and drag her towards the back of the bus, where I plan to have my dirty way with her.

I FOUND you   ***October 5th, 2006***

"I'll tell Eli to hold on for another bumpy ride," Brody yells and I close the door behind us.

We arrived in New York several hours ago and settled into the Marriott in Times Square for the night. The plan was to go out tonight with the crew, but it seems my wife has other plans for me.

And so does Violet's phone, which has been ringing nonstop for the last ten minutes. She keeps telling me to ignore it, but the ringing isn't helping me keep it up.

Not being able to take it anymore, I reach for the phone on the nightstand. Violet stays latched around me as I shift, kissing the inside of my neck, her dripping core moving up and down my achy shaft.

When I see the name on the caller ID, it isn't who I expected it to be and answer, wanting to have a little fun with the person on the other end.

"Violet Reid's phone. She can't talk right now, she's too busy sucking her husband's dick."

"Cooper!" Violet whacks my chest and reaches for the phone, probably thinking it's Brody.

"Put my daughter on the phone right now, Reid," my monster-in-law barks like the bitch she is. Violet freezes for a second, but can't control the small giggle that leaves her lips.

"Sorry, I had to," I say covering the microphone, giving her a wink.

It was too good to pass up, especially after what happened in Arizona last time. I see the spark of remembrance in my baby's eyes and I know she wants to play too—and not very nicely either.

"Put her on speaker," Violet whispers in my ear and I can practically feel her smirk against my neck.

I hit the speaker button and I swear the bitch is growling while she waits.

"Fuck, Cooper..." Violet moans loudly. She's wigging her core on my dick, making me groan in response. I'm not sure if it's for added effect, or to torture me as well, but I'll take it.

"You feel so good, Ace..."

"God, I love you..." she screams, adding to the over exaggerated passionate noises.

"Violet Harper cut that shit out. We need to talk!" Amber bellows, and I swear even through the phone she's shaking the walls with her anger.

"I'm...busy...and there's nothing to talk about." She fake whimpers, and stops rocking on my cock.

"There's lots to talk about, Violet. I read you're pregnant! You're too damn young to have a baby, and you don't want to have a baby with him. He'll just fuck it up like he's fucking up your life now."

"Excuse me?" I growl and Vi puts her hand over my mouth, telling me to hush.

"Who said I was pregnant?" she asks casually.

If I could stop the media, we might avoid the wicked witch from ever knowing.

"I saw you buying those tests in the tabloids."

"Oh, they could've been for anyone. But if I was, what should I do? *Get an abortion?*" she hisses through her teeth.

Amber is silent and Violet continues. "I mean I already had one before right?"

"Vi—" she starts and Vi screeches telling her to shut up.

"Don't even try to play me, Mother. I know all about the papers you made and what you told Evelyn. How could you do something so vile to your own daughter? I

I FOUND you   **October 5th, 2006**

don't care about your messed up reasons. What you did hurt me. Do you even care? Did you enjoy your sick game?" Violet seethes, and her chest heaving with anger.

"Ace," I whisper, while Amber remains quiet. The phone drops to the bed and I maneuver myself to sit up, taking Violet with me to cradle her body in my lap. "Try to breathe, she's not worth it."

The bitch doesn't deserve any of her energy. My hand rubs her back and I feel her relax, but it hasn't killed her fight.

Hell, who am I kidding? She needs this. Get her baby.

Violet picks up the fallen phone, the line still connected. "Do you have nothing to say?"

"I did what I had to do. I'm only trying to protect you. I mean how many celebrity marriages work? I can tell you about one in a million. He'll leave you with nothing after he cheats on you and you get ripped apart by the public."

I can't contain the growl that leaves my throat. I'm so sick of this bitch assuming I would ever do something like cheat on her or leave her. I'm going to get enough bullshit from the media, and her mother should be the last person filling her head with that bullshit.

Vi grabs my hand and squeezes, the same deep throaty growl leaving her throat. "That's never going to fucking happen, Mother. And you know what? Such is life, and it's a lesson I'll have to deal with if it happens, but guess what, it won't because Cooper and I have something different and always have."

"You're so damn blind, Violet. Always had your damn head in the clouds," her mother spits out. "You needed to see how quickly the boy would leave you. I was pissed when Evelyn said she had enough of trying to get you to leave him, so I had to step up." It's like I almost hear her evil leer over the phone.

"Fucking bitch," I mumble, gripping my wife's hips.

"Step up?" Violet laughs sarcastically. "Oh, you're brilliant, Mother. So, when that failed what else would you have you tried to do?"

"I was certain it would have worked, but I was waiting for Evelyn to put it into motion…" she snarls, "I should've known when I didn't hear from her she'd fucked it up. Giving you both a chance to confirm they were wrong."

"The only person who fucked up is you, Mother. I want nothing to do with you. You're no longer a mother to me. I lost her a long time ago."

"He was and is fucking up your life. I'll stand by it," Amber yells.

Vi blows out a large puff of air, annoyed. "Change the fucking record, Mother. Your reasons for not wanting us together are dated because they happened seven years ago. You keep telling me he's going to fuck up my life, yet as we figured out months ago, you are the only one fucking it up. You took the bribe money and you broke my heart countless times. And to get what out of me? I want you to just stay out of my life."

"I am your mother."

"I. HATE. YOU." Violet bellows and her whole body tightens. Her cheeks are bright red, heated from her anger, and when I put my hand on them, I swear they burn me. "I want nothing to do with you. I told you at the Ball I wanted nothing to do with you. I thought you got the point finally when you haven't called me in four months. But here you are again putting in your two cents. Now this is the last time I'm going to say this. Stay out of my life or I'll be forced to take drastic measures."

"Oh? Like what?" Her mother challenges with a bitter hiss, but there's a hint of fear in her voice.

My wife's lips lift maliciously, and her eyes dance savagely. "Wouldn't you like to know? I got lucky; my

I FOUND YOU　　　　　　　　　　　**October 5th, 2006**

husband is famous with huge bodyguards who will protect me from anybody threatening me. His father was a respected lawyer and I'm sure I can get a restraining order, so if you come close to me, I'll have you arrested. Oh, and let's not forget his grandfather is a pretty powerful person. So, just do yourself a favor and stay away from me. Forever."

Lacking any kind of dramatic effect Violet hits the end button, so instead, she screams and throws the phone against the wall, where it breaks into three pieces.

I grip her shoulders and rub them, feeling the tension under my palms. Slowly with each knead and light kisses to her neck, her breathing begins to steady and her body relaxes. She's not crying, just staring ahead, silently at the wall.

"I'm here, baby," I whisper, not knowing what else to say.

She turns around in my arms and straddles my lap. Her breasts squish into my chest and she buries her face into my neck. "I hate her," she murmurs. "You think she'll stay away? I need her to stay away."

"I hope so, but we'll deal with it then if we have to, or we can do something now if you really want to."

Her head lifts, a somber look in her blue eyes. "I don't want to think about her anymore. She only keeps proving how unhappy she wants me to be. That's not what a mother does." Her eyes close and she takes a deep, shaky breath. "And the last thing I need is this stress, right?" Giving me a small smile, she grabs my hand and places it on her belly where our baby is growing.

Our baby.

"No stress." I kiss her gently and look her straight in the eye, "but you'd tell me if you are, right?"

"Yeah, I promise. I cut my mom out of my heart months ago. Now I just need to shut her off in my brain. Doesn't mean she won't pop up from time to time, but I'm not going to let what she's done cause me tears or pain. You're right, she's not worth it."

I really wish I could serve the bitch on a platter.

My mother seems to be trying, but I'm not ready to talk to her yet. She texts me all the time telling me to have a great show or that she loves me, but I would never forgive myself if I let my mom get back in and it ends up being some bigger plan for later.

This time around, for sure, it's me and Vi, against the world. Hopefully with a couple extra little people in our arms.

"I really am alright, Coop. I've been waiting to tell her off since it happened. Now that I did it's like the weight of the world is off my shoulders. If anything, through all of this I learned a valuable lesson."

"What's that?"

"Our children are going to be free to love whoever they want. Make their own mistakes. Let them enjoy their lives, and be whoever they want to be, but most of all we need to talk to them. Listen to them. I refuse to be like my mother."

"Well, when it comes to our daughter, I'm taking after your dad." I laugh and repeat back one of the many threats her dad had used on me, "*Reid. If you ever hurt my daughter, I'll hunt you down with whatever weapon I have and you'll wish you never lived.*"

"Of course you will." She presses her lips to my dimple. "You know what I just realized?" she hums.

"What's that?"

She gives me a bright smile. "Today is the first day we met all those years ago. The day sits in my mind forever, but it didn't click 'till now. It was our true beginning and now we're starting another chapter on the same day. How freakin' odd is that?"

"That is *freakin'* odd." I teasingly mock her because she never just uses the word fuck, well unless she's super

I FOUND YOU   **October 5th, 2006**

pissed. I give her back an equally bright smile. "Meant to be..." my words drift off.

October fifth: who would've known the day I saved her life, we'd also make new life years later? Something you think only happens in movies, is playing out in real life.

Taking her with me again, I lie back on the bed and cuddle her in my arms. I brush her hair back with one hand and the other covers her belly. "We should probably get you in to see someone soon for the baby."

"For what?" Her head shoots up, her eyes widen with a worry which is washing away the dark look she had moments ago.

"Just to confirm and find out our next steps. We'll have to get you some prenatal vitamins and figure out how many times you have to see a doctor, you know to plan it around being on the road. Also, if we need to do anything when we go overseas. Shots and stuff."

Once Violet told me she was ready to start trying, I'd lived in a sea of Google searches and baby books. Most of the shit scared the crap at me. There's so much that can go wrong, and I'm trying to learn everything I can to be prepared.

Instead, it's freaking me out.

"Oh...yeah." Her head falls back on my shoulder. "Good point. I want to do everything right."

"When do you think we should tell people?"

"Um, when we know for sure. Also, I think I heard after fourteen weeks is the best time...you know. We'll see though because I can't tell you why, but I have a good feeling about this baby." Her hand covers mine on her stomach. She smiles, a smile I've genuinely never seen as bright as when it came to talking about having kids. "I expected when we got a positive result I would be freaking out. I am a little. The worry has been trying to seep in for hours and I'm sure it will once in a while.

Despite everything, it feels right."

I'm going to be on my knees every night, praying nothing goes wrong and we have this baby.

"Our Angel, I think, will make sure of it." She pauses, snuggling in closer to me. I press my lips to her forehead and when I glance at her she's grinning, looking peacefully in thought.

Then out of the blue, she starts to giggle.

I shake my head at her sudden change of mood. I wonder if I have to worry about these mood swings already. "What is it, random girl?"

"I was just thinking, but we might have to duct tape Brody's mouth. It wouldn't surprise me if the whole crew knows by now. Especially, if he's taking shots. Actually, we might have to tell Alexa and Julie, because I doubt he'll be able to keep it from Alexa."

"I'm sure Brody will keep his mouth shut. I made sure he will," I say nonchalantly and kiss the top of her head.

"What did you do to him now?"

"I haven't done anything to him." Vi playfully glares at me, telling me, 'yeah right'. I dramatically blow out a breath of air. "Fine. I told him I would chili pepper his Toilet Paper and jizz in his shampoo then put the aftermath on YouTube. No biggie."

She shakes her head, rolling her eyes to the ceiling. "God, who needs kids when I already have two."

I laugh at her annoyance. "To have someone on your side against us?"

"Yeah right. Then I better keep them away from you two then."

"I'll behave. I mean, around our child. Don't worry." I lie, knowing I'll just be glad to have an extra hand to teach my tricks to when they get older.

"Uh-huh. I don't believe you." Violet rolls herself on top of me, straddling my hips. "But it's okay because I have a few tricks up my sleeve for when you misbehave." Her fingers pull roughly on my hair before she sinks herself down on my waiting shaft.

    Everything else around us is forgotten for now.

Erica Marselas

October 12th, 2006
Cooper

My phone buzzes and dances on the table while Violet, Brody, and I dig into our bowls of *Cap'n Crunch*. Brody had kept my childhood favorite hoarded for himself, only for Vi to find it while searching for any type of food she could stomach. Violet suddenly can't stand the smell of eggs, or anything lately, so we're eating the old favorite I haven't had since *I* was a kid.

"You should answer it," Violet says pointing her silver spoon at my phone.

"Why?" I shrug, not interested in talking to the person on the other end. The buzzing stops and a few seconds later it buzzes once more, telling me I have a voicemail.

"Because you should. She's your mother and she's trying. I don't expect you to hug it out or forgive her right away, but I know you want to hear what she has to say. I'd do almost anything to hear my mother utter the words, *'I'm sorry'*, even if I tell her to fuck off after." She shrugs and circles her spoon around in her bowl.

I remain silent and stuff a large spoonful of cereal in my mouth. As I chew I stare at the phone, contemplating my next move. Part of me does want to reach out to her, another part of me is screaming it's a trap.

"I'll be the first to say what she did was fucked up," Brody pipes in, mid-bite, with a red cereal berry and milk dripping off his spoon. "But she knows you and jellybean here might be carrying an actual jellybean now, so she's desperate to make things right. Can't blame her." He shoves the spoon in his mouth, completing his comment.

"Did you tell her?" My eyes narrow at my brother, unable to keep the sudden irritation out of voice.

Brody glares at me. "No," he snaps, his mouth still full as he talks. "Did you forget about the tabloids, dude?"

"Close your mouth," I cover his mouth to avoid particles of red and blue hitting my face. "I don't want to wear your breakfast."

He knocks my hand away and I watch him swallow. "Just talk to her because she's driving me crazy trying to get information out of me about you two and asking how you're doing." He pauses, scooping more cereal on his spoon. "Listen. It's been three months now, she's sorry, you're having a baby, and frankly, I have a permanent headache because of it."

"I'll think about it," I grumble and stand up. Picking up my bowl I throw it in the sink, willing this conversation to end. "Now, can we talk about something else?"

"We can talk about how you're going to rinse that bowl out before I cut you," Violet jabs her finger in my direction, narrowing her eyes at me.

The thing is, she probably will if I don't. Unrinsed dishes drive her crazy.

Note to self: Make sure to stay on her good side with her pet peeves when the pregnancy hormones fully kick in.

"Yes, ma'am." I salute her, as a soggy piece of *Cap'n Crunch* hits me right between the eyes. Her and Brody are laughing at her direct hit.

Abandoning the bowl in the sink, I march the four steps to my wife and grab her hand, pulling her from her seat.

Her eyes dance in amusement while my hand runs down her face, down her arm, and rest on her ass before I lay a nice hard smack to it. She yelps with a giggle.

"Maybe I should give you your birthday spanking early this year." I grab a handful of her luscious ass and yank her to my chest.

"Can't I just have extra?" Her eyes flutter as her tongue darts out of her mouth wetting her lips.

"Oh, come on. I'm right here and I'm eating," Brody groans. "I don't need morning sickness either."

"Shut up," I flip him off and he flips me off right back.

"Will you two behave for one minute?" She grabs my finger and folds it down, tucking it back into my fist. "Now, tell me what we're doing for my birthday?" She gives me her most radiant smile.

"I'm not telling you."

"Please." She folds her hands together, giving me large doe eyes, and a cute pout with her bottom lip puffed out.

I laugh, and push her lip back in, shaking my head. "Not happening, you'll just have to be surprised."

We're going to be in Seattle on her birthday, so I made plans to take her to the space needle for lunch and then to the Ferris wheel. I do have a show that night, but afterward, we're going to a club I rented out, and Alexa and Julie will be joining us as well.

What I really should do is return the favor of throwing a cake in her face on stage like she did on my birthday two months ago, but I want to live.

"I think I have ways of making you talk…" She purrs and runs her hands up my chest, her lips making contact with the bottom of my chin.

"Seriously you guys, I'm right here. And don't even think of running off, we have to get to the radio station for your interview in twenty minutes." Brody stands up and moves to throw his bowl in the sink.

He doesn't wash it out and walks toward his bunk.

"Brody Daniel Reid," Violet snarls, leaving my

I FOUND YOU *October 12th, 2006*

arms, to chase after him, "I'm going to hurt you."

"Good," he retorts, ducking for cover as a pillow comes at his head. "My ears and my eyes will appreciate it."

And she tells us we're the ones who act like children. But now I'm left pouting, knowing I'm not getting laid anytime soon.

With sound check finished, I head to the green room for some water and to chill before the show starts. Last I saw my wife, she was in the pit talking to one of the promoters, while Brody handled the opening act.

I think my favorite part about this is that every show's opening act is a winner from the area's Battle of the Band's contest. Everyone should get a chance at the limelight. I mean it's how I got my start, though my mother storming on stage is what made me memorable to my record producers.

And as if she knew I was thinking about her, my phone pings, lighting up the screen with a text.

Mother: **Have a good show. Love you.**

As always, simple and to the point.

I have about thirty minutes 'till the show starts and I figure if I'm ever going to do this, I might as well do it when I can quickly get her off the phone.

Finding her name, I hit the call button. It rings once before she answers, with a large amount of uncertainty in her voice. "Cooper?"

"It's me. I thought…" I trail off and look around the

empty green room, hoping it will give me an answer, "maybe I'd say hi."

"Hi." She sniffles, and I wonder if she's crying about a phone call.

Though, maybe I would feel the same way if my children stopped talking to me—even if I deserved the silent treatment.

Which is never going to happen. I'll earn my father of the year cup, every year.

It's silent for a moment on both ends, and I realize I should say something, but she jumps the gun, taking the next step. "How are you? Don't you have a show soon?" Her words tumble out of her mouth so fast they sound more like one long Mary Poppins word.

"I'm fine and yes, soon. I just know you've been trying to reach me and I've been…"

"Avoiding…" she answers for me. "I know, and I don't blame you. I only wanted to keep trying, to let you know I'm sorry and that I'm not giving up 'till I show you I want you and Violet to be happy."

My hands push through my hair, willing my mind to believe the sincerity in her voice. Violet believes she's genuine and she hasn't done anything to show otherwise. Brody thinks she's finally returned to the mother I used to know as a kid, but does it mean I should try to forget everything that happened?

Why can't I be more like Violet and let shit go easier?

"Cooper?" She interrupts my inner battle, "listen, I don't expect your forgiveness and I'll never be able to say sorry enough, but with that being said I want to be there for you now and show you I can be the mother you always needed…" She breathes heavily through the line, just as the green room door opens.

"Hold on a sec," I tell her and drop the phone from my ear as Violet comes barreling into the room. Her strawberry hair sways and her subtly larger boobs bounce,

I FOUND YOU   **October 12th, 2006**

as she makes her way over to me. She's all smiles as she wraps her arms around my neck, kissing my cheek.

"We have ten minutes before Fingerpunch comes on." Her blue eyes light up with a mischievous glint and she wiggles her eyebrows. I lightly chuckle in response. She knows ten minutes isn't nearly enough time to satisfy each other.

"Yeah, and?" I ask awaiting her smartass comment.

"Thought we could you *know? Maybe* go on a 7-11 run to get some hot dogs and ho-hos. I'm feeling the need for some meat and cream." Her hand runs down my chest and I shake my head at her comment.

"You've been hanging out with Brody too long." I smirk, lifting her chin and kiss her softly on the lips. "As fun as it all sounds, I'm on the phone with my mother."

Her gorgeous eyes widen and she steps back from me. "You could've told me *that* first."

"Sorry. You know I don't think clearly when you're in the room." I wink at her and she smacks me in the chest.

"Jerk. I'll see you out in ten and be nice. Oh and if she asks about—you know," her hand circles her belly, "you can tell her if you want, but hurry, we got a show to do."

She starts to walk away and I grab her hand, pulling her back before she can get out the door. "Stay."

Her eyes search mine curiously and she nods. "Alright." She cuddles into my side and I bring the phone back to my ear.

My mother is chuckling on the other end and I can't help wonder what she thinks is so funny.

"You were saying?" I snap, and her laughter fades.

"I'm sorry, it's just, you might be right about her hanging out with Brody too much." I instantly soften and glance at my wife who leans on my shoulder, as she listens in on the conversation.

"It's the price I pay to have them with me. I'll reel her

back in after the tour," I jest, surprising myself by talking to her so...*casually*.

"Ha!" Violet remarks into my arm.

"Maybe a tab inappropriate for my ears, but refreshing to hear you two goof around. Your father and I used to be like that."

I don't say anything as she wistfully remembers a time where she might have been fun. But time is a wasting. I open my mouth to say something when she speaks again.

"Anyways, as I was saying before, I want to make up for not being there for you, and be what you need now. I only hope I'm not too late."

I look down at Violet for help. She keeps telling me to let her back in, but I don't know how to trust her again.

I've never felt more confused than I do now on what is right or wrong.

"Don't look at me," Violet smirks. Her hand sweeps through my hair, keeping my attention on her, which tells me she really has something else to say. "*Buttt*...at the end of the day, she's trying, and I for myself want it to be better and behind us. Also, think of your dad and your brothers. All this affects them too. I was lucky and no one else was affected by my mother being a witch, but think about what you will miss with them if you can't be in the same room with her."

Glancing down at her flat belly, I know it will be easier to release my grudge because I have no doubt my brothers and my father are going to want to be around the baby all the time. Also, do I let her in for my kids' sake too? So, they don't have any worries or questions about why their parents dislike their grandmother?

Warm hands grab my face and wet pouty lips kiss me gently on the mouth. "You heard how my mother acted the other day; she's a person who is worth hating and cutting out. Your mom, well, I think she's earning her

I FOUND You **October 12ᵗʰ, 2006**

second chance. One day at a time. *Though,* it doesn't mean I don't have my guard up," she says pointedly and glances at the phone, making sure my mother heard her.

"You're not too late," I mumble, still questioning my sanity, "but only because I'm trusting my wife, and if she's willing, then I guess I have to be too."

"I should've always seen how good she was for you, and how she kept you in line. I wish I saw it before, but I see it now." I swear I can hear her smile over the phone. "She's also going to be a great mom for your children, Coop."

Violet chuckles at my mom's blatant innuendo. I'm actually surprised it took her this long to make any comment about it to me.

"I'm guessing you've seen the tabloids then?"

"I have, but also from *before* when I assumed…" The words drift off, but she doesn't need to finish them—I know.

I close my eyes tightly, pinching the bridge of my nose, remembering the things I said to Vi, believing those stupid papers. Violet's fingers dance along the back of my neck and I try to push myself out of the dark thoughts.

"It's fine. I really would like to forget that day for as long as I live."

"It's not fine. It will never be fine, Cooper. Just know I think you both will be great parents, well if it's true…" She probes again and I groan, covering my hand with the phone.

"I can still lie. She doesn't *need* to know, yet."

"Just tell her, because when you tell your dad, he's not going to keep it from her. Think of it as a test of her trust."

"It is, but we're not telling anyone else 'till the time is right," I grunt, though I almost feel lighter to finally tell someone else the news.

I really would love to tell the world, shout it from

rooftops, but that's never going to happen.

"I understand. Congratulations. Just know if you and Violet need anyone to talk to, I'm here."

"Thanks." My eyes dart to the clock on the wall and know it's time to get a move on. "Listen, I have to go."

"Yes, of course…"

"But before I go, Mother," I snap, cutting her off, needing to have my final peace before I can think about starting over, "just know if you do anything ever again to try to come between us, that's it. There won't be any more chances, and you can go run off and rot with Amber. I refuse to live through that hell again, and I refuse to have Violet or any kids we have go through it either. So, I really do hope you're being honest."

"Never again, I promise. I love you, Son. Now go. Your adoring fans need you," she says sweetly, not even seeming a little put off by my words.

"Bye," I mutter and close the phone when I hear her final farewell.

"See, it wasn't so bad," Violet jokes, nudging my shoulder.

It wasn't, but I'm not going to admit she's right. I'll never hear the end of it.

"It was brutal and awkward. I think yelling at her would've been easier." I hand her my phone, so she can hold on to it for the show. She rolls her baby blues as she stuffs it in her pocket.

"Shut up, you're fine. Now come on, we have a show to do." She grabs me by my belt buckle, yanking it hard to get me to move. She only jolts me forward a little and lets go, knowing she's not going to be able to move me further. "Stop being a pain, Coop."

"Oh, that's not going to happen," I swoop down and grab her by her legs, tossing her over my shoulder. Her high-pitched squeal echoes around the room and in my ear.

"Put me down..." She shrieks and kicks her legs. My hand rubs over her denim ass before I give it a loud resounding smack. "Cooper!"

"What's wrong Ace? If I remember, I owe you some spankings..."

October 25th 2006
Violet

We're back in L.A. for a couple of shows at the final leg of the American tour. In two weeks we'll be heading off to Australia, to start the three-month world tour. Before the show tonight at the Hollywood Bowl, Cooper and I are at the OB/GYN to get the first glimpse of our baby. I'm excited and nervous at the same time. I think when I see our baby's heartbeat I will stop being so anxious with the 'what-ifs' that have been popping into my head since I made this appointment.

I'm about seven weeks and if the heartbeat is good and strong, the chance of miscarriage drops significantly. Also, this morning sickness—or all-day sickness is what they should really call it—is a good sign of a healthy pregnancy. Or so I was told. I only wish it could be healthy without having me bent over a toilet. After we found out, I had blood work drawn in New York, to confirm the pregnancy. Even with the five positive tests, it was nice to know for sure. The doctor there told me my levels were perfect for how far along I was at the time.

I'm sitting on the exam table in only a gown waiting for Dr. Lawrence to come in. She's supposedly one of the best OB's in L.A. and deals with high profile clients.

Not that I'm high profile, just married to someone whose name is always in lights.

My hand goes to my stomach and for a fleeting moment, I think of my own mother. Twenty-two years ago, she was giving birth to me. I envision her holding me, wrapped in a pink blanket looking down at me adoringly. At one time she'd loved me, gave me gifts, and cake on my birthday. Now I can't seem to process how a mother, who carried me for nine months, and took care of me, would do everything she has done to me. To ruin their child's spirit out of spite or jealousy, or whatever fucked up reason my mother had.

Reasons I'll never know for sure.

"Ace, you're clenching your jaw," Cooper says, moving to sit next to me on the exam table, with his arm around my shoulder. I lean into him and take a deep breath, inhaling his new Calvin Klein Cologne I got him the other day.

Forget her Vi, you're already a better mother and your baby isn't even the size of a banana yet.

I have all I need right here next to me and inside of me. She's gone, hasn't even tried to contact me, or even my father. So, I hope she got the point.

"Sorry, thinking too much. You know I hate waiting because my mind drifts to places it doesn't need to go."

He hums his agreement, pressing a kiss to my cheek. "Well, cut it out. I can hear your thoughts all the way over here."

"Then maybe you should give me something else to think about," I purr and run my hand down his chest.

His large hand wraps behind my neck, seconds away from bringing me into a kiss, when there's a knock on the door that separates us.

Heels click on the floor and a woman in a white lab coat walks into the room. She smiles sweetly at us. Her kind hazel eyes put me at ease.

"Mr. and Mrs. Reid, I'm Dr. Lauren Lawrence. According to my chart congratulations are in order. How are you feeling, Mrs. Reid?" She moves to the ultrasound machine sitting next to the bed.

"I'm fine besides the morning sickness and exhaustion."

"Good. Have you been taking your prenatal vitamins and drinking lots of water?" I nod. "It's important even if you can't eat right now to drink to keep yourself from getting dehydrated. Are you able to keep anything down?"

"Yeah. I eat little bits at a time. It seems to help."

"Great. Do you have any questions for me before we get started?"

"Um, yeah we're about to go overseas for a couple of months. I guess I need to worry if there's any shots or precautions I'll need before I go."

"Well, first, do you have anyone who will be able to check you over while you're there. Urine, blood pressure, heartbeat, measurements? Just to make sure you're progressing as expected. The first two things are the most important."

"I have hired an RN to come with us who worked in an Obstetrician office for years," Cooper tells her and the doctor with the tight raven hair bun nods her approval.

"Good, but feel free to call the office if you have any questions or concerns. I know it was mentioned you had a miscarriage about six years ago." Coop grips my hand and gives it a small squeeze. Dr. Lawrence looks at our entwined fingers and continues. "Remember, just because you had one, doesn't mean you'll have another. Just look for any signs of bleeding or extremely painful cramps. Also, don't be afraid to tell your nurse who is with you to check you out, okay. It's better to know if everything is okay, than to worry."

I look over at my husband who gives me a tight smile as we let her words sink in. It's all scary to think about, but I have to remember it'll be alright.

One step at a time, Vi. Day by Day.

"Now, why don't you lay back and we can take a look at your baby. Put your mind to rest."

Cooper stands and moves to stand next to my head when I lay down on the table. Our hands still joined tightly together.

Dr. Lawrence sets up the machine and grabs the internal probe. I remember the thing from when I lost the baby. It's uncomfortable as hell, from what I recall. She rolls a condom on it and squeezes on the lube. My eyes dart to Cooper, waiting for the joke, anything, but he's looking intently at the still blank screen.

I can see the nervous excitement in his eyes, and I feel it in his clammy hand holding mine. The doctor asks me to spread my legs and inserts the probe. My head darts to the screen and it comes to life in blacks and grays. I see the large back area with a tiny white blob in the middle.

"There's your baby, you guys." Dr. Lawrence points to the screen at the tiny white alien in the middle of the black hole. Although, it looks funny, compared to what I've seen online. She moves the probe around and I swear I see two heads.

"Well, lookie there..." Dr. Lawrence grins and points to the screen.

"Is that?" I gulp and turn to glance at Cooper who remains staring at the ultrasound, his eyes wide in confusion. When the doctor moves the probe again, it comes clear as day as to exactly what I'm seeing.

My heart is hammering out of my chest and I wonder if this is really a dream.

But it's not, because Cooper is holding my hand so tight it hurts.

"Congratulations you two, you're having twins."

"Oh my god," the tears are building in my eyes as I gaze at the two babies Coop and I made.

Two.

Holy hell.

I can't help but wonder if this is our angel coming to join us. Twins don't run in either of our families. This is almost like an extra special bonus birthday gift.

Cooper is silent, still looking at the screen when she

points to where their tiny hearts are flickering on the screen. She clicks a couple buttons and what looks like sound waves appear on the screen.

"The heart beats are strong. 155 and 153 beats per minute and they're both measuring seven weeks, which is perfect. I'll print you out some pictures."

"Thank you," I tell her and turn back to my bewildered husband. "Coop?"

"Twins?" Cooper finally says, still not looking down at me. Dr. Lawrence prints out a couple pictures and hands them to me. "Twins?" Cooper whispers again.

"No, it's really quintuplets. Didn't you see the other three?" I tease, thankfully snapping him out of his haze. With his eyes still wide in shock, he falls into his seat.

Dr. Lawrence says she'll give us a minute and walks out of the room. Once the door closes, my hand pushes through his overgrown waves. "You okay there, big guy?"

A slow smile spreads across his face. "Twins." I don't get to say anything more when he grabs me around the waist and his mouth attacks mine, pinning me down to the exam table.

In this moment, I know everything is going to be okay because love really does always win in the end. This time nobody can stand in our way.

We're complete, a family, and becoming whole once again.

THIRTEEN

June 4th, 2007

Violet

Thirty-five weeks pregnant and I look like an over-inflated beach ball, ready to pop. I'm exhausted, the feet I haven't seen in weeks are swollen, and I'm being kicked around because my twins are having a cage fight inside of me. But even with all that, I wouldn't change a second of it.

I think I was pretty lucky and the morning sickness only lasted about twelve weeks. As soon as that was over my sex drive went through the roof. If Cooper wasn't on stage, I was riding his damn dick. I couldn't get enough, and I didn't hear any complaints from my husband.

Just Brody, who kept yelling that Cooper's dick was going to fall off if I didn't lay off.

After we finished the overseas tour, Cooper took me on what he called a long-awaited honeymoon to Maui. Brody had brought Alexa with him and I watched as the couple bloomed. I'd never seen Brody or Alexa so happy. Two of the best people I know might get their happily ever after together. Alexa is now moving to L.A. to be with him, in his house, and found a job working as a PA for some hotshot lawyer.

Julie also joined us for some fun in the sun and met an islander. She has only returned stateside to visit, and

I'm not sure what's she's doing, but I think along with the guy, Maui has stolen her heart.

For Coop and I, the couple of weeks on Maui, turned into a month. Cooper had no obligations for appearances until March and all interviews could be done via Skype or by phone. I also had no urge to get home, enjoying the peace, and my husband, for much needed alone time.

Of course, I only wish we could've stayed forever because as soon as we got home we couldn't go anywhere without the paparazzi following us. The public isn't aware I'm having twins, so guess who's getting made fun of for how 'big' I am?

One article had a picture of me and Cooper outside a donut shop, stuffing our faces with the pastry goodness. I'm mid-bite of a Boston crème when the picture was clicked.

Reid Baby Watch: Violet, when are you *really* due? Because you look ready to pop. Or maybe you should lay off the sweets and carbs, because Cooper is going to have to start rolling you around.

Freakin' rude.

I had only been 29 weeks at the time. Can't a woman be pregnant and enjoy it without having to worry about her size, for one minute? I tried not to let it bother me, but it did hurt. Thankfully, it was only one heartless magazine, and I had Cooper, who always makes me feel as if I'm the most beautiful girl in the world.

His one and only.

His hands always find my belly, telling the babies how much he loves them and their mother. He's always singing to them, which only makes them kick me harder. I don't think there could be a better father for my children;

I FOUND YOU *June 4th, 2007*

he's going to spoil and love them like crazy. It's something I can't wait to see.

Our kids are going to be loved and not just by Cooper and me, but a sea of family, including our closest friends and our 'family' on the road.

It's too bad one of their grandmothers won't be a part of it though.

I guess one way to look at is, she's dead to me.

As for Evelyn Reid, she's proven over and over again how much she's accepted mine and Cooper's relationship. There hasn't been one big thing to show her change, but her words, and efforts of support have shined through. Cooper and Evelyn have started to rebuild their relationship, and I'm finally getting the mother-in-law I should've always had.

We decided this morning to take a drive up the coast to Malibu to enjoy the fresh beach air. There's no tour this summer since we're having the babies, but there are some dates planned for the late fall and winter. I have no idea how it's going to work, but we have a lot of offered help. Because there's no way Cooper wants to be away from us for any long period of time.

"Just a couple more weeks, Ace, and think how full our house will be," Cooper says, helping me out of the car to go into the house.

I look at the house we've now shared for over a year and it's hard to believe sometimes we were ever apart for four years. Those missing years seem to have vanished, and we've picked up where we left off. This is the life we were always supposed to have.

I'm still blown away some days how fate brought us back together in a Vegas bar. I owe Alexa's father everything for giving her the room vouchers.

"Very full." I rub my hand over my swollen belly.

"I can't wait 'till we teach them how to play the guitar…or the drums," he smiles at me wickedly, "maybe start a family garage band."

Oh, my poor ears.

We walk into the house and Cooper leads me to the living room. I stop him and look up at him lustfully, needing my fill of him again. I haven't been as horny in the last couple weeks, but today I suddenly feel recharged. My hand slides down his chest, slowly making its way to his groin. "What are we doing in here? I thought you were going to do unspeakable things to me—"

"Surprise!" A bunch of our friends and family yell, jumping out of nowhere.

I yelp, my heart beating out of my chest from the sudden shock of all the people in my house. Guests who might have gotten a full show if they didn't burst out of the floorboards, stopping me mid-sentence and my hand from its descent down to Cooper's crotch.

With my hand over my heart, I look around the room at the pink and blue streamers and balloons. I spot a cake with blue and pink icing on a table surround by all my favorite foods: tacos, buffalo wings, mini cheeseburgers, and salad. There's also trays of finger foods laying around. It's all very simple and not overdone. Just the way I like it.

"Did you know about this?" I whisper to Cooper.

I mentioned to everyone who offered to throw me a baby shower I didn't need one. Coop and I can afford everything we need, so I didn't want anyone to feel obligated to buy us anything. I'd much rather the stuff go to someone who needs it. He shrugs his shoulders with a sly grin on his face, telling me everything I need to know. Should've known something was up when he wanted to take me out to Malibu so urgently.

Evelyn approaches me and lovingly touches my belly. "I know you didn't want a baby shower, but every mother to be should have a celebration of their upcoming birth, gifts or no gifts. So, I put this together, with a lot of

I FOUND YOU　　　　　　　　　　　　　　**June 4th, 2007**

Cooper's, Alexa's, and your dad's help. I hope you don't mind?"

"No, not at all. Thank you." I don't even have to think when I pull Evelyn into a hug. Maybe it's the hormones; despite trying to make things right, I never thought I would hug this woman, but I'm hugging her, trying not to break down in tears from the sweet gesture.

"You're welcome, honey," she whispers. As she pulls away from me, I catch the few tears swimming in her eyes before she brushes them away.

I guess she was as surprised as I was by the sudden show of emotion.

"Now, I know you didn't want gifts so instead everyone donated what they would have gotten you to the local women's shelters."

"Yeah?" I choke back a sob. Stupid hormones turning me into a ball of mush.

"Yep, and enough diapers to last hopefully a couple of years," Cooper adds.

I reach up and kiss his cheek. "This is wonderful. Thank you."

In the next moment, I'm gathered into hugs from the people who mean the most to me.

"I can't wait to bounce these guys on my knee." My dad puts his hand on my belly skittishly like it's going to bite him, but instead, one of the twins kick him. He chuckles and moves his hand away. "Bet they're going to be a handful like you were when you were a baby."

"Good thing you'll be closer to teach me how to reign them in."

My dad is retiring from the Navy after twenty-four years when his contract ends in August and has decided to move closer to me and Cooper. He refused Cooper's offer to buy a place for him and my offer to live with us.

Cooper vetoed that too, saying, "There are some things a father should never hear or see."

"You're naming the boy little Dustin, right? So, much better than Cooper Junior." Dustin sticks out his tongue pretending to be disgusted at the idea, causing Coop to whack him playfully in the back of the head.

"Who said there's a boy in here?" I ask, rubbing my belly.

We decided not to tell anyone what we're having, wanting it to be a surprise. We have the twins room already set up and all the clothes and essentials picked out, but keep the room locked when people come over. I love all the guessing because it amps up the excitement of the birth.

Also, we figured the fewer people who knew the less chances there would be of the media finding out.

"Oh no little bro, they already decided if they're boys they're naming both of them after me. Hell, even if they're girls. Brodena has a nice ring to it."

"That's not happening, Brody." Cooper rolls his eyes.

"And why not? I think I've earned it for all the shit I've put up with you guys and what I will put up with later," he scoffs.

It's so true though. We are Brody's personal melodrama.

"Yes, you have…" I move to wrap my arms around Brody's neck, giving him a hug, and planting an extra wet kiss his cheek. "But that's why you're the godfather; to corrupt them and teach them Brodyisms." I giggle when he wipes the sloppy kiss from his cheek.

"You're damn straight I will. You two are doomed." He points his finger at us, as I step back over to my husband. I can see Brody's mind over working through all his evil plots to turn our twins into his little minions.

"Only *if* we're not around anymore," Cooper adds forcefully. "So kill whatever ideas are swarming around in your head."

I FOUND you   **June 4th, 2007**

"Yeah, don't let him think he has the permission to do so before. You want to keep them *out* of trouble," Alexa teases, cuddling into Brody.

"That's why you're the godmother, Alexa. To keep him in line," I add, "and to protect them from Brodyisms." I wink.

"Alright, you know I'm feeling a bit ganged up on here. Let's play some games or something."

Playing games was fun 'till I almost ended up throttling Brody. Everyone was supposed to take a roll of yarn and guess how big my belly is. Brody unraveled the whole thing and asked for more.

Jerk

I gave him my best pout and worked up some fake tears, telling him I wasn't that monstrous. In return, he laughed, and said, "Sorry, sis, I thought we were measuring Cooper's new dad gut."

Cooper has put on a *couple* pounds, so he says. I haven't noticed it, but I think he only says it to make me feel better.

It helps...a little.

Now, I'm sitting between Evelyn, and Alexa, and Julie as they try to guess the sex of the twins. Most of the guests have left for the evening. I'm really glad Evelyn threw this party. It was great to see everyone, especially the crew, who I haven't seen in months, and won't again 'till who knows when.

And Evelyn got my favorite cake, triple chocolate.

Cooper comes up to me and kisses my cheek. "I'm going to show our dads and brothers the new 'man cave.'

347

You okay for a bit?"

I snort, at the term man cave. It was made to be an entertainment area. I *guess* you could consider the bar with two large TV screens, oversized, black leather recliners, and sports decals on the wall a manly place. But it's really me who has spent more time in the manly room than Cooper, finding myself falling asleep every night in one of the comfy chairs, watching some sappy romance movie.

So, if we need to be technical, it's Vi's Cave, really.

"Yep, try not to drink all the kegs that are in the bar though." I give him a sweet grin and bat my eyes.

"I think you're confusing me with Brody." He splays his hand on my belly. "You know I'm going to stay sober 'till these two are born."

"One beer won't hurt. Go. I'll be fine talking with the girls."

He glances at his mother and I see the glimpse of uncertainty in his eyes before they dart back to me. "You sure?"

"Go. You're bugging me, Coop." I shove his shoulder and he feigns hurt.

"Geez woman, I thought you loved having me around, but I see how it is." He gives me his dimpled smile before blowing me a kiss and walking away with the other guys.

"I'm still saying it's two boys," Julie continues to the others, pulling me away from staring at Cooper's ass as he leaves the room. "Because I read the lower you carry, it's more likely a boy."

"I'm not carrying low? Am I?" I glance down at my belly, trying to figure out what she means.

"You are now," Alexa points out. "You weren't a couple days ago..."

Evelyn chuckles beside me and I look at her curiously. "It's quite normal in the final weeks for the babies to drop. Did the doctor tell you if they were both in position the other day?"

"Yeah, they're both head down now. One of them was always that way, while the other turned around a lot, and stood on the others head." I giggle remembering watching the left twin twisting all around on top of their sibling.

"You know it would be easier just to say, brother or sister, when you talk about them, right?" Julie raises her eyebrow at me and I respond by sticking out my tongue.

"No, I like keeping you guys on your toes. Plus, don't you all have a bet going on?" I question knowing everyone made a pool to guess the babies' sex, weight, and the day they think I'll pop.

I heard from Big Frank the pool was up to a thousand bucks, but all the money is going to a 'save the music' charity. The winner gets to have their name on the donation though.

And maybe also bragging rights?

"Yeah, but if you tell us, we have time to change the answer," Julie says pointedly and I shake my head.

"Not happening. Only a couple more weeks and you'll know."

"Fine. At least I'll be close for when it does happen." She rubs my belly and tells them to come on the 12th since it's her guess.

Julie is staying with Alexa and Brody 'till the babies are born, then going back to Maui to be with Kahiau, her sexy, buff islander. Julie has little hearts in her eyes, along with her new tan.

"I'm sticking with one of each," Alexa muses.

Evelyn stands and walks over to the kitchen while Julie and Alexa argue about dates and guessing which crazy rock star name we're going to give them. When she comes back she's carrying a gold and silver box. She sits back down next to me, and Alexa and Julie's conversation quiets.

"We're going to go bug the guys." They both stand abruptly, making my curiosity spike, wondering what could be in the box resting on Evelyn's lap.

"You girls don't need to go," Evelyn says and they both shake their head.

"It's okay. We'll be back in a few. I could use a beer." Alexa grabs Julie's hand, pulling her out of the room.

"Wait, I wanted to see…" I hear Julie whisper as she's dragged from the room.

There's a strong double kick to my stomach, as if my twins are also asking 'what the hell is going on?'

"Um…" I hum at the departing figures before turning my attention back to Evelyn.

"I sure know how to clear a room." She laughs modestly.

"Yeah, makes me wonder if I should worry what's in the box." I grin, eyeing the package. If she was Brody or Dustin I would think a stink bomb or something about to jump out at me. But this is Evelyn and the boys definitely didn't get their love of practical jokes from their mother.

That comes from Grandpa Bud

"Now if it was bad, I doubt your best friends would've left the room." She winks, patting my hand. "I got you something. I know you didn't want or need any gifts today, but I had this made up for you." Evelyn hands me the gold and silver box.

"You didn't have to."

"Nonsense, figure this as a very late anniversary gift and to also tell you I'm glad you're my daughter."

Daughter. I don't correct her by adding the in-law part because I think she actually means I'm more than that.

These days it's really hard not to take Evelyn Reid as anything less than genuine. Unlike before, there's no sense of a hidden agenda behind her eyes. This is the mother

I FOUND YOU *June 4th, 2007*

who raised three well-rounded, respectable boys. I used to think it was all Andrew. Now I know a little better.

"Thank you." I open the box and push the tissue paper away to reveal a picture frame. "Oh my god," I gasp, and tears pool in my eyes, from the thoughtfulness of this gift. "This...is...perfect."

It's a sterling silver frame and on the side is an Elvis in a red and yellow bejeweled, white jumpsuit, with his lip curled and large sunglasses. Across the top is the word "Uh-huh" in green jewels and on the bottom etched into the silver is the day Cooper and I were married. The picture is of us kissing after saying our 'uh-huhs' in front of 'The King.'

"I love this. There are no words for how much I do. Coop will get a kick out of it." I sniffle and wipe away the fallen tears from my face.

"I have one for the babies being made, just waiting for names and dates."

"Thank you." I reach over and hug her.

"You're welcome, sweetie. I should've done this for you long ago." She chokes back her tears, embracing me a little tighter.

I still can't get over that I'm hugging her again and letting it happen for more than a second. Maybe it's because it's the welcoming motherly hug I've needed for so long. She's the only one I have for a mother figure from now on, and I think she's shown me just enough where we can begin to have a good relationship.

The hug suddenly turns warm *and wet.* There's a popping sensation in my belly and a trickle down my leg. I pull away and look down at myself, dampness spotting the front of my dress.

"What—I..." My eyes jump to Evelyn's whose eyes grow big in surprise, but there's a faint smile on her lips, so I'm guessing I didn't pee my pants.

"I think your water broke, sweetie. Have you been

having any pain?"

"No," I break into a cold sweat. I'm panicking, knowing it's too soon. They're not ready. "No, it's too early," I mutter in fear.

I've read every baby book known to man and know most babies do well after 34 weeks, but that information doesn't help me now. I'm scared out of my mind something could go wrong. They need more time to grow. They were only last measured a little over four pounds each. The doctor told me thirty-seven weeks was ideal because any potential complications drop significantly.

"Breathe, Violet. Thirty-five weeks is good for twins. They don't have as much room as singletons and when they run out of room, they'll vacate." Evelyn grabs my face, giving me a reassuring smile.

It doesn't do much to ease my worry.

"I'm scared…" I cry, my fear rising, not knowing up from down or left from right.

"Don't be scared, sweet girl. You're not in active labor yet, but these babies are coming sooner than later, and they'll be more than fine. I promise."

I nod, the sweat continuing to drip from my brow, trying to take a deep breath. Because she's right. She's right. It'll be fine.

But no mother wants to worry if their babies are going to have to spend time in the NICU.

"Let me go grab Cooper and I'll call your doctor."

"Evelyn…" I grab her hand before she goes far and hunch over as my stomach feels as if it's twisting.

She glances at her watch on the hand I'm not squeezing to death. "Okay, breathe through it. It'll pass." I take a deep breath and loosen my grip on her hand as the contraction subsides.

"So much for not being in active labor," I jest, placing both my hands on my belly.

"Let me go get your husband and you go clean up. If

I FOUND YOU *June 4th, 2007*

you have another one, let me know so we can time them. It'll be okay, there's plenty of time, they're not going to come flying out of the chute just yet." She chuckles and it makes me giggle in response. I'm glad it's not only me who can find humor at the wrong times. *And who knew Evelyn had a sense of humor?* "Breathe, you're going to be holding both of those beautiful babies soon and they will be more than alright."

She places her hand on my cheek lovingly, much like my dad used to do when I was little and he'd tell me he loved me. I instantly feel at ease with her warm eyes telling me everything is going to be okay before turning to get my babies' father.

.

5 a.m. June 5th, 2007

Ten hours later, I'm finally at ten centimeters and ready to push.

Everyone has been in and out of the room as my labor progressed. My husband hasn't left my side since the second he came flying into our bedroom, concern and excitement etched all over his handsome face. His hair is standing on all ends from pushing his hand through it hundreds of times. He's got worried, anxious wrinkles forming around his eyes, making him look older than he is.

His mother, who also has been with me the whole time, has been doing her best to reign in her son's distress. I know she has mine. Even though his mom is a doctor, it isn't 'till he hears from Dr. Lawrence that the twins will more than likely be perfectly fine, he finally relaxes a bit.

"You're going to do great. I can't wait to meet them,"

Evelyn tells me about to leave the room. I reach out for her hand.

I can't explain any of the reasons why I don't want her to leave: maybe it's everything that happened today, or the exhaustion, or because Cooper is driving me insane suddenly, but I need her.

I need a mom.

"No, don't go," I beg, gripping her hand harder. "Please."

"Of course." She grabs the cool rag from the table to place on my head.

"I'm going to need you to push on your next contraction, Violet," Dr. Lawrence says between my legs, ready for the catch.

It comes with a piercing scream, as I bare down, trying to free one of these babies. It hurts so much.

Silly me thought it would be the best for the babies to do this *without* an epidural.

Never again! I fall back when it's done, catching my breath, and Cooper kisses my head. "You're doing so well, Ace." I squeeze his hand hard, causing him to flinch.

As much as I love his sweetness, he's not the one about to push two four-pound bowling balls from his freakin' vagina.

He just needs to hush right now and let me work.

"You know babe, if you break all my fingers, I won't be able to help with all those dirty diapers." He chortles, and I glare at him. I hate that he's right and I loosen my grip, *a little*.

With his damn perfect smile, he kisses my forehead. "You love me."

"Uh-huh!" I howl as the next contraction hits and I push down.

"I see the head," Dr. Lawrence announces. "I think one or two more pushes, the first one will be here…"

Three minutes later, Dr. Lawrence is pulling out a

screaming baby. "It's your little girl," she announces, the nurses coming up to do a quick clean up. "You want to cut the cord, Dad?"

Cooper readily agrees, taking the scissors and cutting our daughter free.

"She's perfect, Violet," Evelyn coos, staring down at her new granddaughter, who is still wailing that distinct newborn cry.

"She is," I croon, watching the nurse take her over to the table to look her over. Cooper is quickly back to my side, kissing me hard on the lips, thanking me.

"I love you," he whispers pushing back wet strands of hair away from my face.

"I'm going to wait to hand her to you and let the nurses check her over first. Okay? By the way, she's screaming her head off, so I'd say she's good. Her Apgar was 8, which is perfect. Now let's bring the other one into the world…"

Six minutes and three pushes later, our baby boy comes crying into the world, though not nearly as loud as his sister, and Cooper cuts his cord. Once the nurses get the twins cleaned, weighed, and measured, they give me both to feed. As long as they eat, pass a car seat test, and do well overnight, they'll be fine to go home tomorrow.

With some help from a nurse, they both latch on and suck down the colostrum like pros.

Evelyn steps out of the room, giving Cooper and me a few minutes alone.

"I never would've thought I could love you more or that you could be even more beautiful, but seeing you feed our kids blows me away." His long finger runs down our daughter's cheek, and she starts suckling again in her sleep.

"Can you believe we made these?" I murmur, and lean my head on his shoulder. Watching the babies eat is sucking the energy out of me.

"But we did." He kisses my forehead. "You should close your eyes while you can before everyone gets here."

"I'm otay…"

He laughs shaking his head at me. "You can't even say okay correctly. Sleep. I'll put them down."

"I love you," I whisper sleepily before passing out completely once both babies are safely out of my arms.

A couple hours of shut-eye later, my dad, Andrew, Dustin, Brody, Alexa, and Julie join us. Alexa and Dustin high five over picking the correct sexes. Cooper is cradling our son in his arms and Julie looks him over, cooing softly. I'm holding my sleeping daughter on my partially bare chest.

My dad kisses the top of my head, telling me how proud he is of me, and runs his finger over my daughter's full head of soft, dark blonde hair.

"She reminds me of you when you were born…small and wrinkly," he says with a proud smile.

"Alright, now we know what they are, but can we get some names, weights, anything, please?" Brody groans, standing beside Cooper.

"I *guess* you've all waited long enough."

"Nine months, now spill it, Vi," Brody pushes.

"This little girl is Summer Lilly Reid. She's four pounds eleven ounces, and 19 and a half inches." I look at Cooper and nod my head, letting him do the honors for our son.

Cooper hands our baby boy to Brody, who readily accepts him into his arms. "Hey buddy, let's hope they didn't give you some crazy name…"

"Some will think we're crazy for it." Evelyn and I laugh knowing what's about to come. "Dustin might kill me for it, actually."

"Say it already, while we're young Coop," Dustin retorts. "We don't need a speech because I already know you two are crazy."

I FOUND YOU   **June 5th, 2007**

"His name is Axl Brody Reid." Cooper pauses letting the name sink in. Brody's head pops up, his jaw dropping open in surprise. His eyes dart from me to Cooper to the baby.

"Seriously?" he stutters and for once we've rendered Brody speechless.

We wanted our kid's names to have a mix of Rockstar persona and the middle names to be connected to someone special in our lives. Brody is well, Brody, and Lilly was my dad's mother's name. I didn't get to know her well because she passed when I was eight, but she's the reason my dad gave me such a flowery name.

"Yeah, you said it yourself, you deserved it..." I answer, but I'm quickly cut off by Cooper.

"If it wasn't for you dragging my ass to Vegas, who knows if we would be here now."

"Yeah, you do owe me pretty big."

"*But* also, as much as you deserve it, we couldn't give you the first name. We wanted to make sure he only heard Brody when he was in trouble," Cooper adds the extra jab in for good measure. The compliment wouldn't be complete without the sarcastic input from one of them.

"Asshole." Brody glares while everyone laughs. "Be glad I'm holding your son or I'd hit you." His glare quickly washes away and smile replaces it. "Thanks, man."

Once everyone leaves, letting us get some much-needed rest, Cooper lays next to me. I cuddle with him, while our twins cuddle in the bassinet. We tried separating them, and even wrapped up tightly they awoke, wanting to be close to each other. Cooper pushes his lips to my temple, my body ready to crash from the full adventure we've had the last day and a half.

"You know, the day you left Riverside, I knew no matter what we'd be together..." Cooper says, drawing my attention from my restlessness. "I knew, in the end, we'd have to find each other and come back together."

"I thought so too." I cuddle deeper into his side, inhaling him. There's a trace of his cologne underneath the smell of hospital soap.

"As much as I hated not having you around for years," he continues, brushing his hand up and down my shoulder. The gentle caress and the smoothness of his baritone voice is lulling me to sleep. "I don't think we could have had this good of a chapter in our lives if we hadn't been apart. This is better than anything I could have ever dreamt for us."

"Same." I pause, my eyes finally drooping closed. "I never dreamt of us having twins..." I tease, half asleep.

He pulls me closer. "No, that's a nice added surprise to the dream of me finding you again."

"I found you first, buddy," I whisper, drifting off to sleep. Dreaming of what's yet to come.

I FOUND you *August 9th, 2010*

EPILOGUE

August 9th, 2010

Violet

*"I used to be told dreams were only for dreamers
And I shouldn't believe in the make-believe.
I almost believed it—'till I saw you
My everything*

*You were standing in the crowd, your eyes on me.
I dreamed you would be mine.
You quickly became my dream come true
when you told me you loved me too.
My undying love is for you
For only you
'Cause your everything to me.*

Cooper's eyes meet mine with a wink like they do every night, as he performs one of his biggest hits, written for me, on stage to a sold-out crowd. All these years later the man still attracts giant flocks to come and see him. Maybe it's because, now at twenty-six, he's even hotter and the songs keep getting better, or simply because his silky baritone voice makes all the girls melt. Whatever it is, it's keeping his dream alive.

My hand falls to my pregnant belly. We're having

our third child in January. This time I'm only carrying one and it's a boy. Our twins, Summer and Axl, have just turned three and are little handfuls. They both love being on tour with us, hearing their father sing, and helping their mommy and uncle 'plan.' They walk around here with paper and crayons, telling people what to do. Thankfully, the crew finds it adorable.

Our crew is our family too.

"Mommmmy!" my son screams as he comes running over to me. His blond hair is sticking up around his ear muffs as he comes diving into me. I gather him in my arms, his blue eyes glaring behind him at his uncle.

Axl looks just like his father when he's annoyed with Brody.

"What's wrong?"

"Uncle Brody stole my Cheetos." He crosses his arms in a huff.

"I did not," Brody declares as he approaches us with my daughter Summer upside down in his arms. She's in a fit of giggles as he swings her around.

It makes my heart stop, but she loves it.

"Yeah-huh!"

"Nuh-uh," Brody argues back playfully and sticks his tongue out at Axl.

"Stop being a child, Brody." Alexa slaps his chest.

Alexa and Brody are still going strong, but their relationship is a little *rocky*, at the moment. Alexa doesn't know why he won't propose, and then they have their time apart with the tour and it adds to the struggle. She comes on tour with us when she can, but it's not nearly as much as Brody wants, and I think it's where he gets hesitant about asking. Alexa is passionate about her job and doesn't want to give up her dream just because Brody has to travel all the time. I don't know how many times I tell Brody I can handle the job and he can go be with Alexa, but he refuses.

I FOUND you   **August 9th, 2010**

"Down, down." Summer squirms in Brody's arms and he puts her on her feet. I do the same with Axl because the boy weighs a ton now.

"Daddy," Summer yells trying to wave at her daddy as he plays the cords of "Trouble follows you" which is her favorite song.

In the whole wide world, she'll tell you. Over and over again.

Before I can blink, Summer is grabbing Axl's hand and running toward the stage.

"Crap!" Brody is fast on their heels, since I don't move nearly as fast anymore, but I'm right behind him.

There's a large cheer from the crowd when the twins close in on their father. I'm shaking my head, somewhere between embarrassed, and laughing hysterically at the situation. These two know better than anyone not to run onstage, but once in a blue moon, they forget, wanting a piece of the limelight.

Cooper notices them and nods to Van to pick up his cords to take over, while he keeps singing. He bends down to scoop them into his arms. Summer sings the lyrics excitedly and they vibrate through Cooper's head mic. While Axl waves to the crowd as they scream louder. Brody and I stand back waiting for the song to end since Coop has it under control.

The audience is going nuts and I grin watching them together.

"Trouble, Trouble. Follows me." Cooper finishes the final lyrics singing them directly to the handfuls in his arms.

Summer grabs his face and places a kiss on his cheek. All the girls in the audience swoon, while Axl buries his head in Cooper's shoulder.

"I was going to introduce you to the band now, but I'll start with these little troublemakers slash backup singers first. Meet Axl and Summer Reid. Now, they're still in training, but I'm sure soon they'll be where I am."

"I'm gonna be a star—" Summer yells out to the thousands of people. It's almost as if I can see her little ego inflate as the audience goes bonkers for her. My little Summer, since she was born, has been the most vocal and knows what she wants.

My Axl has always been shyer and laid back. I have a feeling he'll end up being more like his uncle and me, behind the scenes. Or maybe Andrew and Evelyn will get that doctor or lawyer they always wanted.

Cooper walks over to where Brody and I are standing. Handing off Summer to me and Axl to his brother. "I know all of you know my brother and tour manager, Brody." The throng of people cheer their love for him. Brody is a bit of a star in his own right, and over the years, has gained his own fan base. The girls think he's *so* cute, especially after he posed for pictures for music magazine about the ins and outs of touring.

Cooper takes my face in his hand, and I bite down on my lip as he looks at me lovingly. "And my beautiful wife, Violet." My skin flushes under the bright lights now pointed at me. I've only been onstage with Cooper a couple of times and it never gets easier to be in front of these large crowds. To this day, I admire Cooper for his ability to get in front of thousands of people. He kisses me on the lips and whispers he loves me, but the words still echo through the sound system making the fans go wild. I wave shyly and take it as my cue to leave. The concert is on a time limit due to a noise ordinance of the town, so we can't have any extra delays. I'm mid-turn on my heel when Cooper calls back out to me.

"Oh, no Mrs. Reid, don't go anywhere yet. I need you around for the next song." I shake my head wildly and mouth 'no'. He smirks and turns to the sea of people. The people who will agree to anything he says.

"Go, mommy…" Summer yells in my ear.

I FOUND YOU *August 9th, 2010*

"Don't you all think my wife should stay?" I'm not sure if my cheeks could get any redder than they are now, when the masses scream out 'yes' all at the same time.

I really should kill him! I'm not dressed to be out in front of thousands. I'm wearing an oversized black t-shirt with the words Crew on the back, and a pair of jean shorts. My hair is also a mess in a high ponytail from running around the last six hours. I don't move, glaring at my husband.

"Kids, bring your mom out here…"

Summer wiggles out of my arms and I put her down and she takes my hand.

Brody drops Axl to the stage and pats my back. "You better go."

"Yeah, mommy, we have a time crush." I laugh at Axl's pronunciation of crunch as he takes my other hand.

They both yank me to the center of the stage beside their father. He slings his arm around me, making sure I can't go anywhere as he introduces the band. Summer goes and runs toward Van and Axl runs to Alex the bass player, where they each lower the mics to their level.

Why do I get the feeling I've been set up? They're too prepared.

Cooper finishes announcing the band and looks to me. "Remember the time when we spent four years away from each other," I nod. "We've been back together for a little over four years now. I'd say life has been pretty good to us." His hand spreads over my stomach, his thumb brushing over my tattoo of our family tree, "Our little Angel has been watching over us pretty good."

I wipe tears from my face. The bastard is making me cry and I'm going to kill him if there are pictures of my mascara running down my face all over Facebook tomorrow.

"I haven't sung this song on stage in a while, and I figured it was due. We went through a lot in the beginning. I think it's safe to say we won…" He winks and lays another kiss on my cheek.

Moving his arm from around me, he grips his guitar, and starts to play the opening chords to "I Found You."

After he performed this song all those years ago, he reserves it only for special moments now. I'm not sure what brought on this one, but I won't complain, as his silky voice rings through my ears and the words land deep into my heart.

*"We'll keep proving them wrong
We won't let them win
This time we'll conquer all.
Because our love is all we need
Love led me back to you."*

My eyes dart to my kids who sing only at the uh-huh's and realize how lucky I am. He's right, despite everything that happened at the beginning of our first and second start, we won. Nobody can stand in our way anymore. Not even tabloids making up lies to try and rip us apart because we know how to handle bullshit stories now. Our mothers taught us something in the end.

Never believe anything without proper sources.

Evelyn is now the perfect mother-in-law, who I now actually call Mom. When I look back and compare her to the woman I knew in the beginning, it's day and night. I'm glad she had her wakeup call because my kids adore their grandmother.

As for my mother, last I heard, she remarried and moved somewhere on the east coast. She tried calling me once after the twins were born, leaving me a voicemail, telling me how disappointed she was I didn't tell her about the twins. Upset she had to hear it through some trashy tabloid. I never called her back, and well, she never did either.

I FOUND YOU August 9th, 2010

In the end, it doesn't matter, because I'm surrounded every day by the only family and friends I'll ever need.

But most importantly, I give thanks every day that I found the love of my life again, to have and to hold for the rest of eternity.

Uh-huh.

The End!

Erica Marselas

ABOUT THE AUTHOR

I'm a wife and a mother always... but a writer in my free time...whatever that is with four little ones hanging around. :P

I've always had a vivid imagination and a passion for writing. All I ever wanted to ever do was share my art with the world. Tell the story that needs to be told.

As long as I have an idea for it... I will write it. Dreams come to us when we sleep—but when you write them down, they come alive.

Erica Marselas
Living The Dream Through Words

If you would Like to Find out more about my next project, sign up for my non-spam
Newsletter.
There's deals, insights, and bonus chapters or stories.
Feel Free to stalk me in these places too:
Facebook:
www.facebook/EricaMarselas
My Author Group: Author Erica Marselas
Reading Group: Three Witches Reading Room
Instagram: @erica_marselas
Pinterest board for this story
Goodreads @ericamarselas
Word press: ericamarselas.wordpress.com

Erica Marselas

Find my other stories on Amazon

Playing With Fire

WATCHING YOU

DIRTY little SECERTS

Erica Marselas

I FOUND YOU — Songs

MY EVERYTHING

"I used to be told dreams were only for dreamers
And I shouldn't believe in the make believe.
I almost believed it - till I saw you
My everything

You were standing in the crowd, you're eyes on me.
I dreamed you would be mine.
You quickly became my dream come true
when you told me you loved me too
My undying love is for you
For only you
Cause you're everything to me.

Chorus: You're the only love I've ever known
I'll never stop loving you.
Or be able to let you go.
You're my soul, my air, my everything...
And I need you back to live again."

It was you whole made complete.
You believed in me when no one else could
Gave me the hope to keep on going
Even after you were gone.
You're my everything, my one and only,
My reason for breathing, my only reason for living...
And I only started living when you were ripped from me
--
.

Chorus: I've never stop loving you.
You're the only love I've ever known
I'm not willing to let you go .
You're my soul, my air, my everything...
And I need you back to live again."

Erica Marselas

You went away, but in my heart, you're always here.
I close my eyes hoping you'll come back to me
Because I can never stop loving you with everything I have.
"Say you still love me. That you'll always be mine.
Because I miss the way you taste and the way your eyes used to shine.
You're my everlasting love, my number one, my everything."

Chorus: *I've never stop loving you.*
You're the only love I've ever known
I'm not willing to let you go .
You're my soul, my air, my everything...
And I need you back to live again."

I FOUND YOU-
Written with Leslie Middleton

You went away
I was lost
Lost without you

Our parents thought we were wrong
Never happy with our young love
Thought our love wasn't strong enough to survive.

They ripped us apart
When you went away
But you remained in my heart.

Then like six years ago
You were across the club
Looking so hot
Our eyes met and you had to know

I FOUND YOU   **Songs**

You'd always be mine
Our story is something divine.
So with a kiss
I let you know , you were missed.
And we finally became one.

Chorus: *I found you*
Made you my wife
I found you

To have, to hold, for the rest of my life.
Uh-huh,
We'll prove to them
They'll never win
You're mine forever
Because I found you

Back then we were up to no good
Remember when
We did all we could
To be together
No one else wanted us whole
We stayed out late
Jumped from planes.
We got tattoos
Branding your name on me
Showing everyone you are mine
And me as yours.

Then like a bad dream
You had to go.
We stayed in touch
Dreaming for when we see each other again.
The darkest day was when

The letters stopped

373

Erica Marselas

And our parents won
Breaking us apart
Breaking us--
Untillllll
Chorus*: I found you*
Made you my wife
I found you
To have, to hold, for the rest of my life.
Uh-huh,
We'll prove to them
They'll never win
You're mine forever
I found you.
I found you
To have to hold, for the rest of my life.
Uh-huh.,
We'll keep proving them wrong
We won't let them win
This time we'll conquer all
Because our love is all we need
Love led me back to you.
Chorus*: I found you*
Made you my wife

I found You
To have, to hold, for the rest of my life.
Uh-huh, your mine forever
Because I found you.

I FOUND YOU

Made in the USA
Monee, IL
16 May 2020